P9-CQV-134

The Secret's
in the Sauce

The Secret's in the Sauce

A Novel

Linda Evans Shepherd and Eva Marie Everson

a division of Baker Publishing Group
Grand Rapids, Michigan

© 2008 by Linda Evans Shepherd and Eva Marie Everson

Published by Revell
a division of Baker Publishing Group
P.O. Box 6287, Grand Rapids, MI 49516-6287
www.revellbooks.com

Printed in the United States of America

All rights reserved. No part of this publication may be reproduced, stored in a retrieval system, or transmitted in any form or by any means—for example, electronic, photocopy, recording—without the prior written permission of the publisher. The only exception is brief quotations in printed reviews.

Library of Congress Cataloging-in-Publication Data
Shepherd, Linda E., 1957–
    The secret's in the sauce : a novel / Linda Evans Shepherd and Eva Marie Everson.
        p.   cm. — (The Potluck Catering Club ; #1)
    ISBN 978-0-8007-3208-0 (pbk.)
    1. Womem—Societies and clubs—Fiction. 2. Caterers and catering—Fiction
3. Women cooks—Fiction. 4. Cookery—Fiction. 5. Female friendship—Fiction.
6. Colorado—Fiction. I. Everson, Eva Marie. II. Title.
PS3619.H456S43 2008
813′.6—dc22   2008012783

This book is a work of fiction. Names, characters, places, and incidents are the product of the authors' imagination or are used fictitiously. Any resemblance to actual events or persons, living or dead, is coincidental.

The Secret's in the Sauce is dedicated to the faithful readers of our first Potluck Club series. Thank you for letting us know you weren't ready to say good-bye to your favorite Potluck characters. Here they are again in our all-new Potluck Catering Club series. Just wait till you discover the secrets they've been keeping. Stir this serving with our love and enjoy!

Contents

Evangeline

1

Peppered Prologue

Saturday, March 25
Summit View, Colorado

Maybe I should begin by telling you how the Potluck Catering Club came about. Quite naturally I am the one to do the telling, too, no matter what Lisa Leann Lambert might think. She, of course, is taking all the credit for this whole thing, but the fact of the matter is the Potluck Catering Club wouldn't even be in business this very minute had it not been for *my* Potluck Club.

I'm rushing ahead of myself, and I don't mean to. So let me start with a little history. My name is Evangeline Benson Vesey—Mrs. Vernon Vesey, to be exact, having been married now for two whole months to the sheriff of Summit View, Colorado.

If anyone is qualified to tell you about Summit View, it's me. Not only am I married to the county's sheriff, but I am also the daughter of the late mayor of the town, the Honorable Daniel Robert Benson.

This makes me something akin to royalty, not that I would ever act like it. After all, we are every one of us God's children.

Nonetheless, people in this community treat me with the utmost respect, though I'd like to think it goes beyond who my daddy was or my husband is and straight to the kind of person I am.

I started the Potluck Club many, many years ago with my friend Ruth Ann, God rest her soul. Over the years we became a six-member union, now made up of Vonnie Westbrook, Lizzie Prattle, Goldie Dippel, Donna Vesey (who is now my stepdaughter), and Lisa Leann Lambert, a Texas transplant who was never actually asked to join the club but rather invited herself with her delectable cinnamon rolls. As much as I was against her and just plain didn't care for her, she has become quite the friend. In fact, when I married Vernon a few months ago, she coordinated our wedding.

Which is, in truth, how the catering business came about. And also why I say I started it . . . in my way.

Before you can really understand how the catering service came to be, it's important to know a little more about the petite package of dynamite known as Lisa Leann Lambert. After she moved to our little town in Colorado's high country and tried to take over my role as the president of the Potluck Club, Lisa Leann opened a charming bridal service. This was before Vernon and I got engaged, and in order to build some sort of Christlike relationship with her, I had offered to let her handle my wedding. This was a big step on my part, entrusting someone I'm not sure I trust at all with something as important as my wedding day. After all, I'm fifty-eight years old, and this would be my one and only wedding to the man I've loved my entire life. Or, at least since I was twelve years old. But that's another story.

So, while it's important to understand how the whole catering business came to be—at least to my way of thinking—it is equally as important to know that in my very humble opinion this business has as much potential for failure as it does for success. The question you might be asking—"What could go wrong?"—is more accurately expressed in my mind as "How much will go wrong?"

While I settled in as the new wife of Sheriff Vernon Vesey, a handsome, silver-haired, blue-eyed teddy bear of a man, Lisa Leann took charge. At first, I thought this was a fact I must quickly change. But like I said to Vonnie, it wouldn't be easy.

"At least Lisa Leann can cook," I had told her over the phone shortly after my return from my honeymoon.

"You can cook, Evangeline. You can cook just as good as the rest of us."

"Oh, get real, Von." I plopped down in one of my kitchen chairs as gracefully as a woman of my age can plop into a piece of brick-hard furniture. "I'm a casserole kind of woman. I go for whatever is easy. If I want to take charge of this catering business, I'm going to have to expand my culinary horizons. Start watching the Food Channel and trying out those recipes in *Woman's World* magazine." I took a moment to rub my derrière, which ached a bit from its recent descent into the chair.

"But why must you take over anything, Evie? Why can't you just be happy with being the president of the prayer group?"

"Vonnie Westbrook, how naïve can you possibly be? Don't you know that if she's in charge of the catering business it will only be a matter of time before she's in charge of the club as a whole? My gosh, I can see it now, the brass nameplate at her counter: 'Lisa Leann Lambert, President of the Potluck Club and COO of the Potluck Catering Club.'"

"Today the Potluck Club, tomorrow the world," Vonnie said. I pictured her raising one fist into the air in a symbol of victory and mock salute.

"You joke, Vonnie Westbrook, but you'll see. You may not be far off from the truth there."

Vonnie laughed then, laughed so loud and so hard I had to pull the phone away from my ear.

"It sounds like a job for Superman," she said when she finally—and I do mean finally—quieted.

Or Super-Evie, I thought. *Surely somewhere in my closet there's a cape I can don.* Indeed, I had a new goal in life—an assignment, so to speak. My job, should I decide to take it, would be to become the best Mrs. Vernon Vesey ever . . . and save the world from Lisa Leann Lambert and her gooey cinnamon rolls.

It was the least I could do, I decided, as president of the Potluck Club.

Well, I've gotten ahead of myself again. I'm good at that. I don't mean to be confusing; it's just that I want you to understand what's happened in the month since my nuptials to Vernon. Then again, I suppose if you're really to understand everything as it pertains to all of us, we'll have to go back a bit. Back to that cold yet beautiful January day when I became more than just the Potluck Club president. I became Mrs. Vernon Vesey.

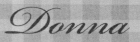
Donna

2

Wedding Punch

Evangeline's Wedding, One Month Earlier

Now, I'm not one to get all misty eyed, but let's just say when I saw my daddy standing at the end of the aisle, dressed in his tux, I had to blink to clear my vision. He was so handsome, so regal, as he waited for his bride. It would have been a perfect moment if it hadn't been for the woman he was marrying.

It was no secret Evie and I had been at war for years. It started when I was in fifth grade and had inadvertently kept her from getting too friendly with Dad, the local sheriff and one of the most eligible bachelors in Summit View.

After that, I was always a target for her cutting remarks. But at least I'd had my Sunday school teacher, Vonnie Westbrook, to stand up for me.

Evie would bark, "Donna, you're slouching, can't you stand up straight?"

Vonnie would say, "Evangeline, why are you speaking to this child in that tone?"

Evie'd put her hands on her hips. "It's just this child needs a mother."

With all innocence, I'd reply, "No, ma'am, not if that mother was to be you."

And now, all these years later, Evangeline was finally marrying my dad. Oh happy day.

So not only did the two of us have a history, though I was willing to forgive if she was willing to play nice, I had other concerns. For instance, I was concerned about Evie's emotional stability. I tried to believe she'd merely had a case of wedding jitters, but in the past few weeks, she flittered from dating my dad then getting engaged to that hideous Bob Barnett before finally walking down the aisle with Daddy.

Talk about an emotional roller coaster.

That, and a couple of public temper tantrums, made me a bit nervous to embrace her as a close relative. But what could I say? Dad obviously loved her, and I was going to have to live with that fact.

Still, I was already missing Tuesday nights, when I'd cook Dad dinner and have him all to myself. Now, he dragged Evie along. It just wasn't the same.

I clutched my bouquet of daisies and roses and stepped into my rehearsed glide, feeling a bit uncomfortable draped in pink satin. This froufrou look was a far cry from the tough girl image I'd so carefully crafted in my role of sheriff's deputy.

Before I could break into a scowl, my eyes locked with the eyes of the man who raised me. His smile shifted from me to the back of the room, where Evie would soon appear.

He looked so happy. I vowed to look happy too. Besides, in recent weeks, Evangeline had seemed to soften toward me. So, I was going to try, really try, to soften toward her.

Just as I turned to join the other bridesmaids, two faces seemed to pop out of the crowded pews.

Both David Harris, fresh from Los Angeles, and Wade Gage, my old high school sweetheart, were staring at me as if I were an angel. The thought struck me so funny that I had to stifle a giggle.

Though I tried to keep my mirth under control, I caught Wade with one of his lopsided grins spreading across his face. He looked both amused and smitten, and I had to hold my breath so I wouldn't laugh out loud. I was saved by the abrupt organ prelude to the "Bridal Chorus."

When the music sounded, it was as if God himself had flipped a switch inside of me. My giggles stopped, and a heavy soberness engulfed me.

The crowd stood and turned as Miss Evangeline Benson, in her Grace Kelly wedding gown, floated toward the altar.

Everyone turned, except David. He was still staring moon-eyed at me. He jumped as his date shot him in the ribs with an elbow jab.

This might have struck me as funny if the jabber hadn't been my long-lost baby sister, Velvet James. She was clad in white as if she were a bride herself. I'm no fashion expert, but I know tacky. Velvet flamed me with her eyes as she twined David's arm into hers.

Her little performance seemed right out of grade school.

The music crescendoed, and I shifted my eyes to Evangeline. She looked lovely as she blushed under the intense gaze of my father.

Sweet. And she'd better stay that way. Otherwise, my niceness might crumble and she'd have to deal with the real me, the me I saved for passing out tickets to speeding tourists.

But what was I thinking? This was her wedding day, and I'd pledged to be on my best behavior.

Later, at the dinner reception, after my duties at the head table had been fulfilled, relief swept over me. I sat in my chair, nibbling on one of Lisa Leann's double chocolate brownies and watching how tender my dad was with Evangeline. She smiled at him, and he kissed her cheek.

I found myself smiling too. Maybe having Evie as a stepmother wouldn't be as bad as I feared. Besides, what was joined together was joined together, and there was not a thing I could do about it.

The DJ hired to play romantic love songs suddenly blasted us with "The Macarena," a wedding tradition still popular in the high country. I rushed to join a growing crowd of celebrants as we began to coordinate the motions to the song. Suddenly Wade was next to me. We both hopped and swung our hips as we tried to match the hand motions to the music. I at least had the moves down, but Wade's elbows were flailing at all the wrong angles. I had to stop just so I could double over in laughter.

He laughed too, then took my hand and pulled me into a standing position before kissing me on top of my head. I felt as though I were in a trance as he led me down a hallway and into an empty room, the church nursery. He pulled me into a corner, next to an empty crib.

I felt my heart pound. I wanted to run, but all I could do was stand as if my feet had been super-glued to the gray plaid linoleum.

He took my hands in his, and I held my breath, uncertain what he would say or how I would respond.

His blue eyes were intense under a wisp of blond hair that had slipped off his forehead. "Today, as I watched you, Donna, I couldn't believe how beautiful you've become."

I tried to laugh off his tenderness. "Yeah, just like I was eighteen again." I hesitated as the warmth of the moment bled into my voice. "Like we were both eighteen again."

He caught my chin in his rough, work-worn hand. "It's like fourteen years of my life have turned to dust. My feelings for you are still alive. They're deeper than ever."

It was too late to escape. I felt hot, then cold, then fear, then peace as he closed his eyes and leaned in for a kiss. As our lips touched, I discovered how hungry I was to kiss him back. His arms encircled me, and my knees felt weak as I became lost in his breath, his scent, his touch, his—

A shrill voice rang out, "Wade, I've been looking for you everywhere."

Startled, Wade let go and stood ramrod straight before turning to face the doorway.

"Mom!"

And there, silhouetted in shadow, stood the littlest, biggest reason why any girl should run away from Wade Gage: one Mrs. Fay Gage.

Mrs. Gage was wearing a lavender knit dress with a matching crocheted sweater studded with shiny black beads. Her graying curls were gently brushed into a rounded orb of hair, carefully sprayed so stiff that no breeze would dare interfere. Her naturally wrinkled face was crafted into a scowl that reminded me of the movie poster for the latest horror flick playing down at the theater.

One hand was on her rather wide hip and the other wagged an index finger through the air. "Wade, did you forget you drove your sister and me to the wedding?" She shot me a glare and nodded. "Donna. Can't say that it's nice to see you."

I tried to wipe the evidence of the kiss from my lips, as if I could. "Same here."

She stared at me without blinking as she spoke to her son. "Wade, why don't you go and meet us at the front door of the fellowship hall. I'm ready to go home now."

Wade stepped away from me, a move I noticed and noted. "Yes, Mom."

He nodded at me, as his mother had. "Donna."

Then he was gone.

Mrs. Gage took two steps toward me and folded her arms across her middle. "What do you think you're doing?"

"Excuse me?"

"What do you think you are doing with my son?"

"Well, I . . ."

She put both hands on her hips. "I will not have you interfering with Wade again. Do you know what my family has been through because of you?"

I tried to tighten the satin shrug that covered my shoulders. "But . . ."

"We just got Wade cleaned up, dear. He's sober now. I'll not have you messing him up again. Is that clear?"

Suddenly Kat Cage Martin, Wade's sister, appeared at the door. She was a tall, dark-headed woman, with chin-length hair. She was dressed in deep purple with a fuchsia scarf tied around her neck. She was in her early thirties and about sixty pounds overweight with sort of a linebacker look. I wasn't so sure, even with my years of police training, if I could wrestle her down in a dark alley. Hopefully I wouldn't have to. "Is everything all right, Mom? Wade said he's bringing the truck around."

Mrs. Gage gave me a hard look. "It is now, dear. Isn't that right, Deputy?"

I had no reply.

Kat looked at me with disdain. "Oh." Then with total disregard, "Come with me, Mother."

Mrs. Gage turned to leave and slid her arm through the crook of her daughter's elbow. "Yes, dear, it's time we left this woman behind us."

Then, they were gone.

I blinked. Wade had left me for his mother.

I was still fuming a few days later when I got the call to come to Lisa Leann's meeting.

I mean, it wasn't that Wade and I hadn't talked. We had.

"What I don't understand," I'd told him on the phone as I leaned back against my kitchen counter, "is why you deserted me like you did." I hugged my gray sweatshirt with my free arm. "Didn't you know your mom would get her claws into me as soon as you turned your back?"

"I don't know what came over me," Wade said. "I guess I just felt like we were in high school again, and she'd just caught us making out on that old sofa in the garage."

I had to laugh at the memory. "Don't remind me. That was *the* most embarrassing day of my life. Especially when she noticed my shirt was inside out."

"She grounded me for a month, you know."

"Well, she just did it again."

"What do you mean?"

I ran my fingers through my short, blonde curls. "Didn't you hear? After you left, she forbade me from seeing you."

Wade let out a sigh. "No wonder you're upset."

I turned and stared at the sunlit peak outside my window and poured myself a cup of coffee. "Yeah, well, you're still afraid of her, and that makes me wonder if we really belong together."

"Donna, wait. We can work this out. I know we can."

"What's to work out? Either you stand up to your mom or you can kiss me good-bye."

Wade laughed.

"What's so funny?"

"After our hello kiss, there's no way I'm kissing you good-bye."

That comment softened my disposition. "Well, then, what are you going to do, Wade? What?"

"Let me talk to her, maybe I can even get us an invitation for one of her famous chicken parmesan dinners."

"If you can do that, then we can talk."

"Uh, I'm interested in more than talk."

This was a subject I wanted to avoid. My voice iced. "I'm not a bad girl anymore. I'll tell you that up front."

"Oh. I didn't mean—"

"Call me when you've patched things up with your mom."

I clicked out of the conversation, not even giving him a chance to reply, and slammed my almost empty mug next to the sink. This whole thing was nothing but a disaster. One I wasn't sure I could weather.

So, when Lisa Leann, one of the members of the Potluck Club prayer group I belonged to, called and told me "her Potluck catering business plan," as she called it, and about the meeting scheduled at her wedding shop the next evening, I knew this was the distraction I needed.

By the time Evie came out of her honeymoon daze, her little Potluck Club world, of which she was president, would be changed. But as she and Dad were so sweet on each other, I thought she'd hardly notice, much less mind.

Maybe, this would lead to a new Evie, an Evie I could get along with.

Only time would tell.

Lisa Leann

3

Reality Bites

The defining moment of my life came the day of Evie's wedding, the very first wedding I'd ever planned and implemented as a professional wedding consultant.

It was too bad I almost missed it.

I had more urgent matters to attend to. When I got the call from Deputy Donna and her (ahem) friend Wade Gage that my sweet daughter Mandy had gone into labor, my world rocked. Suddenly, the last-minute details of putting on the biggest show Summit View had ever seen were no longer important to me. Without even waving good-bye, I tossed off my pink apron with the words "Lisa Leann's High Country Weddings" embroidered across the bib, jumped into my Lincoln, and sped toward the hospital.

Thank heavens I'd left detailed wedding plans that my dear friends, whom I like to refer to as the Potluckers, could implement without me. Otherwise, poor Evie might still be a Miss instead of a Mrs.

When I arrived in the hospital parking lot, ahead of Deputy Donna, I didn't know what to think. Donna had told me they were already en route. Had something gone wrong?

Just as I'd decided to drive to the house, Donna's Bronco with its siren blazing pulled to a stop in front of the emergency room entrance. I rushed to the truck and got the shock of my life. There my daughter sat in the back seat, holding my newly born grandson. So help me, I'm afraid I screamed.

As I recovered my composure, Wade ran inside and grabbed a gurney, then he and Donna helped Mandy climb on board. That's when I experienced my life-defining moment—the moment I took my grandbaby into my arms. If the baby hadn't still been attached to Mandy, I might have burst into song, twirling my grandson through the hospital's parking lot, you know, like Julie Andrews did in that high Alps meadow in *The Sound of Music*.

For there, nestled in my arms, was red-faced Kyle Christopher, wrapped in one of my pale pink bath towels. His little eyes squeezed shut against the bright sunshine.

How precious.

One look into that little face and I went from a woman in her late forties whose main concern was how to fight wrinkles, to Grandmother Extraordinaire.

I may never recover from the shock of seeing my baby with a baby of her own. And I *know* I will never recover from the shock of having to put both my babies on a 737 headed to Houston's Bush International Airport.

I'd known that my time with Mandy was short. And it was only by luck, really, that she'd been with me in Colorado for Kyle's birth. She'd traveled to see "the folks," as she calls her dad and me, over the Thanksgiving holiday, two months earlier. We'd been having a grand visit when she collapsed in my kitchen with the pangs of early labor.

With Mandy confined to bed rest, and Ray, her husband, having to return to Texas, Mandy had been left entirely in my care. It would have been heavenly if she'd not grieved so about missing Ray. "Mom, of course I appreciate what you and Dad are doing for me," she'd say, flopping her strawberry curls against my velvety mauve sofa. "But I'm so homesick."

I'd sit next to her and pull her into my arms. "Of course you are," I'd coo, patting her shoulder. "Just consider this time with us as God's gift. It is, you know, at least from my point of view."

Her little chin would quiver and she'd dab her eyes with a tissue. "Mom, you keep reminding me, but I miss my Ray!"

Then the sobs would start in earnest, and all I could do was hold her. After her tears, I'd comfort her with a slice of my famous chocolate cheesecake, which I always keep in the back of my freezer for emergencies. (Chocolate cheesecake has special power to heal any heartbroken woman, I say.)

But now that the baby was born, it took no time for Ray to come to Summit View to collect his little family. Can't say that I blame him, after all, and I'm happy Mandy has a husband who loves her.

But here's my complaint: Ray made it to Summit View faster than a dignitary on the Concorde, ready to pack my Mandy's suitcase and whisk her and the baby back to Texas. Even then I had to put my foot down to convince him to stay a week after Kyle was born. "It's too soon for Mandy to travel," I'd scolded. "Honestly, is this any way to take care of your wife?"

"But she says she's more than ready," he argued.

Then from the bedroom down the hall, I could hear Mandy's voice sing out, "And willing."

I walked down to her room, where she sat in my rocking chair nursing the baby. She looked so sweet in her pale coral button-down gown that I couldn't be angry.

"Darling, I know you're anxious to get home, but a day, that's all I'm asking. You can wait another few days."

That was all she waited. Before I knew it, it was a week later and Henry was driving us all to DIA.

Little Kyle slept peacefully in his car seat, a gift from the Potluckers, while I sat beside him, gently stroking his silky head as his rosebud lips spread into what almost looked like a grin.

"He smiled!" I crowed to Mandy, who sat just on the other side of him. She giggled. "He's glad to be going home."

"I'd wish you'd let me come with you, to help."

"No," Mandy and Ray chirped in unison.

I looked at the back of Ray's head, then at Mandy. "But how will you manage?"

Ray's announcement almost stopped my heart. "It's not that we don't want your help, it's that we don't need it. My mother is meeting us at the airport."

I fumed the rest of the way to the departure drop-off. I could just imagine Ray's mother, Sandy, with my grandbaby all to herself.

The next thing I knew, we were at curbside with the trunk of the Lincoln popped open. Was it good-bye already?

"Let me go into the terminal."

Mandy held the baby in her arms and kissed me on the cheek. "No, Mom, we'll be okay. Besides, you're not a ticketed passenger; they won't let you through security."

I reached for the baby and kissed his forehead. "Oh little one, your Mimi will miss you so much." I looked back up as Mandy reached to retrieve Kyle. "Listen, I've decided. I'll be down in a couple of weeks. I can stay as long as you need me."

The kids exchanged glances, then Ray cleared his throat. "Appreciate the offer, Mother Lambert, we really do. But that just won't be necessary. We're going to need some time to ourselves."

"To settle in," Mandy said.

Ray nodded. "Yeah, we'll call you when we're ready for company."

My heart lurched. "How long will that take?"

Henry opened the front passenger door. "Time to go, Lisa Leann."

I could feel the color drain out of my face. "But . . ."

Mandy and Ray turned to leave, but Mandy paused. "I'll call you when we get home, love you!"

I wanted to run, to hold her and little Kyle one more time, but Henry was ushering me inside the car, almost as if I was under arrest. All I could manage to do was wave before my vision blurred my family away from me.

Upon arriving back at our condo in Summit View, I needed a slice of chocolate cheesecake, which I vowed to myself to burn as Jane Fonda workout fuel, and half a box of tissues before I could calm down.

Despite my tears, I knew God had used this move from Texas to Colorado. I mean, if I hadn't arrived in town when I did, the Potluck Club would have fallen apart, Goldie might have left Jack for good, Donna might not have ever found herself in Wade's arms, and I doubt Evie could have made it to the altar with Vernon. Yes, God was using me right where I was, but how I missed my grandbaby.

After the kids' departure I sat with Henry as I knitted a pair of booties. I looked up at my husband, who had not that long ago retired from a Houston oil company. "Henry, just out of curiosity, would you ever consider moving back?"

Henry glanced up from his paper. "Not a chance, Lisa Leann. This is *our* time."

I felt my heart skip a beat. There was something about the way that he said "*our* time."

I murmured, more to myself than to him, "Yes, our time."

The Lord knows that through the years we'd let our marriage fall into shambles. We were just now beginning to rebuild. I studied Henry carefully as he said, "It's been nice, you and me growing closer, as a couple, I mean."

I suppose it was only my guilty conscience, but something in his eyes made me catch my breath. *Does he know?*

I smiled. "Yes, I'm glad for that."

I returned to my knitting, my heart beating a little faster.

Secrets, I've always found, are so difficult to carry. But sometimes they're a necessity.

I noticed Henry watching me. I put my knitting aside and stood up. "Ready for a slice of cheesecake?"

He nodded.

I practically bolted for the kitchen, but called over my shoulder, "Coming right up."

Once behind the swinging kitchen door, I braced myself against the kitchen counter. No, in my heart I knew he couldn't know the real reason I'd agreed to this move, and if I could help it, he never would.

I had to smile then. Who would have thought that I, Lisa Leann Lambert, would be so good at holding my tongue?

I was putting the dessert dishes away when I was, once again, struck by my own genius.

Of course, I had inspiration. You see, amid the congratulations I'd received about my new grandbaby, I also was getting a few calls congratulating me on the wonderful spread at the Vesey wedding that the Potluck Club had prepared. Come to think of it, I'd heard that Lizzie, the local school librarian, had teased about opening a catering business. Vonnie told me she'd even called it a catering party.

Joking aside, this was a great idea, and I always have a knack of not only claiming but implementing all great ideas that come my way, whether original or not.

This idea, though inspired by my friends, I would claim as my own, for not only did I have a commercial kitchen at the wedding shop, I had the know-how and I had the team. At last, I had a way to organize the Potluckers as their once-and-for-all leader. I quickly dialed Lizzie to tell her my plan.

After I spilled the details, Lizzie said, "Ah, great minds think alike, Lisa Leann. And I must say, your timing is remarkable. Just tonight, Samuel and I were talking about my retirement. My early retirement is, blessedly, not too far off, and I'll certainly want something to keep me busy and supplied with mad money. Count me in. Let's call a meeting with the girls. How about tomorrow evening?"

"What about Evie? Shouldn't we wait and hold the meeting when she returns?"

"Not this time. Who knows where her head will be when she gets back from her honeymoon. For all we know, she may want to spend all her spare time with *Ver-non*."

I giggled, very pleased to bypass the Potluck Club president. "You can never predict honeymooners," I happily agreed.

The next evening, the Potluckers, minus Evie, met at my wedding shop to discuss the possibilities.

We were seated around my cozy front room, and I'd just put another log on the fire. I poured everyone a cup of Celestial Seasonings apple tea from my bone china teapot.

I, wearing a camel-colored cashmere turtleneck with matching wool pants, was beside myself with excitement.

It had been a slow day at the shop, so I'd spent the afternoon making a PowerPoint presentation, which now played on my laptop placed atop my marble coffee table. The girls watched, perched on the sofa and my wing-backed chairs, as I'd flipped through the slides.

The last of my bulleted points and pie charts faded as I pressed a button. A pink background with the words "Potluck Catering Club" splashed across the screen.

"Girls, we've got a name, we've got a kitchen, and we've got a plan," I told them. "Who's in?"

Vonnie, a retired nurse, raised her plump hand, looking so sweet in her oversized pink sweatshirt embroidered with hearts and butterflies, which I'm sure she purchased at Wal-Mart. Her graying blonde hair was swept up in a do that was held together with a clear plastic banana clip. Soft ringlets of stray curls framed her face. "But do we have a reason?" she asked.

Donna laughed. "Because we can?"

Vonnie lowered her hand and shook her head. "No, what I want to know is, what are we doing this *for*? This looks like a lot of work. I can't make this kind of commitment without a reason. It's not that I couldn't use an extra buck, but I'm comfortable with the way my life is now. Why bother?"

I felt my brows knit together, mainly because I hadn't tried Botox yet, though I was certainly thinking about it. "What about using our little business as a ministry fund-raiser? I mean, we could give 10 percent of our profits away to a good cause, and the rest could be divided among us."

Lizzie got so excited I thought she would spill her tea on her gray velveteen pantsuit. She had a way of looking elegant without even trying. That soft gray had remarkable powers for bringing out the blues of her eyes while highlighting the silver in her short hair.

"Samuel says the church is looking at hiring a youth director. They even have a few candidates in mind, though the budget's a bit tight. What if our new venture was able to help support the church's youth program?"

Vonnie actually applauded. "The youth are our future," she crowed just before taking another sip of tea. "I always say a church is only as strong as its youth program."

The other Potluckers nodded in approval while I beamed. "Why don't we test the waters?" I suggested. "Run a little ad in the paper to see if we get any calls?"

Goldie, still dressed in her work clothes, a light tan dress with a matching blazer with gold buttons, seconded my idea. "Yes, let's test the waters. I mean, I wouldn't dream of quitting my job with the law firm, but I love this possibility of helping the kids at church. I know Chris will help us with the legal paperwork."

"That will save us a buck or two," I gushed. "Wow, this is exciting. We have so much going for us, what could possibly go wrong?"

Evangeline

4

Catering Dreams

A few days after Vernon and I returned home from the paradise of the Bahamas, where we'd honeymooned for eight days, I had the girls over for some leftover wedding cake (still moist and delicious thanks to Lisa Leann's freezing method) and coffee over at the house. Vernon wisely took off for the afternoon.

"I'm going to get in a round of golf." Vernon shoved his arms into his leather sheriff's jacket he'd retrieved from the foyer coatrack.

I placed my hands on my hips. "You don't play golf."

He smiled and then winked. "I don't eat wedding cake and cluck with hens either."

I'd barely kissed him and sent him out the door when Lisa Leann came swooping in, waving a DVD of what I assumed to be the wedding in one hand and carrying the thawed cake, protected by a bakery box, in the other. "Look what I haaaaaaave," she sang as she crossed the front door threshold of my home.

I took the cake from her. "Are you singing about the cake or the video?"

Lisa Leann gave me a "ha-ha" and then followed me into the dining room, where I placed the cake box on the cherry dining room table that at one time belonged to my grandmother. It shone with the patina of time and Pledge and was adorned with soft linen, fine china, and polished silver.

I pulled the cake from the box while Lisa Leann fingered the tablecloth. "Lovely," she said with a pat to the linen. "Always lovely."

I looked at her. As usual, her red hair was styled to perfection and her makeup, which she would never leave the house without, was applied as though by an artist of Hollywood caliber. "Thank you."

She gazed at me full-on then. "And look at you."

I stood upright. "What about me?"

Before she could answer me, the doorbell rang. And before I could answer *it*, Lizzie and Goldie stepped into the house.

"Hello, hello!" Lizzie called out. "It's us, Goldie and Lizzie."

Lisa Leann leaned in to whisper, "You and Goldie pretty much have the same look about you, I'd say."

I didn't have to wonder what she meant by that; Goldie and her husband Jack have recently reunited after a brief, albeit long-time-coming, separation. However, I do believe that certain elements of marriage are best left unspoken.

I headed for the foyer. "Good afternoon, girls," I called back.

They were coming out of their heavy sweaters, and I reached for them as Lisa Leann came up behind me. "Never fear, ladies! I brought the cake and the DVD."

"The DVD?" Goldie asked, just as the front door opened and Donna walked in. Since my marriage to her father, I have insisted that she not knock when we know she's coming. If we don't know that she's coming, that's another story. After all, we are still in the honeymoon phase.

"What DVD?" Donna asked. She was as cute as always, her pixie blonde hair pushed away from her pretty face and—as always—dressed in comfortable yet tasteful clothes. Today's attire was a gray long-sleeved tee tucked into what appeared to be new black jeans. She wore a multicolored belt with flecks of black and gray mixed in with red, pink, and turquoise.

"The DVD of your daddy's wedding to Miss Evie, here," Lisa Leann answered.

"What I want to know," Lizzie said, "is if there is a DVD of the honeymoon." There was a twinkle in her eye I'd never noticed before. What is it about . . . *ahem* . . . married coupling that brings out the devil in a group of women?

Church ladies, no less.

Donna blushed as hot as I felt. "T-M-I." She threw her hands up in surrender. She nodded at me. "I don't smell coffee."

"I haven't started it yet," I answered, hanging up the sweaters I still had gripped in my hands.

"Allow me. Anything to get away from this topic of conversation."

"Where's Vonnie?" Goldie asked.

Lisa Leann raised her chin just a bit. "Oh. She's going to be a tad late. She and"—she lowered her voice to a whisper—"D-A-V-I-D were having lunch today."

D-A-V-I-D, as Lisa Leann called him, is Vonnie's birth son and—at one time—Donna's love interest. Or, at least, Donna was his love interest.

"I heard that," Donna called from the kitchen. I could both hear and smell the coffee beginning to perk. She walked back into the foyer, where the four of us seemed to be glued. "And . . . I can spell." She gave Lisa Leann a cross-eyed look. "Since I was near-bout in the first grade." She sounded like a mixture of Elmer Fudd and Jethro Bodine.

"Let's go into the living room." I motioned toward the opened doorway leading into the Victorian setting. As the hostess I needed to stay in control of my guests, two of which apparently needed to be kept under control.

As we moved into the room Lizzie spied the opened photo album I'd strategically placed on the coffee table before they'd arrived. "Oh, what do we have here? Why, girls, I do believe we have honeymoon pictures!" The others began to cluck around the book.

"I've seen them." Donna dismissed the implied notion of looking at the pictures of her father and me frolicking along the beaches and resorts of Nassau and Freeport. Instead, she walked over to the window and peered out. "There's Vonnie."

"Oh, good," I said. "Girls, feel free to sit and look over the pictures. I did that creative memories thing so each picture practically has its own commentary. You won't need me."

I left the living room and went back into the foyer, opening the door for one of my oldest friends before she could reach the front steps.

"Good afternoon, Vonnie," I said as she ascended them.

She looked up at me. "Good afternoon, Mrs. Vesey. I'm the last to arrive, no doubt."

I stepped out on the front porch and pulled the door nearly shut behind me. "How's David?" I kept my voice low.

Vonnie shook her head sadly. "Pathetic. I understand Donna choosing Wade over David. After all, Donna and Wade have a . . . history."

"I suppose you could call it that." Between me and the lamppost I might call it something else, but that's neither here nor there. After all, Donna is my stepdaughter now and I have to be careful about what I think concerning her.

"But poor David . . . And what really concerns me is his sudden interest in Velvet James."

"Velvet James? That tart?"

Velvet James is Donna's half sister, the daughter of Donna's mother, who left Vernon back when Donna was about four years old. But that's another story, and since I'm not inclined to gossip, I'll avoid saying that Doreen Vesey left with the church's choir director only to live a hard life, marrying a whole handful of times, having a pack of children, living life doing illegal things to support them and her, but in the end losing them to the state or their daddies, whichever was in the best interest of the child.

But, like I said, I don't much care for gossip.

Vonnie shook her head. "Don't get me started. No matter what I say, he thinks he's actually got something going there."

About that time the front door swung open. My hand was still on the doorknob, and my arm was nearly ripped out of its socket. "Ow!"

"Hello, ladies." It was Donna standing before us. "Sorry about that, Evangeline," she said unconvincingly. "Talking about anything interesting?"

Vonnie has always been like a second mother to Donna, so I know this whole situation has been difficult for them both. "Hello, precious," she said to Donna.

Donna gave us her best "uh-huh" look and said, "Don't 'precious' me, Vonnie Westbrook. And do *not* think I don't know about David and Velvet. I am, after all, a deputy sheriff. I get paid to know things."

"Does it bother you?" I asked. "At all?"

"The only thing that bothers me is that David will, no doubt, get hurt." She looked at Vonnie with compassion. "And I really don't want that, Von. He is, if nothing else, my friend."

"That's nice, dear." Vonnie stepped toward her and patted her on the arm. "And I believe you mean it." She took a deep breath and sighed. "Shall we go inside then? I can smell the coffee from here, and I'm anxious for another piece of Lisa Leann's delectable wedding cake."

In other words, subject closed.

Over cake and coffee I heard the story—once again—as to how the catering club came about.

The first time I heard about it was from Vonnie, who came by the morning after Vernon and I had returned from our honeymoon. She and I curled up on the family room sofa like the old friends we are while Vernon went to his old house to help the movers load up the U-Haul truck.

"It all started the morning of your wedding," Vonnie told me. "Actually, it goes back to last year's Christmas tea when we were all saying in jest that we should open a catering service because so many of us were such good cooks."

"I remember that." I pulled my feet closer to me. "You call it last year's tea, but it was a mere few weeks ago." This being the middle of February and the tea occurring just before the New Year, after all.

"Nevertheless, on the morning of the wedding, when everyone was at the boutique helping out, Lisa Leann got a phone call that Mandy had gone into labor."

"I remember that too. But how does that lead to a whole new business venture? For crying out loud, Vonnie, I was gone just a little over a week."

"Well, naturally Lisa Leann had to leave, which of course left the rest of us at the boutique to handle things." Vonnie threw her hand about in the air and tossed her fading blonde hair. "I don't know who said it for sure, but I think it was Lizzie who said something about the Potluck Club Catering party, and the next thing you know, an idea was born." Vonnie grinned, and I could tell that, even at less than two weeks into the venture, she was quite pleased with it. "While you and Vernon were basking in the sunshine, we all met over at Lisa Leann's and put everything on paper."

"A game plan," I commented.

"So to speak. Anyway, we managed to get an advertisement in the paper, which came out on Thursday, and two days after that we got a call to do our very first event."

"Which is?"

"Hannah Lowenstein's bat mitzvah. They had hired a caterer from Breck," Vonnie explained, referring to Breckenridge as the locals so typically do. "But apparently Mrs. Lowenstein and the woman who owned the service had something of a misunderstanding . . . don't ask me about what."

"Hannah Lowenstein? Is she Ed Lowenstein's girl?" I asked. When Vonnie nodded, I added, "I had no idea she was that old." The Lowensteins live right down the street from Vernon and me. I discreetly cleared my throat. "I don't mean to throw a monkey wrench into this, but you say you have a game plan."

"We do."

"But what about some sort of legal business agreement? In my line of work I see all sorts of disasters when you don't have a good legal agreement." I own an accounting service that I operate from my home.

Vonnie laughed lightly. "Don't worry, Evie. We will. And, yes, you will be very much a part of this too."

I hate it that she knows me so well.

It nearly killed me not to participate in the Potluck Catering Club's first event (I was still focusing on getting Vernon moved in, which included helping him get rid of some of the tackiest household items I've ever seen, not to mention a few things I knew were left over from his marriage to Doreen, and not to mention that this is my busy season). However, I heard all about it immediately afterward when Lizzie came by to fill me in, telling me that Lisa Leann practiced making chocolate macaroons with matzah cake meal at least five times before she felt she'd gotten it right.

I smiled. It was now three weeks since my wedding, one week since our little coffee-and-cake get-together.

"So how do you think it's going to go?" I asked. "Any more calls for business?"

"Not yet."

I'd poured us some homemade lemonade, and she took a long sip as we stood in my kitchen, leaning our hips against the countertop. "I'm going to take this whole thing very slowly," she said. "So I'm glad we're not bombarded with business so far. After all, school is still in session, and I'm not about to leave my job when I'm so close to retirement. When we see where this thing is going, I'll rethink it. Not to mention that I'm still taking care of Mom."

Well, I can't say that I blame her. Like she said, she is close to retirement and her mother is somewhat senile and living in a nearby assisted living center. Goldie has a good job with Chris Lowe, who is an attorney, Donna has her position with the sheriff's office, and I'm heading toward April 15th.

Vonnie is the only one of us fully retired, but she has her hands full taking care of *her* cantankerous mother, and beyond all that . . . with Lisa Leann at the helm, who knows where this ship will go?

So, yeah. I vote for taking this one step at a time too, at least until I can get into the real swing of things. I've said it before and I'll say it again: if it weren't for me, there'd be no catering club.

Goldie

5

Chilling News

I am beginning to think I'm married to a pretty wonderful guy.

Not that I always felt this way. For far too long Jack Dippel was an adulterer. I have to say, though, that since the fall of last year when I left him and his cheating ways and he started counseling with our pastor, he's become something of a Prince Charming.

Take last evening, for example. I returned home from work completely exhausted. I work for Chris Lowe, Attorney at Law, and we are in what is known as trial term—a two-week period that rolls around every so often so that the courts hear current cases on the docket. Or, at least as many of them as they can. For those of us who work within the court's system, it's a time of great stress and physical fatigue, but necessary nonetheless.

On my way home I nearly fell asleep at the wheel. If it hadn't been for Lisa Leann's call, I would have.

"Goldie," she said in that Texas way she has that always gives me the impression she has a nonstop party going on inside her head. "Darlin', do I have news for you!"

I blinked at the red traffic light before me. "It must be good. You sound even more excited than usual."

"And I am. Listen, now. I just got a phone call from Beverly Jackson. Do you know who I'm talking about?"

"Of course I do, Lisa Leann. I've lived in this town since I was a child bride. She's married to Steve Jackson."

"Vice president of the bank."

The light turned green, and I drove through the intersection. With every turn of the wheel, I was getting closer to home. "I know that. So?"

"So, Miss-Hurry-Me-Along, she and the ladies of the bank—meaning the female employees and the wives of the male employees—want to throw a bridal shower of unforgettable proportions for Michelle Prattle and—"

"They want us to cater it!" I squealed.

Lisa Leann laughed. "You've got it, girl."

I pressed my hand against my breast and took a deep breath. "Whew! When? Where? How many?"

Lisa Leann continued to laugh. "One month from today. That gives us just the right amount of time, but we'll have to keep our noses to the grindstone, as they say. I don't want anything to go wrong."

My mind was suddenly wide open. "I have an idea, want to hear it?"

"You know I do."

"It's a bank function, right?" I didn't wait for an answer. I kept talking as I turned onto the street where Jack and I live. "Why not have a 'money tree' for the kids. We can get some silk ficus trees with the little white lights—"

"I'm liking where this is going."

"White lights everywhere."

"An entire theme of white and green."

I pulled into our driveway and shut off the car's engine. "People can bring money cards that can be clipped to the leaves."

"Elegant dinner wear."

"Oh, absolutely. Not to sound materialistic, but you said it right when you said 'posh.'"

"I didn't say 'posh,'" Lisa Leann said with another giggle. "But I should have."

"Let's ask if they'd like to make it a couples event. The women may be throwing it, but I'm thinking black tie."

"We're on the same page, my friend. I'll let you know more as soon as I know more."

I pulled myself out of the car. "Have you talked to Lizzie yet?"

"Her line was busy. I hear you getting out of the car. Enjoy your evening."

I felt my shoulders droop of their own accord. "I'm so tired. I'm going to beg Jack to go to Higher Grounds and pick us up something while I soak in a tub of hot water."

"Now that's the way to train a man. I'm thinking I'll have Henry do the same thing. Ciao for now, baby."

I closed my cell phone with a smile, then trudged up the walkway to the front door, keeping my eyes on my feet. It wasn't until I'd reached the bottom step of the front porch that I saw the large wicker basket lined in white linen and graced with a simple pink bow along the side of the handle. I stopped for a brief moment, then carefully approached and squatted down. I felt my light overcoat pool around my feet as I fingered the contents of the basket.

Lavender-scented bath salts, complementary body lotion and spray, a thirsty lavender-colored towel, a terry cloth sponge, and half a dozen lavender-scented floating candles. Tucked between the towel and the sponge was a CD of American standards sung by none other than . . .

"Frank Sinatra," I whispered.

It was then that the front door opened. I looked up to see my husband standing there, looking fairly fine in a pair of dark khaki chinos and a navy blue V-neck sweater over a plaid oxford shirt. There was a time when I rarely saw him out of sweats, but since our reunion he seemed to take special care of his appearance when we were together. "There's a tub of hot water and a new terry robe with matching slippers waiting for you in the bathroom."

I grew uncomfortably nervous; an old voice whispered to my still-fragile heart. *Is Jack having another affair?* In the past, the end of an affair meant some eye-boggling piece of jewelry for me. This wasn't jewelry, but . . .

Jack must have read my thoughts. He frowned at me and said, "Can't a man buy a gift for his wife without having . . ." He looked away for a moment. "Goldie, I love you. I'm trying to get it right this time."

I pursed my lips to keep from laughing (or perhaps crying) at the whole thing. Relief does strange things to a woman's emotions, especially a woman married to Jack Dippel. Even in his early fifties he managed to look so handsome. His face bore hardly a wrinkle, his gray hair only making him look all the more striking. He kept a year-round tan, and his glasses only served to give him a studious appearance.

I stood, bringing the basket up with me. "What made you think to do this?" I asked, calling something akin to a truce with my words.

"Hard day, right?"

"Very." I took a step toward him, and he met me, the basket keeping us physically separated. But I managed to nuzzle his neck. "I'm sorry for the slight lack of trust."

"It's going to take time, I know." Then to change the subject: "I've got dinner warm in the oven, straight from Higher Grounds."

I pulled back. "Now you really have read my mind."

He kissed me gently. "I'm good at that. Now scoot and take

that bath. I want you in the robe and slippers when you come to the table."

I looked up at him coyly. "Who says love gets stale when a couple gets old."

He stepped aside, and I took steps to pass him. He swatted me on my fanny, which as a coach has always been one of his trademark endearment touches. "Who says we're old?" When I looked over my shoulder at him, he winked at me. And I at him.

I soaked up to my chin in the sweet-scented water as Old Blue Eyes serenaded me from the CD player that rested on the tank of the toilet. It wasn't piped in stereo, but it was perfect, especially with the lights turned down and the lit floating candles bobbing atop the water, adding to the delicious aroma that filled the room in a misty cloud. At some point Jack brought me a cup of hot tea, and though he gave me quite the stare, he didn't bother my respite.

"I have died and gone to heaven," I whispered to him, closing my eyes.

"Not quite, baby," he said softly. "But I'll do my best to get you as close as possible."

When the water had turned tepid and my fingers had shriveled along the tips, I reluctantly sat up, blew out the candles, and drew myself up to the cool of the room. I wrapped myself in the new robe and tied the sash tight around my waist, then pushed my feet into the slippers. I walked over to the vanity, picked up my brush, and ran it through my hair for two or three strokes, and then left the room as the tub gurgled the last bit of water into the pipes.

Jack had lit candles on the dining room table and put steaming hot lemon chicken from the café on china plates out of my grandmother's set. I'd inherited them after she died about ten years ago. Ten years later and I'm still stunned that she even thought to leave them to me. I'd never exactly been her favorite; my moving to Colorado practically sealed my fate of being plucked from her side of the family tree.

I pointed to the table. "Grandmother Hampton's china, I see."

Jack smiled at me. "We don't use it enough." He pulled my chair out for me, and I sat, watching over my shoulder as he poured a glass of lemon water into two of the stemmed crystal glasses we'd gotten as a wedding gift. He brought them over to the table and then sat, placing one at my plate, one at his.

"Jack, this is lovely." I leaned over for a kiss. "Thank you."

Jack blessed the food and then picked up a remote control I hadn't noticed before. With a press of a button the stereo in the adjacent living room clicked on: more American standards, this time performed by Rod Stewart, wafted in.

"Jack," I whispered, then spoke in a teasing tone. "What was it Julia Roberts said in *Pretty Woman*? 'I appreciate this whole seduction scene you've got going here, but I'm a sure thing.'"

Jack shook his head. "Nah-ah. I'm never taking you for granted again."

I sat up straight and picked up my fork. "I like that."

A moment later I pulled my foot out of one of the slippers; we spent the rest of the meal playing footsy under the table.

I sat long-ways on the sofa, my feet in Jack's lap while he rubbed them with some of the lavender body lotion from the basket. "The worst part of trial term is having to wear heels all day," I said with a moan.

"But think how pretty your legs look in them," my husband teased.

"You say that, but you don't have to wear them."

We sat in silence, and Jack continued to rub. Frank and Rod had long ago sung their last stanza, but Jack continued to hum "Bewitched, Bothered, and Bewildered." He was, oddly enough, in perfect pitch.

"I'm going to have to get some sleep pretty soon," he finally said. "Four-thirty comes awful early every morning."

I opened my eyes from my near-reverie and said, "Spring break is just a few weeks away. Then you can watch *The Tonight Show* and sleep late like we used to when we were first married."

Jack furrowed his brow. "Are you planning to go back to Georgia again this year?"

I paused briefly before nodding. "I'm sure I will. I talked to Daddy the other night, and he says the livestock festival will be held the end of next month, so if I go, I'll go then. If I can get the time off."

"How's your daddy doing?"

I wrapped my arms tight around my middle, warm at the thought of Daddy. Like most Southern daughters, I'm a daddy's girl. Always have been, always will be. "Good, as usual."

"Your daddy wouldn't have it any other way."

"Still working too hard. I talked with Mama on the way to work this morning, and she said she's wishing he'd slow down a bit. You'd think at seventy-eight the man would be moving toward the recliner, but no. Mama says he and my brother argue all the time over how hard Daddy continues to work the farm."

"Like I said, your daddy wouldn't have it any other way. If the man ever gets sick, he'll die from being miserable at having to lie around all day."

"Yes, he would." I pulled my feet from his hands. "Let's go to bed, Mr. Dippel. I'm tired, you're tired, and tomorrow is another day."

"Yes, it is." Hand in hand we stepped down the dark hallway. Without turning on a single light we found our way to the rumpled covers of our bed and slipped under the coolness of them.

I believe I fell asleep, happy and content, before I even closed my eyes.

My eyes shot wide open, and I bolted up in the bed as my heart hammered in my chest. "What is that?" I asked, aware of a shrillness piercing through the dark and silence of night.

Jack sat up beside me. "It's the phone, Goldie."

I pressed my hand to my chest and fumbled for the lamp on the bedside table as Jack did the same from his side of the bed. I peered at the digital clock. It stared back at me: 4:15. *Who would be calling at 4:15 in the morning?*

Jack answered the phone, which was on his bedside table. "Hello? . . . Hey . . . yeah . . . yeah . . . that's okay . . . oh no . . . okay, I . . . I will . . . sure . . . sure . . ." He cradled the phone against his chest and looked at me, his hair tousled and his eyes squinting against the harshness of the light behind me. "Goldie, it's your brother."

"Which brother?"

"Tom. It's Tom . . . he . . . well, here." He extended the phone toward me. "Talk to him."

I took the phone slowly, instinctively knowing something was wrong. Tom would never call at such an ungodly hour. "Tom?"

"It's Daddy, Goldie," he said, coming right to the point. "He's had a heart attack. We're at the hospital now and . . . Mama wants to know how soon you can get back home."

Lizzie

6

A Little Mixer

The things I once held dear about returning to my home after a long day at work have gone by the wayside. There was a time, not so long ago, when I would leave the high school where I am the head librarian (or, as they say these days, media specialist) by 4:00 in the afternoon. I would drive home slowly, taking in the sights of my beloved Summit View—its magnificent wildflowers blazing color along the mountainsides in spring, its deep greens in summer, the bright yellow aspen groves zigzagging up the mountainsides in autumn, and the evergreens bent from heavy snows in winter. This was my time to reflect on the day that had just passed and to contemplate the evening ahead, usually spent with my husband Samuel and adult daughter Michelle. With Samuel and me being quiet by nature and Michelle being deaf by God's design, ours was a peaceful home where I could slip in and enjoy a cup of tea before Samuel's arrival from the bank, where he is president, and Michelle's return from Breckenridge, where she works at one of the resorts as an advertising executive. Then I would cook a simple dinner—meals like Texas hash (one of Samuel's favorites)—that was hearty and filling but didn't take all night to prepare. We would eat around the kitchen table and speak of our individual days. After dinner Michelle and I would clean the kitchen and Samuel would take a peek at the news so he could, as he says, stay informed. Then together we'd watch *Law and Order* reruns on TNT, and at some point Michelle and I would each grab a favorite book and read until time for bed.

But all that was behind me; that season of life over. Now I have a houseful of people living under one roof. Our thirty-one-year-old son Tim and his wife Samantha, along with their children, ten-year-old Kaci and six-year-old Brent, moved back home just before Christmas last year in an effort to salvage their marriage. Though they actively looked for their own house, so far nothing had "jumped out" at them.

"At least nothing in my price range," Tim said just a few nights ago, having spent the entire day, Saturday, looking while I was busy with the Lowenstein Bat Mitzvah over in Breckenridge.

I walked over to where my purse rested on the nearby kitchen countertop. "Here." I reached in and pulled out a thin stack of folded papers. "I picked up some house information papers on a few of the places I saw while in Breck. You should consider there as well. It's where you work, after all."

Tim shot me an "I can't believe you" look as he reached for the papers. "Mom, first of all, I couldn't afford a one-room shack up there, and second of all, if we move to Breck it will mean the kids having to relocate schools again. You should have thought of that, being a school employee and all."

"Silly me," I muttered, then went into the living room, where my husband continued to recuperate in his recliner, having sustained a back injury in December. He was doing what he was always doing these days, watching television. With TiVo he had managed to record every judge show, every *Law and Order*, and every cold case show ever filmed. Today, however, he was actually watching a classic, *To Kill a Mockingbird*.

I halted behind Samuel's chair long enough to watch the scene where Gregory Peck is putting papers back in his briefcase and every black man, woman, and child—relegated to the balcony—rise in honor of what he has attempted to do, to acquit an innocent black man in rural Alabama, circa 1930. I placed my hand over my heart and took in a deep breath as the preacher tapped Scout on the shoulder and said, "Stand up. Your daddy is passing by."

When I exhaled, Samuel turned and looked toward me. "Hey, there. I didn't hear you come in." He turned the volume down. "How was the bar mitzvah?"

"Bat mitzvah," I corrected, walking over to the side of his chair. "*Bat* not *bar*. Bat is for girls. Bar is for boys."

He smiled at me, reached for my hand, and tugged me to sit on the armrest. "You learn that today or did you know it already?"

"I knew it already. And do you know how I knew it already?"

He playfully rolled his eyes. "No, but I think you are going to tell me."

"I knew it because I read books. Books, Samuel. I don't insist on getting my sole entertainment from television or movies." I glanced toward the television. "Even movies well done such as this old great."

"Makes me want to rush to the library and get the oldest, mustiest copy of 'this old great,' as you call it, and actually read it, if that's any consolation."

I leaned over and braced myself by placing my hand on the opposite armrest. "Mmm-hmm. How's your back today?"

"Much better. I walked to the kitchen and back without my cane. How's that for progress?"

I frowned. "It's slow, if you want my opinion."

"Doc says I'm beginning to heal nicely. He thinks I'll be back at the bank within the next few weeks."

I sighed at the thought of even the tiniest number of weeks with Samuel hanging about the house all day—whether I was here or not—but gave his lips a quick peck anyway. "Watch your movie while I throw a frozen lasagna in the oven." I rose. "I'm going to run over to the retirement home and see Mom while it bakes, so keep an eye on it for me, will you?"

Samuel nodded as he reached for the remote and increased the volume on the television. I took a few steps and looked back at the picture of Atticus Finch and his son Jem sitting close as they drove toward the home of Tom Robinson. For a moment I thought of my own father.

I missed him terribly.

My mother, who is in the beginning stages of Alzheimer's, lives in a nearby assisted living facility. Until recently she lived with my brother Charles and his wife Mildred. Then Mildred had a heart attack and Charles called, informing me it was now "my turn" to take care of our mother. His hands were full of taking care of Mildred, who has—like Samuel—returned to health at a snail's pace. With Tim and family living in the house and Michelle's new fiancé Adam practically a fixture in our home, I couldn't move Mom in *with* us. Samuel and I chose, rather, to place her at the Good Samaritan Assisted Living Facility, located near Lake Dillon. In this way, I could stop by on my way home from school or if need be before school, or—in this case—before or after everything else I had to do on a Saturday.

I shivered as I made my way from the parking lot to the front door, but not because of the February cold that hung today like an old gray coat. I shivered, instead, because I knew that Mom—if she were lucid enough—would know it was Saturday and that I had waited until dark to come by.

Mom's "place" is a studio—450 square feet of what she has left of the furniture she once filled my childhood home with—and is next to the elevator on the second floor. I tapped on her door and pulled leather gloves from my hands as I waited for her to answer. "Mom?" I called out. "It's me. Lizzie."

She swung the door open wide and stood before me, dressed in the black slacks and light pink sweater set I'd given her for her birthday last November. "I know your name," she spouted at me. "If a woman's voice calls me Mom, I surely don't think it's your brother Charles."

I squared my shoulders and smiled at her as I walked through the threshold. "Good to see you at your best, Mom." I kissed her overly powdered cheek.

She closed the door behind me. "What took you so long?"

"Beg pardon?" As though I didn't know where this was going.

"It's practically bedtime."

I pulled myself out of my coat. "Mom, it's hardly six o'clock. Pipe down."

"But it's a Saturday. You couldn't come by this morning? There's a bridge tournament going on downstairs in the game room at seven, and I want to get there early enough to ensure I'm on a good team."

I crossed my arms and tilted my head a bit to the right. "Why don't you and Mrs. Chismar from the fourth floor go down together? You know you want to team up with her, and that way you won't chance her teaming with someone else."

Mom lifted her chin. "Hadn't thought of that. I'll call her in a few and see what she thinks of that." Mom shuffled to her favorite place on the love seat and sat down. "So, where have you been all day?"

I took a seat next to her, folding my hands in my lap. "Our catering business had a job to do today. Do you remember me telling you about the catering business the Potluck girls and I put together?"

"Of course I do." She didn't look at me as she spoke. I noted a faint reminder of my kiss on her cheek and reached over to wipe it away with my thumb. She looked at me then. "What kind of job did you have today?"

I sat back, relieved that she actually wanted to talk. *Someone to hear about my day*, I thought. *She may or may not remember it this time tomorrow, but at least she's listening now.* "We catered a bat mitzvah for a little Jewish girl from Evie's neighborhood."

Mom laughed. "Well, I wouldn't expect you to cater a bat mitzvah for a little Protestant girl, now would I?"

I laughed too. And for a moment it felt good to be with my mother.

Luke Nelson, the administrator of the Good Samaritan, stopped me as I walked from the game room where I'd left Mom and Mrs. Chismar happily plotting their evening. "Mrs. Prattle, may I speak with you a minute?"

I looked at my watch. The lasagna should come out of the oven within fifteen minutes, which gave me just enough time to get home. "A minute?" I asked.

He gave me a firm but sympathetic look. "More like ten minutes."

I studied him for a moment. He was a man in his early thirties, too thin by my standards, with deep-set gray eyes and thinning brown hair. He wore a coat and tie, the consummate professional, with Nike sneakers, appropriate for keeping up with six floors of elderly citizens and a full staff of dedicated employees. "I'll just need to call home."

"You can use my office phone." He turned and began down the hallway from which I had just come.

I followed close behind. "I would use my cell phone, but I left it and my purse in the car."

He paused for a moment and waited for me to catch up to him. "It's not a problem. How is Mr. Prattle?"

"Getting better."

We reached a closed door with a brass nameplate next to the

frame. "Luke Nelson, Administrator," it read. "Tell him I miss seeing him when I go into the bank." He opened the door for me.

I stepped into the plush office—too plush for my taste. The wallpaper was black, splattered with oversized images of lavender hydrangeas, and had the appearance of having aged over an extended period of time, though it was perfectly obvious it was new. Along the thick and ornate crown molding was the matching border with both lavender and pale pink hydrangeas. The few wall hangings the room boasted were large, thick-matted, and framed in gold leaf. Cases of solid cherry held the books they were made for and photographs of Luke, his wife, and three children. The photos were also framed in gold leaf, though none were larger than five-by-seven.

Against the left wall was a small pink settee and an occasional arm chair, two end tables with Waterford crystal lamps, and a coffee table with a large but low centerpiece of silk lavender and pink hydrangeas. Near the back was a large cherry desk with an impressive black executive's chair. Behind them, a wall of windows flanked by heavy draperies that matched the wallpaper. The room smelled of lilacs and aftershave.

"My goodness," I said without thinking. "Isn't this lovely."

Luke laughed. "It's my wife's doings. If it were up to me, we'd have a lighthouse theme. Phone's on the desk. Would you like something to drink? I have coffee, water . . ."

I walked toward the desk. "No. No thank you. I'll just make my call. I'm sure you want to go home too." And then I thought, *Too?* Because to be honest, I wasn't really sure that's what I wanted to do at all.

I drove home without the car radio or CD player turned on, taking the long way rather than a direct route, allowing myself more time to think. Luke Nelson's words had nearly floored me.

"Your mother came to Pajama Party Night dressed in a teddy," he said.

I could hardly believe the words. "A what?"

"You heard me. A teddy."

"But where on earth would she get a teddy? My mother has never owned any such thing, I can assure you."

Luke blushed. "I have pictures to prove it. Would you care to see them?"

I felt my jaw go slack. "I most assuredly would not." The very thought was more than I could bear.

Luke, sitting in the chair, braced his elbows on his knees and cracked his knuckles for a moment before continuing. "We had a group of college kids that came a few weeks ago to entertain. They're a dance company." He cleared his throat. "Your mother managed to befriend a young woman named Kimberly."

"Kimberly."

"And Kimberly brought her the teddy."

"Did you speak to this . . . Kimberly?"

Luke leaned back and nodded. "I did. She reports that your mother told her she was married and she was going to use it to spice up her . . . um . . . love life."

I gulped. "Oh, dear heavens. I can't imagine my mother thinking anything like that, much less saying it."

"Mrs. Prattle, these are the kinds of things we begin to look for in cases such as your mother's. What I am gently trying to tell you is that pretty soon you will need to move her from this facility and into round-the-clock care. Whether in your home or at a nursing facility. It's coming. It could be a month from now or a year from now, but it's coming."

I looked toward the door for a moment, then back at Luke. "But she seemed fine awhile ago."

His look registered both empathy and something akin to "get real." "I know. And you and I both know that's how this disease works, Mrs. Prattle." He slapped his knees with the palm of his hands. "Now, I'm not saying you have to do anything right now.

After all, her meds are helping . . . some. But they aren't a miracle cure, and I'm . . ." He cleared his throat of the knot I'm sure was forming there. "I'm suggesting you begin to think about this re-alistically."

Realistically, I thought as I pulled up to a traffic light on Main Street. To one side of the road was Higher Grounds Café. To the other, closest to me, Apple's Restaurant. I powered down the driver's window and allowed the aroma of fresh-baked Italian food to titil-late my senses. The next thing I knew I was calling home on my cell phone, instructing everyone to start dinner without me.

I entered Apple's. It was Saturday night and packed out. The hostess informed me that the only available seat was at the bar. I glanced over and saw that, sure enough, there was one seat empty at the far end. "I'll take it."

She escorted me, and I climbed onto the barstool. Brad, the bartender, came over. "Mrs. Prattle? What brings you to my bar on such a cold night?" Brad had been one of my students many years ago. He's also a good friend to Clay Whitefield, our town's star reporter who is engaged to Adam's sister Britney. He leaned over the bar and smiled at me, sporting a deep dimple on one side of his mouth. "In fact, what brings you to my bar? I'm positive I've never seen you here before." He pointed to the bar with his index finger.

I laughed lightly as I settled in, slipping out of my coat and gloves. "No, I should say not."

"You look to me like you could use a drink. How about a brandy? It'll warm you all over before you have to go back out in the cold."

I have never been one for taking "a drink," but I'd certainly heard about brandy, that it was good for warming a body. "No, I—"

He leaned on one elbow and turned a bit. "How about a cof-fee?"

"That sounds wonderful. I wouldn't mind a nice Caesar salad with grilled chicken too."

The coffee came first, in a pedestal mug, topped with whipped cream and sprinkled with what appeared to be chocolate shavings. Two narrow straws jutted from its depths. "My, my. What is this?"

"To your health," Brad said, sliding it closer to me on a cocktail napkin embellished with the restaurant's name and logo. He took a step away. "I'll have that salad for you in a few."

I watched him walk down the length of the bar and into the kitchen area before I took a sip of my coffee. I swallowed hard. There was a strong under taste, something I'd never experienced in coffee. I licked my lips and took another sip, this one long and savored. I felt a warmth slide down my spine, slipping into the veins of my arms and legs. When Brad returned I grinned at him. "Did you put that Irish cream flavoring in my drink?" I asked.

He grinned back. "Something like that." He chuckled. "Here, Mrs. Prattle," he said, setting a basket of hot garlic bread before me. "You'd better eat some of this bread here before you fall off the stool."

My eyes widened. "Do you mean to tell me this is an alcoholic drink?"

Brad's ice blue eyes seemed to dance before me. "Just sip it slow and easy. I promise it won't kill you." He leaned his elbows on the bar again. "In fact," he said, "it just may help you forget whatever it is that's going wrong in your life."

I wrestled with it, of course. I'm not a prude by any means—at least I don't think I am—but I've never resorted to "having a drink" to lessen life's tension. I've not even had anything "to drink" just for the sake of having a drink. But as I took another sip (and I must admit, it was delicious) I reckoned that one little bit of alcohol in a large cup of coffee surely wouldn't hurt me. It's not like I'd be heading to AA anytime soon. It was just an enjoyable hot drink on a rather cold, stressful evening.

That's all it was.

On Tuesday evening, as I felt the world closing in on me once again, I picked up my purse and headed for the front door of our home. In the family room Samuel was watching *Cold Case Files*. Michelle and Adam, as pretty a picture of an in-love couple as there could ever be, were giggling over honeymoon destination brochures spread across the dining room table. Brent was playing an excruciatingly loud game on the computer his parents had put in the downstairs room he slept in. Tim and Samantha sounded as though they were arguing over another house they'd looked at during some point of the day. And Kaci was yakking on the phone with one of her new school chums. I had visited with Mom on the way home and, as was sometimes the case, she didn't recognize me. Instead of greeting me with her usual friendly bark, she'd cursed at me.

I signed to Michelle that I was "going out."

"Where?" she signed back, looking more than a little perplexed.

I ran the palm of my hand along the cascade of her dark hair, then lovingly patted her porcelain cheek with my fingertips before saying, "Just out."

I gave a cordial smile to Adam, who returned it with a dimpled smile of his own. It was easy to see what had attracted my daughter to this young man. He was storybook handsome and tall enough to have to duck a bit when entering through a doorway. He was genuinely kind, soft spoken, and he loved my daughter in spite of her handicap. Not once had I ever heard him make excuse for her inability to hear. To Adam—who had learned to sign from the start of their relationship—Michelle's deafness was both endearing and natural. "You two pick a good enough place for your honeymoon,"

I said to him while signing to Michelle, "and I'll be forced to stow away in Michelle's luggage."

I didn't even tell Samuel I was leaving, and by the time I returned the house was dark and quiet and everyone had apparently gone to bed. I stepped into the family room, which was still warm from the dying fire behind the fireplace screen. I folded the throw Samuel had left on the floor next to his chair and straightened the pillows on the sofa. I then sat down and kicked out of my shoes, stretching as I lay across the deep cushions, feeling the residual effects of the coffee I'd—this time—ordered at Apple's bar. My head did a lazy somersault backward, and I closed my eyes.

"Delicious," I whispered, though I'm not sure why, then fell asleep.

Goldie

7

Plane Pickings

It took everything I had to get on that plane.

Of course, I was anxious to get back home to Georgia, to find out how my daddy was doing. But boarding without Jack—this time—was doubly difficult.

In previous years, during my springtime vacations, I would board with the full knowledge that while the proverbial cat was away the mouse was gonna play. Jack would, no doubt, spend as much time as possible hitting a few girly clubs and seeing his current mistress (unless he cheated on her too), and then I would return home to a lovely bracelet or brooch or some other offering of penance. While on some level I had been fully aware of what was going on, I had also chosen denial as my boarding companion, if that makes any sense. But this time it was all in the open, and a little voice kept whispering in my ear that if I were not home to be in Jack's bedroom, then he just might stray again.

"But why can't you come with me?" I'd asked him as I placed a few pairs of neatly folded slacks in the open suitcase lying across our bed. It was about 7:30 on the morning of Tom's phone call.

"Goldie, honey. There's no way I can take off right now. Not with spring break just around the corner. And there's no way you can be sure how long you'll be gone. Besides, I'm just a phone call away if you need me."

I rubbed my forehead with the fingertips of my right hand. "I don't know if I can do this, Jack. I don't know if I can do this by myself."

"Olivia said she'd go with you," he reminded me.

I had called Olivia as soon as the digital numbers on my bedside clock read 6:00 and told her about her grandfather.

"Olivia doesn't need to be traveling in her condition." I shook my head. "Not with her as far along as she is now."

"Women give birth on planes. Happens all the time," Jack said, handing a sweater to me that I'd laid near the suitcase for packing.

"Jack!"

He chuckled. "I'm just saying that women travel in their last trimester all the time, Goldie."

"Not my daughter." I was going to remain firm on that, so the conversation might as well end right there.

And so I got on the plane alone. Seat 16A, right next to the window, which is good for sleeping but just awful when you have to get up and go to the lavatory. Practically announcing to the whole world that you have to go to the bathroom is bad enough; stepping over two strangers to get there just adds insult to injury. No chance of my not having to make the trip; a woman my age nearly always has to go at some point during cross-country flights.

The plane taxied down the runway, and I closed my eyes and pressed my lips together, my fingers clutching the book I'd brought with me, though God only knows why. I wasn't sure that I could concentrate on anything other than Daddy and his heart attack.

Please, Lord, don't let my daddy die. Especially don't let him die—if he is going to die—until I can get there.

I felt the nose of the plane lift, pointing its way skyward. My back pressed against the seat until we leveled out and once again I was sitting upright. When I opened my eyes I saw that the man who sat in 16B—short, balding, and with large round glasses—was staring at me. "Never flown before?" His voice was somewhat nasal.

"What?" I swallowed. The air pressure that had built up in my ears during takeoff popped.

"I used to be just like you. Scared to death to fly. But I fly all the time now. It's part of my job, you know." He reached into his shirt pocket, whipped out a business card, and handed it to me. "Reginald McPhearson." He pointed to his name. "That's me, right there." He laughed lightly. "And right here." He pointed to himself.

"I, uh—"

"I work for a software company." He grinned as he spoke. "But then again, who doesn't these days, huh?"

"Huh?"

"What about you? What do you do?"

"Do?"

"For a job? A living? I assume you aren't one of those women who stays at home and raises babies. Well, for one thing, you look a bit too old to be having babies—not meaning to insult you."

"No, I'm not—"

"And for another, you have that look about you. Sophisticated. A woman of the world, I'd say. So, let me guess. You are . . . not a teacher, no. You are . . . now give me a minute . . . a lawyer."

"I work for an attorney, but I'm not a lawyer. I'm his secretary."

His round face seemed to only grow rounder as he smiled a toothy grin and nodded. "Yep. One thing I'm good at is guessing what people do for a living. It's a gift."

"I see."

"You know my name." Again he pointed to the card. "Yours?"

"Goldie."

"Goldie?"

"Yes."

He stuck out his hand for a shake. "Nice to meet you, Goldie." He pumped my hand until I thought my arm would come out of its socket. "And don't you worry your pretty little head about flying. Anything you need to know, you ask me."

I opened my mouth to speak but could get nothing to come out, so I just closed it and smiled, nodding back at him as I pulled my now-sore hand from his.

He leaned closer to me. "Tell me something, Goldie. You heading to Atlanta on some big classified case?"

I shook my head. "No. This is a personal trip." In fact, I thought, I'd rather be working right now. Poor Chris. When I'd called him to tell him that Jack had managed to get me on a flight at noon that day and that I wouldn't be in court to assist him, I could hear his anxiety level flying off the scale, even over the phone.

"Got family down South, do you?" Reginald asked.

I looked down at my book and nodded, willing myself not to begin tearing up again. *I will not share my problems with this complete stranger. I will not.* I no sooner had the thought than I could hear Lisa Leann saying, "Now, Goldie. You never know when you might meet an angel unaware."

Just as quickly I heard Donna saying, "Angels, smangels. Never trust a man with a bald head and round glasses."

I glanced up at my stranger—my angel unaware, perhaps—and smiled. "My father had a heart attack last night. I'm heading down to my home to be with him."

"So sorry to hear that. Fathers are important."

"Especially to their daughters. Do you have children, Reginald?"

"I've never married," he said. "Just never had time to settle down.

You know, buy a house, work the old nine-to-five, dinner with the in-laws on Sunday . . ."

I nodded. Yeah, I knew *all* about that.

"Tell you what, Goldie. Why don't you tell me about your family, and I'm sure the time up here in the air will seem like only a minute." He grinned at me again. "Help you to relax a little."

I sighed, deciding not to burst the "angel's" bubble of belief that I was actually afraid to fly. "Well, Daddy and Mama have been married since 1954."

"Over fifty years. I imagine your family celebrated the big day?"

"We did." I turned in my seat so as not to twist my neck. "They had five children, me being the middle child."

Reginald twisted in his seat too, I suppose in an effort to also be more comfortable. "What is it they say about middle children?"

I shrugged. "I really don't know. Whatever it is, I can assure you I had a wonderful childhood and never felt neglected or any of those things." I paused for a moment before continuing, and, just as Reginald said, our time in the air—all two hours of it—went by as though it were a minute. Somewhere in our conversation we'd been served soft drinks and then, later, coffee by perky flight attendants. As the plane glided toward Atlanta's Hartsfield-Jackson airport, I settled back in my seat and sighed deeply. I was almost home. I had an hour or so layover and then a short flight to Savannah, where Tom's wife Melody would pick me up.

Reginald and I had been silent for about five minutes when he leaned over and murmured in my ear, "Who is picking you up in *Hot*-lanta?"

I turned my neck toward him. "Oh no. I'm flying on to Savannah."

He touched my arm ever so gently with his fingertips. "Got a long layover? I was thinking that maybe we might have a drink together."

So much for Lisa Leann's angel theory, I thought, frowning. *Donna, you are my hero!* I jerked my arm away from his touch. "I told you. I'm married."

He pulled his glasses from his face. "But are you *real* married."

I'm just sure my mouth fell open. "Of course I'm *real* married! What kind of question is that?"

Reginald began to shush me, and nearby passengers turned to stare, but I didn't care. "Don't you shush me, Jack Dippel!"

"Who? Who's Jack Dippel?"

I blushed at my twist of words, if they were indeed that. "He's my husband, that's who!"

"Look, Goldie . . . I didn't mean . . . I only thought that you . . . that you and I . . . that you were feeling the same thing I was feeling."

"All I'm feeling right now is nausea!"

Reginald turned beet red, then shifted in his seat and mumbled, "Sorry."

Well, I never!

"Well, I never," I said to Lizzie on the phone as I waited at Gate B-2 in Atlanta's massive and remarkably hectic airport. "I mean, what a slap in the face that was for me, Liz."

"What do you mean?"

"You know. Jack and all his consorts."

"Consorts? Goldie, have you been reading romance novels again?"

I crossed one leg over the other and took a long swig of my Starbucks café latte with a shot of caramel. My favorite, though I rarely get to splurge on it. "I have never nor do I now read romance novels. Not those kind, anyway." I glanced down at the latest Beverly Lewis bit of Amish fiction I'd brought with me but had not yet read.

Lizzie paused before continuing. "I understand what you're saying, Goldie. It's easy to see how quickly women might fall for a smooth-talking man."

"Like Jack."

63

"You said it, I didn't."

"I know." I looked over at the gate, where the flight crew was heading into the Jetway. "Lizzie, keep your eyes on Jack, okay?"

"Goldie, you either trust Jack or you don't."

"I don't. Not yet, anyway."

"Well, my friend, I don't know what to say about that."

"I know. So, you will keep an eye on him?"

"Now, how do you expect me to do that, Goldie?"

"He works at the high school . . . you work at the high school . . ."

Lizzie gave a deep sigh. "I'll see what I can do."

"That's all I ask." Then I paused before adding, "You sound upset this morning."

"I have a throbbing headache."

"Did you take anything for it?"

"Mmm . . . yes. It just hasn't kicked in yet. What's the news on your father?"

"I called Tom's cell phone before I called you, but he didn't answer. His wife is supposed to pick me up at the Savannah airport."

"Is your whole family there? At the hospital, I mean."

"Yeah. Daddy's been moved to one of the hospitals in Savannah— St. Joseph's—and so pretty much everyone is there. When I spoke to Tom in Denver he said that Preston was driving down from Atlanta." Preston is our older brother. Hoy Jr. was the oldest in the family, but he died years ago.

"It's a shame Preston couldn't just wait for you to get there. You could have ridden together."

I hadn't thought of that. "I'll let you go, Lizzie. I'll be boarding shortly."

The flight between Atlanta and Savannah was short. We barely lifted off the ground but what we were making our "initial descent," as the pilot informed us. The seat beside me was, blessedly, empty.

As soon as we landed and it was safe to use our cell phones, I turned mine on and waited for it to boot up. Before I could dial Melody's number my phone indicated that I had three messages waiting.

The first was from Olivia. "Hi, Mom. You're obviously in the air still. Call me when you get to the hospital and let me know how Pa-Pa's doing. I love you. Don't worry about anything on the home front, okay?"

Hmm. My daughter knew enough about me to know where my concerns were.

The second call was from Jack. "Hey, babe. I'm taking a break at work and wanted to call you. I don't know if you tried to get me earlier or not, but it's been a crazy morning around here. Senioritis is already striking, if you know what I mean. Well, anyway . . . let me know what's going on and know that I love you. My prayers are with you and your father."

I played the message back again, this time listening for any background voices. Specifically, background voices of the female persuasion. But there were none, and I mentally kicked myself in the rear for having made such an effort.

The third message was from my baby brother, Tom, who worked the farm with Daddy. I couldn't imagine the stress Daddy's heart attack might be on him from the business point of view. "Goldie. Call me when you land. I'm at the airport—not Melody—and I've got my cell phone with me."

I hung up and started to dial Tom's number, then stopped and put my phone in my purse. Our small aircraft had reached the gate and we were about to deplane. When I was inside Savannah's airport, I stepped into the women's restroom for personal matters, then walked over to a row of chairs and sat down to call my brother.

"Hey, Goldie." He sounded so tired.

"I'm here, Tom. I'm just outside my gate. What happened to Melody picking me up?" Melody and Tom live, as Mama puts it, "a good hollerin' distance" from the family home with their six children, so either one of them could easily have made the trip. But, between dealing with Mama and Daddy at the hospital and the kids everywhere else, Melody's plate was, no doubt, full.

"I'm here. I'll meet you at baggage claim. I'm at carousel three. That's where your luggage will be."

I stood, hoisted my purse over my shoulder, and began to walk toward baggage claim. "How's Daddy?"

Tom didn't answer right away.

"Tom? Did I lose you?" I glanced over at a small shop that boasted Georgia pecans and peanuts, Georgia T-shirts, and books about Georgia, including recipe books from every ladies group in the state, each one complete with a recipe for Southern pecan pie. I decided that on my way back through I'd pick up a few for our catering company. Lisa Leann would be nearly beside herself with glee knowing she could throw a Southern-style party of the Georgia kind. "Tom?"

"I'm here, Goldie. I'm waiting for you at baggage claim."

Another turn and I'd be seeing him face to face, so I decided to just let him tell me about Daddy's condition once I saw him. "I'm almost there. See you in a minute." I hung up my phone, rounded a corner or two, and then spotted my brother standing along the line of luggage carousels. He looked ten years older than the last time I'd seen him, which was nearly a year ago. Dark circles bagged under his eyes, and his hair—still dark but thinning—looked as though it hadn't seen a comb in days.

I waved and he waved back, taking the steps necessary to meet me in the middle.

As he wrapped me in a tender hug I hooked my chin over his shoulder. "Oh, Tom." I squeezed him. "How's Daddy?" I attempted to pull away from him.

But Tom held me all the tighter. "Daddy died," he said, the words choked back in a whisper.

My knees buckled and I felt myself sliding, held up only by the strength of his arms.

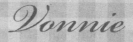

8

Dinner Guests

When David called and said he was bringing a friend to dinner, it was as if a chill had seeped in from my closed kitchen window and frosted the room.

Oh boy.

I held the phone between my ear and my shoulder as I took the whistling teakettle off the burner. "That's fine, David, as long as your friend likes Italian."

"Of course. Are you making your famous apple pie?"

"I've already sliced the apples."

Mother began to ring her bedside bell. "Hold on." I put my hand over the receiver. "Mother, I'm on the phone, I'll be there in a minute."

The impatience in my mother's voice outdid my own. "Vonnie, I need you now."

"Okay, Mother, okay."

"Sorry, David, I gotta run. I'll see you and your friend at seven?"

"We'll be there."

I hung up and ran toward the guest bedroom as the bell continued to clatter. "Vonnieeeeee!"

Mother was sitting in her rocker, rubbing her leg. "I've gotta get to the bathroom."

I grabbed Mother by an elbow and pulled her into a standing position. "Why didn't you just use your crutches? They're right here."

"My ankle just hurts too much," Mother huffed as she leaned on me and hobbled toward the bathroom.

"It's probably just irritated from the cast." I gritted my teeth as she rested her ninety-five-pound frame on me. "You see the doc Friday, maybe he'll take it off. Won't that be a relief?"

She was wearing her favorite pink velour jogging suit and would have looked cute if it weren't for her sour expression. She ran her fingers through her short but stylish white hair. Her blue eyes flashed. "I don't think I can last till Friday."

I got Mother to the bathroom door. She practically slammed the door in my face. "I can manage from here."

I let out a sigh and tried not to cross my eyes. It was bad enough Mother had slipped on the ice outside her condo in Frisco and broken her ankle those weeks back, but when Dad dropped her on my doorstep, she'd become my problem.

Oh sure, Dad visited, but I think the man was enjoying his freedom from her crabby disposition. I knew I was looking forward to saying good-bye.

I headed back to the kitchen, straightening the pillows on the couch as I passed. The house never looked tidy when I played caregiver. But it helped to be surrounded by so many friendly faces from my doll collection.

But that was only one more thing Mother hated about moving into my house.

"Aren't you ever going to grow up?" she'd ask as she'd shove my favorite dolls off the couch. "There's no room for real people in here."

I stopped and straightened a newly framed photo of David that was propped on the hearth. He was the spitting image of his handsome father, Joseph Ray Jewell. Joseph had been killed in Nam and had been my first husband, a husband I'd never mentioned to my Fred—that is, until David had showed up on our doorstep. I was happy to have found my son after a lifetime forced apart, a separation for which I blamed Mother. So, in many ways David still felt like company as Fred and I were just getting to know him. Though I had to hand it to Fred. He was starting to adjust to the news that I'd held such a secret for three decades of marriage. *Surprise, dear. Here's David, my long-lost son who was raised by that famed Hollywood actress, Harmony Harris.*

It had been touchy between the two of us for a while, but Fred was beginning to accept David as the child the two of us never had, God bless him.

Once in the kitchen, I finished slicing the apples and sprinkled them with cinnamon, sugar, and butter. It wouldn't be long until my little house smelled sweet and cozy.

My mother's voice shrilled, "Vonnie! How do you expect me to get back to my room?"

"Coming!"

I slid the pie into the oven then rinsed my hands in the sink.

"Vonnie, what's taking so long?"

"Just a minute." I sprinted across the house to find her holding on to the doorjamb. I offered her my arm, and she locked on with a vise grip as she hobbled back toward her room. "Does your ankle hurt more than usual?"

She nodded.

"We'll have to ask Dr. Galloway about that when we see him." I helped her back to her rocking chair, daring a smile. "Aren't you looking forward to moving back home with Dad?"

The deep line between her eyebrows furrowed. "I can just imagine the mess he's made of the place."

"Fred says it's not so bad. He was over there helping Dad install your new microwave after dinner last night. He said Dad seemed to be doing well."

"Humph. Well, the man's had all his evening meals here with us," Mother said. "So hopefully I won't have to face a sink full of dirty dishes. But I know he's not dusted or swept. And I can just imagine the laundry. It will take me forever to get the place in shape."

"I'm sure things will get back to normal quicker than you think," I tried to encourage. "I'll come over and help."

As I lowered Mother into her rocker, she winced. "Careful."

"Sorry. Is there anything I can bring you?"

"You already promised me a cup of tea, and don't forget my lemon wedge this time."

I hurried back to the kitchen. "Coming right up," I called over my shoulder.

I was glad I hadn't asked David the identity of his mystery guest, though I could have guessed. But at least this way, I could try to feign ignorance. *Don't fret about it. There's no need to borrow trouble*, I repeated to myself for the umpteenth time that afternoon.

I was in the kitchen pulling the pie out of the oven when David and his date scampered in from the cold February evening. I could see into the entryway from my vantage point in the kitchen. The couple and their coats were dusted with a few stray snowflakes. David called out, "Smells good, Mom."

I set the pie down, speechless.

David's eyes twinkled as he helped Velvet out of her coat. "Mom, you've met Velvet James?"

I nodded as I felt the corners of my mouth twitch into a smile that didn't connect with my heart. I looked into Velvet's thinly veiled glare and saw Donna's look-alike sister. An evil twin sort, if you ask me. And the way she was dressed. Let's just say the poor girl hadn't been taught a thing about modesty.

She was wearing skintight black jeans and a shimmering black top that was so low cut it was almost no-cut. She had Donna's blue eyes and blonde curls, though her hair was longer and pulled up into a high ponytail. Sprigs of ringlets framed her face, making her look even more like Donna, which had me asking, *Is this why he's dating her, because he's still in love with Donna?* I mean, it hadn't been that long ago that he'd proposed to Donna, though she'd turned him down. It appeared to me David was dating Velvet on the rebound.

"David, Velvet, welcome," I managed to stammer as I wiped my hands on the white bib apron I'd tossed over my red sweatshirt and jeans.

Mother's bell started to ring, and I turned to David. "Be a dear and help your grandmother to the table."

"Sure thing." He turned with the blonde still attached to his arm. They dropped their coats on the couch and headed for the back.

I took a deep breath and tried to look calm as I reminded myself, *Velvet is only his date, not his fiancée.* A relieved smile curled my lips until I thought, *At least, not yet.*

I was busy putting a basket of fresh hot rolls on the table when David returned with his grandmother hanging on to his elbow. Velvet sulked behind them.

I hesitated for a moment, watching Mother with David. Something struck me about the way she looked, a little too frail, a little too pained. *Goodness.*

Fred was coming up from the basement, where he'd been tinkering in his workshop, and Dad had just walked through the front door, wearing his fleece-lined denim jacket over his khakis and his black-and-red-plaid flannel shirt. He hung his jacket in the hall closet and shook off the snowflakes that were rapidly melting into his thick gray hair. It's funny how a home-cooked meal has a way of gathering men.

"What's for dinner?" Dad called, rushing in to pull out a chair for his wife.

"Italian casserole." I plopped the bubbling dish on the ceramic Raggedy Ann trivet in the middle of the table.

Dad looked up. "Well, hello, young lady, who might you be?"

Velvet had reattached herself to David as soon as his elbow was free.

David grinned. "Hi, Grandpa, this is my date, Velvet James."

"Did anyone ever tell you that you look just like Donna Vesey?" Dad asked.

Velvet shifted her weight and cocked her head in an almost defiant look. "Unfortunately, she's my sister. My half sister."

Dad's gray eyebrows shot up his forehead, and he glanced at me to see how to respond. I'm guessing my smile must have been stoic if my dad's expression was any indication. "I see."

Mother shot Velvet a glare. "Young lady, you look like you're going to catch pneumonia, dressed like that."

Velvet laughed as she took a seat next to David. "Flaunt what you've got, I always say."

Fred had been busy washing his hands in the sink. "Want me to get the iced tea?" he asked me.

I sat down. "Please."

Fred was soon seated beside me. I asked, "Fred, could you say our blessing?"

He bowed his balding head and reached for my hand. "Sure thing."

One thing I could always count on with Fred was his long-winded blessings. And for once, I didn't mind that the food was getting cold. I needed to catch my breath. I needed to ask God to help me get through this evening.

It was bad enough that Mother had never warmed up to David. Not that he'd seemed to notice. But I did. She was the reason why David had been adopted out to that Hollywood actress in the first place.

She'd only gotten away with it because she'd taken advantage of the circumstances.

She and her foolish pride. She'd been embarrassed that I'd married a man who was half-Mexican. She was even more appalled that I, her precious Swedish daughter, was carrying his baby. So, when she learned that Joe had been killed in Vietnam, she'd swooped in. There I was, out cold in an L.A. hospital because of the shock of Joe's death, the onset of labor, and a cocktail of heavy medications given to me by the labor and delivery team. My lack of consciousness had set the stage to her advantage. As soon as David was born, but while I was still sleeping, she'd called in a Hollywood attorney.

"Here's the release you need to sign for the baby's burial," she'd told me the moment I'd opened my eyes.

In my shock, I'd had no idea I was signing David's adoption papers.

I'd only discovered the truth when he'd shown up in Summit View last fall, looking for me.

I still couldn't get over the fact that my son had been raised by Harmony Harris, the star of the musicals of the sixties, God rest her soul.

So, it was ironic that Mother had moved in with me, only months after I'd learned of her betrayal. How I'd managed to hold my tongue these past few weeks, I don't know. Because to tell you the truth, I was still seething.

But I kept telling myself, "Hang on, Vonnie; it's only a few more days till she gets her cast off. You can make it."

Velvet sighed at Fred's continued prayer. Fred was saying, "Thank you for the loving hands that prepared this meal. Thank you for all who are gathered here. And dear Lord, we thank thee for all the blessings you've bestowed upon our family . . ."

I smiled. Poor Velvet, she wasn't used to prayer time with Fred.

I tried to concentrate on Fred's prayer, but my mind drifted back to Mother. I knew I'd have to forgive her, one day. I mean, I wanted to, but honestly, I didn't know how.

Fred was winding down. "In Jesus's name, amen."

I looked up and exchanged smiles with my dear husband. His extra long prayer had helped me center myself so I could play hostess. Besides, this family needed all the prayer it could get.

I picked up the basket of rolls and handed it to David, who was sitting next to me.

"Thanks, Mom."

Velvet was already helping herself to the casserole. "I sure hope this is a vegetarian dish. I don't do meat."

David looked surprised, which was a relief to me; I wondered if this was actually their first dinner date. I mean, maybe up until now they'd only done breakfast. *Ugh*. I blinked and tried not to shudder. Mother said, "Why not?"

"I don't like to mess with the universe like that. I mean, we're all one. The animals and us, I mean."

Mother snorted. "Where'd you get that crazy notion?"

I looked up. "Mother, be nice."

Dad reached over and patted her hand, which she pulled away. Mother looked incredulous. "I am being nice. I'm curious, that's all."

I looked up at Velvet and noticed that fury lit her eyes. "Don't mind Mother, she doesn't mean that the way it sounded."

David tried to defuse the situation. "Are these rolls homemade? They're really good."

Mother interrupted. "There's no need to apologize for me, Vonnie. I know exactly what I'm saying."

My eyes snapped back to Velvet, whose cheeks were growing pink.

"Well, excuse me, old woman, for living and breathing," Velvet said.

Fred turned to David. "You're right, son. These rolls are good."

Mother's eyes sparked. "Young lady, I *am* trying to excuse you."

Dad asked, "Vonnie, does this casserole have oregano in it?"

I nodded. "Yes, and garlic."

Fred said, "Ah. That's why it's so good."

I realized I was still posing with my first bite on the end of my fork. "Thanks, Fred."

I put the bite of casserole into my mouth and tried to chew it, but my mouth was too dry. I reached for my glass of iced tea but somehow sent it spilling across the table, straight for Velvet's lap. Direct hit.

She leapt into the air.

"Oh! I'm so sorry, dear."

Velvet turned to David. "I think it's time to leave."

David looked from Velvet to me, then put another bite of roll in his mouth and chewed. "Uh . . ."

Velvet looked down at him in disgust. "Let's get out of here."

He washed the bite down with his tea. "Okay, uh . . . sorry, folks, guess we've got to run."

"And take your date with you," Mother said, triumphant.

I was busy with the paper towels, trying to blot up the mess. I handed a handful to Velvet. "I'm so sorry, dear."

She looked me up and down. "I doubt that."

Before I could respond, she and David had donned their coats and were heading into the night. She slammed the door behind them.

I turned back to Mother, who looked so pleased with herself.

"Mother, why do you have to act like that?" I asked.

"Do not take that tone with me," she snapped.

Dad lifted his glass. "Vonnie, can I get you another glass of tea?"

I shot him a look. "Dad, let me finish. I've got something to say."

Fred reached up and gently touched my arm, "Vonnie, now's not the time."

I put my hands on my hips. "Not the time? Then when? How long are we going to let my mother get away with her childish behavior?"

Mother's eyes began to bulge. "Childish? You'd like me to be as silent as one of your silly dolls, wouldn't you? You're the one with a bit of growing up to do, if you ask me."

I looked down at her. "What?" I felt myself tremble with rage. It was like all the frustration I'd been hiding was pushing its way toward my mouth. I knew if I released a word of it, I wouldn't be able to stop.

The phone rang, and Fred ran to answer it.

It was too late; I could taste my anger. "Mother, if you think for one minute that—"

"Vonnie," Fred called. "It's for you."

I had to take a breath before I could answer. I turned to him. "Tell whoever it is I'll call back."

He turned his back and repeated my wishes to the caller. He paused then looked back at me. "It's Lizzie. She says it's an emergency."

I turned my back on the family and walked to my bedroom to take the call. I shut the door behind me and sat down on the bed as I reached for the receiver.

"Lizzie?"

"I hope I'm not interrupting."

"No, no. Is something wrong?"

"It's Goldie. She just called me from Georgia. Her dad died this morning."

I rubbed my forehead with my free hand. "Oh, poor Goldie."

"Yeah."

I paused. There was something funny about Lizzie's voice. *She's probably grieving for Goldie.*

Lizzie continued. "Goldie says things aren't good back there, and she's asked us to pray."

"Will do. Prayer sounds like a really good idea."

"Um, Vonnie. Would you mind calling the other girls? I'm really tired and need to get to bed."

"Sure," I said as though I'd be happy to do it. I hung up the receiver, though I continued my conversation with Lizzie in my head. *But I have to call on someone else first.*

I sat down on the edge of my bed and leaned my face into my hands. "Oh Father" was all I could say before my tears interrupted me. I got up and took the box of tissue from the dresser then locked the bedroom door. I sat back on the bed, allowing my shoulders to quake with both anger at Mother's shenanigans and despair over Goldie's loss.

I dabbed at my eyes and blew my nose. It looked like I was going to be here awhile. My saving grace was that Mother had left her bell in her bedroom.

9

Cookbook Dilemma

I stood in the checkout line at Wal-Mart, my arms stretched to the point of aching as my fingers gripped the handles of a shopping basket full of magazines, cookbooks (including the latest from Paula Deen, which my sister Peg said no self-respecting cook would be without), and even one of those magazine books (would that be a magabook?) titled *Operating a Successful Catering Business from the Comfort of Your Home*, if one can believe that title. Comfort? I didn't know about that. But, I was determined to be as knowledge-able about cooking and catering as Lisa Leann any given day of the week. My plan was to study from the privacy of my living room and then shock the Crisco and cream of tartar out of Mrs. Lambert at our next meeting, which was—unfortunately—that afternoon.

I berated myself for having waited until Saturday morning to do this, even as I studied the endless covers of rag-mags that lined the shelves before me. Somehow despite the latest in the sagas and gossip headlines of the Hollywood elite, I managed to focus on the fact that Lisa Leann had insisted that we all get together early in the afternoon to start planning Michelle's shower and here I was feeling as ill prepared as I could possibly be. I'd intended to do this days ago, but between continuing to settle Vernon in, beginning to see clients again, and the ins and outs of running a household, I'd found it impossible.

When it was finally my turn at the checkout I heaved my basket up and onto the conveyor belt, then began removing the items one at a time.

"You're Miz Benson, aren't you?" I heard a voice drawl from the other side of the counter.

Looking up, I immediately recognized Velvet James, all decked out in the trademark royal blue vest over a dark blue long-sleeved oxford shirt worn tucked into a pair of belted black slacks. She looked so remarkably like her sister I felt my words catch in my throat before I managed to state, "I am Mrs. Vesey."

She gave me a half smile before she began scanning my merchandise. "Oh, that's right. I remember now. You married my mama's first husband."

"I will ignore that."

"I'm sure Mama sends you her condolences." She continued to scan, studying my purchases as she went along. "Is the new bride learning to cook?"

"I know how to cook." I placed my purse on the small counter near the credit card scanner and pulled out my wallet. "I'm simply expanding my already vast culinary skills."

As my luck would have it, at that moment she picked up the catering book, waving it at me like a parade queen greeting her fans. "What's this? Are you thinking of catering a party with all your culinary skills?"

"If I do, I'll be sure to let you know." I sounded as sarcastic as I dared allow myself to sound, considering my status in this community.

With the exception of the gum popping between her molars, Velvet wisely stayed quiet until she announced, "That'll be $83.59."

I tried to remain calm. But $83.59 for a bunch of cookbooks? I pulled a credit card from my wallet and slid it through the machine, then waited for approval, feeling quite uncomfortable as Velvet kept her eyes on me. I scanned the rows of checkout lines as though on a mission, then stopped short when I saw David Harris dressed in his paramedic garb stepping through the front door, a thin cloud of snow blowing in with him. I suppose my gaze caught Velvet's attention because the next thing I knew, she was looking in his direction, a broad smile coming to her face. "There's my sweetie now," she cooed, then looked at me with an arched brow. "I suppose you know that David and me are dating now."

"So I've heard. And it's David and I, not David and me."

"You say potato," she commented, shocking me that she even knew the line from that old song. The register began spitting out my receipt, and Velvet returned her attention to it, reaching for it with manicured fingertips that looked as though they'd been dipped in blood.

Donna's, no doubt.

David spotted Velvet and walked toward us, stopping at the end of the register. "Mrs. Vesey," he said.

"Mr. Harris."

"Hi, honey," Velvet gushed.

I couldn't help notice that, though he said nothing, David blushed.

"He blushed?" Vonnie asked when I called her from home. "Are you sure he blushed?"

"Like a schoolboy. Vonnie, what in the world is your son thinking? And since when does Velvet James work at Wal-Mart?"

"I have no idea what that girl is up to. As for David, I don't know the answer to that either, Evie, but I can hardly say anything to him, can I? After all, he's a grown man. And it's not like I raised him.

I'm barely getting to know him myself. I just don't think I can tell him what I really think."

"Well, let me tell you what I think," I said, pulling books and magazines from plastic shopping bags.

"You don't have to tell me, Evangeline. I know what you think."

"Well, maybe you do and maybe you don't."

"You think David is rebounding with Velvet."

I simply hate it that she knows me so well.

"Did I tell you he brought her to the house the other night?"

"You did not."

For the next few minutes Vonnie entertained me with a less than positive story of her dinner guests from a few nights before. I was horrified.

"Wouldn't you think that David would have known Velvet was a vegetarian?"

"I don't know what to think anymore."

In the background I could hear Vonnie's mother hollering like a banshee for her daughter. "Oh, Evie. I've got to run. See you at Lisa Leann's shop at two?"

"Two o'clock it is." I glanced down at my watch. That gave me all of a few hours to read as much as possible of my new catering book. By the time this day was over, Lisa Leann would be a little impressed by my savvy and a lot worried about what I might know about the business side of cooking.

We Potluckers, sans Goldie, sat in the parlor of Lisa Leann's wedding boutique. Lisa Leann had romantic instrumental music piped in at just a breath above a whisper. She was, as usual, dressed to the nines for a Saturday afternoon, wearing (what appeared to be) a new outfit: dark blue jeans, a creamy white, long-sleeved sweater, and Ugg boots. I know they were Ugg boots because she told us so. "They're the latest thing. Very chichi." She said the last bit with a wrinkle of her nose.

I frowned at her words, mainly because while she was out spending her money on "chichi" boots, I had been spending mine on cookbooks.

I was the fourth to arrive. Donna pulled up the rear five minutes late. Before we got to the business side of the meeting, we talked about Goldie, who had called Lizzie that morning.

"The funeral is today," Lizzie said. "This afternoon at 4:00 eastern time." She glanced at her watch. "Which would be right now."

"We should pray," Vonnie said.

"I was going to suggest that." I cast a sideward glance at my friend. Unlike Lisa Leann, she was looking less than fashionable today. In spite of our having a business meeting, she appeared more like a frazzled beggar woman than a business owner, even if only a one-sixth share. I, on the other hand, had taken special care in choosing what I would wear. After all, I was the wife of the sheriff now. Keeping up appearances was important in my role.

From the other side of the room, Donna rested her elbows on her knees. She was sitting in one of the occasional chairs, unlike the rest of us who sat on the settees. She cracked her knuckles and cleared her throat before saying "I can't imagine losing my father" in a tone so faint we almost didn't hear her.

My heart leapt to my throat and then to my chest again. "I can." I looked around at the group and added, "Not Vernon, of course. What I mean to say is that the feelings of losing my father are as real to me today as the day of the accident."

Vonnie, who sat next to me, patted my knee. "God love you, dear friend. You had the double whammy of losing both parents at the same time."

I nodded and straightened my back. "Let's pray, then."

And we did. We prayed for Goldie, for her kin—as she called them—and for the peace that passes all understanding. Knowing as little as we did about the dynamics of Goldie's family, it was the best we could do.

With the last amen, Lisa Leann stood, walked over to the countertop near the front door, and retrieved a clipboard and four white notebooks, the latter which she passed around the room. "Ladies, I have taken the liberty of speaking at length with Beverly Jackson, whom I'm certain you all know."

We all mumbled our affirmations.

Lisa Leann sat again, this time in a chair opposite Donna. She crossed her petite legs and placed the clipboard firmly in her lap. But before she could open her mouth to speak again, I interjected, "Might I inquire about our business? A few questions, if you will, seeing as I was away previously."

Lisa Leann turned a shade of pink complementary to the red in her hair. "Well, Evangeline, we have gone over all the details in earlier meetings, but I can see why you are . . . in the dark, so to speak." She scanned the others in the room before returning her attention to me. "What do you need to know?"

"For one, legalities." I jutted my chin forward a bit. "As I'm sure you are aware, the Department of Agriculture and Consumer Services requires that all cooking be done in a kitchen separate from a personal or residential kitchen."

Lisa Leann's jaw dropped. For a sliver of a second I felt a shimmer of victory. But only for a sliver. "Evangeline," she said calmly, waving her hand toward the back of the building. "What do you think the kitchen in the back is for?"

She had me there. "What about the labeling of the food? The Department of Agriculture and Consumer Services requires that all food be labeled properly and—"

"Evie, I know all this. I know how each individual container must be labeled. I know all about inspections." She lightly touched the single row of pearls at her throat. "I thought you and I were friends."

"We are friends. What does our being friends have to do with this?"

"Then, why are you challenging me?"

"I am not—"

Lizzie stepped in, so to speak. "Girls! What *is* going on here?"

Donna chuckled. "Looks to me like the church ladies are at it again." She cocked a brow at me. I narrowed my eyes at her, flashing a warning that read: I'm married to your daddy now.

Not that I knew exactly what I meant by that, but that's what I meant.

I raised my hands in protest. "I'm not trying to argue. I'm merely trying to ascertain whether or not we've got all our bases covered."

Lizzie answered in her usual gentle tone. "Evie, Goldie had Chris draw up all the necessary papers—"

"Which I have for you to sign today, Evangeline." Lisa Leann pulled papers from the back of the clipboard. "Right here. Once you've signed, I'll take them to Chris and he'll file everything for us. He's ready to file for corporate status—"

I opened my mouth, but Lisa Leann kept going.

"As far as taxes—which is truly your forte—I was going to chat with you about that after our meeting today, which, may I remind you, is supposed to be to discuss Michelle's bridal shower to be given by the bank employees. And, by the way, a most important event because this one party could put us firmly in the black."

"We're in the red?" Donna asked.

Lisa Leann answered, but not before taking a deep breath and exhaling. "Girls, girls. To start a business, one must have the necessary tools of the trade . . . so to speak. Now, we got off easy with the Lowenstein bat mitzvah. But this soirée that the bank is planning for our Michelle"—she paused long enough to beam at Lizzie—"is a very big deal. As I was saying before this little . . . interruption . . . I have already spoken at length to Beverly Jackson. Now, if you will open your notebooks . . ."

I had been dismissed. Me, Evangeline Benson Vesey. Daughter

of the late mayor. Wife of the local sheriff. President of the Potluck Club. I had been dismissed with an instruction to open a
notebook.

I glanced down at the hardback, three-ring binder in my lap.
Lisa Leann had printed pink decorative cover sheets with the words
"Prattle Bridal Cocktail Party" and slipped them into the front
sleeve.

"How lovely," Lizzie commented. I glanced up at her momentarily as she went on. "I apologize that I haven't had time to talk
to Beverly myself."

"Never you mind, darlin'," Lisa Leann said. "She came by the
other day. We had tea and petit fours, absolutely delicious, if I may
say so myself. She insists that we serve them, by the way, and you
will get your own taste after our meeting. I have tea, coffee, and
these marvelous little cakes for us once we're done. Now, notice
on page one . . ."

We all looked at our notebooks. Lisa Leann had carefully laid
out the details, page after page of them, to be exact, beginning with
the particulars of what Beverly wanted.

"A cocktail party?" Vonnie asked. "Do they intend to serve alcohol?"

"We talked about that."

"Because I don't think I could justify this from a spiritual stand-
point."

"What are you saying?" Lizzie asked. All eyes went to her. "Even
Jesus drank wine."

"Go, Jesus." Donna chuckled. Then, taking in our expressions,
added, "No disrespect intended."

"And I'm sure none taken." Lisa Leann was clearly trying to get
the meeting back on track.

"A lot of the bank employees drink cocktails, wine with dinner," Lizzie added. She paused for a moment. "Not Samuel. He's

always been a teetotaler, but we're looking to please the customer, right?"

"Ladies, if I might have your attention," Lisa Leann all but yelled. "Beverly and I have already discussed this. She would like to have the party in the fellowship hall of the church—the only place in town large enough to hold the number of attendees we're expecting. So this is really a moot point. There will be no alcohol served. Just lots of pretty punch."

"Really?" Lizzie asked. "A lot of people for my baby girl's party? I am touched. I am so touched." Lizzie truly glowed. "Michelle is going to be tickled pink."

Pink? I suddenly had a flash of brilliance. "Speaking of pink, what are Michelle's colors?" I looked at Lisa Leann. "Quite often the colors the bride chooses are the colors for the parties."

"That's true," Lisa Leann confirmed with a smile. Lisa Leann looked to Lizzie for an answer.

"Michelle has chosen—now I know this sounds odd, but I've seen it and it is fabulous—black and metallic silver."

"I've seen that too," Donna said. "And it's pretty awesome."

"Black?" Vonnie asked. "What bride chooses black? Not that I'm being critical, Lizzie, but . . . black?"

"Von, wait till you see it," Donna answered for Lizzie. "I'm telling you, it's gonna knock your socks off."

"Just what I need." Vonnie wrinkled her brow. She looked nearly pathetic.

I giggled. "Vonnie, you're so funny sometimes."

"Can we talk about the menu?" Lisa Leann asked.

"Before we do," I said, "do we have a date for this . . . soirée, as you called it?"

"One month from today," Lizzie answered. "March 25th."

"Which is a Saturday," Lisa Leann noted. "I have a calendar in the back of your notebooks."

We all flipped to the back.

"The wedding is June 24th. That's four months from now. The shower is in one month. We're going to have to concentrate and stay on task, girls, if we're going to pull this off."

"And we're minus one right now," Vonnie noted.

"Does anyone know when Goldie is planning to return?" I asked.

We all looked at each other. "I'm planning to call Goldie tonight," Lizzie said. "Somewhere between seeing Mom and cooking dinner for the motley crew I call my family."

"I hear you," Vonnie said.

"Details, girls," Lisa Leann continued. "Before she left for Georgia, Goldie suggested a money tree theme, which Beverly just loved, by the way. We're going to get lighted ficus trees, and instead of gifts, the attendees will bring money cards to attach to the leaves . . . to help the new couple get settled financially."

"I love it," Lizzie said. "What a wonderful idea!"

"I'd love to take credit for it," Lisa Leann said. "But it was Goldie's idea."

"What about entertainment?" I asked.

Lisa Leann took a long look at me. "Evie, you've been doing your homework, haven't you?"

I felt my face grow hot. "I was at a disadvantage. Having just been married and going on my honeymoon and all."

I heard Donna sigh.

Vonnie giggled. "I wouldn't call a honeymoon a disadvantage."

"Not to mention that wedding I threw for you," Lisa Leann added.

I pursed my lips. "Entertainment? What about entertainment?"

"The bank is hiring a string quartet from Denver."

Lizzie clapped her hands. "I am loving this!"

Lisa Leann waved her hands to get everyone's attention again.

"If you look at page three, you'll see the menu Beverly has chosen for the event."

"A chocolate fountain?" Vonnie asked, reading over the page.

"I'm glad you brought that up," Lisa Leann said. "We need to buy a chocolate fountain."

"With what money?" Vonnie asked.

I scooted forward in my seat. "Surely we have the bank personnel—or whoever is in charge—putting down a deposit."

Lisa Leann pulled a pen I'd not previously seen from somewhere within the strands of her teased hair and behind her ear and pointed it at me. "Yes. But, that's not going to cover everything. So what I propose to do is loan the Potluck Catering Club some money from my personal finances."

"Why not just take out a loan at the bank? A small business loan?" I asked. Now this is where I could really shine.

"I didn't plan to charge interest. After all, I'll be paid back in a month. I'll hardly miss it."

I looked her dead in the eye and pondered her proposition. Blast it all, I had nothing to say in return. "Oh."

"How much is a chocolate fountain?" Vonnie asked.

"I've done some research and found one that would be appropriate for our use. It'll run between $250 and $300."

"What will we serve with it?" I asked. "Berries?"

"Yes," Lisa Leann answered. "Strawberries, marshmallows, apples, cherries . . ."

"Yum," Donna interjected.

Lizzie was studying the menu. "Poached salmon mousse, pumpernickel crisps, cheese straws, crimini mushrooms with lemon-glazed scallops and prosciutto . . ."

Donna continued for her. "Bok choy spring rolls."

"And," Lisa Leann concluded, "petit fours, coffee, decaf, and tea for dessert. Which, by the way, I have ready in the back." She stood. "Girls, give me a few minutes; I'll return momentarily. We'll talk more about the details and our specific and individual roles in all this." With a flutter of pressed denim and the muffled shuffle of Ugg boots she was out of the room, leaving the rest of us to stare after her in silence.

"Do you need any help?" I finally called out.

"No, no! I've got everything under control!"

Mmm-hmm, I thought. *I'll just bet she thinks she does.*

10

Half-Baked Valentine

It was the predawn of a Monday morning when I slid to a stop on the ice-glazed highway that wound its way between town and the high school. I was careful not to rear-end the red pickup that had slammed into the guardrail. The slightest shove from my bumper would send the wreckage tumbling over the bluff I called the Ice Gallows, in memory of blue-tarped accident mop-ups that came with visits from the local coroner.

Under the pulsating red and blue lights of my Bronco, I walked to the truck as the driver powered down his window, revealing the pale face of Charlie Wilson, Summit View High's star basketball player.

"Charlie, you okay?" I asked, shining my flashlight into the cab. From my vantage point I could see a bone protruding from his ankle.

His eyes were round. "I think so, 'cept my ankle hurts."

In the distance, I could hear the whine of the local ambulance company. "You just sit tight; the paramedics are on their way."

"I gotta get to practice. Coach Dippel's gonna kill me."

"Don't you worry about Coach. I'll give him a call and let him know you're running late." Realizing the kid was going into shock, I walked back to the cab of my truck to grab the extra bottle of water I always carried for these kinds of emergencies.

I unscrewed the cap and handed it to Charlie. "Take a couple of sips." When the ambulance approached, I stepped out into the roadway with my flashlight and waved a warning so the driver would slow down before he too skidded out of control.

A few moments later David and his partner pulled in beside me. When David hopped out of his truck I tried not to notice how good he looked in his dark blue uniform. As I set up the traffic cones around the accident, I watched as David talked to Charlie about bracing his leg. I could catch enough of the conversation to be impressed; David certainly knew his way around trauma victims.

David and his partner Randall Holmes, a teddy bear of a man with a bushy mustache and a wide grin, loaded Charlie into the ambulance while I waved the ever-building traffic past the wreckage. As I stood in the middle of the freeway, I unhooked my cell phone from my belt and pulled Coach's cell number off my contact list before dialing it.

"Coach Dippel?" A blast of icy wind cut me in half as I continued to direct the cars. "Ah, Coach, I know you're busy with practice, but it's Charlie Wilson. Looks like he broke his leg out here on the highway this morning. They're transporting him to the hospital now."

"Have you reached his parents?" Coach asked.

"Yeah, just got off the phone with his mom."

"Thank you for letting me know, Donna. I'll touch base with his parents during my lunch break to check on him."

"Good idea. Ah . . . Coach, since I have you, how's Goldie?"

"I was with her at her dad's funeral just a couple of days ago, and, well, she's pretty broken up."

"Yeah, I know they were close. Do you know when she's coming home?"

"That's still under discussion. She's still needed out there in Georgia, but her homecoming can't happen soon enough for me."

It could have been the windchill, but I felt a shiver of relief. I could only hope that the fact Coach missed his wife meant he hadn't taken advantage of her absence to strike up his old friendship with Charlene Hopefield. At least I hadn't seen their cars parked at the local tavern or the hotels or anywhere else suspicious. And yes, I had been keeping a watch out—for Goldie's sake. "Okay, tell her I asked about her; tell her she's in my prayers."

"Will do."

I must have smiled as I ended the call because David, who was just shutting the rear ambulance door, gave me a wave and jogged over. "We're about finished here. See you at Higher Grounds later?"

"Probably." I glanced over at the tow truck driver hooking Charlie's smashed pickup to his winch. "I'll need to thaw out while I finish up my accident report."

David nodded and with a wave went back to the ambulance. He swung open the door and turned back as the glow of the dawn blushed his face. "Catch you later."

I watched the ambulance pull away, lights rotating, sirens blaring, and wondered, *How could such a nice guy get stuck with my sister?*

I was dying for a cup of fresh hot coffee when I stopped at the local Wal-Mart to pick up the prescription they were holding for me at the service center.

Though it was sealed in a brown bag with my name on it, I was careful to avoid Velvet's checkout line. I barely knew the girl and didn't need her snooping into my business, even if my business only consisted of a prescription for nail fungal cream.

Once I paid for my purchase, I gave her a glance as I hurried past her cash register on the way out.

She nodded. "Donna."

"Velvet."

I exited into the frosty morning, which by this time was bright with pale yellow light that reflected on the snow. I squinted into the glare as I slid my package onto the seat beside me then pulled out of the parking lot for Higher Grounds. Once there, I grabbed my clipboard and headed for the café. Even in the morning sunshine the place glowed from the inside out. As I slipped inside, the bell chimed above my head.

"Donna! Come sit by me."

I saw Clay parked at his usual window seat. He waved. "Back from working that accident?"

"Yeah." I pulled off my gloves and rubbed my hands together in an effort to warm up. "Where were you?"

"I just got the call . . . I'm about to head out to the hospital to see Charlie and then to the wrecker service to see if I can photograph the truck." He reached for his reporter's notebook as I sat down across from him. "But first, care to tell me about it?"

I caught Sally's eye as I pointed to my coffee cup. She picked up a freshly brewed pot and headed our way.

"Looks like Charlie Wilson lost control of his truck. Not a big surprise in these wintry conditions. I mean, the snow stopped about midnight, but it's still icy out."

"So, it was black ice that caused the accident?"

"Yeah, that and the kid might have been in a hurry to get to basketball practice."

Clay jotted a few notes. "Tough break."

"No kidding. Charlie broke his ankle."

Clay groaned. "There go our hopes for the Gold Diggers basketball season."

I nodded as Sally poured me a cup. "The special?"

93

I nodded again. "Thanks, Sally."

"Speaking of news, Clay, I've been expecting to read your en-gagement announcement in the *Gold Rush News*. I mean, I see you sitting with Britney in church every Sunday, looking very cozy, but where's the ring you gave her?"

Clay blushed. "Not to worry. One of the stones was loose, and as soon as we get the ring back from the jewelers, you'll see our wedding news in the paper."

"What I can't believe is that she's got you going to church. All I can say is you must really be in love."

"Britney's been helping me with this faith thing," Clay said, as if this were a simple matter. "I'm starting to see God from a different perspective."

"That's a news flash."

He chuckled. "Not to change the subject, but what's going on with you and Wade these days?"

The door jingled behind me. "Beats me."

"What did ya do for Valentine's? I took Britney out to the Whales Tail in Breck. Kinda expected to see you and Wade out there stroll-ing the sidewalks in front of one of the restaurants."

I rolled my eyes. "No."

Clay looked amused and leaned in as he took a sip of his coffee. "So tell me, how's it going?"

Images of Valentine's Day swam before me.

Me dressed in new jeans and a red turtleneck, Wade at my door with a huge bouquet of red carnations and baby's breath.

"They're beautiful." I felt the soft petals against my face as I breathed in their fragrance.

Wade stood at the door as tiny snowflakes waltzed behind him in a halo of porch light. "You look great."

I looked back at the man I had loved a lifetime earlier. The rav-ages of alcoholism had not taken the little-boy shine out of his eyes. I could only thank God he'd found his way back to sobriety, at least so far.

I almost giggled. "Why do you make me feel like I'm eighteen?" I asked as he stepped inside.

"Do I?" he asked.

I had just started to turn toward the kitchen to grab a vase when his arms caught me and pulled me to him, tucking my head just beneath his chin. He nuzzled his face in my hair.

"Funny, you feel eighteen to me too."

I laughed as I turned to him, wrapping my arms around his waist. I sealed the knot with the bouquet.

"Are you nervous?" I asked, my ear pressed against his heart.

He pushed me far enough away so he could look down at me. "Nervous? About?"

"Taking me to your mom's house for dinner."

He stepped back, turning to shut the door as he pulled off his denim jacket. He tossed it across the back of a chair.

"Mom? Well, she's not, she . . ."

"She's not what?"

"Having us for dinner after all."

"But, you said . . ."

Wade sat down on my rust-colored couch. "Donna, she's just not ready, for *us*."

I put my hands on my hips. "But, you said you'd talk to her, that you'd work things out."

Wade stood. "It's not like I'm asking you to date my mother."

I folded my arms and walked to the window that overlooked the two trucks side by side in my driveway. It was just warm enough that the dancing snow instantly melted as it landed on the windshields.

Wade walked toward me and gently touched my shoulders.

"Donna?"

I shrugged off his touch.

"Donna, why is my mother's approval so important to you?"

I continued to stare into the darkness. "How can we ever find happiness if your family hates me?"

I could see the reflection of Wade's face in the window as he started to reach for me again, but he hesitated. "I . . ." He hung his head.

I angrily flicked away a stray tear that had dared to betray my hurt. "Then just go."

"But Donna."

I turned and looked up at him. "Go home to your mother."

He stepped toward me, but before he could recapture me with his embrace, I tossed the flowers into the kitchen trash can, flounced to the coat closet, grabbed my jacket, and bolted to my Bronco before roaring it into reverse and down the drive.

Wade stood in my doorway, watching as the snowflakes dropped an ever-widening veil between us.

Trouble was, I didn't know where to go. I'd have gone to Vonnie's, but I wasn't so sure her mother liked me either. So I just drove the streets as if I were on patrol, looking for an answer while I swiped at my eyes with the back of my hand.

I just wasn't strong enough for rejection from yet another mother. *Why am I so unworthy of maternal love?*

It was after midnight by the time I returned home to a dark and empty house.

I went to the trash can and gathered my flowers, gingerly stroking some of the broken stems before placing the bouquet in a vase of water. How could I love a man who couldn't face his mother like an adult? But maybe the question really wasn't *how* could I love him, but *why*.

Two weeks later, I was sitting in Higher Grounds blinking back my Valentine's memory as Clay waited for me to say something. Thing was, I didn't want to say that I hadn't heard from Wade since that night.

I shrugged. "Things are a little rocky between us."

"What happened?"

"Let's just say he stood me up for our Valentine's dinner and leave it at that."

"Wade stood you up?" a voice from behind me asked.

I turned to see David.

I shooed him away. "Mind your own business."

David laughed and walked toward the counter, where he sat down. "I'll catch up with you later," he called over his shoulder.

I shook my head then turned back to Clay. "See what you've done? You've gone and started rumors about me."

Clay held up his hands in mock defense. "But, Donna, don't you . . ." His phone rang, and he looked to see who called. "Gotta take this."

I hate it when other people's cell phones interrupt my conversations with them.

Clay actually pinked. "Britney," he gushed. "Good morning to you too . . . Nothing . . . Breakfast at the café is all . . . Uh-hum."

I tried not to roll my eyes as I imagined Britney flirting with Clay on the other end of the phone line. But I'll admit, a small part of me wished I could act like that instead of my old angry self. Then maybe I wouldn't have "relationship problems."

I tried not to stare as Clay suddenly stood to his feet. "I'm on my way now, sweetie. I miss you too." He ended the call. "Donna, gotta run." Clay made a quick wave, then he was gone. I took another sip of my coffee as Sally plopped a steaming plate of eggs florentine in front of me.

I unrolled my silverware from my napkin before digging in.

Whoa. Too hot.

I sipped from the glass of ice water, and while I waited for my eggs to cool, I reached for my clipboard so I could jot down some of my observations on the accident report.

I looked up to see David standing before me, holding a plate of pancakes. "Can I join you?" he asked. "I thought maybe we could go over some of our notes from the crash."

I pointed to Clay's abandoned seat as Sally whisked away the remains of Clay's breakfast.

I looked up from my clipboard and took a bite of my breakfast. "Help yourself." David waited while Sally wiped away Clay's coffee ring with her sponge, then he sat down.

"You handled yourself pretty well out there, Deputy."

I looked up. "All in the line of duty. How was Charlie when you got him to the hospital?"

His chuckle was low. "He was okay, but his mom wasn't."

"Yeah, Louie's a bit of a drama queen."

"Too bad about Charlie's ankle. I hear he's the local basketball star."

I nodded. "That's a dangerous curve. It could have been a lot worse."

David nodded then took a bite of his pancake while I continued scratching out my report.

He watched me for a while then asked, "So you broke up with Wade?"

I looked up and frowned before returning to my writing. "I don't want to talk about it."

He took another bite of his pancakes and stared at me. "Okay."

When I finally finished, he'd already pushed his plate to the side. He leaned toward me on his elbows. "Deputy, just know that I'm here for you."

I felt my eyebrows arch. "What?"

The door jingled and David leaned closer, but before he could say anything more, I asked, "Don't you have a girlfriend?"

"She's not you."

"That's not the way I see it. Seems to me like you've pretty much got someone who looks exactly like me."

"Looks like you, yes. But she's not you." He chuckled. "She doesn't even come close, not that I'd want you to repeat that."

"Consider the vault locked on that one." I stood. "I've gotta get this report filed." I picked up my clipboard and turned and almost stepped into Wade.

"Didn't mean to interrupt," he said.

"Hi. I, ah . . ."

But before I could blurt out anything more, Wade turned around and left the way he'd come.

I tossed a bill on the table, grabbed my jacket, and hurried after him, only to see his truck pull into the morning traffic of Main Street.

He didn't even look back.

I walked to my Bronco, opened the door, and slid inside, noticing the brown bag on the seat next to me.

I patted it. I deserved to be alone, I decided. Just me and my little secrets.

11

Spicy Shocker

I'd just poured a fresh cup of coffee into one of my favorite rosebud-covered ceramic mugs and sat down to log on to my online service. I took a sip and smiled as an email from Mandy caught my eye. It had attachments, which I hoped meant baby pictures!

I clicked the email open.

> Hi, Mom. How did you keep the surprise baby shower Sandy threw for me a secret???

I felt my brows furrow. *That's easy. Nobody told me,* I answered as I continued to read.

> When Sandy invited the baby and me to the Green Beanery for lunch, what a surprise to find all my friends there. But I have to admit, I was even more surprised you weren't there. But Sandy said you couldn't come. So I've attached a few pictures for you to enjoy.

For Pete's sake, it sounded like Mandy's mother-in-law used the pretense of "keeping a secret from Mandy" to keep the secret from me, knowing I'd try to keep the peace between myself, my daughter, and her mother-in-law even when I learned of her deception.

I opened the attachment to see what I'd missed.

Ah. There was my baby, Mandy, looking as cute as a bug's ear, dressed in a pale peach cable-knit sweater that complemented her strawberry curls. Her bright brown eyes sparkled as her lightly freckled cheek pressed against the sleeping face of my grandbaby, Kyle Christopher Richardson. Kyle, looking adorable, was wrapped in the pale lavender-blue blanket sweet Vonnie had crocheted for him.

How precious. I put my hand above my heart before opening the next picture.

I studied a redhead dressed in a shimmery bronze outfit, right off the cover of my latest Chico's catalogue. Lilly Lorraine Appleton, my baby sister. I shook my head. *You mean to tell me that Lilly was invited and didn't call to tell me to come? Ugh.*

She must have fallen under Sandy's spell, which meant I was going to have to put "call Lilly and complain" at the top of my day's to-do list.

I clicked open the next picture, and my ruffled feathers instantly smoothed. *How sweet.* There was little Kyle Christopher held tight in Mandy's arms. He was awake now, balanced on her blanket-covered shoulder, as if he were admiring the pile of presents on the center of the table.

My heart sang to see that little face. As I blinked back tears of delight, the sad face of Goldie unexpectedly floated into my mind, intruding into my joy. I took another sip of coffee and leaned back into my office chair and reached for my Bible. "Aw, Goldie," I said to no one but the Lord. I flipped to Ecclesiastes 3:4 and read, "A time to weep and a time to laugh, a time to mourn and a time to dance."

I stared at the words on the page and continued to talk to the Lord. "That's the way of things. Goldie's grief coincides with my joy."

There was nothing to do but bow my head and pray for her. I mean, why else had the Lord suddenly brought her to my thoughts?

When I finished, I typed Mandy a quick message.

> Loved the pictures. Say hi to Aunt Lilly. Hope to see you soon.
> Mom

I put my hand on the mouse and opened my Aunt Ellen Explains Everything file, a popular column I write for the local *Gold Rush News*.

It was fun being anonymous, though the Potluckers all knew I was "the Auntie," as I liked to call her. Writing the column was a hoot, though I occasionally got into trouble when any of the Potluckers happened to recognize themselves in my letters. But strangely enough, it happened less often than one would think.

Now that the column was such a success, I actually had letters I could answer, but on a slow letter day I resorted to answering a letter of my own design, like today . . .

To come up with a letter, I think of a friend with an issue that I'd like to address.

As I thought, Evangeline danced into my imagination. I thought about her latest power play at the Catering Club meeting. Poor dear, if she could but trust me, we'd be better friends. I smiled and started typing first the question:

> Dear Aunt Ellen,
>
> I have a friend I'd like to get closer to, but I don't know how. We've had our share of misunderstandings, but now that she's reaching out to me I'm not sure how to respond. Do I trust her?

I mean, I hesitate because my mother always told me, "Never drop your gun to hug a grizzly."

But what if my friend isn't a grizzly? How do I know for sure?

Signed,
A Friend?

I smiled to myself. Now for the answer:

Dear Friend,

Why not take a chance? If your friend's reaching out to you, well, why don't you reach back to her and find out if she's really a teddy bear? Misunderstandings are exactly that, misunderstandings. It's possible your friend never meant to hurt you. So, put the misunderstanding aside to see if your friendship grows.

Bear hugs,
Aunt Ellen

I saved the letter then attached it to an email to Clay. "Here's the rest of my column," I typed then paused as I thought about how I should word what I wanted to say next. My fingers sprang to action. "Now, you know I'm not the pushy sort, but I do hope you'll let me coordinate your wedding. You will, won't you, Clay?—With love, Lisa Leann."

I hit *send*.

Of course Clay would let me coordinate his wedding, that was a given. I just had to be sure he understood he had no choice. So, not only did I have the Britney/Clay wedding wrapped up, I had a lot of other leads. The fact I'd held up a sign about my wedding services during a live broadcast of the TV show *Hollywood Nightly* had certainly helped business. The TV crew had been in town because of reports that David Harris, whose adopted mother had been Hollywood royalty, was in town getting himself engaged to our own Donna Vesey. The rumor had proved false, but still I'd gotten a lot of national exposure. Not only that, but my new column in the *Gold Rush News* had actually sparked quite a few romances across Summit View, since it often touted advice to the area's lonely hearts. In fact, a couple from the singles class I taught at church, Allen and Becky, were coming in at four o'clock to sign a contract for my wedding services.

Of course, I was also keeping my eye on Donna and Wade, who I now knew had more than a little history between them. Surely I'd land that contract too, considering Donna would get a discount as she was part owner of the catering company.

The phone rang.

"Hello, Lisa Leann?"

It was Beverly. "Hi, Beverly, how are you this beautiful Friday morning?" I asked.

"Good, but I have news."

"Oh?"

"This shower for Michelle, we've decided to change the location."

"Really?"

"The church setting would have been nice, but we've decided to move the party down to Breck to the Mountain Bell Tower Resort, mainly to accommodate the invitation list, which grows bigger by the minute. Plus, this way we can serve cocktails."

I was surprised. "I thought you'd decided against cocktails."

"Well, some on the committee are insisting."

"I see." I wondered how Vonnie would take the news. I kept a smile in my voice. "So the venue will be at the Mountain Bell Tower Resort?"

"Have you seen their facility?" Beverly asked.

"No, I haven't."

"Well, then, how about meeting me over there for lunch?"

"A lovely idea. About noon?"

"See you then."

I hung up the phone then stood up and stretched. Goodness. The day was getting away from me and here I was still in my fuzzy pink robe. I looked at my list of things to do and noted that I'd have to call Lilly later. It was time to get to the shop. I had some calls and orders to make before lunch, and I had to get moving.

A few hours later, after taking care of business down at the boutique, I put the "will return" sign in my shop window but not before moving the hands of the plastic clock to two o'clock. I locked the front door then hurried out the back to my awaiting Lincoln.

After I buckled myself in and started the ignition, I put my Bluetooth in my ear and dialed my sister. I got her answering machine, which twanged, "Hi, this is Lilly Lorraine. Sorry I missed your call but leave me a message. *BEEP.*"

"Lilly Loraine, just got the pictures from the shower, but I could see someone was missing. Me! Why didn't you tell me about it? You got some explaining to do, sister."

I hung up and pulled out of the parking lot. I took a deep breath. Lilly would call me later. For now, I'd concentrate on my drive to Breck.

Once I pulled out of the upper valley Summit View's located in, I enjoyed the scenic downhill drive. I've always said there was no grander drive anywhere, at least not with such gorgeous drop-offs and heart-stopping views. My favorite spot was the switchback that faced the Breckenridge ski slopes and looked down upon the town of Breckenridge itself. The snow, of course, made it picture perfect. White majestic mountains, bright blue sky.

I love snow. It reminds me that God's love covers our sins. That especially appeals to me, a woman who moved across the country to start a whole new life. I turned up K-LOVE on my radio and listened to Out of Eden sing "Every Move I Make."

How appropriate, Lord, I prayed. *I'm making all my moves in you. Thanks for the confirmation.*

Soon enough I was pulling into the parking lot at the resort. As I scampered across the snow-glazed parking lot, I passed a car that looked familiar. A cream-colored Lexus with a caramel interior. I noted its Texas plates caked with icy sludge and felt a shiver run down my spine.

Though I knew this car couldn't be the one I remembered from back home, the memory jolted me just the same. I guess what they say is true. No matter where you move, guilt has a way of following.

I shot off another prayer, one I'm sure I'd prayed a million times already. *Lord, I'm sorry for the past; you know I am. And I know you've forgiven me. At least, I know I should know.*

I sighed at the emptiness I felt. *Will I ever be free?* I wondered.

I grabbed the handrail and walked up the metal mesh steps, holding tight just in case the heels of my camel boots slipped on the ice deposits left by the snow boots that had gone before.

I reached for the brass handle of the resort's front door and swung it open, revealing a world of latte-colored marble that glowed across the floor of the upscale lobby. The added illusion was that everything—furniture, drapes, pottery, decorative tassels and throw pillow fringe—was dipped in gold. A wide garnet-red Oriental rug nestled in front of a roaring fire inviting one to step out of the cold and defrost in front of the dancing flames. As I stepped through the door and past the potted trees that lined the entrance, my cell phone rang. I checked and saw Lilly's name. I stepped to the side and took the call.

"Lisa Leann, I had no idea you didn't know about Mandy's shower. Oh, will you ever forgive me?"

I smiled because I just can't help but enjoy a good apology. "Next time, you'll call, right?"

"Right. But I wish you could have been there. You should have seen all the lovely presents. Besides, you'd have died for a slice of that cake. I ate two pieces and now I feel as fat as the town hog."

I spotted Beverly waiting for me on one of the jacquard-print ivory couches that was tucked into a nook not far from the fireplace.

"Lisa Leann!" she called as she stood and waved.

I finished my phone chat. "Gotta go. I'll catch you later this afternoon. Okay?"

We hung up, and I hurried toward Beverly. As always, she looked charming. As a bank executive's wife, she didn't have that "I don't believe in wearing makeup or cold cream" look that seemed to prematurely wrinkle the faces of many of these high-country women.

In fact, Beverly's face glowed with a well-blended palette of pigments that blushed her cheeks and lips and highlighted the coppery browns of her eyes as well as the tastefully chosen auburn of her fringe of short but stylish hair.

She gave me a quick hug and led me up a couple of steps toward the great hall.

"You're going to love this place." She let go to spread her arm in a wide gesture. "Before we dine, let me take you by the conference room we're going to use for the reception."

I followed her down the hallway to a large open room half set with round tables. Several hotel employees were rolling brown tables in place before popping their legs out, setting them up, and covering them with white tablecloths.

Beverly gestured again. "These walls open up to make a bigger room." I nodded as she continued. "They have a lot of corporate and conference events here. From the look of things, there's some sort of banquet here tonight."

I turned and saw the back of a man with dark wavy hair and wearing a dark navy suit duck out and into the hallway. From the back, it looked exactly like . . .

No!

I steadied myself and turned to Beverly. "What's the name of the sales manager you're working with?"

"He was right here a minute ago." She looked around. "Now, where'd he go?"

I felt as if I was having a hot flash, though I took a deep breath, keeping my voice smooth as silk. "His name?" I asked.

"Let's see, where'd I put his card?" Beverly dug through her designer black Fendi handbag with the most adorable gold lock. I made a mental note to check it out at the Fendi website when I got home. "Here it is." She handed it to me.

My eyes darted from the name on the card back to Bev's face as if she owed me an explanation.

She tried to oblige. "He's new. Fresh from Texas." She chuckled. "Hey, maybe you two were neighbors."

Neighbors? I remembered to close my mouth. After all, I couldn't make a public spectacle. Though doing so crossed my mind. My unease was contagious because Beverly continued to look around, as if she felt alarmed that he was missing. It didn't take long before the object of her hunt waltzed through the open door.

Beverly looked relieved and motioned him over. "Oh, here he is now. Lisa Leann, I'd like you to meet Clark Wilkes."

I tried not to die on that thick forest green carpet of the banquet hall. I suppose I could have run. I suppose I could have slapped him. But I decided to play it cool. "Hello."

"Believe we've met, good to see you again, Lisa Leann," Clark was saying as he reached for my hand. His dark chocolate eyes glinted fire. As he stared down at me he caressed the back of my hand with a slow circular rub of this thumb.

I felt a flame rush up my neck and into my face. I was definitely having a hot flash.

Clark looked satisfied, as if his eyes had delved into my soul and read a secret I wanted to keep.

I broke the moment by looking down at his shoes, a shiny pair of black lace-up Versaces. I looked up again and put on the performance of my life. "Really? I don't recall you. Though I hear you, like me, are from Texas. I'm wondering if we've visited some of the same country clubs, been invited to some of the same parties . . ."

I pulled my hand from his and resisted the urge to wipe it off.

He just stood there and grinned, his brown eyes glinting beneath his long black eyelashes. I wanted to roll my eyes and sing "You're So Vain." But I didn't dare, mainly because Beverly didn't need to witness anything more than she'd already seen.

Beverly interrupted my thoughts. "Shall we go to lunch?" she was asking. At least, that's what I think she was saying, since I was finding it hard to focus.

"Maybe I'm mistaken," Clark was saying. "It's just that you look like someone I used to *know*."

He'd said the word *know* with such intimate intonation.

Though I was having trouble breathing, I let a peal of polite laughter ring out. "I guess everyone has a double."

He looked amused and folded his arms across his chest. "And a history. I'd love to catch up on yours."

Beverly, who had been watching the exchange, looked shocked at such a comment. I tried to force another laugh. "How sweet. But my Henry doesn't allow me to share histories with other men." I stepped back and looked at my watch and turned to Beverly. "What time was our reservation?"

"About now." Beverly waved good-bye to Clark as we left the ballroom. "I'll call you later." Once in the safety of the hallway, she giggled a conspiratorial whisper into my ear. "No wonder you started a dating service. You seem to be able to zero in on the lovelorn with amazing accuracy. And here I had no idea the man was even single."

"He's not."

She stopped dead and looked at me. "I thought you said you didn't know him?"

I pointed at my diamond ring. "Didn't you see his wedding ring? He's married, all right."

Beverly laughed as I followed her to our awaiting table. She looked back over her shoulder. "And obviously on the prowl."

When we sat down at the table, I reached for the ice water the busboy had just finished pouring for me and took a swig.

"Are you okay?"

I rolled my eyes. "Oh, I feel as if one of my migraines is coming on."

"That's too bad. My sister gets those too."

"I haven't had one in a while, not since I left Houston."

"Maybe your migraines are related to allergies," Beverly was saying as she scanned the entrees.

Yeah, I thought to myself. *I am allergic to something, all right, or should I say, someone.*

Beverly was studying the menu. "This thyme roasted chicken with vegetables looks good."

I tried to focus. "I think I'll have the same."

Beverly reached into her purse and pulled out a brochure and handed it to me. "I wanted to thank you for recommending these bartenders for our cash bar."

I took the brochure in hand and stared at it, realizing the bartenders were none other than Velvet and Dee Dee, Donna's blood relatives.

"I recommended them?"

"They said so." She hesitated. "Didn't you?"

I shook my head. "I'm not saying they wouldn't be good, it's just I've never worked with them."

Beverly frowned. "Then maybe I misunderstood."

Misunderstood, my eye, I thought, wondering how devious this mother and daughter pair might really be.

"What will you ladies have?" a cute blonde with a slicked-back ponytail asked as she pulled a pen and order pad out of the pocket of her black pants.

She jotted notes as Beverly gave her the order.

"And to drink?"

"Iced tea." I turned to look at the brochure in my hand. If I could make my mind focus, maybe I could figure out what this bartender thing was about.

But for now, I needed to sit and try not to bolt out of this resort, this town, and this state. Maybe what I really needed to do was hightail it to Houston and hug my grandbaby for a few days.

It might be the safest thing to do, at least under the circumstances.

My cell rang again. I checked the number; it simply said "Clark." I frowned. Somehow I'd sworn I'd taken his name out of my directory.

"Are you going to get that?"

I turned off my phone. "I can let this go to message."

"Are you sure you're okay?"

I nodded. "I'm fine. Really."

The waitress brought me my tea, and I took a big sip as Beverly watched with one eyebrow cocked higher than the other.

Does she suspect?

I smiled as sincerely as I could. "Just a hot flash. Now, where were we? Any more thoughts on what you want printed on the party napkins?"

12

In a Crunch

I felt like I was embraced in a clumsy dance as I pulled a seven-foot-tall artificial tree up my front steps then slid it across the thin layer of snow on my porch. Its outstretched branches, made from a real tree limb, grabbed at me as it waved green fabric leaves into my face and hair. I squinted at the assault and kept tugging backward. I had to lift the plant in its cement-filled planter, just a bit, to clear the threshold. I felt the weight of it topple toward me and took a couple of steps inside the house to keep my balance.

Through the leaves that tickled my face, I could catch a glimpse of my mother still sitting in my husband's pickup truck, which I'd borrowed for the day. I stopped to catch my breath and caught a glint of sunlight on the car's passenger window as it lowered, revealing Mother's pruned face. *Here she goes again*, I thought, bracing myself for yet another round of complaints. But in this frigid air, I could not only hear her grievances but I could see them rise in a vapor cloud that dissipated somewhere above her head.

She whined, "This is the limit. How long are you going to keep me sitting here? Vonnie, I want to go to my room."

As I was still standing in the doorway, with only the tree between us, I parted the leaves with my hands so she could see my face. "I'll be there in a minute, Mother."

I clumped the tree to its place alongside the wall to join the mini-forest I had accumulated from Wal-Mart.

I rolled my eyes. How in heaven's name did I let Lisa Leann talk me into picking up more money trees for Michelle's shower?

"They're half price today only," she'd said on our early morning phone call. "If you could pick them up, I'll drop by later tonight and help you decorate them with lights and clips to hold the money."

I was always glad to save a buck, so I said, "Sure, but will we have enough?"

"I already have half a dozen in my garage and that in addition to the hotel's greenery and my fine decorating skills, and I think we'll be good to go."

But now that I'd been at this for hours, with several repeat trips, the few bucks we were saving didn't seem so important. No wonder Mother was cross.

"Vonnie!"

"Mother, I tried to talk you into staying home this last trip. Besides, it's almost one o'clock and time for your doctor's appointment."

"Aren't we going to have lunch first?"

"We'll have cream of potato soup when we get home."

"I need to go to the bathroom."

"Can't you go at the doctor's office?"

"Absolutely not. Help me inside, please."

I finished pushing the tree into its spot by the doll-adorned fireplace and tried to stand up straight, a process that proved no easy task. I put a hand on my back and arched out the kinks. "Coming, Mother."

I hurried down to her only to make the trip up the steps once more, but this time as a crutch.

I felt my mother's grip tighten on my arm as she sucked in her breath.

I looked down on her head of white hair. "Are you okay?"

She nodded. "Just hurts a bit is all."

By the time I got her to the bathroom door I was sure I'd have a permanent purple handprint on my upper arm.

I couldn't wait till the doctor removed that awful cast off Mother's ankle; then we'd all be a lot happier as Mother would finally go home with Dad.

I couldn't help but wince. *Poor Dad.* Though it was hard to feel too sorry for him because he was the one who'd dumped Mother on me in the first place.

In truth, I was still angry with her for the distant past. Plus her constant whining and complaining had done nothing to soften my heart. I'd only honored her with my caregiving because I'd felt it was my duty. After all, the Word says we're supposed to honor our parents, so I was trying, really trying. But knowing the end was in sight made my "trying circumstance" bearable.

I looked at my watch. It was almost one. What was taking so long in there?

I knocked on the door. "Mother? We're going to be late."

No answer, though I heard the swoosh of the plumbing. I knocked on the door again. "Mother?"

A faint voice called out from behind the door. "Vonnie?"

I sighed. "What is it, Mother?"

"I can't get up."

I felt a wave of exasperation. "What do you mean, you can't get up?"

"I need help."

For goodness sake. I tried the doorknob. Locked. I rapped on the door with my knuckles. "You locked the door."

Her voice sounded tired. "Don't you have a key?"

"Yes, Mother. Just a second."

I rushed to my catchall drawer in the kitchen. I pulled it out and dumped it on the table while pens, pencils, and even an old marble rolled onto the floor. What remained in the large pile were old sugar packets, paperclips, rubber bands, a wad of string, my stapler, a collection of coins, and a hodgepodge of keys.

I picked up the proper key and rushed back to the bathroom door. "I'm back."

"What took you so long?"

I ignored the question and unlocked the door. It opened into a tiny, yellow-painted room. The sink was backsplashed in yellow tile printed with inky blue designs of flowers. There Mother sat, prim and proper on the white porcelain toilet bowl.

"What seems to be the trouble?" I asked.

"I told you, I can't get up."

I tried to pull her up by her elbow, but she winced. "That's not working."

In the limited space I tried another tactic. I stood in front of her and took her hands in mine and tugged.

"Please stop," she cried at last. I sat down, exhausted, on the worn, white rug, which covered the hardwood floor. "Your ankle hurts that much?"

She nodded.

"Well, what do you want me to do?"

"What do you think? Get me off of this thing."

I stood up.

"Where are you going?"

"To call the paramedics."

Mother was aghast. "You can't do that! They'd see me."

"Then I'll call David. He's a paramedic, he worked last night, and I know he's off duty this afternoon. He'll come over."

"No! I just won't have it."

"Mother, I'll get you a blanket and you can put it over your lap. He won't see anything. Don't you think that would work?"

She considered it for a moment. "I guess that would be okay."

I dialed David's number and he answered on the first ring. I could tell I'd awakened him. "Hello?"

"David, it's my mother; I need your help."

His voice perked. "What's wrong?"

"I know this sounds silly, but I can't get her off the toilet. I mean, she can't stand up."

"I'll be right there." He hung up before I could explain further.

A few minutes later, his black Mazda 3 pulled up, and I hurried to meet him at the front porch.

Though his tennis shoes were untied, he bounded toward me, dressed in a pair of frayed jeans and an old gray sweatshirt. The word *Raiders* was barely legible beneath his unzipped parka. He was clutching a well-worn paramedic's kit.

I led the way to the bathroom, where Miss Priss looked as if she had just summoned a gentleman to tea. Her pink blanket covered her lap, making her white top look like the top of a flowing ball gown. "Hello, David."

"Gram." He knelt on one knee and reached for her hand to take her pulse. "How are you this afternoon?"

"I'm fine."

He let go of her hand and asked with gentle intensity, "What seems to be the problem?"

"I can't get up," she answered as if she was talking to a thick-headed schoolboy.

David took her grumpiness in stride. "But why, Gram? Why can't you get up?"

She pointed to the cast on her ankle. "It hurts too much."

"Where?"

She pointed to her leg, just above the cast. "It won't take my weight."

"Can I see?"

She smiled then, like a shy schoolgirl, and shifted the pink blanket off her ankle. David gently touched her leg.

"Ouch."

He stood up and pulled me into the hallway. "Mom, her leg's pretty swollen. Has she fallen?"

I shook my head. "No. At least, not that she's told me."

"I'm thinking she might have a secondary fracture."

I think I gasped, but David's eyes held mine with that same gentleness he'd used with my mother. He was saying, "Now, we can call the fire department or I can help you get her to the car. What do you think?"

"I'm not deaf," Mother scolded from the bathroom. "And I'll not sit here while the whole of Summit View comes to gawk."

David walked back to the bathroom door and told her, "Okay, then do you think you can help me?"

"I can try."

"I'm going to bend over, and when I do I want you to put your arms around my neck. Then when I stand straight, I'm going to pull you up with me."

"That won't work, and I won't do it."

"Why not, Mother?" I asked.

She sighed heavily, like she thought I was an idiot. "I'll be exposed."

"What if I shut my eyes?" David asked.

"And I pulled up your slacks?" I added.

Mother hesitated. "Don't announce that out loud. Someone might hear you."

I put my hand on my hip. "Mother, honestly. No one is here but us."

Mother sat straighter as if trying to muster every ounce of dignity she possessed. "Well, I suppose we could try."

We all got into position, with David grasping Mother beneath her armpits. "On the count of three," David said. "One, two . . . three!"

Like a well-oiled machine, we had Mother standing and dressed in the same moment.

David helped her hobble out of the bathroom, then scooped her in his arms and carried her to my car while I grabbed my purse.

"I'm assuming we're heading for the hospital?" David said.

I looked at my watch. "No, I was trying to get her to her doctor's appointment when this happened. She's an hour late, but we always wait at least that. Go ahead and get her into the truck while I call to see what the doctor wants to do."

A few minutes later, we were heading for the doctor's office with David trailing behind us in his car. Both David and I pulled into the circular driveway by the front door, and he jumped out to get Mother's folding wheelchair out of the back of the pickup. Once we got her seated, he wheeled her into Dr. Galloway's office.

David moved the vehicles to the parking lot and came back to the waiting room. I'd rolled Mother up to the end of a line of chairs and was sitting beside her. I said to him, "Why don't you go on home?"

"Nothing doing. I'm in this with you."

The earnestness in his eyes reminded me so much of his father, Joseph Ray Jewell, my late first husband, that my vision blurred.

He said, "It's going to be okay."

I nodded.

The young redheaded receptionist called for my mother, and David pushed her back to one of the exam rooms while I followed behind. As we were positioning her wheelchair in the only open spot in the room, Dr. Galloway joined us. He was a short man wearing an oversized white lab coat that split wide in the middle to reveal his rounded belly. He wore silver bifocals on his turned-up nose. His thinning dark hair was combed over his bald palette, making him look like a man who'd long passed his prime, if he'd ever had one.

Mother took his hand. "It's so nice to see you, Doctor Galloway. I've been having a little trouble with this cast, you see."

"A little trouble?" I said. "You should have seen how she got stuck—"

"I'm perfectly capable of talking to my own doctor. You and David can go to the waiting room. I've got privacy rights, you know."

David and I looked at each other and then at the doctor. He looked over his bifocals and smiled. "That will be fine," he said as much to us as to Mother.

Honestly, I felt as if I'd been sent to my room. As I shuffled out the door, David turned back. "Gram, just let me know if you need me."

"I will."

A moment later, David sat next to me in one of the navy plastic and chrome chairs. The receptionist must have gone to lunch because the place was deserted. I shook my head. "Mother banished us. How do you like that?"

David patted my hand. "She's losing her sense of control," he said. "That's why she lashes out sometimes."

I wanted to say, *Sometimes? She's lashed out at me my whole life, and at my first husband and at you. How is it you don't walk away?*

I wanted to say that, but in truth, I couldn't out of fear that David *would* walk. I needed him, and in his grief over Harmony's passing, he needed me too.

I leaned back against the clinic gray wall and closed my eyes. "She's been a bit difficult."

David grinned. "I get what you're going through. I went through much of the same thing when Harmony got sick."

I looked at him then. I'd never thought about what it was like for him with Harmony's cancer. *Oh, bless him.* I looked into his brown eyes, which were looking beyond me and into his past. "That must have been hard for you."

119

His eyes focused on mine, and I squeezed his hand. "It was. But I survived it and—"

The front door of the office flew open, and Donna ran in, looking ragged. Had she worked last night too?

Her cheeks were pinked from the chill of the day, and her curls were just long enough to give her a windblown look. It was a nice effect, even though she was dressed in her ratty black sweats.

I stood up. "Donna! What are you doing here?"

She stopped and stared at David and me as if she'd forgotten our names. "Is everything okay? I mean, Fred called and said something had happened to Mrs. Swenson's leg."

"How did Fred know?" I asked, amazed.

David looked a bit sheepish. "I called him on my cell, on the way over here."

"You did?"

"Yeah, I'm supposed to call him with a report when we're done."

I had to blink back my surprise. David really was becoming part of the family.

David pointed at the empty seat next to him. "We don't know much of anything yet. Wanna join the wait?"

Donna ignored his gesture and sat down in a chair just opposite of us. "What happened?"

"She got stuck in the bathroom. She couldn't get off the toilet, and David thinks she may have another fracture."

"Oh no."

"David helped us get her here," I said.

I could tell Donna was impressed, though she tried to hide it. "Oh."

David grinned. "Long time no see, Donna."

Donna, so help her, smiled back. "Yeah, right. Seems like we were just working a scene together, when was that? Four days ago?"

Hmm. What is going on here? My heart quickened. I mean, I'd

120

have loved for David to stop dating Velvet, but I wasn't so sure I wanted him to take Donna away from Wade. But come to think of it, Donna hadn't had a lot to say about Wade lately. In fact, he barely nodded our way at church. Had something happened?

Nurse Penny, a tall brunette, stood at the entrance to the inner hallway. She looked professional dressed in a blue snap-down cotton shirt, which she wore over white pants. She glanced down at her clipboard. "David, I was wondering if you could help us get Mrs. Swenson on the X-ray table."

David practically leaped into the air. I stood too.

Penny shifted her weight. "No, just David."

I sat down and watched as my only son darted out of the room. Donna and I stared into space for a while, each lost in our own thoughts. I slowly looked at her, wishing I could ask her a question that she'd think was none of my business.

"What?" she finally asked. "Do I have a second head?"

I chuckled. "Dear, I'd never tell you if you did. But won't you come sit by me? We haven't had a talk in ages."

Reluctantly she sat down beside me.

"So, what's going on with you and Wade these days?"

She hung her head. "I think we broke up."

I grabbed her hand. "Donna, no. What happened?"

When she looked up, her eyes were glistening. "Not only do I have the little problem of his mother, but I think I'm pushing him away."

"You're having a problem with Fay Gage?" I sniffed a laugh. "Who doesn't? That woman is the reason he became an alcoholic."

Donna's lips parted. "Vonnie! I'm surprised you said that out loud. But from the way Fay tells it, I'm the one responsible for everything that happened to Wade. She never wants me near her son again."

"So, how are you and Wade handling this?"

Donna shrugged. "We're not; we're not even speaking."

I reached for her then and pulled her to my soft shoulder. "Oh Donna, I'm so sorry."

But before I could say more, I caught movement out of the corner of my eye. I looked up to see David watching from the hallway. How much had he heard? He answered that question by quietly disappearing the way he'd come. But I'd seen the answer in his eyes.

Everything.

I patted Donna's shoulder, and she pulled away and brushed at her eyes with her fingertips. Had she seen David?

No, I could tell she hadn't. Suddenly David reappeared and sat across from us.

"How is Mother?" I asked him.

"She's all smiles for the doctor, but he won't know anything more until the films are developed. He may run a couple of blood tests too."

"For what?" Donna asked.

The nurse in me kicked in, and I answered, "To see if there could be another organic reason for her troubles."

Donna looked concerned. "Organic? You mean like osteoporosis, cancer, or some horrible disease?"

I leaned back and spent a moment contemplating the worst of the possibilities, and it was as if Mother had slapped me herself. I admit it, I was mad at her. But right now, whatever was happening to her was happening to me. I fell silent, and the three of us sat together for what seemed an eternity. I would occasionally swat at the dirt stains on my light blue sweatshirt and jeans, then break the silence with a light sniffle.

Donna gave me a hug. "Aw, Vonnie, it'll be okay."

I wasn't so sure as I searched in my purse for a tissue. David handed me one from the box on the nearby coffee table. He said, "I know I'm new to the family and I don't know much about God. But maybe this would be a good time to pray?"

I dabbed at my eyes and nodded.

"Let me." He reached for my hand, then for Donna's as he bowed his head. The three of us formed a tight circle. "Lord, help my grandmother and my mother. Be with us. And show me what it means to believe in you the way I should. Teach me how to pray for Gram. Amen."

My head bobbed up. "Oh David . . ."

Before I could say more, Nurse Penny was standing at the hallway door, pushing Mother's wheelchair. Mother was sporting a new and larger cast. "I haven't died, you know."

I jumped up and ran to her. "What did the doctor say?"

"That's my business. All you need to know is I've got another six weeks before Doctor Galloway takes this thing off. So, let's go home. I missed lunch and I'm starving. Vonnie, didn't you say you made cream of potato soup?"

David walked over so he could push Mother's wheelchair to the car. Donna and I followed.

"There's enough for everyone." I turned to Donna. "Care to join us?"

Donna crossed her arms. "Okay, but only to help you."

David said, "Count me in."

Mother looked up at the three of us. "Then, let's hit it."

"Cream of potato soup, coming right up," I said.

13

Pressure Cooker

I awoke on Saturday morning with a nagging headache, something I was doing more frequently of late. It began in the nape of my neck and wrapped itself like a giant hand with splayed fingers across my skull. I opened first one eye and then another to the haze of sunlight entering through my bedroom draperies, swearing to either stop the nonsense of my secret obsession or to drive over to one of the outlets in Silverthorne and purchase some blackout curtains. I closed my eyes again, begging God for more sleep as phrases from our catering club business meeting played ping-pong within the recesses of my brain.

Vonnie:	*Do they intend to serve alcohol?*
Lisa Leann:	*We talked about that.*
Vonnie:	*Because I don't think I could justify this from a spiritual standpoint.*

Brad (How'd he get in there?):	*What brings you to my bar on such a cold night? I'm positive I've never seen you here before.*
Me:	*No, I should say not.*

I heard the tape of events rewinding, screeching like nails down a blackboard along the way.

Me:	*Good evening, Brad. I'll have an Irish coffee, just like the one you prepared for me last time. Only this time, a little more Irish and a little less coffee.*
Vonnie:	*Did you hear me, Lizzie? I said that I just don't think I can justify this from a—*
Me:	*I heard you, I heard you. Must you shout in my ear like that? And stop being so self-righteous, Vonnie Westbrook. There's surely more skeletons in your closet than just the old bones David Harris brought with him . . .*

Where did that come from? Where did that come from? Where did that—

Me:	*Even Jesus drank wine.*
Donna:	*Go Jesus.*
Brad:	*Go, Mrs. Prattle.* (deep dimple showing)
Lisa Leann:	*Beverly and I have already discussed this. She would like to have the party in the fellowship hall of the church . . . the church . . . the church—*

The phone by my bedside rang with a shrill. I bolted upright, grabbing my head and holding it onto my shoulders.

"Are you going to answer that?" Samuel asked from his side of the bed.

125

I reached for the phone, glancing at the clock as I did so. It was 8:30 in the morning.

"Hullo."

"Lizzie? Lisa Leann. Glad you're awake already."

"Mmm." My tongue felt as though it were sticking to the roof of my mouth. "Lisa Leann? What's wrong?"

"I suppose you've heard from Beverly Jackson?"

Lisa Leann sounded even more animated than usual.

"Beverly." I closed my eyes and kept them shut.

"Lizzie, this is awful. It's just awful. I can't tell you how awful it is. I mean, what is poor Donna going to think? And Evangeline too, no less?"

"What are you talking about, Lisa Leann?" I said. Or at least what I tried to say. To my ears it sounded more like, "Wha-a-you-tal-but-Lee-Leeaaaa . . ."

She paused, but only for the most minute of moments. "Lizzie? What's ailing you, girl? You sound like you just woke up."

"I did," I whispered back to her.

"Oh. Oh," she said, then continued. "Well, here's the deal, and I won't get into the whole thing now. You probably won't remember this anyway, but I'm calling an emergency meeting at my shop at one o'clock this afternoon. I'll call you back in about an hour or so to make sure you heard me."

"I hear you, Lisa Leann. I don't need another call. Meeting at one o'clock."

"That's right. One. On the button. I'll see you then."

I hung up the phone.

"Who was that?"

"Lisa Leann." I looked over at my groggy husband, then ever so gently laid my head back against the pillow.

"What in the world did she want at this hour?"

"For the life of me, I have no idea."

"Mmm." He shifted a bit in the bed, turning it into something akin to a boat in the middle of a stormy sea. "What time did you get home last night?"

"I'm not sure." *Yes, you are. You know. It was 2:00 in the morning.*

"How's your mother?"

I felt my face grow warm. I'd told Samuel I was going to spend my Friday evening with Mom. Anything, I'd said, to get out of this zoo of a house. It was a lie, of course. But, I hadn't gone to Apple's. No longer willing to take a chance on being seen by someone who knew me, I'd gone to an intimate tavern located in the back of a Swiss inn in Silverthorne; a place where I'd blend in with the locals and the tourists. A place where I could sip red wine and read a book by dim lighting, or close my eyes and relax in the hum of soft music that played from overhead.

It was quite simple, wasn't it? And I had hardly become a lush. So why did my head hurt so badly?

"She's fine," I lied.

"Lucid?"

"Pretty much." *O Lord . . . I'm sorry . . . I'm sorry . . . I'm sorry . . .*

"What did you two do with yourselves for the whole night?"

I turned my head to look at him. "What is this? Twenty questions?"

He looked at me square in the eye. "No, I was just wondering what you did. Because I know you weren't in her apartment just hanging out. I thought maybe you'd gone down to see a movie, or game night, or—"

"What do you mean you know we weren't in her room?"

Samuel propped up on his elbows. "I tried to call you once. You didn't answer your cell phone either."

"You called my cell?"

"Went right to voice mail. I didn't bother to leave a message. I figured you had it off."

I sighed. "I must have forgotten to turn it on." *No, you didn't.*

You didn't want to be found out . . . in case it rang . . . and you had to explain background noise.

"A lot of good it'll do you like that."

"Sorry."

Samuel raised himself up a bit more. "What's wrong with you, Lizzie?"

I reached for his pillow and placed it over my face. "I'm just tired. I was really looking forward to sleeping in this morning, and now . . ."

Samuel pulled the pillow away from me, and I automatically closed my eyes. "I know you better than that, woman. What's going on with you?" When I didn't answer, he continued. "Is it the kids being here? Is that it?"

I pondered his question before answering. Opening my eyes ever so slowly, I nodded. "This is driving me crazy. I love my children. My precious grandchildren. You know I do.

Samuel leaned over then and pecked my lips with his. "Ah, Lizzie Prattle is human after all." He placed his head back on his pillow and then turned it so as to keep his gaze on my face.

I frowned. "What do you mean by that crack?"

He smiled at me in that way he has that still melts my heart. "Nothing ever seems to faze you, Liz. Your mother moves here in a less-than-healthy state and you bend your life around it. When the kids mess up, you take it in stride. When your husband gets sick and hangs out entirely too much in front of the television, you take that in stride too. No matter what goes on at work, you survive it. Your daughter's wedding plans, with all that they involve, don't seem to faze you any more than one of her childhood birthday parties did. So, we'll blow up a few colorful balloons and serve cake. That's always been your way." I watched a shadow fall over his face. "But not so much lately." He took in a deep breath then let it out so slowly I was nearly unaware of it. "I'd be lying if I said I wasn't worried about you. Even if just a little bit."

I stared at him for a moment before answering. This conversation was starting to get too close for comfort, and I needed a road out. "Lisa Leann has called a meeting for one o'clock. Apparently something has happened concerning Michelle's bridal shower."

"You're changing the subject."

"Not really. You're talking about all the things going on in my life, and I'm telling you about another thing going on in my life."

"Lizzie, Lizzie."

"Samuel, Samuel."

"We've got to get some of this chaos out of our lives."

"Hold that thought," I said, then ever-so-carefully swung my legs over the side of the bed, feeling the chill of the room as it slapped them awake.

Since Tim and Samantha and their kids had moved in with us, I had moved a small coffeepot with all the fixings and two large mugs to one of the occasional tables in our bedroom, thereby allowing us a private place for coffee and quiet on mornings such as this when no one had anyplace special to be by any certain time. I always prepared the coffee the afternoon before so all I had to do was push the "on" switch, which I now did, then climbed back into the warmth of our bed.

The aroma of fresh-brewed coffee permeated the air, sending with it waves of anticipation on my part. "Moving that little coffeepot up here has to be one of the best ideas I've ever had."

"I'll say," Samuel seconded the thought.

"Now, back to what you were saying." I pushed my back against the headboard and pulled the covers around me.

"What *was* I saying?" Samuel moved to sit like me.

"Chaos. Getting it out of our lives."

"Oh yeah. The way I see it is this: Michelle and Adam. That's not going to change until the end of June. We're giving our daughter her Cinderella wedding, come what may. She deserves it, if nothing else."

"Agreed."

"Your son, on the other hand . . ."

"*My* son?" I shifted a bit to look at him more fully. "I do believe he is *our* son."

Samuel grinned at me. "Well, that's what you keep telling me."

"Samuel Prattle." I pretended to be offended. I crossed my arms over my middle.

"I think we should give him a deadline."

"A deadline? What do you mean by that?"

"What I mean is—and I love my son very much—"

"Oh, now he's *your* son," I toyed.

"Don't split hairs." The coffee sputtered its "come and get it."

I slipped back out of the bed to prepare our coffee. "I wish I had some of Mom's apple rolls right now. They'd be perfect with our coffee on a morning like this."

"You're changing the subject again."

I brought the filled mugs over to our bed and smiled at my husband. "But this time not on purpose."

Samuel reached to take the mugs from me so I could better maneuver into the bed. "Aha." He winked. "I knew it."

I'd settled back in and took the first hallelujah sip of coffee. "Back to the deadline, Samuel. You really are making it difficult for me to follow you this morning."

"A deadline, yes. I think we should give them until the first of April to find a house."

"That's nearly another whole month." I frowned, then grinned at Samuel. "I was thinking more along the lines of next weekend. I know people who have found houses to buy in far less time."

"Compromise, then. Two weeks. Today's the 4th; we'll give them to the 18th. The shower is a week after that, and you'll need every bit of your sanity to be both mother of the bride and be a part of the catering team."

I took another sip of coffee. "I need to talk to Lisa Leann about that. I really can't do both."

"I should say not." Samuel took a long swallow from his mug, then leaned his head back and closed his eyes as though savoring both the thought of our home in less disarray than it was now and the delicious flavor of Chock Full o'Nuts. When he opened them again he said, "Next: I'm going back to work."

I felt a surge of joy so strong my headache all but disappeared. "What? When? Are you sure you're ready? Have you talked to the doctor about this?"

Samuel chuckled. "Take a breath, Liz. I know I've been underfoot—"

"That's not your fault, Samuel. You were hurt and—"

"Oh, don't try to soften it, now."

I felt myself blush. "It's not that I haven't cared."

Samuel leaned over and nuzzled my neck, sending shivers from my nose to my toes. "I know," he whispered. "But you're pretty sick of me being here, aren't you?"

I tilted my head toward his, encouraging the sign of affection to continue. "Samuel," I whispered back. Then, realizing where the nuzzling was heading, "Are you sure you're well enough? For this?"

Samuel leaned back, slipped the coffee mug from my hands, and then placed it along with his on the bedside table beside me. He pulled me into his arms then and drew me back down into the bed, teasing me with nothing more than the twinkle in his eyes. He peered over me. "Doctor's orders. Which you would have known if you'd been home last night."

I laughed out loud. "Oh, shame on me."

Later, as I took a long, hot shower, I made two vows. One: to stop leaving home in the evenings to drink my cares away, even if

131

only with a single glass of wine. I reckoned with myself that even though, yes, Jesus did drink wine, it simply wasn't for me. Otherwise, I wouldn't have such a headache on the mornings after nor would I be lying to the people I love most.

Two: to visit my mother before heading over to Lisa Leann's shop for whatever crisis had arisen since the day before.

I pulled into the parking lot of the Good Samaritan an hour or so later. Glancing at my watch as I exited my SUV, I reasoned that I'd have at least another hour with Mom before I'd have to leave. I only hoped that it would be enough time for her. As things were going, it was plenty for me.

I entered the building and then took the elevator up to Mom's apartment. When I knocked on the door she didn't answer right away, and when she did I saw to my horror that her hair was disheveled—pressed against one side of her head and sticking straight out on the other—and that she wasn't yet dressed for the day. "Mom?" I stepped over the threshold. "Are you okay?"

"I can't get Papa on the phone."

I closed the door behind me, thinking that it was going to be one of *those* days. "Mom, let's get you dressed." I turned her toward the bedroom door.

"I've called and called and called, and he just doesn't answer."

I kept my hands on her shoulders as I guided her into her room. I helped her to sit on the unmade bed, then shivered. "Mom, do you have your heat on at all?" I asked, searching for the thermostat.

"Papa works at the gas company, you know," she mumbled after me as I stepped back into the entryway. The thermostat was to the left of the kitchen door. A quick look told me it had been turned down to 50.

"Mom, who turned your heat down?" I called out, turning the dial to 70.

"But today is Saturday, isn't it?"

I went back into the bedroom and saw that she was now taking off her gown, a floral flannel with snaps from the collar to the hem. "Mom, what are you doing? Let me get your clothes before you start taking off your gown. You'll catch pneumonia in this meat locker."

"Papa likes to go hiking on Saturdays." She was pulling the gown from her shoulders. Of course I've seen my mother's naked body before, but this was too much for the first five minutes of my visit.

I pulled the gown back over her shoulders and snapped the top button, then looked her in the eye. "Mom! Stop. Let me get you some clothes before you start taking your gown off."

Mom blinked a few times. "Lizzie, when did you get here?"

I sighed, then wrapped Mom in my arms for a quick hug. "Just a minute ago." I stepped toward the closet. "What do you want to wear today?"

Mom laughed lightly. "Oh, whatever you choose. I'm not too picky."

"Since when?" I asked in jest. I pulled a pair of gray wool slacks and a cream-colored turtleneck from the closet. "How about this?"

"It'll do." I wasn't sure if she was being playful or obnoxious.

I brought the clothes over to her, then helped her in the task of undressing, then dressing again. I went into the bathroom and retrieved her comb and brush, then came back and worked a bit on her hair.

She glanced over at her bedside large-numbered digital clock. "What time is it? Surely it's not as late as that."

"I'm afraid it is," I said, gently tugging at her hair with a small curling brush. "You've slept nearly half the day away."

She sighed. "I wonder sometimes, what's the point of getting up these days?"

I stopped in my brushing and felt my eyes fill with tears. *Will this be me someday? Would this be Michelle or Sissy, brushing my tangled mess of hair, helping me to get dressed?* "Now, Mom."

Mom turned her head just enough to look up at me. "You don't know," she said. "You don't know."

I looked deeply into her eyes for a moment, then smiled at her. "Do you remember when you used to make those scrumptious apple rolls for breakfast?"

Mom turned to look forward. "Your father loved those things more than he loved me, I'd bet you," she said. This time I knew she was teasing. My father had nearly worshipped the ground Mom walked on, and she'd adored him equally in return. "Of course I remember them. I'd as soon forget my sweet Horace before I'd forget those apple rolls. I'll bet I made them three or four times a week."

"You made them every Saturday." I started brushing her hair again. "And only on Saturdays. They were our special treat."

Mom chuckled before saying, "I made them for you and your brother every Saturday. For your father, I made them three or four times a week."

I sat next to Mom and dropped my hands in my lap. "Are you serious?"

Mom smiled at me. "Your father and I had a very special relationship," she said. "We kept secrets you children never knew about."

"Like what?" I was suddenly very curious about what private relationship my parents had had, even thinking to the passion that—after all these years of marriage—Samuel and I had, though our children were, no doubt, very unaware of it.

"Like none of your business," Mom replied tartly. "We kept our secrets and I'll continue to keep them."

I remembered the teddy Luke Nelson had informed me Mom had "ordered" from the schoolgirl, Kimberly. But, before I would allow my mind to go *there*, I said, "I understand." I kissed her on her cheek.

"What I wouldn't give for some of those apple rolls. With your father, of course."

"Mmm . . . I was saying to Samuel this morning that I wished I had some to eat with our coffee. I haven't made them in ages, and I'm not even sure I'd remember how."

"Do you remember the secret ingredient?" Mom asked me, taking the brush and comb from my hand and walking toward the bathroom with them.

"Secret ingredient?" I rose, following behind her, then resting my shoulder on the door facing. "What secret ingredient?"

Mom paused at the vanity, then set the brush and comb on the countertop. I watched in the mirror as her face grew pensive, and when she looked back up at me in the reflection, I noticed her eyes had filled with misty tears. She swallowed hard. "I don't know, Lizzie." The tears spilled from the corners of her eyes. "Oh, Lizzie. I just don't know!"

Evangeline

14

Honeymoon Jam

My new husband was fit to be tied.

"What do you mean you have a meeting today?"

I stood in the kitchen near the window that overlooked a snow-covered blanket where my spring garden would again soon be, pouring a cup of coffee for myself and another for Vernon. "Lisa Leann sounds like the world is coming to an end, Vernon. But whatever it is, it can't take longer than an hour. And as fast as that little Texan talks, thirty minutes at best."

Vernon was sitting at the head of the table. He was dressed in jeans and a black sweatshirt with "SVHS L&O" in bold gold lettering worn over a light gray tee whose collar peeked just over the neckline. I knew the sweatshirt had been a special gift from the Summit View High School Law & Order Club, something Vernon had helped form with the help of the principal, for students who were looking into law enforcement as a career goal. He was as adorable in that shirt as he'd been himself in high school and even cuter with his little-boy pout. "But I made sure I wasn't working today, just so you and I could spend the day together. Seems to me that since we came back from our honeymoon, we've hardly said 'boo' to each other."

I brought the cups of coffee to the table and sat next to him. "The club meets at one. I'll be home by two. We have what's left of the morning and then what's left of the afternoon." I smiled at him. "Not to mention the whole night long."

Vernon pinked like a schoolboy, then continued whining his debate. "But the morning is nearly over, Evie-girl."

We'd slept in. From my viewpoint—as a woman who has rarely slept in a single morning her whole life—it had been glorious. When we'd finally forced ourselves from the bedroom and into the kitchen, I found to my dismay the answering machine light blinking madly that I'd missed five calls and had five messages. Wouldn't you know; they'd all been from Lisa Leann?

"Call me back immediately, Evangeline," she said. "We have to talk."

"Evangeline Vesey! Where are you?"

"Hello? It's Saturday morning, 9:15. I need to talk to you. Where are you?"

"Evie. Lisa Leann. I'm going to drive over if I don't hear from you soon."

And the last call: "I'm giving you ten minutes, and then I'll proceed to break down your door. It's now nearly 10:00." Pause. "Call me."

I knew it was an emergency, or at least as close to one as a person can have when dealing with Lisa Leann. And, I had a sneaking suspicion that everything in her world was akin to a catastrophe.

"Where have you been?" she asked when I called her. "I called at 8:30 this morning and you're just now calling me back?"

"We slept in."

"Didn't you hear the phone ring? How could you sleep through five phone calls?"

I had turned the ringer off our bedroom phone just so we could sleep late this morning and without interruption. When I told her this she merely said, "Oh."

"What's this great trauma about?"

"I'll tell you when I see you. And believe me, it's a big one."

"Why can't you tell me now?"

"Because I don't intend to repeat myself five ways to Sunday."

I had no idea what that little Southernism meant, but I could figure it out . . . with a cup of coffee . . . which I now sipped with Vernon at our kitchen table.

"I promise I'll be back by two," I said, patting Vernon's hand that rested on the table. "If not, you have my permission to be mad at me for a whole five minutes."

He smiled then. "I could never be mad at you for five minutes, Evie."

I stood and began walking out of the room, pushing him a bit on his shoulders with my fingertips as I walked past. "Oh yes, you could."

I arrived at Lisa Leann's at ten till one, not wanting to be late. After all, the sooner we could get the show on the road, the sooner I'd be out and back with Vernon. When I'd left the house he promised me an afternoon and evening I'd not soon forget *if* I made it home by two. I vowed right then and there to leave the meeting by quarter till, no matter what.

On the way there I called Donna cell to cell, to see how she was doing on time.

"I'm practically there. What is all this about, anyway? Do you have any idea?"

"None whatsoever. But it had better be as big a calamity as she's making it out to be, that's all I have to say. Your father and I had big plans for our day together, and Lisa Leann has put a crimp in our style, so to speak."

"Spare me the details."

I could almost see her rolling her eyes, and for a tiny little moment, I felt a shiver of glee at the whole thing. Every so often watching Donna cringe was—quite honestly—worth the effort it took to see it happen.

Unfortunately, right then, I could only *hear* her exasperation.

"Oh, well," I continued. "I'll see you there in a few and we'll find out just what this latest Texan tragedy is all about."

"Whatever it is . . . it sounds like a . . . how would Lisa Leann put it? . . . A doozy."

I laughed. "You've certainly got her pegged."

We said our good-byes, and within seconds I was turning onto Main Street, ever so careful in the fresh shroud of snow that had fallen during the morning. I wasn't sure what Vernon had in mind for this afternoon, but it had best include a fireplace and a cup of hot cocoa if the man knew what was good for him. According to the weather forecast, we'd be lucky to hit 20 degrees by the day's end. I shivered, even with my car's heater going full blast and my coat wrapped tightly around me.

When I arrived at Lisa Leann's I saw to my delight that I was pulling in at the same time as Donna and Lizzie. Lizzie looked about as thrilled as Donna and I did. Vonnie's car was parked next to mine, and I pointed it out to the other girls as I exited my car. "Looks like we're the last to arrive. Good. The gang's all here."

"Good is right." Donna slammed the door of her Bronco. She gave me a stare and said, "Not that I have any big plans for the night like some people I know, but I don't necessarily like having my Saturday cut in half." She looked at Lizzie as we all stepped gingerly onto the snow-shoveled sidewalk. "You look like I feel, Lizzie. What's up in your world?"

Lizzie waved a leather-gloved hand as though fanning a pesky insect from her face. "Oh, nothing. I just came from seeing Mom. One day she's as coherent as you and me and the next the Alzheimer's seems to be taking its toll. Today I saw both sides of the coin within a half hour. I just don't know how much longer this can go on."

I wrapped my arm around her shoulder as we ascended the stairs leading to Lisa Leann's front door. "There will be times when you think it will never end. But we're here to help get you through it. Is there anything I can do to help?" With my grip around her shoulder, we'd stopped just one step above Donna and two from the door.

"You can start," Donna said from behind us, "by escorting her into the shop."

Lizzie and I turned to look at a scowling Donna. "Hold your horses," I reprimanded. "Can't you see our friend is in turmoil?" I looked at Lizzie. "I apologize for my stepdaughter, Lizzie. I don't know what's gotten into her lately."

"For one," Donna responded, "I'm freezing my back end off out here. For another, nothing has gotten into me lately. I'm happy as a bird, can't you see?" Then she faked a grin at us, and Lizzie burst into laughter so hard I thought we were going to tumble down the stairs and take Donna with us.

"We'll talk about this later, Evangeline." Lizzie took another step to the door, which now opened with Lisa Leann screeching like a parrot.

"What in the world are you doing just standing around out here? Hurry up and let's get this meeting called to order."

Oh yes. Let's.

Lisa Leann nearly had a heart attack when she realized that Vonnie was the only one of us intelligent enough to bring her catering club binder to the meeting. "Ladies, you must bring the binders to every meeting," she said, sighing like a stiff wind through the pines. "Honestly. How can you possibly take notes if you don't have your binders?"

We'd all taken off our coats and gotten seated in the parlor, as we'd done in our previous meeting.

"Can you just fill us in on what today's problem is?" Donna asked from her usual place. "I'm tired, I need a nap, and I have to work tonight so *somebody*"—she cut her eyes at me—"also known as my father, can take a day off to play with somebody else."

I beamed. "She's talking about me," I said, as though they didn't know.

"Ladies," Lisa Leann continued. "We have a problem. A very big problem. I received a call from Beverly Jackson. She invited me to lunch in Breck." For a moment Lisa Leann's face seemed to flush, I wasn't sure for what reason. Then she looked at Lizzie. "Over at Mountain Bell Tower Resort, where your children work, I might add."

Lizzie smiled and Lisa Leann continued.

"Ladies, we have a problem," she said, leaving me to think, *We know this already.* "The shower given by the bank employees has been moved from the church to the resort."

"How is that a problem?" Vonnie asked. Until now, she'd been as silent as a corpse.

"I will tell you," Lisa Leann said with a sigh, "if you just won't interrupt me every two seconds."

Vonnie bustled in her seat, muttering, "Sorry."

"That's perfectly all right." Another deep breath and another sigh. "The problem is that the bank employees have hired an independent bartending service to provide a cash bar at the shower." She all but glared at Lizzie. "Like you said before, Lizzie, the bank employees are known to drink. And, they want the shower moved to the resort."

"Oh, dear," Vonnie said. "I just don't know if I can go along with this."

"Come on now, Von," Donna said, crossing one short leg over the other. "This is no reflection on you. So they want to have a cash bar. So what's the big deal?"

"When you say 'to the resort,'" Lizzie began, "do you mean to Mountain Bell Tower Resort where Michelle and Adam and Tim work?"

Lisa Leann blushed again. "Them and one more," she said, though I have no idea what she meant, nor did I have time to ask because she stomped her little foot and said, "If you will let me finish, I'll tell you why this is such a problem." Another deep breath and another sigh. Her shoulders sagged as though under some heavy weight, and she looked dead on at Donna. "Donna," she began. "Your mother and half sister have started their own independent bartending service."

We all shifted our eyes to Donna, who paled. "Say that again."

We shifted again to Lisa Leann, who was now holding up a lavender-colored flyer with "Bar-None" as bold as could be across the top. I reached for it, snatching it from Lisa Leann's finger grip, and began to read it out loud. "Our service is the best Bar-None," I read. "We provide a full-service cash bar, open bar, tiki bar . . . oh my . . . blah blah blah . . . Call for a free estimate . . . ask for Velvet or Dee Dee." I slapped the flyer onto my knee. "How dare they?"

"Give me that." Donna crossed over to me. I handed her the flyer and watched as she stood over me, reading. Her jaw flexed as her eyes darted back and forth, back and forth. Then she looked at Lisa Leann. "What does this mean? They're bartending the party?"

"According to Beverly—" Lisa Leann began, but was quickly interrupted as Donna continued.

"I'm going to have to be in the same room with those two?" She looked over at Lizzie. "Michelle's party is just the beginning." She walked over to the window overlooking Main Street and Higher Grounds across the street. Her hands rested lightly on her hips, and she bobbed up and down a bit on her heels. "You know why, don't you?" she finally said, breaking the silence no one else dared break. She turned then and looked at us, tears forming in her eyes. "It's because of me. They're trying to get to me."

"Oh, Donna," Vonnie said. "You're crying."

Donna wiped a tear from the corner of her eye, then raised her hand almost in protest. "No. These aren't hurt tears, Von. These are tears of anger. Those two make me madder than . . . first the wedding shower . . . then David . . . now this."

"David?" Vonnie repeated so quietly that if anyone else had been talking we'd not have heard her.

Donna jerked a bit, looking first at Vonnie, then at me, then back to Vonnie. "Everybody wants to know how I feel about David and Velvet." She pointed to Lisa Leann. "And don't go reading anything into this either. But of all the women he could get involved with, he's got to go and choose that one. And for what? Well, we all know for what. He's trying to get under my skin."

"Looks to me like he's succeeding," Lisa Leann said.

Donna turned such a hot shade of red I thought she was going to explode. "Oh, why don't you go bake something, Lisa Leann?" she asked, then stomped over to the coat tree, grabbed her leather jacket, and stormed out the door without even putting it on. We all scampered to the front window and watched as she descended the stairs, all the while shoving her arms into the jacket's sleeves, then shrugging before sprinting across the street to Higher Grounds.

"She's looking for Clay," Vonnie said from beside me.

"What makes you say that?" I asked.

Vonnie stared straight ahead. "I just know," she said. "Call it maternal instinct, if you want, but I just know. A cup of coffee, some of Sally's bread pudding, and a chat with Clay and she'll be all right." Then she turned to me. "Don't worry, Evie. She'll be all right."

I drove my car toward the tavern, all the while forgetting my promise to be home by two. I didn't even bother to call Vernon, a choice I knew I'd regret later, but I was too angry to think about that at the time. Vernon would understand when I told him everything, I decided. Especially the part about Donna crying.

When I arrived at the tavern I was relieved to see Dee Dee's beat-up old car parked near the rear. I parked, stomped out of my car, and slammed the door, then proceeded to the bar's front door, yanking it open with such force I nearly jerked my arm out of the socket.

The room looked like I knew it would. A few ne'er-do-wells sitting at various tables, sipping on glasses and bottles of whatever and whatnot. The large-screen TV blared a basketball game as a haze of cigarette smoke assaulted my nostrils.

As soon as my eyes adjusted to the light (or lack thereof) I scanned the room for Dee Dee, also known as Doreen, my childhood rival. She was behind the bar, washing out a few glasses, best I could tell. I strolled over to the bar, and without looking up she said, "What'll you have?"

"A word, if you don't mind."

She looked up with a frown. "For the love of Pete. What is it this time?"

The "this time" was in no doubt due to the "last time" I had come to the tavern. Worried that Doreen would cause problems for Donna around my wedding, I'd been brazen enough to fly in here and demand to know whether or not Vernon was Velvet's father.

"We need to talk. We can do it out here or in your office. Makes no difference to me."

Doreen rolled her eyes. "I thought you and I had buried the hatchet a few months ago." She had a point. Still, she'd made Donna cry. When I didn't answer, Dee Dee called toward the back, "Hey! One of you boys come out here for a minute, will ya? I need to take a break." She reached into her shirt pocket and brought out a pack of cigarettes. "You don't mind if I take a cigarette break while you chew me out, do you? It'll make it set easier."

"I have no intention of chewing you out," I said. The very thought was beneath me.

A lanky young man with shaggy hair came bopping from the kitchen to where Doreen stood. "I'll man the bar for you," he said.

Doreen smiled her crooked smile at him and said, "Thanks, Shelton. I'll be back in a few." Then she headed around to the front of the bar, where I stood staring at the young man.

"Shelton? Are you Shelton Brodock? Treena and Travis Brodock's son?"

He peered at me through the light hair that covered over his eyes. "Yeah."

"Don't let her bother you, Shel," Doreen said from beside me. "She just thinks she's God's gift to Summit View because of who her daddy was and who she's married to now." Then she leaned over the bar and exaggerated a whisper, "But let me tell you, I was married to him first, and he isn't anything to get so uppity about." The two of them laughed as though they shared some dark secret about my Vernon. Then Shelton looked at me. "Yeah, I'm Treena and Travis's son. I'll be sure to tell them I saw you here," he said, then looked at Doreen again. The two of them shared another laugh at my expense before I turned away and began making my way to the front door.

Doreen was on my heels. "You asked for it." Another congested laugh barked out of her lungs.

"I am not speaking to you further until we reach the dead of winter outside these doors," I said.

We exited the tavern. I now followed Doreen to the side of the building and then to where her car was parked. She propped her backside against its trunk, then bent forward slightly to light her cigarette. I stood in front of her, wrapping my arms around myself, hugging my winter coat as close to my body as I could. *This conversation had better be a short one or I'll freeze to death in the process.*

Doreen blew a combination of cigarette smoke and winter air toward me. "So, what can I do you for?" She sounded like a dumb girl from the wrong side of the tracks. Of course I knew better. Doreen had grown up not too far from my house. She and I had even been something close to friends at one time. That is, before she stole Vernon away from me at the age of twelve. From that moment on, she was my sworn enemy.

Before I could answer her question, she went on to another one. "And how's my ex-husband doing these days? You making him *happy*?" The emphasis on *happy* was a clear one, and I blushed.

"That's not why I'm here."

"Well, just why are you here?"

"I want you to cancel out of the Prattle bridal shower over in Breckenridge."

Doreen drew on her cigarette. "Now, why'd I want to go and do that?" she asked, blowing billows of smoke as she spoke.

"Because."

Doreen laughed again. "Oh, you're going to have to do better than that."

In all honesty, I was a little unsure as to how to answer. But with not a lot of time to wrestle with it, I finally decided that honesty was the best policy. "Look, Doreen."

"Dee Dee."

"Whatever. Donna knows you're going to bartend this little party, and she's very upset. I'm asking you to do this for Donna . . . for your daughter. She is your daughter, after all, and I'd think you'd be interested in how this might affect her."

Doreen (or Dee Dee or whatever she wanted to be called these days) threw the remainder of her cigarette to the ground below, then stamped it out under the toe of her scuffed boot. "Of course she's my daughter," she said. "And of course I'm interested." She looked up at me with fire in her eyes. "Don't you even think about insinuating that I don't care about her none. Because I do. She's my baby girl, and I love her."

"Then show it."

Dee Dee took a quick step toward me then, and I took another quick step back. "Now you listen here, Evangeline Vesey. Don't you dare come out here to my place of business and start this show, you hear me? My little girl has a problem with me working an extra job and helping her own sister start a good business in town, then she can come to me and tell me so. She knows how to speak out of her own mouth. I ought to know, I was there when she spoke her first words while your darling husband was out working all the blessed day and night."

The sound of a vehicle crunching across the front parking lot caught my attention before I could answer the jab. We both turned in time to see Donna's Bronco come to a stop. She stared at us for a minute, then spun the car in reverse and sped out of the parking lot as fast as I would assume she dared.

I looked back at Dee Dee and saw the same tear-filled eyes as I'd seen earlier on Donna's pretty face.

"Now look what you've done," she said through clenched teeth, then jogged to the front and then around the tavern, leaving me alone in the cold of the day.

15

Takeout

I sat in my Bronco in the parking lot of the Gold Rush Tavern. There before me stood my new stepmother, Evangeline Benson Vesey, screaming at Dee Dee McGurk, my birth mother. I was too stunned to speak. How could Evie think it was her place to fight my battles?

This is the limit.

I pulled out of the parking lot, crossing Main to the side street that ran behind the gas station. I did a U-turn and pulled to the side of the building.

From there, I watched as Evie hopped in her tan Camry and drove through the parking lot. She stopped, waiting to turn left onto Main Street, while I speed-dialed her number.

"Evie, meet me behind the gas station," I said just before clicking out of the call.

She snapped her head in my direction and gave me a wave,

obviously proud that I'd caught her doing "mission work" on my behalf.

I didn't wave back.

When she arrived, I got out of my car and slid into her passenger seat.

"That woman . . ." Evie started.

I kept my voice low. "Evie?"

She patted my arm as if she thought I was a cat. "All she does is hurt you, Donna."

I took a deep breath and lifted my chin as I turned to face my stepmother. "That woman is my mother."

Evie snorted. "For what that's worth."

"Dee Dee and I are related by blood."

"But that doesn't mean—"

"You and I are only related by marriage."

I watched as Evie's jaw dropped. "What are you saying?"

I crossed my arms as the leather in my jacket crackled. "I'm saying this is something I need to handle myself."

Evangeline shrugged and extended her palms in an upward thrust. "But why? Your father told me all about her; the hard living, the men, the . . ."

I rubbed my temples. "I know. But I've been sitting over here thinking. Why is Dee Dee intruding on my life now? What does she want?"

Evie's face contorted. "I can tell you. Dee Dee's sneaky and—"

My head started to pound, and I held up one hand to stop her flow of words. "I understand how you feel, but after I left the meeting at the bridal shop I began to think, what if Dee Dee's trying to reach out to me and . . ."

"You mean like how she embarrassed you at our Christmas party?"

I nodded quietly. "Yeah. She does lack tact."

Evie snorted. "Just let me handle her."

I sighed deeply, realizing Evie wasn't about to let go. "Don't make me take this up with my father, Evangeline. I don't want to, but I will. It's time you backed off."

She sat up ramrod straight. "I'm not the one who deserves a reprimand."

"I appreciate your help, I do. But, really, it's time you minded your own business."

Evie's face darkened, and I got out of her car and shut the door before she could spew a response.

I slipped back into my Bronco and watched as Evie spun out of the parking lot. Seconds later, I pulled out behind her, watching as she talked on her cell phone, to my dad, no doubt. She was probably telling him what an ungrateful little daughter I was.

Minutes later, Dad rang my cell phone. "Donna, what is going on out there?"

"Don't jump to conclusions."

"Did you really pull Evie over?"

"No. I had her meet me at the gas station parking lot."

"But I thought Evie was at one of your Potluck Catering Club meetings at the bridal shop, right?"

"She was. But afterward she stopped at Gold Rush Tavern to have a screaming match with my mother. I felt that called for a little chat."

The silence hung on the other end of the line. "Oh, good night!"

"Listen, I'm sure Evie will tell you about it when she gets home, and then we can talk later. I've gotta get back to my house so I can catch a few z's before my shift tonight. Okay?"

"All right. But you may have started a war with my new wife, one I may not be able to save you from. You realize that, don't you?"

I scrunched my forehead. "Sorry."

"Well, I'm the one who's going to be stuck in the middle of this."

I hung up and watched Evie turn off Main, pushing a heavy foot over the speed limit. I narrowed my eyes, tempted to hand out one of my famous speeding tickets.

I was heading home for a nap because I could already tell this day was going to come with a very long night. As it turned out, it was a night shift that started a bit too early for my liking. Just before my alarm could hum me into a wakeful state, my cell phone rang.

Without opening my eyes, I grabbed it off my nightstand, flipped it open, and held it to my ear. "Hello."

"Well, if it isn't Deputy Donna."

I sat up, trying to rub the sleep from my eyes. "Who's this?"

"Oh, someone of little consequence. I'm just the woman who brought you into the world."

"Dee Dee?"

"Most of the people I've given birth to call me Mother."

I rubbed my eyes and stretched. "Most of the people? How many people are we talking about?"

A harsh laugh sounded in my ear. "Wouldn't you like to know?"

There was something strange about her voice. "Dee Dee, have you been drinking?"

"Who? Me?" She laughed sarcastically. "Course not. I'm still at work."

"Yeah. When's your shift over?"

"Six."

I climbed out of bed and walked to my closet, where I slid my black sweatpants off my legs, then reached for my uniform pants. "Ah, you're not planning to drive, are you?"

"What do you mean?"

"Well, are you okay?"

I could hear her hack a laugh as I stepped one leg into my pants with one-hand efficiency. The surprise hum of my bedside alarm clock caused me to look up and teeter just a bit. I tucked the phone under my chin so I could grab the doorjamb for balance. Just my luck, the phone clattered to the floor. I dove for it and stuck it back to my ear.

"What's all that noise?"

"Just my alarm." I pulled up my pants and scampered over to switch the alarm off. "Time to get ready for work."

"So, I'm interrupting . . ."

"No, but I've been meaning to drop by for a talk, and today would be good. I could meet you at the end of your shift."

"Well . . . you'd get off your high horse to talk to me?"

"I'm not sure that's how I'd put it. But yes, I'd like to see you."

"This ought to be good; I'll be waiting." The line went dead.

I finished dressing, then brewed a pot of coffee, which I poured into my jumbo thermos. I grabbed one of my famous pre-wrapped hero sandwiches I'd made the day before.

Zipping my leather jacket, I walked into the dusk. The sky must have grayed while I was sleeping, and the clouds overhead glowed in a pale yellow light. Muted sunsets that faded from golden-gray to black always had a way of unsettling me, especially as a night shift was starting. I rubbed my hands together and peered up at the sky. I hadn't heard the weather report, but from the look of things we were in for some flurries. Despite the fact that the spring thaw was on its way, the news of its arrival hadn't yet reached the high country. It would be another couple of months before the calendar would turn the page from spring ski season to mud season.

As I pulled out of my driveway, my heater purred warmth into the chill. I hit the windshield wipers in an effort to dust off a spritz of condensation before it frosted my view.

A few minutes later, when I pulled into the Gold Rush parking lot, I'd already checked in at the sheriff's office. It wasn't that my call on Dee Dee was official business, but I already knew the sight of me in uniform had a calming effect on her.

Darkness was settling around the shabby bar, cloaking it with a respectability that would soon be stolen by the bar's neon sign that stood over the parking lot.

I walked past a dark figure leaning against the side of the building.

"Donna?"

I turned. "David, what are you doing out here?"

"Waiting for Velvet."

David stepped toward me just as the Gold Rush Tavern sign blinked on, turning him pumpkin orange in its glow.

"You mean Velvet's here?"

"Yeah, I was going to drive her home, then I'm off for my night shift."

That's when I noticed he was in uniform.

"Yeah, I'm working tonight too."

"Wanna meet up for dinner?"

"No, no. I'm brown bagging it."

"Okay. Maybe I'll see you later, then."

"David?" a voice called from behind me.

We both turned around as Velvet approached. "Excuse me, Velvet," I said nonchalantly as I brushed past her.

Velvet's voice rose just loud enough for me to hear. "Why were you talking to *her*?"

I paused at the door of the tavern and stole a look at the couple.

Velvet was standing in the orange light in her barmaid's outfit, which consisted of a white blouse tucked into a pair of black pants. With her hands on her hips, she'd tilted her head to one side. Even from a distance I could see a scowl playing in the shadows that partially hid her face.

David stood with hands in his pockets, a wide-eyed look of innocence on his face.

"Just saying hello. Donna's a friend."

153

Velvet grabbed David by the arm and pulled him toward his car. "Not anymore. Understand?"

"But she's your sister."

Velvet turned and gave me a glare. "That woman is no relation of mine. She couldn't be. All she does is hurt Mom."

I turned my back on that remark and pulled open the door and slipped into the warmth of the tavern. It was almost as dark inside the joint as it was outside. Through the haze of yellow light and cigarette smoke, I spotted Dee Dee sitting in a corner booth. She hunkered over a bottleneck beer as she blew a stream of cigarette smoke in my direction. I froze, taking in the scene. She must have changed from her uniform into her street clothes because she was wearing a loose pair of jeans topped with a white sweatshirt that said "Dangerous" in large red letters. I had one just like it.

She looked up at me with glassy eyes. "What are you staring at, Officer?"

I sat down on the bench opposite her. "Nice shirt."

"Thanks, I got it last year in Las Vegas."

"Really?"

"Yeah." She stared back at me. "So?"

"So, listen, I'm really sorry about Evie today. But don't worry; she won't bother you again."

Dee Dee hacked another one of her laughs. "What'd ya do, arrest her?"

I could feel a grin spread across my face. "No, but I should have."

Dee Dee's eyes locked with mine. "Well! Maybe you really are my daughter." She took a sip of her beer. "But that doesn't explain the way you've treated me."

"We got off on the wrong foot. If I'd known you were my mother, before you took up that microphone to announce it at the Christmas tea, then maybe the two of us would be in a different place now."

Dee Dee took another drag on her cigarette and stared at me.

"Leave it to me to do the thing up wrong. That's one thing I always get right."

I shrugged. "I didn't handle it well either. I'm sorry for that."

She took another sip of her beer. "Well, you certainly took long enough to say so."

"I know. I had issues."

She grunted an agreement. "Yeah, I understand issues."

I felt myself warming toward her. "So, here you are, Dee Dee McGurk, my mother. You know, I was only four when you left, but I remember you."

"Do you?" She smiled softly. "What do you remember about me, Donna?"

I looked out the only window in the joint as a busboy sat a glass of water in front of me. "Gonna order?"

I shook my head and patted my radio, which was attached to my belt. "I'm on call from dispatch. Wish I could stay and eat, but it's too early for my lunch break."

The boy shrugged and disappeared, and I returned my gaze to the orange darkness outside. My voice was soft. "I remember your scent—lilacs."

"You really remember that?"

I looked back into her wrinkled face. "Yeah, and I remember you rocking me in your arms in that old rocking chair in my room, singing round after round of 'Clementine' . . . Oh my darling . . . Lost forever, Clementine."

Dee Dee smiled. "That was our song."

"Yeah? Well, the song was prophetic. Somehow you were lost to me. I wasn't sure what I'd done to make you leave."

Dee Dee's tired blue eyes widened. "No, Donna, you have to understand. It wasn't you."

"Now that I'm an adult I know you were having problems with Dad. I know you had dreams of singing on a stage somewhere."

Dee Dee nodded. "Yeah, me and my dumb dreams."

"But knowing you had dreams made it all the worse."

"Why?"

I simply shrugged and took a sip of my water. "I wasn't enough."

Dee Dee snubbed out her cigarette and leaned back in her chair. "Ouch. Okay, I know I deserve that. Hey, I'll just add it to my load of guilt, and I'll be off." She stood unsteadily and dug in her pocket for her keys. "I'm sorry, Donna. I don't know what I was thinking or what I expected, but I guess it was a mistake coming back to town."

I stood too. "No, don't say that." I reached for her keys. "I'm driving you home."

"Naw, I'm okay for the road."

"Not if I say you're not."

She held up her hands. "After that evil stepmother of yours told me off this morning, I tipped a few back, I'll admit it. But I'm okay. Really."

I put her keys in my pocket. "You'll ride shotgun with me."

She looked suddenly interested. "In your Bronco?"

"Yeah."

She gave me a sort of shy smile that surprised me. "Okay. I'd like that."

We walked to the coatrack, where she slipped into her dark blue jacket while I zipped up my leather coat before we walked into the night and through the lazy snowflakes spiraling through the orange haze.

I opened the door of the passenger side of my cab, and she slipped in. I walked around the front of my truck then climbed into the driver's side. "I'm glad we had this chance to visit tonight."

She looked at me and smiled. "Yeah, me too."

I could see the sadness in her eyes, sadness that told me we'd both lived through some of the same story—a story of heartache and loss.

I powered up the truck and pulled into Main Street and turned right. A few blocks later, I'd turned into the trailer park, past Wade's humble abode, and in front of Dee Dee's white and turquoise trailer. It was an older model, maybe from the seventies. I saw the interior blinds twitch. Velvet. My sister was home and watching.

I handed Dee Dee her keys. "Well, Dee Dee. I trust you'll remember where you parked your car?"

She nodded as if to herself. "Yeah. I won't forget this night for a long time."

My radio crackled to life. "Donna, we have a juv over forty at the Stop and Shop."

I unclipped my radio and held it to my mouth. "Ten-four, Clarice. I'm on my way."

Dee Dee's eyes sparked. "Never heard of a juvenile over forty."

"Oh, that's cop talk for a young shoplifter with expensive tastes—I'd better go check it out."

"All right."

"See you soon, okay?"

She climbed out of my Bronco as the trailer blinds twitched in the window again. "Yeah. I'd like that."

"Besides, I want to hear your side of the Bar-None and the Michelle Prattle bridal shower story."

She turned and put her hands on her hips. "I wondered when you were going to get around to that."

I leaned toward the passenger door. "Just trying to understand."

"Well, you know that living up here in the high country ain't cheap. Velvet and I, we're not trying to do anything but make a living. Is there a law against that?"

"No, but it feels like you're trying to interfere with my life and the catering company's business."

"Everything isn't about you, Donna."

With that she flounced unsteadily to her door then disappeared inside without looking back.

A few blocks later I was pulling into the parking lot of the famed Stop and Shop, Summit View's only twenty-four-hour gas station and convenience store. I hopped out of my Bronco, and through the window I could see the proprietor, old man Carter, holding fast to a kid's arm.

I pushed through the front door with my clipboard in hand. "What have we got here?"

"Pete Horn, caught in the act," Carter said, dropping the youth's arm from his plump hand.

Pete rubbed his upper arm and looked up through his coppery bangs. "I said I was sorry. I said he could have it back."

I turned to Carter. "So, you wanna press charges?"

Carter, a man in his fifties, squinted his blue eyes at me as he folded his arms over his maroon knit shirt. His dark but graying hair was slicked back with too much hair gel. "I can't afford to send the message that these kids can come into my store and help themselves to whatever they want."

I looked at the kid in question, Peter Horn. He was small for his age and he wore a too-big jacket that had seen a lot of wear before it had made its way to him. "Pete, now, this isn't my first run-in with you, is it?"

The twelve-year-old shook his head and looked down at his worn tennis shoes.

I stared at him. "So, what'd ya do? Bring a couple of shopping bags and fill her up?"

He nodded as I looked over the items spread on the counter in front of me. "Okay, I get the candy and pop. But you got a lot of frozen burritos in there. I didn't even know those were edible."

Carter folded his beefy arms. "Deputy, I happen to sell a lot of frozen burritos. That's what my microwave is for."

I ignored Carter and continued to stare at Pete's loot. "And a carton of milk and premade sandwiches? Peter, what were you going to do? Have yourself a party?"

He shook his head. "No. I was picking up some takeout."

Carter exploded. "Is that what you call this, you steal off my shelves and call it your takeout?"

"Sorry," Peter muttered. "The kids are hungry."

I gave the boy a hard look in an attempt to prompt a better explanation. "Your buddies?"

Peter looked up at me. "No, my little brother and sister."

"How come, Peter? Why is your family hungry?"

He shrugged. "Dad's out of work again."

"I see." I looked up at Carter to see how he'd take that piece of news.

He puffed out his lower lip and frowned. "Look, his family's misfortune is not my fault; I've got a business to run. I can't take on charity cases."

"No one's asking you to, Carter. But say . . ." I pulled out my wallet. "I owe Peter's dad a few bucks."

Peter looked up at me, surprised. I continued, "Carter, I don't suppose it's against any of your rules for me to make good on my loan by paying you what I owe Mike Horn?"

Carter gave me a look that would have killed me if I'd let it. But he didn't hesitate as he grabbed my two twenties plus a fiver. "This ought to cover it," he said. "But you're not going to get anywhere if you give all your money away, I can tell you that right now."

I turned my back on Mr. Compassion. "Come on, Pete, let me drive you home. All right?"

Carter busied himself repacking Pete's plastic shopping bag before handing it to him. "Next time, kid, you're not going to be so lucky. If I catch you stealing my stock again, you're going to jail, understand?"

Pete nodded and followed me outside.

"I'm driving out your way," I told the boy. "Get in, I'll take you home."

Pete hesitated but complied, appearing to be too afraid to disobey.

We rode together in silence as the evening's white precipitation slow-danced in front of my headlights.

"Everything okay at home?"

Pete nodded. "Yeah, though Dad's been drinking again."

I turned onto Quail Road, and as we approached the small log house where Pete and his family lived, he spoke up. "Ah, Deputy, would you mind letting me out here?"

I pulled over to the side of the road.

"Don't wanna scare my parents."

"This time. But next time I'm coming in to talk about your adventures to your mom."

Pete nodded solemnly. "Okay."

He got out and trudged down the road, carrying his load of groceries. He looked lonely as he made his way to his front door. I slowly pulled away and drove past the house, wondering about his family. My job had taught me that no one really knew what some families went through. Maybe I'd make a point to drop in and talk to his mom in the morning, make sure things were okay. If they were really hungry, I'd see what the church could do about filling the Horns' pantry.

Later that evening, as my truck idled in my secret nighttime hideout, the drive-thru of the Gold Rush Bank, I munched on my hero sandwich and sipped coffee from the cup of my thermos.

So help me, I couldn't get that image of Dee Dee wearing that "Dangerous" sweatshirt out of my mind. Were we so alike that we picked the same clothing? I shuddered as I thought of her tired eyes and deeply lined face. Would I soon look like her?

I rolled my eyes at my own self-pity. Yep, I was following Dee

Dee's footsteps, all right. Like her I was sad and alone. Soon my lifestyle would reflect in my face just as it did hers.

There was a tap on my window, and I jumped, spilling a drop of coffee onto my pants.

David peered in at me, grinning. I could see his paramedic's truck parked just behind him. How had I let him sneak up on me like that? I lowered the window.

"Aha!" he said. "I knew I'd find your hiding spot sooner or later. Care for a little company?"

"Suit yourself." I pointed toward the passenger door as I rubbed at the coffee spill with my napkin.

He waved at his partner, Randall Holmes, who was munching a sandwich. Randall lifted it in a greeting.

In a flash, David was sitting beside me. He'd brought an empty coffee mug and a white paper bag.

"Picked up a few of Larry's cookies before they closed up the Higher Grounds."

That perked my interest. "What kind?"

"Peanut butter. Help yourself."

He needn't have told me because as he poured coffee from my thermos, I was already munching away. I dusted the crumbs from my hands and asked, "Should you be here?"

"What do you mean?"

"You're dating my sister."

"Not seriously."

"Does she know that?"

"We've discussed it, yes."

I sighed deeply. "David, I don't need more trouble."

He grinned at me in a way that made my frown soften. "I know it. I'm really sorry for causing a problem."

"Well, it's not our relationship that's a problem, because like you told Velvet, we're only friends."

"For now," he said quietly.

I looked at him hard. "I don't think I'm up for you."

"Why not? You and Wade are a thing of the past, right?"

I shrugged. "Maybe. It's just, my life is complicated enough. I wouldn't feel right about starting anything with you, especially with Velvet in the picture."

"What if she wasn't?"

So help me, I balled my fist and hit him in the arm. "You *are* asking for trouble."

My radio interrupted our conversation with a sudden crackle, then a voice. "Donna, there's an abuse report up on Quail Road."

I reached for my radio. "What's that address?"

"It's the Horn place, 2224."

"Ten-four."

David leaned toward me. "Any injuries reported?"

But before I could shrug an answer, I saw the lights start to flash on top of the paramedic van. "Looks that way," I said as the radio crackled again.

"Reports of a juv with a broken arm," Clarice confirmed.

David hopped out of my cab and scurried through the icy parking lot to his truck. "En route," I said into the radio. "Got a prelim report?"

"Report is the juv was trying to stop his father from returning family groceries for beer."

"Ah, Pete," I said out loud to myself. "What kind of life do you have?"

I pulled onto Main and turned left. The paramedic truck was right behind me.

I hit my lights too and sighed. My previous assessment was correct: this was going to be a very long night, and the flurries had only begun.

16

Steamy Pair

I kicked off the covers and sat straight up, my heart pounding in my ears. I looked at the digital clock. It was 3:00 a.m. I could see Henry's sleeping form as he nestled deep in the blankets.

I wiped the sweat off my neck with the palm of my hand as my heart continued its wild beat. Goodness. If this wasn't a hot flash, then my sins had caught up with me and my soul was roasting somewhere just above . . . Hello! I knew this was one of those moments God wakes a person up so she will spend some quality time in prayer. Okay, I had something to ask God, and seeing as I was awake with nowhere else to go, I bowed my head. *Why, God, why?* I prayed as my heart continued to hammer. *I've confessed my sin to you. I've repented, turned away from my sin—two thousand miles away—but yet my sin has followed me. Help me!* An image of Clark's smile flashed in my mind. I sighed then. *Help me, Lord!*

I got up and slipped into my velveteen house shoes and padded to the kitchen for a glass of water from the fridge door. As I sipped

163

it, I looked out the kitchen window. The ice-glazed lake gleamed in the moonlight as the dark shapes of the mountains blackened a portion of the starry sky.

Hoping to cool off, I picked up a throw blanket and pulled it around my pink satin-covered shoulders before slipping out the sliding glass door. As I felt the cold air of the early morning hit my cheeks, I sighed.

I had run from the truth, blocked it from my mind, but yet my past haunted me with an affair I'd tried to forget. I sat down in my rocker to contemplate my past.

Clark, a marvelous baritone, and I were both on the church choir steering committee. Sometimes the leadership would meet in the back room of the local pancake house to discuss the month's agenda. Clark and I were usually the last ones left at the table, and we'd sit together with a fresh cup of coffee—talking about our lives.

Everything had been so sweet and innocent. He looked so handsome as he'd confided to me his frustrations with life married to dumpy little Jane, a woman forty pounds overweight who never took care of herself or seemed to have a fresh thought.

Sometimes he'd whisper, "I wish Jane could be more like you."

The flattery only enhanced the growing intimacy between us. Soon, I found Clark was a safe place to share my frustrations over Henry's lack of interest. I'd told him about my lonely nights at home while Henry worked late at the office. I'd discussed our failure to connect and reviewed my hurt feelings.

"Maybe you're just too much woman for him," Clark would tease, his brown eyes sending sparkles of healing to my wounded spirit.

His flattery was charming. Clark was charming. And to have found a friend who admired me? Well, how could a girl walk away from that?

Long before Clark and I opened the door to our first motel room, the affair started in my imagination. First I imagined what it would have been like if I'd married Clark instead of Henry. Then I began to wish I had, even imagining what the most intimate of moments of married life would be like with Clark. And even though, as a mature Christian who would never stoop to have an affair, so I'd thought, I longed to connect my soul to his on a more intimate level. These daydreams would haunt me those evenings Henry left me alone, either emotionally by ignoring me with one of his prerecorded *CSI* shows or physically by staying late at the office to work on some rush project.

I wasn't alone in my struggle. Late one night, after choir practice, after everyone had left for home, I locked the side door of the church with my key and Clark walked me to my car.

He looked so adorable in his jeans and black open-collared golf shirt. He opened the door for me, but instead of climbing inside, I just stood there, caught in the moonlight and the hunger in his eyes.

"Lisa Leann," he whispered.

"Clark?"

But there was no way to express what we were feeling until his lips touched mine. I felt my body relax into his arms, and I experienced a different sort of hot flash. I was the first to pull away from the moment. "Someone will see us."

He looked down at me, brushing a stray curl from my face as his dark eyes streamed pure love. "I'm sorry; I didn't mean to do that."

"Me either," I said bravely as I stepped into my car. "We'll talk about it later."

And we did, after the very next choir rehearsal as we sat in his dark car hidden in a wooded area near the church. "We shouldn't have kissed," I said.

"I agree."

I looked into his moonlit face. "Then, it's over, right?"

Instead of answering me, his eyes glistened.

"Clark, what's wrong?"

He hung his head, ready to confess what I already knew. "I think I'm in love with you."

I closed my eyes against the pain of his admission and leaned my shoulder against his. In that moment, he reached to cup my face in his hands and his lips found mine once more. There was no stopping what happened next.

After that first night we began to frequent a quiet motel across town after every choir rehearsal.

I knew what we were doing was wrong. But I didn't want to stop. Living a lie was complicated, and lies of the heart, I discovered, are difficult to hide from both yourself and the others in your life. Not only did I have to deal with the guilt of betraying my marriage vows, I had to deal with Clark's growing sense of entitlement.

In forbidden moments, he'd whisper into my ear, "You belong to me, Lisa Leann."

"If only that were true," I'd say, brushing my fingers through his dark curls.

He would hug me tighter. "But you do. You may not share my name, but you're mine just the same."

I guess I really didn't understand what he meant until, out of overwhelming feelings of guilt, I tried to cool things down. Finally, one evening after choir rehearsal was over, he gruffly pulled me into an empty Sunday school classroom and closed the door.

He didn't bother to hide his agitation. "Why won't you meet me at the motel tonight? It's been weeks."

"Don't you ever feel guilty?"

"For what?"

I felt my cheeks burn. "For what we've done."

He reached for me, but I stepped away.

"Lisa Leann, you're mine. You know that."

I walked to the front of the room and looked back at him. "But we're not married to each other. You're married to Jane, I'm married to Henry."

"What are you saying?"

"You, Clark, despite my feelings for you, you're not my husband."

"But you know all the reasons we can't change that."

I hung my head. "Clark, what we're doing is wrong."

He took a step toward me. "Don't you think God wants us to be happy?"

I looked up and into his handsome eyes and felt such a longing to run into his arms and to taste that happiness, if only for a fleeting moment. But I resisted and hugged my arms across my flat belly. "Well, Clark, when Jesus said to love your neighbor, I don't think this is what he had in mind."

Clark shook his head. "Lisa Leann, I don't get it. After a year and a half you suddenly grow a conscience?"

I turned my back on him to walk behind the pine lectern. I turned around and leaned on it. "Come on, we both know the Ten Commandments say 'Thou shalt not commit adultery.' Don't you feel the guilt of our relationship? I do, and sometimes it's so overwhelming I can hardly breathe. And when Henry looks at me, it's like he *knows*." I shuddered. "The thought of discovery makes my heart literally stop beating."

Clark held up his hands and shrugged. "We can't help that we're married to the wrong people. But we're not hurting anyone."

"Really? We've betrayed both Henry and Jane. And have you thought that maybe we're hurting each other?"

"Meaning?"

"What if this isn't God's best for us?"

He rolled his eyes at that and walked to stand in front of the lectern. "But our marriages are loveless. Does God want us trapped in a world without love?"

"Clark, I know I don't have the best marriage in the world, but how can I work on it with you in the picture?"

Clark chuckled and folded his arms. "Why would you want to?"

I looked up at him. "Now, see? That's my point."

I held on to the lectern that separated us, and Clark rested his hands on top of mine. "But we belong together."

"No, Clark, we don't. In fact, our time together was only for a moment."

"What do you mean?"

"Henry's taking an early retirement. We're moving to Colorado."

Clark's face grayed, and he entwined his fingers through mine. "No."

"Clark, you've had to sense I was pulling away, and, well, in fact I'm ending this affair tonight. What we've been doing isn't right. Now, I've got a fresh chance with my husband; a time to start over. Clark, I'm taking it."

His grip almost crushed my hands. "What about me?"

"I'm not your wife." I pulled my hands away to wipe the tears that now kissed my cheek. Blindly, I pushed past him. Just before I opened the classroom door, I said, "I'm sorry, Clark; it's over."

That night, as I walked into the church parking lot, I did the hardest thing I'd ever done. I walked into a new life, a life where I could concentrate on my marriage and on my relationship with God. A life that had taken me to Summit View, Colorado, and to the Potluck Club, a life that did not include Clark William Wilkes. I had put him out of my mind . . . mostly, that is. And my new life had been working, it really had.

The freezing temperature of the predawn had done the trick. Now, instead of broiling in my skin, I felt chilled. I stood and entered my condo, shutting the sliding door behind me. I walked into the kitchen and put my glass in the sink before heading down the hall. I hugged my blanket shawl closer to my shoulders as I leaned onto the bedroom doorway, watching my husband as he slept. He looked so peaceful, so undisturbed by my terrible secret.

I smiled at the sight of him. Things were better for us. We'd been growing closer like a husband and wife should. Sure, it still felt at times that Clark was wedged between us, but that was now the past. I mean, it wasn't as if Clark lived in town. Did he? Well, at least he didn't attend our church; for that I could be grateful. So, I was safe. I took a deep breath. *I'm safe, right, Lord?*

My eyes focused on the bedside clock. It was almost five in the morning. I turned off the alarm and returned to the kitchen and switched on the light. It was too late to try to go back to sleep, so I figured I might as well start my day. I opened the kitchen cabinet and pulled out my mixing bowl. I'd planned to make a fresh batch of pineapple muffins, in honor of Becky and Allen's recent engagement announcement. My baking had already made me one of the favorite leaders in the church's singles group. Besides, I was really starting to love those young adults, and I could tell they looked up to me. And I wouldn't let them down.

My muffins had been a hit at the Sunday school hour. I'd caught up with Henry and found our seats in the sanctuary. We were early, so I looked for Evie. I found her sitting in her usual spot with Vernon. They looked so cute together, Vernon in a gray suit that complemented his blue eyes and gray hair, and Evie, so lovely in a swishy black velvet skirt topped with a scooped long-sleeved velvet top in maroon. *Has she been shopping Coldwater Creek?* I wondered. *Good for her.*

"Evie, how are you today?"

"Fine," she said, not looking like she meant it. She asked, "Did you get the situation with Bar-None worked out?"

I shook my head. "No, that's what I wanted to talk to you about. I saw you and Donna discussing things on the roadside yesterday, and I was wondering if you two had come up with a plan?"

Vernon's eyes widened, and he quickly turned his face from me to hide what looked like a mixture of both mirth and terror.

"Well, I did drop by the tavern to talk to Dee Dee, but I'm afraid I didn't get anywhere with her."

My mouth fell open. "You dropped by the tavern? Does Donna know?"

Vernon muffled a cough and . . . what, a grin?

Evie sat straighter. "She does."

"And?"

"You'll have to talk to her about her own plans to speak to her mother."

"Okay. I will."

As I bade Evie and Vernon good-bye, I spotted Donna sitting in her usual spot with Vonnie, Vonnie's mother and father, and Fred on one side and David on the other. She was wearing a new red turtleneck with a pair of black slacks. I knew she'd worked the night shift, so she'd probably head for home as soon as church was over. I'd try to grab her now.

I blinked. Was Wade sitting behind her? Sure enough! My, what a cozy little party they made, a little party I would love to crash.

Just as I began to make my way across the sanctuary, I heard my name ring out in a deep baritone. "Lisa Leann Lambert!"

I turned to find myself face-to-face with Clark Wilkes and his wife Jane. I pasted on my best smile and turned my attention to Jane, ignoring the look of "gotcha!" Clark was sending me with his wide grin.

Jane's unmade face looked grim, and her flat gray eyes seemed to shield me from a secret. *Yikes!* There was something about this woman that scared me. I gave her a hug anyway. "Why, it's the Wilkes from the Woodlands, Texas. Imagine seeing you two here. Are you on vacation?"

Jane, dressed in a long denim shift over a long-sleeved red tee, simply stated, "We moved here."

"Oh! Ah, that's nice. To Summit View, you mean?"

"Yes."

I could see Clark standing just behind her, his eyes glittering, looking handsome in a chocolate-colored designer suit. *The brute.* I made momentary eye contact with him, then said, "Well, nobody told me you were coming to town."

Jane said, "It was a sudden decision to—"

Clark interrupted. "Yep, and here we are and looking for a church home. We knew if we visited around enough we'd eventually run into you and Henry. And here you are."

I tried to sound unimpressed. "Well, Henry and I like it here, but I don't think the music style is what you're really used to. You know, they go for all those newfangled praise songs. Not the majestic hymns you two are used to singing back at First."

Clark glanced at his wife. "Oh, I'm sure we can adjust. Besides, I think it would be nice to have friends here, like the Lamberts."

Jane gave me an unconvincing nod. Clark continued, "Where are you and Henry sitting?"

I pointed. "Over there."

"Lead the way, it'll be good to say hello to Henry."

I turned and headed back the way I'd come, my heart hammering despite my cool facade. "I'm sure he'll be glad to see you," I said as the couple followed me to my seat.

Henry looked up as we approached. "Henry," I called out, just as the pianist entered from the side door to sit at the piano bench. "You'll never guess who I just found."

The look of surprise on Henry's face broke my heart. No, he didn't know. He didn't suspect a thing. He shook hands with Clark and said his hellos to Jane while my fake smile practically froze my face.

As the Wilkes settled beside us, I was glad Jane sat between Clark and me. It prevented him from quietly touching me with a shoulder or thigh. *Lord, please, don't let him touch me. I don't know if I could bear it.*

As the piano began to call us to worship, I continued my prayer. *Lord, my sin has found me, now help me not to be found out. Please. Give me strength.*

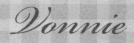

17

Deviled Lunch

Sunday lunchtime at my house was becoming a habit with my family, a habit with responsibility that rested solely on me. I mean, I counted my blessings, glad that Fred and I could have each other, my son David, and my mom and dad at our table. But to tell the truth, I was about Sundayed out.

With mom's care demands, then the disappointing news she had a fresh ankle fracture, I was stressed to the max. How could I survive another six weeks as her personal caregiver? And how could I do that while I played cook and housemaid to both her and our men?

All I knew was I needed help. In fact, "help!" was the theme of my morning prayers as I somehow managed to peel potatoes, chop carrots, and slice an onion before dumping them, along with my roast, into my trusty Crock-Pot. Of course, all the while I ran in and out of the kitchen in an effort to get both myself and my cantankerous mother ready for church.

173

By the time I sat down in the pew with Mother, Dad, and Fred on one side and David and Donna on the other, I was ready for a mid-morning nap. And I would have taken one too, if the sermon's topic hadn't been based on the text of Psalm 37. As the pastor read it in his NIV, I'd underlined bits of text from verses eight through eleven in my Living Bible: "Stop your anger! Turn off your wrath. Don't fret and worry—it only leads to harm. . . . But all who humble themselves before the Lord shall be given every blessing and shall have wonderful peace."

Peace? What would that be like? And as for anger, I'd been more than a little familiar with the feeling of late.

I stole a look at my mother sitting so straight in her pale pink knit suit. Judging by her elegant appearance, no one would suspect how difficult she'd been.

My mind began to wander from the sermon. . . . It wasn't that Mother had mistreated me as a child. She'd been decent enough, but she'd hurt me over my first husband. Then, she'd betrayed me over my baby, tricking me into signing David's adoption papers after she told me he died at childbirth, a birth I'd slept through due to the strong medications I'd been given. Yes, I was angry. Yes, I'd love to turn off that feeling, but how? How does one get to that "wonderful peace"?

The only solution I could think of was for God to heal my mother so she could go back home. *Lord, please?*

But it was my home she would return to this afternoon. Mother and a band of hungry men would soon be expecting Sunday lunch, compliments of Vonnie, cook and self-sacrificing slave to all.

So help me, I sighed as I thought about getting everything on the table, taking care of Mother, then cleaning up the mountain of dirty dinner plates that would be left behind.

How I missed having Donna around. She'd been like a daughter to me and was such good company, as she always stayed until the last dish was clean and resting in the cabinet. But lately, she'd pretty much disappeared from my life. I mean, I was glad to have found my son David, but how I missed my time with Donna.

I was comforted by the fact she still sat with us at church. And this morning, though she sported a new red turtleneck that made her look like the fabulous young woman she was, her eyes told me her very soul was weary. I raised my brows. "Tough night?"

She settled beside me and sighed. "Yeah, we had a rough child abuse case."

I put an arm around her and patted her shoulder. "Oh, Donna, I'm so sorry."

"Yeah, me too."

When David joined us, dressed in black slacks and matching turtleneck a few moments later, he looked at her. "Surprised you're not home sleeping."

"Too much adrenaline."

"Yeah, me too."

I felt guilty then and silently prayed, *Oh Lord, here I am complaining when there are others out there with real problems.*

After the message, Donna turned to leave and gave me a quick hug. "Gonna head for bed."

I grabbed her by the arm. "Donna, wait."

When she turned to look at me I blurted, "Donna, I know I ask every Sunday, but won't you join us for lunch, please?"

She shifted uneasily. "No, I couldn't."

I squeezed her arm tighter and pulled her closer, to whisper in her ear. "Donna, I know you're uncomfortable with David and all, since your breakup, but you have to understand something."

"What's that?" She seemed startled by my unusual boldness.

"I need you to come."

"Need me?"

"Donna, I'm overwhelmed. Could you, as a friend, please come and help me this afternoon?"

175

She stood straight, as she suddenly understood my plight. "Oh! Vonnie, I hadn't realized."

I patted her arm. "Then, you will come?"

"Of course."

David, who overheard her last comment, looked overjoyed. "That's great news."

Something like irritation flicked across her eyes, but before she could answer, Wade, who had been loitering just behind us, piped up. "Uh, I hate to be a bother, Vonnie, but are you still having problems with that leaky faucet?"

I looked at him then to see the cowboy he was, dressed in his jeans, boots, and a dark blue flannel shirt, with a big silver buckle at his waist. "Are you still planning to come over to take a look?"

He smiled, first staring at me, then at Donna. "How about right now?"

I realized I'd have to set yet another plate at the table. "Sure. That would be fine. You'll join us for lunch?"

I wasn't terribly surprised when Wade grinned. "Why, I'd love to come."

What a full house we had. But what a help Donna was, setting the table, filling the glasses with iced tea while I helped Mother change out of her Sunday clothes. Soon Donna and I were in the kitchen, pulling the dinner rolls and green bean casserole out of the oven while the men, minus Wade, who was fixing the leaky faucet in the master bedroom, hovered over ESPN in the living room.

Donna turned to me just before we called them to the table. "Why didn't you tell me you needed my help before now?"

"I knew things were tense between you and David and I didn't want to put you in an uncomfortable situation. But now that Mother's going to be here another six weeks, I . . . well, I've missed you."

"Don't worry about David. I can handle him. Besides, he's still dating Velvet."

I must have looked stricken because Donna patted my shoulder. "He says it's not serious. For his sake, let's hope not."

I nodded as I put the steaming platter of sliced roast on the table, surrounded by my onions, carrots, and potatoes. I wiped my hands on the dishcloth and called to the crowd, "Lunch is ready."

David and my dad helped get Mother to the table, while Wade hovered near Donna, determined to sit next to her. He landed in the chair to her right, while David, undeterred, sat on her left. *Oh my.*

It was comical, really; every time Wade got her attention, David tried to steal it, and so it went for the entire meal.

"Donna, didn't you like the pastor's sermon?" Wade asked.

"Of course she did," David would answer. "Say, Donna, maybe we could try the singles group next week."

Wade would respond, "Well, if you two are going, you can count me in."

I finally interrupted the seesaw. "Uh, Donna, I need your help to scoop the ice cream."

She hopped up. "Sure." We slipped into the kitchen, and I lowered my voice. "My heavens, Donna, you've got those two men coming and going."

She rolled her eyes. "Wade hasn't spoken to me in weeks, but as soon as he thinks David's interested, he's all about protecting his turf." She crossed her arms and leaned back on the kitchen counter. "Then there's David." She shook her head. "If he's so interested in me, why is he dating my sister?"

She turned to pull my blue glass bowls out of the cabinet while I got the tub of ice cream from the freezer side of the refrigerator.

"Still, Donna, are you interested in either of the guys?" I opened the top to the ice cream, and Donna pulled my scoop out of the drawer and dug it through the creamy vanilla.

"I don't know, Vonnie. I think I'd be better off to live my life alone, you know?"

I looked at her then, seeing her pain. "You don't mean that, Donna."

She handed me a bowl with one large scoop in the middle. "I think I do."

I trotted the bowl to the living room and plopped it in front of Mother, who looked delighted. "More ice cream, coming right up," I said to the boys, hurrying back to the kitchen.

Soon everyone was seated around the table while I passed the squeeze container of chocolate syrup around.

"Can't stay much longer," David said after wolfing down his last bite. "I'm going to run by the hospital to check on Pete."

"Who's Pete?" I asked, taking another slow bite of the cold dessert.

"Our child abuse case from last night," Donna answered.

"Whoa," Wade said. "Ours, as in yours and David's."

"That's right," David said. "Donna and I are on the same beat."

Wade stared hard at Donna. "Is that so." He turned and looked back at David. "I wonder how your girlfriend feels about that."

Donna raised her eyebrows while David looked chagrined. "Velvet? Well, she's not really my girlfriend."

"That's not what she told me," Wade challenged. "When I had lunch at the café with her the other day, she seemed to think you two were an item."

Donna turned to Wade. "You and Velvet had lunch together?"

Wade shrugged. "What if we did?"

Both David and Donna stared at him. David said, "Like I say, we're free to see other people. And, well, maybe Velvet is your type."

"My type would be Donna," Wade said.

"Really?" David said. "I heard you stood Donna up for Valentines. That's not how I treat a girl."

Wade shot a look at Donna. "Is that what you heard? As I recall, it was Donna who stood me up."

"No kidding!" David looked at Donna. "That's good to know."

Donna held up her hands. "Okay, stop it, you two. It doesn't seem to me that I'm dating either one of you knuckleheads."

The boys fell silent until David stood and said, "Well, I'm off to check on Pete."

"What happened to him?" I asked, standing up to pick up the dirty plates and bowls.

Donna did the same. "His dad broke his arm, and he's in the hospital."

"How sad," Wade said.

Donna nodded. "Yeah, he's only twelve, and now it looks like he and his little brother and sister are going into the system."

"Meaning?" I asked.

"They'll have to go into foster care unless a suitable relative can be found."

"What's Pete's last name?" Wade asked.

Donna looked alarmed then. "I can't tell you, unless of course you're a relative." She furrowed her brows and frowned. "But in this case, I believe you are. Wade, aren't you related to the Horns?"

Wade looked alarmed. "The Horns? I have a cousin named Mike and he's got three kids, including a boy named Pete. It's not Pete Horn who's in the hospital, is it?"

Donna nodded. "Yeah, I'm afraid so. I'm telling you officially. Wade, it looks like it's your family who will get a call from social services."

Wade turned to David. "I'm going to follow you to the hospital, do you mind?"

The men got up to grab their coats from the coat closet, and Wade picked up his tool kit. "Guess not," David said, zipping up his jacket. "See you there."

Mother, who had until now been entertained by the romantic suspense at the table, said, "I'm ready to go to my room, Vonnie."

"Sure, okay," I said as Dad and I stood up to help.

"I'll start the dishes," Donna said, "then I've gotta get home to bed."

"Thanks, Donna, I'll join you in just a minute."

Soon, it was just the two of us standing in the kitchen, wiping and stacking the freshly washed and rinsed dishes.

"So, Donna," I teased, "about your love life."

She laughed. "Despite appearances, Vonnie, I really don't have one."

I smiled. "I really wouldn't be so sure about that, dear. There was more going on at my dinner table than meets the eye."

"Maybe, but what I saw didn't impress me."

So help me if I didn't laugh. "Well, I can understand Wade and David's frustration."

She looked surprised. "You can?"

"You're a pretty girl, Donna, and those two are smitten."

Donna hung her damp, blue dish towel over the edge of the sink and put a hand on one hip. "Well, they put on a show today, but I don't hear my phone ringing."

"You will." I smiled knowingly. "It's inevitable. The only question is, whose call will you take?"

Goldie

18

Deep-Fried Secrets

"Two weeks," I said to my sister Diane. "I can't believe I've been here this long already." We were in the bedroom we'd shared as children, the one Mama had changed from a girly shade of pink to deep hunter green, trimmed in white and decorated in the popular palm tree motif. Though the windows still boasted old but dustless Venetian blinds that clattered like dropped plates when opened and closed, the window treatments were new and flowing, pooling on the floor, and the framed artwork was sparse, complementing the new theme of the room. The only thing that remained from our past was our antique sleigh bed and the two of us perched upon its downy covers.

Diane, leaning against the footboard of the bed, took a long sip of hot cocoa then closed and reopened her eyes before speaking. "When do you think you'll go home?"

My eyes left the loveliness of my baby sister—her dark hair that held no strands of gray and olive skin that showed few signs of aging—and scanned the room until they rested on my suitcase in a corner of the room. "Friday," I said, just above a whisper. "I need to get back to work . . . to Olivia . . . and to Jack."

Diane had never much cared for Jack, even when the rest fell in love with him. When we were younger and Jack had come for his first visit to our home the Christmas after we'd met and months after we'd secretly corresponded, I thought her cool demeanor toward him was jealousy. Over the years, however, as Diane fell in love and married a local boy named Jeff and had a child of her own, her attitude still hadn't warmed up much. So, I figured it was something else. Exactly what that something was, I had never been brave enough to ask.

"Jack," she said in response. "I'm still a little shocked that he didn't stay any longer than he did after Daddy's funeral. After all, a man's place is with his wife in situations like this, Goldie."

My back was against the headboard, the pillows carefully moved to one side so as not to upset Mama. "I explained it to you." I felt the hair on the back of my neck prickle as I pressed my spine against the wood. "He would have found it difficult to be away for this long from work, and I . . . I . . ."

Diane pursed her lips. "You . . . you . . . what?" She slipped off the end of the bed, careful not to spill her cocoa. She placed the mug on the bedside table, then walked around the footboard and leaned her forearms against the curvature of the weathered oak. "Tell me the truth, Goldie. What's it been like, married to someone like Jack Dippel all these years?"

I didn't answer right away. Instead I wrestled with what I wanted to say as opposed to what I should say. What I wanted to say was: "No, Diane. You tell me the truth. Why have you always had such negative feelings toward Jack?" But I couldn't bring myself to do it. I couldn't risk having Diane tell me that during that first visit he'd tried something with my sister, who would have been all of fifteen at the time. But she'd been a voluptuous fifteen and so much prettier than I'd ever dreamed of being. My only consolation over the years had been that, when pregnant with her son twenty-two years ago, she'd put on weight she'd never quite managed to get off while I had returned to my, as Jack put it, not-thin-but-not-heavy-just-right-pre-pregnancy weight and stayed there.

What I did say was, "We've had our ups and downs. I guess most couples do." I wanted to change the subject. "What about you? Being married to Jeff?"

Jeff was a part-time piano player for a traveling Southern gospel group and a full-time piano teacher in their home. Between his two jobs and Diane's employment in our family produce store, they managed to eek out a fairly good living. Though, I had to admit, Diane lived and breathed as if they were the crème de la crème of society around these parts. Jack has always said that they live way beyond their means—owning a new brick house with an inground pool and substantial acreage—and that Diane liked to put on the dog (as we say in these parts) so people would think she and Jeff were doing better than they were.

"Being Jeff's wife is just fine." She frowned. "Except for the traveling he does." She returned to her place on the bed. "Sometimes I . . . I worry."

I shifted a bit. This wasn't what I was expecting. "What do you mean? You worry about what?"

Diane shrugged. "You know. All those women out there, sitting in the pews. Thinking about getting more than spiritual food from my husband. Jeff's a good-looking man, and I . . ."

She was right about that. Jeff was a good-looking man. "But, he's a piano player in a gospel group."

She coughed out a chuckle. "Don't be naïve, Goldie. Your husband stays home, except for out-of-town football games, and even then he returns at night. You're lucky you've never had to wonder what Jack was up to like I have with Jeff." She stared down at the bedspread and began to trace its stitched pattern with a finger.

This time I laughed, but it wasn't for humor's sake. "Diane." She continued to trace the pattern. "Look at me," I said in my best big-sister voice. When she did I lowered my lids and moistened my lips before going on. "You're right when you say I never had to wonder. But I never had to wonder because I always knew. Until recently Jack's been carousing like a seventeen-year-old boy with his first set of wheels."

I could see Diane was clearly shocked, which—for the moment—was sheer relief for me. Maybe he'd not tried anything with Diane after all. Maybe her coolness toward him was for another reason. "Are you serious?"

I shook my head. "I wouldn't make something like that up, Diane." I leaned over and patted her hand, then straightened. "He and I are both in therapy right now. Mainly him. He's had a very serious problem over the years, and I've been stupid enough and insecure enough to put up with it. Which means we both had a problem."

"Oh, Goldie." She released a deep sigh. "I honestly don't know what to say."

"Let me ask you this: do you have any proof against Jeff?"

"Only that, for some reason, he never wants me to join him on these gigs he and the boys go out of town on. He used to say that I needed to be home with Jeff Junior, but now that Jeffy's in college he can't use that excuse anymore."

"So what does he say now?"

Silent tears began to slip down her cheeks. "That he and the boys only get two rooms at the motels and it wouldn't be right if I went and we got a private room, meaning one of the boys would have to pay for the price of a room alone."

"Well, it makes sense."

"Mama says let sleeping dogs lie."

I crossed my arms over my middle. "Mama never had to worry about Daddy. Daddy loved Mama more than any man has ever loved a woman, I do believe."

184

Diane and I were silent then. Silent for so long the shadows shifted in the room as the sun began its descent behind the bare oaks and tall pines beyond the window. "I sure do miss Daddy," Diane finally said. When she burst into tears, I joined her, reaching for her, sobbing loud enough to bring Mama and anybody else in the family that was in the house bounding up the stairs to see what might be the matter.

But no one came. For the past two weeks we'd allowed one another to grieve as loudly or as quietly as we wanted.

During those times when we weren't dealing with the legalities of living and dying, I took long walks alone down the lane toward the main road that led to town. I spent that time praying and crying, thanking God for giving me my daddy and questioning God's wisdom at having taken him so soon. "You could have waited," I boldly proclaimed on one such walk. "At least waited until I got home. Couldn't heaven have waited a few more hours?" I'd no sooner proclaimed my unhappiness at the sovereignty of God than the sky turned a darker shade of gray, sending showers of icy rain to pelt against my body as I hurried back to the house, vowing never to question God again on such issues.

We'd buried Daddy three days after I'd arrived in Georgia, giving as many family members as could make it a chance to come. That included Jack. He flew in on Saturday and out again on Monday morning. My brother Preston came in Friday morning from Atlanta with his wife Elizabeth but without their daughter Shauna, a twenty-five-year-old beauty who was blessed (or cursed, according to how you look at it) with my golden red hair. Preston and Elizabeth said Shauna "simply couldn't get away" for the funeral. We all thought that was pretty odd, but their closed-mouth attitude about the whole thing kept us from prying any further. Like I told Tom, Shauna lives and works in Toronto now, a grown woman with her own life to live.

"It's her grandfather's funeral," Tom said matter-of-factly. "There's no excuse."

I love my brothers—both of them—and have never liked talking about one to the other. Especially in the midst of grief. "Tom," I said. "May I remind you that my Olivia is not here either."

"She's pregnant. She doesn't need to be on an airplane."

I elected not to comment further. With everything else going on, why add family friction to deepest sorrow? Still, when I was alone and not thinking about Daddy, I did find it rather odd.

Daddy's funeral was an event I wasn't sure I would remember in detail, at least not any time soon. Even as I sat in the front pew of the church and tried to listen to his pastor, all I could hear was a tiny voice inside my head saying, *So this is how it feels . . . so this is how it feels . . .* Only problem was, I couldn't quite figure out *how* it felt. I was numb. Too much had happened too quickly. The middle-of-the-night phone call, the flight, the sudden news that Daddy was gone. Rushing back to the house, to Mama, to the safety and surety of her ample arms, wondering if she were holding me up or if I were holding her up as we cried together. If I live to be a hundred, I'll always remember the cupping of her hand on my shoulder—*pat-pat, pat-pat*—and the sound of her voice whispering in my ear, "It's all right now, it's all right. You're here. You're here." As though life had somehow been suspended from the time Daddy died until I arrived.

I knew that wasn't so. By the time I arrived, Diane and Jeff had already met with the funeral director, according to Melody, because Mama had asked them to. "She said she just couldn't do it," my sister-in-law told me as she helped me take my luggage up the stairs to my old bedroom. I couldn't help but notice that Melody, in spite of the long night at the hospital and having enough children to start her own one-room schoolhouse, managed to look so cute and perky on such a day. Then again, she always did, no matter what. It was as though, even with death all around us, Melody was in our family to remind us of one who enjoys life to its fullest, meeting it head-on each and every day.

Diane and Jeff picked a lovely casket—ocean blue stainless steel lined in baby blue crepe, which I noted matched the color of Daddy's eyes. Stitched on the inside of the lid was a hillside scene bearing a few trees and three crosses—one prominent—supported by the words: In God's Care. Because of Daddy's military service, the American flag was draped and pulled back in an accordion fold until after the casket was closed, then it fell over it like a proud sheet, with corners stiffly pointing downward, reminding me of a soldier standing at attention.

I asked Tom if he would take me to the funeral home on the evening of visitation before anyone else could arrive. I hadn't seen Daddy in a year and I wanted some time alone with him before everyone and their brother showed up to pay respects.

DeLoach's Funeral Home is, like so many Southern funeral homes, located in what was once a sprawling Victorian on Main Street. Its wraparound porch is lined with old rockers and plant stands supporting enormous ferns, offering a familial welcome. The front door—half glass, half paneled wood with chipped paint— had to be jerked to be opened, and it rattled when Tom gave it his all. Inside what used to be the front hall was a split staircase and on either side of that four sets of double doors leading to rooms where the dead lay in wait for the living. At one time, of course, these rooms had been parlors and dining rooms and such. But not now.

Someone, a reedlike woman I neither recognized nor knew, came down from a back room and up the hallway. Tom met her halfway while I stared at each set of closed doors, wondering which one my daddy was behind. I heard Tom mumble something, bringing my attention back to him. He stepped back to me. "She said for us to take our time." He cupped my elbow and turned me to the left, to the first set of doors. He slid one of them open just enough for us to step through. Inside the room my senses were nearly assaulted by the smell of roses and carnations, of lilies and mums. But by this time my gaze was solely on my feet and the long narrow floorboards beneath them.

I didn't look up until we'd reached the casket bathed in soft sunlight made all the more ethereal by stained glass windows on the west side of the room. Raising my eyes I saw a man lying in repose. He looked vaguely like my father and yet did not. He appeared younger somehow than the last time I'd seen him, and that had been a year ago. Instead of his favorite faded denim overalls and worn cotton shirt, he was dressed in a dark blue suit, white dress shirt, and a blue tie striped in blood red.

I placed my hand on his chest as though feeling for a heartbeat and, finding none, wept. "Oh, Daddy . . ."

Tom's arm came around me, pulling me to his side, supporting me, I suppose for fear that I might collapse. I knew I wouldn't. Couldn't. My hand was on Daddy, and Daddy was all the support I needed.

The following days were hard. We'd no sooner laid Daddy to rest and begun to make our way to the line of cars than old Mr. DeLoach approached me with a zippered vinyl case and said, "Give this to your mama when you get home. It's everything she'll need. Paperwork and the like."

I looked into the eyes of a man who'd been a friend to my father since they'd been children, and noted the kindness there. What manner of man, I wondered, chose death as his occupation? A kind one, to be sure. "Thank you." I took the case and held it against the black wool of a dress I'd borrowed from my childhood friend Laci. "I'll be sure she gets it."

"Your daddy was a good man. I don't know if I'll ever know another one like him."

Jack came up behind me just then and placed his hand on my shoulder. "You want me to take that, Goldie?" He nodded toward the case. I handed it to him, and he shook Mr. DeLoach's hand and then said to me, "I'll be in the car."

I gave him a fleeting glance, then looked back at Mr. DeLoach. "Thank you again."

I started to turn away, but before I could the old gentleman stopped me with words. "Did your daddy ever tell you about how he'd bring us banana pudding up to the funeral home?"

"No, sir. I'm afraid he didn't."

"Well, he sure did. Your mama would make it, of course. Then Hoy would say, 'Bake two of 'em, Doris, and I'll take one over to Kenny and his bunch of gravediggers.'" He chuckled. "That's what he always called me. A gravedigger. I'd say, 'Hoy, now you know I've got men out there to do the digging,' and he'd say, 'Yeah, but that don't stop you none from dropping the casket in the hole, now does it?' Your daddy . . . he was a character." Mr. DeLoach choked on his final words.

I'd heard those words more in the last few days than I'd been able to count. I tried to smile but failed. "Yes, he was."

"I'm gonna miss him. I'm going to miss his puddin' too."

I placed my hand on his arm, leaned over, and said, "I'll be sure to tell Mama to bake you a banana pudding next time she's baking one for the family."

"Nobody bakes 'em like your mama." He gave a sad shake of his head. He turned then and walked away.

The day after my eye-opening conversation with Diane I stood alone in the kitchen and pulled Mama's recipe book out of one of the cabinets, laid it on the counter, and began to skim it.

"What'cha doin'?" Mama said from behind me.

I'm sure I jumped a country mile. "Mama! You scared me nearly to death." I took a quick breath. Funny how something as ordinary as "scared me nearly to death" suddenly didn't suit.

"Only the guilty jump." She smiled at me.

"Mr. DeLoach said Daddy used to take him some of your banana pudding, and I thought I'd make some for the funeral home before I leave tomorrow."

Mama picked up the recipe book and placed it back on the shelf. "You won't find it in there," she said, straining a bit. Then she looked at me and pointed to her temple. "It's all up here, sister."

I put my fists on my hips. "Well, Martha Stewart, will you talk me through it then?"

"Go get yourself a mixing bowl over there," she began, reaching for an apron hung on a hook near the sink. I believe Mama is one of the few women left in this world who still cooks wearing an apron, and I said so as I retrieved the bowl and brought it to her.

She blushed a pretty shade of pink. "Your daddy always said it made me look sexy."

My eyes widened. "Mama . . . my, my. The devil you say." I cut my eyes in jest.

"Your daddy was a lover, honey. I never talked to you children much about it, but he was that. A hard worker and a fine lover. That man was mad about me, and I was mad about him." She paused. "Hand me the bowl."

I did.

"Get me four eggs from the icebox, and the milk too."

I did as I was told, and Mama began pulling other items from the pantry: sugar, flour, a box of vanilla wafers. . . . I joined her back at the counter and said, "Don't stop there."

"What do you mean?"

"Aren't you going to tell me some more saucy stuff about you and Daddy?"

"Nope. Now, get me four bananas from over in the fruit bowl, and while you're doing that, *you* can tell *me* more about this catering club I heard you talking to Diane about the other day . . ."

Preston drove me to the airport Friday morning. He and Elizabeth had come in the night before to spend the weekend with Mama and so Preston could see me off. I spent the better part of the evening packing and crying, so I welcomed the time alone in the car with my oldest living brother.

"How's Mama doing, you think?" he asked me when we'd pulled onto the main highway in his Escalade rich with the scent of leather.

"Mama's made of pure butter fat and starch. She'll hold up. Besides, she's got Diane and Tom right there with her, so neither you nor I have to worry, Preston."

I'm sure my tone was a bit icy; for the life of me I don't know why. He whipped his head to face me, then turned back to the road. "Where'd *that* come from?"

"I'm sorry. I'm just . . . I don't know." I took a breath and let it out, all the while pressing the front of my slacks with the palms of my hands. "You and I used to be close, and I guess I just came to realize with Daddy's dying and all, you and I have become familiar strangers. To our own family as well as to each other." I looked at him, pondering his profile for a moment as he studied the highway that stretched out before us. He looked so much like Daddy. Tall and lanky but with a little extra poundage brought about by age. His hair was salt and pepper like Daddy's, not quite as wavy, and combed back from his face. I thought for a moment that he looked more like Daddy than Hoy Jr., whom Daddy now lay beside in the church's adjoining graveyard. "I mean, when was the last time we talked, Preston? Really talked?"

"I don't know. Seems like life has a way of getting in front of what's really important." He flexed his hands on the wheel, then continued. "I've been thinking a lot since I got the call that Daddy was sick. Here we lived just a few hours from home, and Elizabeth and I barely made it down to see the folks."

"Don't feel bad, Preston. We live in the jet age; I could be here in a matter of hours myself, if you think about it. And I come home once a year. We have families, and Mama and Daddy always understood that."

"I should have called more often."

I felt tears sting the back of my eyes. "If we'd known we only had a little more time, we'd have called every day, several times a day. Both of us would have. You know that."

"Years ago, after I'd moved up to Atlanta, it was all about work, getting settled in my career. Then, I met Elizabeth and we got married. Suddenly life was about building a home and a family with her rather than staying so much connected to the family I'd grown up with."

"*C'est la vie*," I said. "Of such things is life, brother."

He cleared his throat before going on. "I asked to be the one to drive you to the airport because I thought it was time we really talked again, Goldie. Like you said, we used to be so close."

I smiled at him. "Oh, sure," I said with a lilt in my voice. "Never has a brother so mercilessly picked on a little sister."

He chuckled. "It made you tough."

I grew pensive. "And tough is what I'd need to be to get through this life."

He looked at me momentarily. "How's Olivia? Mama says she's expecting."

I nodded. "Baby number two. What about Shauna? Anyone special in her life?"

I watched Preston turn pale, then flush red. "Shauna has someone special, Goldie. In fact, she's married to him."

"What? Preston! Why haven't you told anyone?"

Preston swallowed. "He's a man of color; or at least that's the way Elizabeth puts it . . . when she can bring herself to discuss it."

I took in a breath, my fingers lightly touching my chest. "He's black?"

"That's why Shauna didn't come to the funeral. In Canada it's not so big a deal, but here in the South . . ."

"It's not something Dixie is altogether ready to deal with," I said.

Preston chuckled. "Noooo . . ."

"Is he nice?"

"Very."

"Does Shauna love him?"

Preston reached into his coat pocket and pulled out a photo. "You tell me. I've been holding on to this . . . in case I . . . we . . . talked."

I took the photo from him and then stared at the image of my beautiful niece and a handsome black man. They both bore wide smiles, and I noted the way his dark hand was gently draped over a pale one, his fingertips lightly touching hers. It was a loving caress, evident even on photo paper.

"He obviously makes her happy."

"Like no one I've ever seen."

"Personally I'd rather have Olivia happy with a black man than miserable with a white man." I swallowed. "Believe me."

He looked over at me again, then back to the road. "What are you saying, little sister?"

I shrugged. Jack had changed. There was no need to open this can of worms.

"Jack?" Preston finally asked. "Something with Jack?"

I looked at my brother, his face growing hot in the cold of winter. "Preston, the nightmares of my marriage are all over now. We've worked through some issues and . . . you've always liked Jack. I don't want to say anything that might make you not like him."

Preston exhaled loud enough for me to hear him. "Why do we do this, Goldie? Why do we keep secrets from the people who love us and who we love?"

"I don't know." My voice was barely audible.

He reached over and took my hand, squeezing lightly. "Remember when we were kids? There was that bully—what was his name?"

"Biff Davis." *How could he forget?*

Preston laughed at my quick answer. "He used to pick on you all the time when you were, what? Third grade?"

"And fourth."

"Then you came home and told me."

"He made fun of my hair," I said with a pretend pout and a touch of my red locks.

"So the next day, I held him down while you poured red paint all over his head." Preston laughed heartily, and I joined him.

"Daddy was so mad at us. We could hardly sit down for a week."

Preston shook his head. "Not without a pillow." Then he laughed again. "Look, Goldie, let's not do this anymore, okay? Let's stay in touch. Let's share our hurts and our fears and our . . . secrets. The way I see it, it's a simple matter of trust."

Trust. Indeed.

I leaned over as best as my seat belt would allow and kissed his cheek. "Agreed."

We rode in silence for a while longer until he said, "You and Jack okay now?"

"We're better than okay. We're in counseling. I actually moved out of the house last year and got my own place for a few months, then moved back."

Preston shook his head again. "You should have told me. It makes me sick to think that you lived somewhere else for months and I didn't even know it."

"So then, what about you? How long are you going to keep your secret a secret?"

"Give it some time, Goldie. You're living proof that we share our secrets when we're ready and not a minute before."

I thought about that for a moment, and about the truthfulness behind it. I thought about how long I'd kept my secret, how Diane was holding her fears secret, how Mama had worn aprons all these years because Daddy thought it was sexy, and how even a good secret is a secret nonetheless. I looked out at the flat farmlands stretching before me and thought about my mountain home in Summit View. I thought about Donna and Vonnie and Evie, about how each of them had kept secrets over the years that had kept them emotionally imprisoned for so long. Then I thought about Lizzie and Lisa Leann, the only ones of our little group who didn't seem to have secrets at all.

But surely they do, I thought. *Because all God's children have secrets.*

19

Boiling Over

An entire week had gone by since I'd made my resolution to stop drinking on the DL, a phrase a couple of the kids at school had recently introduced me to.

"The DL, Mrs. Prattle," Jennifer Brown said to me while in the media center one chilly afternoon. "You know, R. Kelly's song? 'The Down Low'? Nobody has to know?"

Jennifer's best friend (at least as far as I could tell), Patrick Noone, chimed in. "Mrs. Prattle probably doesn't listen to R. Kelly, Jen."

I admit it. I'd never even heard of R. Kelly.

"He's a singer, Mrs. Prattle," Jennifer said with a giggle. "You know, 'Bump and Grind'?"

I frowned in response.

Patrick, an adorable young man if I've ever seen one, shook his head. "No, no, no. She's not going to know that one." Then he shot a dimpled grin my way. "But I'd be willing to bet you know 'I Believe I Can Fly.' Right?"

I nodded. "Now, that song I know." I'd heard it recently in a bar, in fact, but I wouldn't go there with my students.

"Totally," Jennifer said. "So, he has this song called 'The Down Low.' It means, on the sly. Hidden."

"Secret," Patrick added.

"Secret?"

"Hey, look at her," Patrick said to Jennifer. "She's blushing."

Jennifer's eyes twinkled as she said, "Maybe Mrs. Prattle has something she's keeping on the DL."

I frowned again. "Maybe it's the grades you're going to get in library science," I said.

"Oops," Patrick said with a wink. "And I'd appreciate it, Mrs. Prattle, if they stayed on the DL."

So, I'd kept my drinking on the DL, and now it was done. Good. A week without a drink had left me a little shaken at times and craving the taste of a glass of red wine at others, but I'd managed just fine. Even last night, a Friday with enough noise in the house to bring a small earthquake to envy, I'd stayed home, read in the semi-quiet of my bedroom, and managed to get to sleep by a decent hour without the aid of alcohol. My short-lived indiscretion was safely over.

On Saturday I woke early, feeling refreshed. I had a long list of things on my to-do list, including a Potluck meeting and tea with Michelle, Adam, and Adam's mother. Later, Michelle and I were going to head over to Denver to shop for a wedding dress. Lisa Leann would have a fit if she knew that Michelle and I were looking at dresses without her expertise, but I had dreamed of this day since the day Michelle was born, and I wanted no one else involved.

Of course I would allow Michelle to pick out her own dress. I'd certainly allowed her sister the privilege for her wedding. Over the past couple of months, Michelle and I had studied stacks of bridal magazines and had pretty much decided that her dress would be a strapless sheath with lots of beads or lace, and in white. Her bridesmaids would wear black trimmed in metallic silver. It would be an en vogue wedding. And I would be the sober mother of the bride.

On my way to our Potluck Club, which was meeting at Evie's despite Lisa Leann's protests to have it at her boutique, I stopped by Goldie's. Samuel had seen Jack in the bank the day before, and Jack had told him that Goldie would be flying in later in the day but that she wasn't ready for a lot of company. I understood, having also lost my father and still missing him as though his death were yesterday. But Jack had told Samuel that if anyone would be welcome right now, it would be me. I took that as a sign to keep her arrival quiet and to slip over for a few minutes.

Goldie looked to have lost about ten pounds in the last few weeks. But her hair was nicely styled, her makeup had been lightly applied, and she was dressed as though she were going to the club meeting.

"Lizzie," she said when she answered the door. "I'm so glad you came."

I had brought a cake. I extended it toward her. "Got coffee?"

"Is that your mystery mocha cake?"

"It is."

Then she smiled. "Then I have coffee."

As we gathered around her kitchen table I noted the strong scent of Pine-Sol wafting through the house and the sound of both the washer and dryer doing their jobs from the adjoining laundry room. No doubt Goldie was working overtime in the housecleaning department since her return. I felt good knowing I'd given Goldie what had to be a much-needed break from her labors.

With thick slices of the cake and steaming cups of coffee before us, Goldie shared with me about her time away, her father's life, his death and funeral. She cried, and I supplied tissues from a small pack I keep in the tidy crevices of my purse. At one point, my emotions raw with memory of the loss of my own father, I cried with her.

When we'd dried our tears and finished off the last moist crumbs of our cake slices, Goldie asked, "So what's on your agenda today?"

"I'm having tea with Michelle, Adam, and his mother, and then Michelle and I are going to a shop in Denver to narrow down the search for her gown."

"Oh, what fun. I remember doing the same for Olivia. Of course, she didn't like anything I liked."

"So far Michelle and I have agreed on everything. At least what we've seen in the magazines and catalogues."

"Good for you," she said sincerely.

I took a deep breath and exhaled. "And we have the club meeting in a bit."

Goldie looked appalled. "Oh no! I forgot!"

"Don't worry about it, Goldie. No one expects you to show up. Heavens, no one even knows you're back in town."

She nodded. "Secrets," she said after a time.

"What?"

"Keeping secrets. My brother Preston and I were talking about it just yesterday. 'No one knows,' you said. He's been carrying a secret from the family and I've been carrying a secret from them since nearly the year Jack and I married. You know, our problems . . . our secrets."

I straightened my shoulders. "Where is Jack?"

"Grocery store. I gave him a very long list. I told him I'm just not ready to handle seeing a lot of people yet, but we need some real food in this house."

I nodded in understanding but said nothing. When I stood to carry my dishes to the sink, I gathered hers as well.

"We share our secrets when we're ready and not a minute before."

I whirled around. "I'm sorry?"

"That's what Preston said to me yesterday." Goldie rested her chin in the palm of her hand. She stared straight ahead, but not at me. "Do you ever wonder what secrets our friends carry, Lizzie?"

I crossed my arms. "No. That wouldn't be right."

She cut her eyes over at me, then gave a slow smile. "Liz . . ."

I sat again at the table. "Would you want them wondering the same about you?"

"No one has to wonder about me," she said. "Everybody in this town knows."

I touched her hand lightly. "Not everyone."

She didn't answer, but her eyes narrowed as though she were deep in thought. "Lisa Leann. Now there's a woman with secrets, I'd be willing to bet you."

"Goldie!"

Goldie shrugged. "Maybe being in the South for a while has brought out the stinker in me. Southern ladies sure do love a good tale, and they don't really care who it's about."

I stood. It was best I leave. "Who doesn't? I have to go. What can I do for you?"

Goldie stood too. "Ask the girls to pray for Mama. For my family. For me. But tell them I'm not ready for company just yet. Make that point especially with Lisa Leann."

We walked to the door. "When will you go back to work?"

"Monday. Chris was kind to let me off as long as he did, but I need to get back to normal as soon as possible. I just don't want to have to recount the story of Daddy's passing over and over to everybody and their sister. Not right now."

I gave her a hug at the door. "I understand totally," I said. "I'll be in touch."

Lisa Leann was still less than happy that we weren't having the meeting at her boutique.

"I told you, Lisa Leann," Evie said to her after several sighs from our favorite Texan, "that our club meetings should be here and our catering meetings should be at your place. Thus, we do not get the two confused."

"But you're a newlywed," Lisa Leann countered. "I was just trying to relieve you of any unnecessary work."

"Get over it, Lisa Leann," Donna said, then popped a meatball in her mouth.

Lisa Leann was nonetheless gloating about something.

"What are you grinning at, Lisa Leann?" I asked her. "What do you know that we don't know?"

She merely raised her perfectly penciled eyebrows and said, "Not we. You."

I pointed to myself. "Me?"

With a wave of her hand she walked away, saying, "I'm not saying another word. You can't make me. Take away all my makeup and make me wear hand-me-downs and I'll still not say another word."

Evie walked up and stood shoulder to shoulder with me, peering after the tiny bit of dynamite that had left the scene. "Good grief, I think she's serious."

"A bare-faced, Goodwill-dressed Lisa Leann," Donna said from behind us. "Who can imagine that?"

All through our lunch and prayer meeting Lisa Leann kept grinning at me. I narrowed my eyes at her (as best I could . . . I'm not good at veiled threats), but whatever little hush-hush was going on in her brain was staying confidential.

Oh well, I thought later as I pulled my car out of Evie's driveway. *I have enough on my plate without wondering what Lisa Leann is up to.*

I rushed to see my mother before meeting Michelle, Adam, and his mother Esther at the teahouse. I found Mom curled up in her bed like a little girl, sound asleep. I didn't want to disturb her so I slipped back out of her apartment and headed back for the parking lot, only to be stopped by Luke Nelson. He was at the front doorway, and I had a sneaking suspicion someone had alerted him of my arrival. It was just too convenient that he was at this particular place at this particular time. He looked more like a roadblock than the handsome administrator of the Good Samaritan Assisted Living Facility.

"Why, hello, Luke," I said with a forced smile. "Do you work *every* Saturday?"

"Every other." He sighed as though he'd been holding his breath since the last time I'd seen him, when he'd told me my mother had worn a teddy to the residents' pajama party. "Mrs. Prattle . . ."

"What has she done now?"

Luke shook his head. "It's not one particular thing. But she's slipping rather quickly."

I closed my eyes and nodded, then opened them again. "What do you want me to do, Luke?"

Luke smiled at me, I suppose in hopes of softening whatever blow he was about to deliver. "My records on your mother indicate that you and your brother are co-executors of her estate." He nodded his head as though he agreed with his own statement.

"You think my mother is dying?"

"Oh no, no, no. Nothing like that." He swung his head from side to side. "But do the two of you take care of the decisions concerning your mother? Together?"

"I suppose so."

Again he nodded. He was beginning to remind me of one of those bobbing head dogs that my father kept on the dashboard of his car back when my brother and I were children. "I would simply suggest that you contact your brother and talk. Start looking into something more along the lines of a nursing home. A twenty-four/seven care facility."

I sighed. "Luke, my brother's wife is still recovering from a very serious heart attack. My daughter is getting married soon. You remember those last few weeks and months just before you got married, don't you? I'm dealing with senioritis at the high school—spring break is just around the corner, not to mention prom—a new business venture and the wedding, and now you want me to find my mother a new care facility when we just got her settled here?" My voice managed to raise an entire octave as I spoke. My chest tightened, and for a moment I thought I was going to have my own heart attack.

"I'm sorry, Mrs. Prattle. I'd say within the next month or so, you'll want to have her in another facility."

I looked beyond Luke to the glass doors of the Good Samaritan. Outside, the gray clouds that had been gathering all day began to break apart and the sun was shining. God, I reasoned, was—in his own way—reminding me that in the midst of trial there was hope. I just had to stay focused. "I'll see what I can do," I said. "I'll call my brother later this evening or perhaps tomorrow after church."

"That's a good idea," he said. "I'll be here to help in any way I can."

I took several steps toward the doors.

"And, Mrs. Prattle . . ."

I stopped, but I didn't turn around.

"I'm so sorry about all this."

"Me too," I said. "Me too."

Michelle had asked that we meet at a new and quaint teahouse called Abigail's. It had been open for less than a month, and I'd not had the opportunity to go yet, so I thought it was the perfect choice. Not only was it different from what I was accustomed to, it wasn't Apple's. Right now, I didn't trust myself at Apple's. Tension was mounting in my shoulders. I either needed a drink or a massage.

I had the desire for one, no time for the other, so a relaxing teahouse on a lovely Saturday in mid-March was the perfect solution. "See, Lizzie," I said to myself as I pulled into the parking lot in front of the new establishment. "You can make good choices. Tea. Not wine. Plain ole coffee. Not Irish."

Adam's car was parked two cars down, so I knew that the others had arrived. I stepped out of my car and into a pile of slush, frowned, but kept going. Inside Abigail's small foyer, I stomped my shoes free of excess snow and sludge onto the damp welcome mat, then removed my coat, hanging it on a nearby antique coat tree. I had no sooner done so when a dark-haired woman who appeared to be in her midthirties met me. "Welcome to Abigail's," she said. "I'm Abigail Bohman."

"Hello, Abigail," I said. "I'm meeting my daughter and her—"

"Michelle and Adam?"

"Yes." I beamed.

"They're here and are waiting for you." She turned and led me into a charming, brightly lit room laden with Victorian furnishings. Painted white tables covered in pristine and crisp white linen displayed fine Victorian china and heavy silver. The walls were papered in a pale yellow and white stripe and bordered with a floral pattern. One window was topped with an ornate stained glass insert that sent prisms of color and light across the room.

In the far corner, at a table for four, my daughter, Adam, and his mother smiled toward me. Michelle was so excited; she actually spoke "Mom!" as she waved me over.

I waved back and was soon seated to the left of my future son-in-law (who politely stood when I arrived at the table and pulled my chair out for me), to the right of my daughter, and across from Esther Peterson.

Adam's mother is an attractive woman who carries about fifteen pounds too many. She has porcelain skin and medium length dark blonde hair that is worn straight and pulled away from her square face. I've seen her at church a good number of times and have, of course, spoken to her over these past few months, but haven't yet felt we were even close to being friends. Just friendly.

Adam looks more like his father—tall and dark—and Britney like their mother sans the extra weight, I thought as I said, "Good to see you, Esther."

"Lizzie. It's always good to see you." She glowed as she spoke and spread her hands over the table as though she were showing it on *The Price Is Right*. "I hope that this tea will be the beginnings of a new and long-lasting friendship."

I looked over at Michelle. She was reading Esther's lips, and once Esther was finished speaking, she turned to me to read my response.

As is my habit with my daughter, I signed, "Hear, hear!"

Michelle applauded lightly and then signed, "I'm so excited."

Out of habit, I spoke her words for her, but before I could finish Esther signed back, "You have every right to be, sweetheart."

Something inside me stirred, and it wasn't pretty. As the mother-in-law of Sis's husband Isaac, Samuel Jr.'s wife Mariah, and Tim's wife Samantha, I was accustomed to loving them as my own children and my own children being loved and endeared by their in-laws. But Michelle is my baby. She's the one I spent the most time with over the years, taking her to the deaf academy, learning sign language with her, teaching the others in the family, speaking for her, all the while encouraging her that she could do anything a hearing person could do . . . except hear.

There was something about Esther calling Michelle "sweetheart" that rubbed me the wrong way. And I felt something even darker about her being able to sign so fluently. I hated the feeling, but there it was.

Michelle signed to me, "Are you okay?"

And I nodded, yes. "I'm fine," I said and signed. "I guess I'm just a little tired."

Over the next hour we were treated to tea and petit fours, finger sandwiches, and easy listening music from an overhead system. Adam shared with us his work on securing the details of their honeymoon (they'd decided on an Alaskan cruise) and—no surprise to me—a find on their starter home, which would be in Breckenridge, close to their work.

"Apparently," I quickly signed to Michelle, hoping the others weren't quite as fast at interpreting sign language, "I need to send Adam out with Tim; Adam was so quick to find a house."

Michelle laughed, then shared with the others what I had said. I had not meant for her to do that, but what was done was done.

We talked about the upcoming shower that the club would be catering and in which I would be an honorary guest; the bridesmaid shower; another shower that had just been scheduled by a few of the ladies at Grace Church; and a final dinner that was to be given in the bridal couple's honor by their fellow employees. All the while, Esther and Michelle kept giving each other knowing glances, as though they were in on some secret I wasn't yet privy to. It reminded me too much of Lisa Leann's expression earlier.

I was beginning to smell a rat. "What's going on?"

It was then that Michelle became her most animated. "Mom," she signed. "I know you and I talked about going to Denver to look in the bridal shops, but I showed Mrs. Peterson a few of the gowns you and I were looking at—"

Esther jumped in. "Now, Lizzie," she began as tactfully as anyone could in this situation. "I know you and Michelle were looking at a more straight-lined gown, strapless, and that sort of thing. But what I have suggested to Michelle is this: because of her princess-like beauty"—she paused to beam at Michelle—"my suggestion is that she goes with a more princess-like dress. Think of your Michelle as Cinderella and my handsome son as her Prince Charming."

"Ah—"

The next thing I knew, Esther was whipping out pages of bridal gown designs in clear protective sleeves, each one more elaborate and . . . princess-like . . . than the next. Adam excused himself from the table. "I'll get a breath of fresh air," he said, pointing toward the door. We women watched him leave, then turned back to one another.

"Now," Esther said, sliding one of the pages toward me. "This is our favorite."

Our favorite?

"Right, Michelle?" Esther said.

"I like it, Mom," Michelle said.

I looked down at the glossy picture before me. It was, indeed, an exquisite gown. Sleeveless. Alençon lace. Hand-sewn pearls and authentic crystals on a tulle overlay. The hem was detailed and the skirt was full. Most importantly, it sported a black satin sash that trailed from the tied bow at the base of the spine to halfway down the back of the skirt. This would tie in with her bridesmaids' dresses.

"But do you love it?" I asked my daughter.

"I do," she signed. The look on her face confirmed it. She must have read my face because she reached over and touched my hand. "Don't be mad, Mom," she spoke.

"Oh no. I'm not—"

Esther prickled a bit. "Oh, Lizzie. I'm so sorry if I've stepped on toes. After all, Britney will be marrying Clay next year, and then it will be my turn to be the mother of the bride. But I just couldn't help myself. After all, this is a first wedding for us . . . but for you . . . well, this is old hat for you by now, no doubt."

Old hat? How could picking out a wedding dress with your baby girl ever be old hat? But I said nothing. Right now, I needed only to smile and look pleased.

"That's fine."

And then the blade fell. "Here's the best part," Esther said. "Lisa Leann Lambert, who you know well, of course, has ordered this gown and two or three others for us to swing by and look at as soon as we're done here." She clapped her hands together. "Isn't that wonderful?"

Aha. The smell of a rat had led to the rat.

At this news, I decided, I didn't need to smile and look pleased. This was the sweet icing on the wedding cake as far as my day had gone. For this news, I needed a drink.

Donna

20

Poached Boyfriends

I pulled out of the parking lot to start my evening shift, hoping for the kind of slow night that would give me time to reflect on my so-called life. Despite the drama of recent days, my phone had barely a chance to perform the new Newsboys tune I'd programmed into my ring tones. The only calls I'd received had come from Dad or one of the Potluckers. The boys, it seemed, were only interested in me when they were in the mood to compete.

I flipped on my blinker and sighed as I pulled onto the highway. My life was pathetic, but not as pathetic as what was happening to the Horn family. I'd been able to keep up with the latest from Dad, who was keeping a sharp eye on the situation. I'd learned that since last Monday, when Pete was released from the hospital, social services had awarded Wade temporary custody of the boy while Wade's sister, Kat Cage Martin, took Pete's two younger siblings, Molly and Jeffrey. At least, that was the plan as long as Pete's dad sat in jail for child abuse and Pete's mom stayed missing. Though

I'd heard through the grapevine that Thelma had left town a week back to "visit relatives." Personally, I hoped I wouldn't find her buried somewhere in the backyard.

I shivered at that thought. That kind of thing didn't usually happen up here in the high country, especially not when the ground was still frozen.

That was really all I knew, as Wade had apparently been too busy to call me and as I'd steered clear of "the Kat," as I called her.

I jumped as my cell phone performed "Wherever We Go" as it tattled Wade's name across its screen. *Well, speak of the devil.* I picked up. "Deputy Donna, here."

Wade sounded hesitant. "Donna, Pete and I wanted to know if you could drop by for a bowl of my homemade mean bean chili, just the three of us."

I laughed. "Wade, don't tell me you're using children to lure women to your trailer?"

"Whatever works. Can you make it?"

"I'm on duty, but it's almost dinnertime. I guess I could drop over for a . . . ah . . . dinner and a wellness check."

"Wellness check?"

"Yeah, I'd like to see how well you two are getting along, you know, in case I get called to testify for any reason."

"Well, the chili's on the stove, and we'll keep it hot till you get here."

"Don't worry, you don't have to call this girl to dinner twice."

Within minutes I'd pulled my Bronco to a stop in front of Wade's trailer and hurried up his steps. I knocked as I stepped through his front door, impressed to find the living room tidied and the table set for three. Pete, with his arm in a sling, was putting some paper napkins at each place setting while Wade stirred a pot on the stove, a few steps away in the kitchen.

"Make yourself at home," Wade called as I folded my leather jacket over the top of his rust-colored recliner. As I did, I noted the absence of his longneck bottle collection that had bouqueted his coffee table for years. Yep, things were looking up around here.

I ruffled a hand through Pete's red hair. "How's your arm?"

Pete adjusted the navy sling that cradled his cast next to his red flannel shirt.

He shrugged. "It itches a lot."

"Ugh, I hate that. Let's see, got any famous autographs on that cast?"

"Saw you on *Hollywood Nightly* awhile back, so you're the most famous person I know. I was kinda hoping you'd sign it." He handed me a red marker from the string-entwined soup can on a small writing table next to a wall. If I didn't know better, I'd say the can was a leftover craft from Wade's grade school days, especially as I had one just like it on my desk.

I scrawled "Deputy Donna" across the white plaster in my angular print. "Wade treating you okay?"

"Yeah, we've been hanging out."

Wade rounded the corner, holding two steaming bowls of chili. "Sit down, Pete, Donna," he said. He turned to me with a sly grin. "I know it's not my mother's chicken parmesan, Officer, but I promise it's edible."

He turned back to the kitchen to grab a third bowl. When he returned, he sat down at the table with us. "I'll say grace." We bowed our heads and Wade prayed, "Father, please bless our little family."

Is he including me in this "family" business? My eyes burned at the thought of Wade and me having a family-like moment with a child who was just a little younger than the one we'd lost when we were mere teenagers. Wade continued, "And guide us, Father. Guide our steps. In Jesus's name, amen."

The food warmed my spirits. Not only was Wade's chili good, but dinner with the boys was actually pleasant as we carefully avoided the elephant topic of how Pete had come to be with Wade.

Near the end of the meal, Pete asked me, "Catch any jewel thieves lately?"

I exchanged amused glances with Wade. "Jewel thieves?"

"Yeah, Wade says you've been looking for a diamond."

I gave Wade a sideways glance. "I hadn't heard of anyone losing a diamond," I said.

"Well, Wade says you've been talking to David Harris about a ring."

I stared Wade down. "Is that so? What else did your cousin say?"

Wade jumped up, his face a bit red. "Nothing. Pete, let's get these dirty bowls to the sink."

I followed the boys to the kitchen with the glasses.

Wade turned to Pete. "I'll start the dishes and you get started on your homework."

Pete looked disappointed but walked back toward the kitchen table, where he sat with his history book. Though the book appeared to be more of a prop to help him eavesdrop on the adults. My suspicion was confirmed when I said, "Wade, I've never seen you in an apron before, it's so you," and I noted Pete's shoulders bounced in silent laughter.

When Wade said, "I don't look nearly as good as you do, with those yellow rubber gloves on," and I said, "You can't expect a deputy to have dishpan hands," I heard the boy's chuckle.

Soon, rubber gloves in the dish rack, I found myself waving goodbye to the boys as I hurried back into the night and back on duty.

I glanced into my rearview mirror to see Wade and Pete still standing on their stoop, looking sad to see me go. Their melancholy settled on me as I drove through the darkness that had enveloped the town.

A nighttime later, I yawned as I watched the evening stars fade and the sun's pale rays stretch over the white mountains and into the void of dark turquoise.

Good one, God, I prayed, glad to be reminded that his love was new every morning. I smiled. Soon I would be in my toasty warm bed.

My cell rang and I saw it was Dad. I flipped open the phone. He said, "Hate to tell you, but Clarence called in with the flu."

"So? Make him work sick."

"He has a temp of 104 and can't stray too far from his bathroom, if you know what I mean."

I groaned.

"So, ah, if you'd be willing to pull another few hours, I'll work the first half of your night shift."

I sighed. "Do I have a choice?"

Dad laughed. "No. Why do you ask?"

"Hope springs eternal."

"See you at the office around one."

Late morning found me still aimlessly driving the streets of Summit View, sipping a fresh cup of Sally's coffee and trying to stay focused. So far, except for a little fender bender on the highway into Breckenridge, it had been a pretty slow morning. Mainly, I'd just made long, slow circles through town, crisscrossing the path of the shuttle bus that carted tourists to the ski resort and other stops.

Despite my fatigue, it was easy to take the pulse of the community as I swept past the church and restaurant parking lots. The cars themselves told me the stories of both the faithful and the hungry on this sunny but cold morning.

Earlier, I'd spied Clay's Jeep down at the paper, meaning he was hot on some deadline. That was fine, as long as he wasn't writing about me. I'd noticed David's car had finally left Higher Grounds Café to be found again at the church parking lot along with the vehicles of the entire Potluck gang. I saw Wade's truck there too, though I didn't have to peek through the double doors to know that at least this morning he wasn't sitting alone. He had his little cousin Pete Horn by his side.

I'd continued patrolling my route through town, and now hours later, I squinted into the bright light of the midday and tried to think about the matters at hand. For instance, where was Vonnie's car? It wasn't at church anymore. I knew it wasn't parked at her house, though David's black Mazda sat next to Fred's truck on their snow-packed driveway. *Don't tell me David's alone with Grandma*, I thought as I passed by for the third time that hour.

My trained eyes helped me put the story together. It was apparent Vonnie and Fred were at the café having lunch with my dad and Evie. (So Dad and his Mrs. had lunch plans with the Westbrooks. No wonder he hadn't wanted to relieve me until one.) That meant David was grand-sitting Mrs. Swenson. I grinned and wondered how that was going.

As I passed Vonnie's house and headed toward the nearby bus stop, my cell phone began its up-tempo song.

Without checking caller ID, I picked up. "Hello."

"Donna," David's voice said with enough enthusiasm to make me check the house in the rearview mirror. "Is that you still on patrol?"

"Yeah, Clarence has the flu. Dad'll relieve me in an hour or two."

His voice teased, "Well, as a private citizen, I certainly appreciate you taking the time to check on our neighborhood. I was wondering if you had a minute to stop by the house and check on our situation personally?"

I chuckled as I began to make the block again. "I might. You in there alone with Mrs. Swenson?"

"'Fraid so, and I think I could use a hand."

I felt a grin glide across my face. "She's being difficult, is she?"

"She responds well to you, and, well, she's hobbling around the kitchen trying to clean up our lunch before Vonnie and Fred get back."

That caught my attention. "Lunch?"

"Yeah, Vonnie made her pot roast again. There's plenty if you'd like a plate."

"I'm on the job." I pulled into the driveway, parking behind David's car. I hopped out and continued the conversation, "Can't say no to Vonnie's roast beef, can I?"

David opened the door for me as we both closed our cell phones. "Come in."

I pulled the radio off my belt and called dispatch. "I'm on lunch break, at the Westbrook house."

"Ten-four," Betty crackled back.

I bypassed David and walked into Vonnie's kitchen, where I found Mrs. Swenson drying dishes. There was something funny about her. Her eyes were too wide, and she had what appeared to be a grin on her face, something I honestly had never seen before. I put my hands on my hips. "You go sit down, young lady; I'll take over from here."

She turned and looked at me with a twinkle in her eye. "Wouldn't want you to arrest me." She hobbled to the kitchen table and sat down.

I had to stare at her for a moment. I've been in law enforcement my entire career, and I'd have to say Mrs. Swenson's performance of surrender seemed a bit too staged. I mean, the old woman was almost as giddy as her grandson, who come to think of it, was leaning on the kitchen cabinet, arms folded across his pects, looking a little too amused. Then it hit me. *Had these two jokers seen me drive by and decided to . . . to what? Bring me in from the cold so they could have me all to themselves?*

I felt my eyes narrow as I looked at David. He was so cute; not that I usually noticed things like that. He was dressed in his black chinos and turtleneck, and that expression on his face could make a girl's heart race.

Trying to be cool, I studied the back of Mrs. Swenson's white curls. She was dressed in her hot pink jogging suit, and she turned and gave me a quick smile. *I was right! These two are conspirators.* Mrs. Swenson was trying to set me up with her grandson. I had to consider the implications of that. I mean, I knew her history. I knew how she'd tried to keep Vonnie away from her first husband because he was part Hispanic. I knew how she'd been the force behind having baby David adopted out, probably for the same reason. So now why was I detecting this conspiracy? Was her new attitude because she was older and wiser, and perhaps a little kinder, or was she trying to dump David on me in an effort to get him out of her life? That was a question I couldn't answer. Still, she looked kinda sweet playing matchmaker. I felt the corners of my mouth twitch. I guess there was no harm in playing along if it meant I got to eat one of Vonnie's home-cooked meals, right?

David helped me put the last of the dishes away before dishing up a plate of food for me. A few minutes later, I sat down at the kitchen table, under their intense stares.

"Working today?" Mrs. Swenson asked.

I put a big creamy bite of gravy-covered mashed potatoes into my mouth. "Mmm-hmm."

David smiled at me. "It's a pleasure to see you eat," he said. "Not like those Hollywood girls who only pretend."

So help me, I broke the magic of the moment, but not before devouring another mouthwatering bite of Vonnie's roast. "Speaking of girls, David, how's your girlfriend?"

Mrs. Swenson answered for him. "Velvet? She's not David's girlfriend. Is she, son?"

I held a fork of steaming roast beef in midair as my eyes shifted to David. He shrugged. There was a tap on the front door, and David got up to answer it while I continued to plow through the meal. I was hungrier than I'd realized.

"Grandma's right. Velvet and I, we're not really dating anymore," he called over his shoulder.

He swung open the door, and a familiar voice asked, "What do you mean, 'We're not really dating anymore'?"

"Velvet, what are you doing here?" David said, stepping back as my sister stormed into the foyer. She was dressed in jeans topped with a white rabbit fur coat and matching snow boots, which she'd probably purchased at the second-hand clothing store that was so popular with the tourists.

Her eyes rested on me sitting at the kitchen table, where I probably looked like a cat with a mouth full of canary. Velvet turned to David. "Having a party without me?"

Mrs. Swenson said, "It's beef, dear. You don't do beef."

Velvet crossed her arms. "Honestly, David."

I put another bite in my mouth and began to chew so I would have an alibi to not get involved in this little drama.

"It's not what it looks like," David said.

Mrs. Swenson interrupted, "It certainly is. David and Donna are having lunch together, dear, without you."

I knew my eyes widened, and to cover, I reached for my glass of iced tea and took a long sip.

Velvet's full attention rested on me. "Why do you hate me?" she whispered.

I swallowed. "I don't hate you, Velvet. As I've said before, I don't even know you."

She put her hands on her hips. "Only because you avoid me. But maybe that's so you can be alone with my boyfriend."

"Velvet, David is not your boyfriend," Mrs. Swenson said. "You just heard him say so."

Velvet looked at David hard. When he didn't respond, she turned her full attention on me. "You just can't stand that David might be interested in me, can you?"

I shrugged. "This isn't a date."

Mrs. Swenson looked a little too smug. "It certainly is."

I gave Grandma a withering look before turning to my sister. "Velvet, I just stopped by the house to help."

She glared. "You mean, to help yourself."

"Donna's a sly one," Mrs. Swenson said.

Velvet put her hands on her hips. "You know why I agreed to follow Mom to this Podunk town? I don't mean to flatter you, Donna, but I wanted to meet my big sister. The big sister I never knew I had until a few months ago. What a fantasy that was."

I pushed my chair back. "Velvet, I'm sorry I haven't made time for you, but—"

"I never dreamed my big sis would go after my boyfriend."

I stood up just as my cell phone rang. I welcomed the distraction and said to Velvet, "Sorry, I'm still on duty. This could be an emergency." I picked up. "Hello?"

It was Wade. "Donna, Pete and I are in Vonnie's driveway. I thought I'd drop by to fix the loose basement step I noticed last time I was there, but I'd hate to interrupt."

"Ah, Wade, hi."

"So is Vonnie even there?"

"I'm sure she'll be home shortly," I said.

"Then, it's just you and David? Alone?"

"Not exactly."

"Then you don't mind if we come in?"

"No," I said. Wade must have already been climbing the front steps because he tapped on the door. David answered his knock. But by that time, Velvet had worked herself into a full rage. She bellowed, "Well, Donna, here's a couple more of your boyfriends."

"Hello, Wade, Pete," I said as the two stepped inside, their eyes round at Velvet's performance.

"What's going on in here?" Wade asked no one in particular.

Mrs. Swenson answered. "David and Donna are having a date."

Wade's eyes shot to me. "Is that so?"

217

"No, no, I'm on duty."

"Yes, they are," Mrs. Swenson replied, in full glee. "They're having a lunch date."

David stood by silently while Velvet continued to rage. "I'm so outta here."

She flounced toward the door and brushed past Pete and Wade. Wade asked, "Velvet, you don't have a car, do you?"

"I took the town shuttle, though I didn't know my little trip would be so educational."

"I'm thinking it's time we left too." Wade turned to Velvet. "Need a lift?"

Velvet glared back at me. "I do. You know, Donna, you can't have every man in town. Why don't you make up your mind so the rest of us will know who's available?"

"Well put," Mrs. Swenson chirped. "Velvet, Wade, you know where the door is, and while you're at it, take that boy with you. I don't babysit, you know."

And with that, our trio of visitors disappeared. I walked to the front door and watched Wade as he helped my sobbing sister into the cab of his truck, with Pete squeezed in between them. I turned around and looked up at David. "Aren't you going to go after her?"

David, who looked a bit shell-shocked, slowly closed the door. "I'll call later to check on her. But, aren't you going after Wade?"

I shook my head. "I'll call him later, to explain."

David turned his full attention on me. "And just how will you explain?"

I shrugged. "I'm not sure. How will you explain to Velvet? I mean, it doesn't seem to me you're being very fair to her."

Before he could reply, Mrs. Swenson cackled. "Fair? Velvet crashed your date. And from the way Velvet left with Wade, those two are an item, but then, so are you and David."

David smiled apologetically for Mrs. Swenson's remarks. "Donna,

I know this is awkward. But maybe we should consider the possibilities just presented to us."

I took my dish to the sink and rinsed it. "You mean the possibility of an 'us'?"

I turned to face David, and he nodded. "Why not?"

"David, I don't know. I mean, Velvet is your girl, not me. Plus, we're friends. Good friends, but we've never dated, unless you count the time you took me to lunch and proposed marriage."

David smiled. "I only started dating Velvet when I thought I'd lost my chance with you. Velvet's a sweet girl, but she's just not my type. I've been trying to break it off with her for the past few weeks, but I've been having trouble getting through to her."

"Congratulations, I think you just resolved that little problem."

David frowned. "I'm sorry she got hurt and I'm sorry you were there."

"Tell me about it."

"Still, the question remains; do you think there's still a chance for us?"

"This is awkward, David."

"I know. The timing stinks." His brown eyes softened. "But if you agree to go out with me, I promise not to pop the question."

I had to laugh at that. "I don't know." I suddenly felt exhausted from the extra hours of my shift. I looked at my watch, then stood and headed for the front door. "I gotta get back to work. So, ah, let's talk about it later."

David blocked my path and stared down at me. "Why not answer my question now?"

I looked up and hesitated. "It's just that I don't know what to say."

Hope filled his smile. "Say yes."

I closed my eyes and shook my head, and against my better judgment said, "Okay . . . yes." But before he could respond, I turned and hurried down the front steps and opened the door of my Bronco.

I paused for a moment and looked back. "Call me tonight, okay? I gotta run."

I could see David grinning from the front door as Mrs. Swenson hobbled up next to him. He draped an arm around her shoulder and gave her a celebratory squeeze.

I waved before backing out of the driveway, feeling more than a little confused. Twenty minutes later, as part of my patrol route, I pulled into the Higher Grounds trailer park. Sure enough, Wade's truck was still parked in front of my mother's and Velvet's trailer. I felt my forehead brake hard into my hairline as I frowned. How nice for Velvet to have a friend to console her.

I slowly drove past Wade's trailer and pulled back onto Main Street. Well, Wade and Velvet were neighbors, after all. And I suppose it was natural for them to hang out. Why was it I so hated the thought of that? But there was no need to fret. Soon my shift would be over, and I'd get a good afternoon's sleep. Then maybe I could figure out why Wade had kept me in a state of limbo for fourteen years. Could it be that David could finally break me free of his lady-in-waiting spell?

Perhaps David and I were supposed to get together. Maybe this *was* the answer to Wade's prayer, and God was guiding me in a whole new direction, a direction I had yet to kiss.

Evangeline

21

Marriage Hash

Vernon and I had invited Fred and Vonnie to have lunch with us at Higher Grounds Café after church on Sunday afternoon. I'm not sure who suggested it first, but to be sure it was probably done more so to keep us from being alone with each other one minute more than we had to be than to give Fred and Vonnie the much-needed break from her mother, who would be taken care of by David for a few hours.

Since the Saturday before, when Donna and I had our little "falling out," Vernon and I had lived in a thin layer of tension I had not yet experienced in my adult life. I've had friends and family a little miffed with me from time to time, or vice versa, but I never had to sleep in the same bed with them at the end of the day.

When I'd returned home the previous Saturday I was met by one very upset man standing in the foyer of our home, arms crossed, legs braced apart. I shrugged out of my coat with a "What? You too?"

"Evie, you shouldn't have gone to the tavern," he said. "Surely you know that. Donna's a grown woman. She can handle her feelings concerning her mother."

I stared at him. "Did you talk to her?" I hung my coat on the coat tree and stormed past him. "Did you?"

He emitted what sounded like a chuckle, but for the sake of our new marriage, I didn't turn around to see if my suspicions were true.

"I did." He was right behind me on my way to the kitchen, where I began to prepare a pot of coffee. In spite of my hot anger, the very marrow of my bones was freezing.

"And? Did you set her straight? Did you put her on the right track where Doreen is concerned? Explain a few things your daughter obviously missed concerning her mother over the past twenty-some-odd years?" I scooped coffee into the filter with such vigor that little black grounds went flying along the counter and then skipped to the floor. "Now look what she's made me do," I mumbled, reaching for a nearby dishcloth.

Vernon leaned against the door frame of the dining room entry-way and again crossed his arms. "Oh yeah, I see her now. Standing right there beside you, bumping your elbow . . ."

I jerked my head up and glared at him until he physically straightened, furrowed his brow, and left my presence.

It had been pretty much like that ever since.

At Higher Grounds Vernon and I managed to pretend that everything was okay in Honeymoon Land as we all four dined on Sally's famous meatloaf sandwich with curly fries, though Vernon had ordered onion rings with his. It wasn't until Vonnie and I went to the ladies' room that I, seeing that we were alone in the spacious and nicely decorated washroom (complete with music from overhead), turned to her and said, "Got a minute?"

"What?" Her hand was on the silver handle of the stall door.

"I need to talk." I walked over to one of the two white wicker armchairs sitting in the far corner of the room. A short white wicker table, adorned only by a lit and fragrant incense burner atop it, was between them. I nearly collapsed into the nearest chair.

"And I need to . . . you know . . . go . . ."

Vonnie was too much a lady to say the word, and that made me smile, probably my first real smile in over a week. I crossed my legs and placed my purse on the little table. Having seen a news segment about what's on the floor of a public restroom, I'd vowed never to place my purse on one again, even if I had to hold the strap with my teeth. "Give me your purse. I'll hold it for you."

"Don't you have to . . . go?" Vonnie asked, reaching me.

"No." I took her purse, and she crossed the room again. "I didn't come here to . . . go. I came in here to talk."

"Have it your way, then." She entered the stall. "What's so important we have to talk in a public bathroom of all places, Evangeline?" she asked from the other side of the door.

"I need advice from someone who's been married for a while." I scanned the room, taking in the slight inconsistencies of the wallpaper. Whoever had hung it had missed a few places in matching the pattern. I hoped Sally hadn't paid them too much, whoever they were.

"Oh, dear," Vonnie called back.

The toilet flushed, and within moments she exited the stall and went to the sink to wash her hands. I noted her method for doing so was still left over from her days as a nurse. Wash thoroughly, rinse from the wrist (or elbow if your sleeve so allows) down, and then turn off the water with a bump of the elbow.

She shook her hands free of excess water, reached for a paper towel, dried her hands, and then joined me in the nearby chair.

I glanced at the six-paneled white door to our left. "Let's just hope no one comes in while we are talking."

"Won't we look a sight?" It wasn't really a question. "Now, Evangeline. Tell me what's going on."

I frowned. "Vonnie . . . how long did it take you . . . after you'd married . . . until you . . ." I trailed off. I wasn't really sure how I wanted to say what was on my mind.

Before I could get my thoughts together, Vonnie reached over and patted my hand. "I see."

"You see? You see what?"

Placing her hands properly in her lap she said, "You're having problems getting used to the more . . . intimate side of your marriage."

I felt my lips draw to a straight line. "The what?"

"Sex, Evangeline."

Maybe Vonnie wasn't the one I should have come to. "I know what intimate means, Vonnie. And, no, that's not what I'm talking about."

"Oh, good."

"What I'm talking about—"

"So everything is okay in that department?"

"What department?"

"The bedroom. I know it can take some getting used to, especially after being single for so long." She nodded at me, and for a moment I wondered if my best friend had suddenly become Dr. Ruth. "And I've been a little concerned about you, though I certainly didn't want to ask."

"I, uh . . ."

"Now with Fred it wasn't so much a big deal. After all, I'd been married before. Of course I didn't want him to know that, so I had to pretend to be a virgin . . ."

I raised my brow. "How do you pretend to be a virgin?"

Vonnie blushed. "Well, you know . . . I acted very . . . you know . . . shy and prudish."

Quite frankly, I couldn't imagine her any other way, even after a multitude of years living and loving with Fred. "Vonnie, I'm not talking about sex."

Vonnie straightened her shoulders. "Oh. What are you talking about then?"

"Well, I'm not even sure how to say this. Okay, last week, after the meeting, I went to the tavern to see Doreen."

"Oh, Evie, you shouldn't have done that."

"That's neither here nor there."

"You really have to stay out of this or you are going to cause problems between you and Donna." Her eyes widened. "Not to mention you and Vernon."

"It has caused problems. But not because I went to see Doreen . . . so much. But because Donna saw me having words with her mother."

About that time the door opened. Vonnie and I remained quiet while the woman—obviously a resort visitor by her clothing, which was too Hollywood ski country than true high country—took her turn in the restroom. When she'd washed her hands—never once looking at us throughout the entire episode of being there—she left, swinging the door shut behind her.

"Evangeline, what is going on? If you don't hurry up and talk, the men will be in here thinking we've been flushed down the toilets."

I shifted a little in the chair. "Maybe we should talk later."

"Maybe we should talk now." She pointed her index finger toward her knee.

"Okay," I said, blowing out a pent-up breath. "Here's the thing. Vernon and I have hardly spoken all week."

"Why?"

"Because he hasn't set his daughter straight, that's why."

Vonnie chuckled. "What do you expect him to do?"

I struggled for an answer, but when it came it was a good one. "He should arrest Doreen or Dee Dee or whatever she's calling herself and Velvet for impersonating a mother and daughter, that's what. Doreen—Dee Dee—may have given birth to Donna, but she's not

225

acting much like a mother, if you ask me. And that Velvet James can just go back to whatever Podunk she was born in."

Vonnie looked truly horrified. "Evangeline, I've never seen you like this."

"They have practically sabotaged my marriage, Vonnie."

"I thought Donna did."

"Don't split hairs."

"I'm not splitting hairs."

"See, that's the problem, it's all the little things. Ever since last Saturday, all I can see is that Vernon squeezes the toothpaste tube from the center and that he plays the TV too loud and that he can actually watch Home Shopping Network for hours on end."

"Who can't?"

"'The Coin Show'?" I asked, then lay back in the chair and splayed my arms and legs as though I were dying.

Vonnie burst out laughing. "Evie, you are too funny. Sit up and listen to me."

I obeyed, but only because Vonnie has been married for so long. And, to the same man. She was surely to have valuable advice.

"Whatever happened last Saturday is over and done with. When it comes to arguments with your husband, you need to keep your focus on the hills you truly want to die on. And let me tell you, whatever little tirade you had with Donna is not worth it. It's just not worth the fight. Furthermore—and really pay attention to me here, Evie—Donna is Vernon's daughter. And she is Doreen's."

"Doreen prefers to be called Dee Dee," I corrected her, remembering how Doreen had corrected me at the tavern, though why I was placating her was beyond me.

"I don't care if she prefers to be called the queen of England, she is and always will be Donna's mother. You must understand that. And, even though she left Vernon all alone to raise that poor sweet girl, to him she will always be the mother of his child. His only child. Listen to me, Evie. I know what I'm talking about here. It's been quite the strain on Fred and me since my birth child came to this town looking for me. But Fred's been smart enough to realize that David is my flesh and blood. And that he always will be."

Vonnie made good sense. I mulled it over before asking, "So then, what do we do about the bridal shower? About Doreen—Dee Dee—and Velvet bartending it?"

"We let them. The best thing you can do right now is to do nothing at all. Either their business venture will fail or it will succeed, but either way it won't be because of something you did or didn't do."

I stood up. "Mmm-hmm."

"In the meantime," Vonnie said, standing with me and reaching for her purse, "you keep the fires burning at home with your honey of a hubby." She winked at me. "There's no little fuss or fight that a little lovemaking can't handle."

"Why, Vonnie Westbrook," I said, grabbing my purse and smiling. "Sometimes you floor me." When she giggled, I added, "And I don't floor easily."

Lisa Leann

22

In a Pickle

Men! I inwardly groaned to myself as I lifted the head of my industrial-strength mixer out of the stainless steel mixing bowl. I scraped the excess dough off the beaters with my spatula while I silently replayed my latest phone conversation with Clark, my third one this morning.

"Who's girl are you?" he flirted just as Henry brushed past me on his way to meet the UPS guy at the back door.

I gritted my teeth as soon as I thought Henry was out of earshot. "Not yours." Before Clark could say more, I'd hung up.

What nerve! I sighed. Clark felt entitled to call me at will, simply because I had to work with him on the Prattle bridal shower, which unfortunately was to be held at his hotel. Talk about unfair. But Clark was playing this fiasco to his full advantage. Which made me wonder, *Does he really think that following me to Colorado will change the fact we're over?*

I bit my lip. Not only was our affair over, it should have never been. Yes, I was ashamed of what had happened. Yes, I regretted my foolishness. But now, despite my efforts to leave the affair behind me, the risk of discovery was greater than ever. I had so much to lose—my husband first and foremost, not to mention the respect of my family and any and everyone who'd ever known me. If this thing got out, it would give the gossips from Houston to Summit View enough fuel to wag their tongues until doomsday. I could hear them now: "Did you hear about Lisa Leann Lambert and Clark Wilkes? Shameful! Having an affair that started in the church choir. Can you imagine that? Think of Henry, think of Jane!"

I sucked in my breath. How could I have justified this? I'd sinned against both God and my husband. If news of this got out, I'd have to move to Alaska and find a deserted igloo to hide in. Then again, maybe Dee Dee McGurk would let me stay with her in her trailer. I bet we had more in common than most folks knew.

With Henry helping me at the shop this morning, Clark's frequent calls had been more than troublesome. They'd been dangerous. It was ironic, really. There was my unsuspecting Henry in his jeans and denim work shirt, carefully wrapping my dishwasher-fresh serving bowls with protective plastic wrap for their upcoming venture to Breckenridge. While Henry worked, I'd been trying to cook while playing cat and mouse with Clark via the phone. If Henry could have heard Clark's side of the conversations, he'd probably divorce me on the spot.

Using my spatula, I shoveled the thick cheesy dough out of the mixing bowl and onto the wax paper I'd spread on the stainless steel countertop.

At least I'd soon be able to check this job off my long list of today's "must do's." Patting and pulling the dough, I stuffed large globs of it into freezer bags. How glad I was Vonnie had promised to come in the Friday before the shower and hand squeeze the dough into long cheese sticks so we could bake them. At this point, I was going to need every pair of hands I could get. It was already Tuesday of the week before the shower, and the girls were all scheduled to drop by to work their job assignments from now until showtime.

Henry stepped into my kitchen from the back room, carrying yet another tray of plastic-wrapped bowls. "Where do you want these?"

"Put them in the shelves in the storage closet."

"Do you want me to wrap the plates?"

"No, we're renting the china and silverware from the hotel."

"Good girl. That will save you some cleanup."

"Yeah, but we'll soon have to invest in our own service of fine china if we're going to be competitive."

Henry chuckled. "Hope you make lots of money on this gig then; you're going to need it."

"Yeah, there are a few hidden expenses I hadn't counted on," I said with a sigh. "Though I'm glad I shelled out for that catering software package. It's an organizational whiz, and it's helping me avoid some nasty surprises."

Henry shook his head back and forth like he felt sorry for us. "Well, so much for our relaxing retirement years in the mountains." He turned to go to the back room, which we'd outfitted as a workroom. He hesitated and looked over his shoulder. "Say, I think I'll saw up that PVC pipe you want to use as leg extenders for your work stations."

I smiled. "Good idea. Raising the table legs will surely save on our old backs. Can't have my crew at the chiropractor's after each event."

I continued to divide the dough, thinking about all the expenses of running a catering service. Yeah, the girls and I knew what we were up against, but I was counting on my sharp business mind and their cheap supply of labor to make way to a great bottom line. Henry reappeared. "Forgot my toolbox," he said as he looked around the kitchen.

"It's on the floor, to the left of the refrigerator."

Henry strode over to the box and bent over to pick it up, reveal-ing a tiny circle of baldness in the crown of his gray hair.

I turned to grab the ringing phone. I put on my hands-free headset and picked up.

It was Clark again. "Lisa Leann, how are things coming to-gether?"

I was terse. "Fine."

"Anything you need from me or the hotel?"

I walked to the freezer and stuffed the dough onto one of the upper trays. "Everything's under control."

"I called to check and see if you had enough help for the night of the event. I could rent you some wait staff."

I slammed the freezer door and took a deep breath. "I've got Grace's singles department to cover and *Henry*." I emphasized Henry's name in a slow drawl. "He'll be there too," I said, hoping his name would protect me from Clark's continued pursuit.

A snicker played through my headset. "Really? That's not what I heard."

I sat down on the pink vinyl-padded stool and clicked my nails on the built-in writing desk. "I assure you, you heard wrong." I smoothed my hand against the lap of my pink apron. "Henry wouldn't dream of being anywhere but with me."

Clark chuckled again. "You mean, he'd even miss the annual youth mission trip with the First Church of the Woodlands?"

"Of course he would, he . . ." Suddenly my heart landed in my stomach with a sickening thud.

"Are you still there?"

My voice sounded an octave too high. "What have you gone and done?"

"Nothing, really. It's just the church back home was so desperate for some more sponsors that when they called and begged me to go, I suggested they call good old Henry. After all, he hasn't missed a trip to that Mexican orphanage in ten years, now has he? I'm sure you remember the week he left us alone last year. With him gone we didn't even have to rent a hotel room."

I closed my eyes and frowned. "I'm sure he'll say no to that trip."

Clark laughed again. "You mean he hasn't told you yet?"

I stomped to the sink, squirting a couple of drops of liquid soap into my hands then turning on the warm water to rinse them. My words were slow. "Told me what?" I asked as I dried my hands on a dish towel.

"I heard they called him last night while you were working at the shop, and he said yes."

I could hear Henry sawing in the back room.

"You wish! Ah . . . gotta run."

"We'll talk soon," Clark practically sang.

"Yeah, I'm sure."

I clicked out of the call and hung my headset on the wall hook then walked to the back room. I found my husband with a length of PVC pipe stretched across a pair of sawhorses. The walls of the workroom were surrounded by Vonnie's forest of money trees decorated with gold and silver clips that were ready for all the cash envelopes and gift cards.

Henry was wearing his safety glasses while he sawed the pipe. Tiny shards of white plastic streamed to the floor.

"Henry?"

He looked up, his sweet grin tugging at my heart. "Is it time for lunch?"

"I'm going to make sandwiches soon," I said. "But I came to ask you a question."

Henry popped his goggles on top of his head and stood straight, laying his saw on the workbench behind him. "I'm all yours, what's up?"

"What's this I hear about you traveling to Mexico next week, to go to the Matamoros orphanage?"

He leaned back and folded his arms. "Who told you? One of your old choir friends from back home?"

I put my hands on my hips. "Yes, as a matter of fact. Henry, you can't leave me in the lurch like this next week. I need your help at the shower."

Henry gave me an apologetic smile. "I'd planned to take you out to dinner tonight and break the news gently. But I guess the cat's out of the bag. Hope you're not too mad."

I felt my hands clench. I was desperate to make him understand how much I needed him. "I can't do this job without you."

He scratched the whisker stubble on his chin. "Lisa Leann, if there's one thing I know about you, it is that you will carry on with or without me."

I felt my face burn at that remark, spoken in innocence, or so I hoped. I walked toward him and slipped my arms around his waist. He in turn slipped his arms around mine and pulled me close. I could feel his breath on my face as I looked up at him. With his arms still holding me. "Please, Henry, you don't know what it would mean to me if you didn't go on that trip."

He let go of me and picked up his saw, turning to hang it on a hook on the pegboard over the workbench. He turned back. "Well, Lisa Leann, let me put it to you this way. Steven Salmen called me last night and said I was his last hope. If I couldn't go, this year's mission trip was off." He shrugged. "What else could I do? Think how disappointed those orphans would be if the youth group couldn't come see them. They rely on us to bring them the clothes, money, and vitamins the teens have collected all year. Plus, can you imagine not hosting their annual Vacation Bible School? I had to say yes. I knew you'd understand."

I gave him another hug and put my cheek against his chest, listening to his heartbeat. I kept my voice steady. "I do understand, but isn't there anyone else who could go in your place?"

He lifted my head with his rough hand. "Are you crying?" He

wiped a tear from my cheek with his thumb. "Trust me, Lisa Leann, I believe in you."

"Do you?"

"You're my girl," he said before he kissed the top of my forehead. "Now, how about those sandwiches before I make a quick run to the hardware store?"

I sniffed my nose and pulled away. "Got some errands?"

"Yeah, I need another PVC pipe; they're holding it for me at the counter at Todd's Hardware just down the block."

I nodded and dutifully went back to the kitchen, where I prepared turkey on pumpernickel slathered in mayo and spicy mustard, which I topped with baby Swiss, a slice of tomato, and a leaf of lettuce. I placed the sandwiches along with small bunches of green grapes onto two of my Lenox Eternal place settings. I plopped the plates onto a small lacy cloth, which I'd draped over a section of my large stainless steel island counter. Next, I folded a couple of my fine linen napkins into tight triangles and arranged them next to the plates. Finally, I pulled up a couple of my pink-topped stools.

The whole time I worked, I knew I was pouting. Not so much at Henry but at me. The extent of my betrayal of my husband continued to pummel me. What had I been thinking? Except for a better taste in men's shoes, Clark didn't stand up to my husband in any way. How could I not have seen that before?

I continued to sniffle as I poured iced tea into crystal glasses and placed them by our gold-rimmed plates. I slipped into the hall bathroom for a makeup check. I looked into my moist brown eyes and wondered how, without Henry, I would protect myself from Clark at that hotel. I tried to put on a happier face as I powdered the tip of my rosy-pink nose, hoping to hide the fact I hadn't stopped sniveling since I'd heard Henry's travel plans. With a semblance of calm, I stepped out of the bathroom and walked back to the workroom. "Lunch," I called, sounding a bit too cheery.

Fifteen minutes later, just as we were finishing the last of our grapes, the phone rang. I checked the caller ID and with relief saw Donna's number pop up.

I slipped on my headset as Henry took his dishes to the sink and rinsed them off.

"Hi, girlfriend. Coming by to get the grocery list and our company credit card?"

"Yeah, I'm on my way now. I have to go down to Denver this afternoon anyway, for an Amber Alert seminar, so I can make the Sam's Club stop on my way back home. I'll be off duty by then anyway."

"Perfect," I said before we exchanged good-byes.

I waved at Henry as he headed out the back door. I turned to start the lunch cleanup when the phone rang again. It was the hotel. I wouldn't have picked up except for the off chance it wasn't Clark but someone from the back office. "Hello?" I heard only laughter. "Clark?"

"I told you."

My silence acted as an affirmation, and he said, "So, looks like I'll be your date at the shower after all."

"I don't think so. In case you've forgotten, it's over between you and me."

His voice softened. "Not for me, never for me."

I touched my hand to my throat. "What is it going to take to get rid of you?"

"Just some of your loving. In fact, I'm reserving a room for us for that Saturday night. For old times' sake. Our little pre- and post-party treat."

I trembled with rage. "I don't think so."

"I'm afraid I can't take no for an answer, not and keep our secret."

I swallowed hard. "You wouldn't tell."

"Wouldn't I? At this point, I don't care if Jane knows or not.

She'd go to Henry, and then we wouldn't have anything to hide, would we."

"Listen, if you don't stop calling me, I'll . . . I'll call the sheriff. This has turned into harassment."

"Isn't that deputy one of your friends? I'm sure she'd be interested to hear my side of our story."

I felt my face flame. "You wouldn't dare."

"Wouldn't I?"

"Look, it's over between us. Get it through your head, no means no!"

His voice took on a menacing tone. "You belong to me, don't you ever forget that."

"I never belonged to you, now stop calling me," I said as I hung up. When I turned around, I realized Donna was leaning into the doorway, her arms crossed. I suddenly felt faint.

Her eyes held mine prisoner, and she spoke in a voice brimming with authority. "Lisa Leann, who were you talking to?"

I scratched my elbow and tried to look puzzled. "Wrong number, I think." I picked up what was left of my iced tea and took a sip, hoping Donna wouldn't notice my hand was shaking.

Donna perched on the stool that Henry had deserted and watched me. "Wrong number, my eye. You're shaking like a leaf. What are you involved in, my friend?"

I turned around and stared into Donna's blue eyes. My voice trembled. "How much did you hear?" I took another sip.

With her elbows on the countertop, she leaned toward me. "Enough to know you're in trouble. Care to tell me about it?"

I took my dirty dishes to the sink and rinsed them, trying to sound nonchalant. "I . . . I can't." I could feel heat rush up my neck and into my face. I took a deep breath and tried to look calm.

"Well, I'm not leaving till you do."

I walked over to where she was sitting and sat on the stool next to hers. I emphasized my words with outspread hands. "It's best to agree it was just a wrong number. Trust me."

Donna sat quietly for a moment, then said, "Sometimes, Lisa Leann, the only way to come back from the brink of disaster is to find a friend who can help you. I know. Vonnie just helped me through a really rough spot last year." She took a deep breath. "She saved my life."

I dared to wonder if I'd missed something major. But I could tell she was too focused on me to reveal any of her own secrets.

She continued, "Now, I know I'm not Vonnie. But do you count me as your friend?"

I nodded, not really sure I did.

"Look at me, Lisa Leann. Whether you believe it or not, I am your friend. I never gossip, and that's saying a lot because I know more secrets in this town than anyone."

I felt my eyebrows arch, mainly because I knew she was speaking truth.

She placed her hands palms-down on the lace. "Plus, I'm a pretty good listener, a little skill that comes with my badge."

I looked into her unblinking eyes. She was serious, but still a cutie with the way those tiny freckles kissed her nose and her curls had grown to frame her face. No wonder all the young men around here were wild about her, especially now that she wore a hint of that blush and lip gloss I'd sold her.

I looked down at my pink manicured nails. "Donna, I wish I could tell you, but some things, well, there are secrets you have to carry all by yourself. It's safer."

She almost whispered, "You mean a secret like having an affair turn sour?"

I looked up and opened my mouth to protest, but couldn't find my voice.

"That's what I thought." She started to rise.

"Wait," I said, putting my hand on her arm. "Nobody knows. I

. . . I made a mistake, the biggest mistake of my life, and, well, it's followed me here." My eyes focused on a smudge of dirt on the floor, which my mop must have missed. "I feel so ashamed."

Donna sighed and sat back down. "Well, if you tell me more I might be able to help you get this creep to leave you alone."

I shook my head, my voice low. "I . . . I can't tell."

The phone rang and I jumped. Donna stood and walked across the floor to check the caller ID. "It's the hotel. Want me to pick up?"

"No!"

She answered anyway with the handheld receiver. "Potluck Catering. Who's calling? . . . Clark?" Her eyes sparked. "The Clark I met at church a couple weeks ago, from Texas? . . . I remember you. I met your wife too. What was her name? . . . Jane. How is Jane? . . . She seems like such a nice woman. . . . Tell her I said hello. . . . Why, it's me, Donna Vesey. . . . Yep, the deputy."

Donna turned her back to me. "No, Lisa Leann's not here. Stepped out with her husband, you know, for their afternoon date. I don't think she'll be back for hours. Gotta message? . . . Yeah, I can remember that. . . . Okay, then. See you around. . . . Oh, sure, at the hotel for the shower. . . . Oh! You're the new sales manager there; I didn't know. How nice. Bye now." She hung up and stood staring at the phone. Finally, she turned and walked back to where I was sitting. She climbed back on her stool without speaking.

"What did he say?"

"He said he'd call you later."

I stood then sat down again. "Will this never end?"

Donna nodded and put a hand on my shoulder. "I'm on your team, Lisa Leann, and I'm going to have a word with this Clark person."

"No, you mustn't. He's threatened to tell Henry if I don't, ah, play along. Though, so far, I've kept him at bay."

Donna's brows furrowed. "Just wait till I get through with him."

"Donna, no. You don't know who you're dealing with."

She gave a low laugh. "Well, neither does he. Besides, not to sound corny or to shock you or anything, but thanks to Vonnie, I've recently learned how to pray. I suggest you do the same."

"I have prayed."

She stood. "Then it's settled."

"I don't know, Donna. I . . . what are you going to do?"

Before she could answer the back door swung open and Henry came whistling in, hauling a long piece of PVC pipe. "Hello, ladies!" He stopped and looked at us. "Is something wrong?"

With every ounce of acting skill I possessed I said, "No, Henry, I just remembered I forgot to call the florist. It may be too late to get the ivy Lizzie wanted, but I'll take care of it."

Henry's grin stretched across his handsome face. "You always do."

Evangeline

23

Sweet Understandings

"Evangeline."

The voice came toward me from the recesses of what felt like a hot tunnel.

"Evie."

And there it was again, stirring me from something I couldn't quite determine.

"Evie-girl."

Only one person in the whole world called me that. I opened my eyes to see Vernon staring down at me, his hair a silver fuzzy mess and his eyes sleep crusted.

"Evie-girl?"

My tongue felt as though it were glued to the roof of my mouth. After a few seconds of dislodging it, I asked, "What's wrong?"

"You were having a bad dream."

I squinted my eyes as I tried to remember what I had been dreaming, but nothing registered. "I was?"

"Sounded to me like it." He rested on his side next to me.

"Oh." I stared up at the ceiling, then ran my fingers through my tussled hair. "What'd I do?"

"You were just breathing really fast."

I looked over at him. "I didn't say anything?"

"No."

I shrugged my shoulders, then sat up. "I have no idea what I was dreaming." I blinked my eyes a few times and the room came into view. Though I'd lived in this house alone from the day of my parents' death until Vernon and I had returned from our honeymoon, I had not changed the décor from my mother's touch. She was a no-nonsense woman, and though her home was Victorian, it was practical. There was a wrought-iron bed with its headboard against the far wall, floral wallpaper that never seemed to go out of style, and only necessary pieces of furniture placed along the walls. A large oval gold leaf mirror hung from a wide satin ribbon over the bed's headboard, and clusters of small framed prints brought the room together. The wardrobe was topped with a stack of quilts dating back from my great-grandmother's day. When Vernon moved in, he said it was a little froufrou but that he'd learn to live with it as long as I came with the package. That thought alone could keep me smiling forever.

I swung my legs over the side of the bed. "I'll make the coffee. Maybe it'll come back to me later."

"Sounds to me like it's best forgotten," he called after me as I slipped into my terry robe and out the bedroom door.

It wasn't until I was sitting in my home office, buried behind a maze of thick stacks of papers along the floor and atop the desk, and preparing the taxes of Buddy and Geneva Youngblood, that I felt that stirring of memory that attempts to draw our nighttime dreams into the daylight hours. Though I tried to dismiss it, I couldn't.

Finally I pushed away from my computer and desk and walked

into the kitchen, where I made the day's second pot of coffee. While it brewed, I called my sister Peggy in West Virginia.

"Is something wrong?" she asked after I greeted her.

"No, why? Does something have to be wrong for me to call my favorite sister?"

I shuffled into the family room with the cordless clutched at my ear.

"I'm your only sister," she said as I sat on the three-cushion sofa. "And it's a Wednesday. You never call on a Wednesday."

I sighed at her candor. "Okay. I had a dream last night and I . . . Peg, do you remember when we were kids? How much time we used to spend over at Doreen Roberts's house?"

"Doreen Roberts? Of course I remember. What is it she's calling herself these days?"

"Dee Dee. Dee Dee McGurk. And you know her daughter is living here with her too." I heard the last gurgle and sputter of the coffeemaker, so I rose from my comfy spot and returned to the kitchen. "The two of them have started a bartending business."

"Really? The freelancers around here do very well. Several of the bartenders at the country club have their own businesses on the side. For private parties and such."

"Yeah, yeah. The point is," I said, pouring the coffee into my mug, "they are causing a bit of a stir around here and somehow managing to wreck my family and seep into my dreams." I returned to the family room and peered out the frosty window while giving her the lowdown on the latest. When I'd finished with the necessary information, I concluded with: "Which leads me to my dream."

"I'm listening."

"I dreamed we were all children again. We were playing that game where you fold a piece of paper this way and that, then write numbers and names under the flaps. Do you remember that?"

"Huh . . . I haven't thought about that in years. We'd stick our

242

fingers into the folds, then go back and forth after asking questions about our futures."

"And we'd find the answers under the folds." I shook my head. "I can't remember exactly how we made them, but we made them. And what I dreamed was that Doreen and I were playing the game and that it said she would marry a lawyer named Robert and that she would have three children and live in a wooden house."

Peggy giggled. "Well, that just goes to show you that we should put our faith and hope in the Lord and not in origami."

"I just think it's sad, Peggy. I mean, Doreen—or Dee Dee as she now likes to be called—had the same opportunities as the rest of us. And she's really a sad example of life gone bad. I mean, she's been in jail, she's estranged from her firstborn, and she's done things I don't even want to think about."

Peggy didn't say anything for a moment. Then, "So what are you thinking, Evangeline?"

"I think the Lord wants me to do something more than respond to her in the way I've responded for so many years."

"Since you were twelve years old, I'd say."

"Forty-six years is a long time to hold a grudge for something a child did to me."

"Stealing Vernon away from you."

I got up and returned to the kitchen for a second cup. "Now it all seems so silly. We were children."

Peggy cleared her throat. "Well, one thing I'll say for Doreen Roberts. She always knew what she wanted and she went after it and the devil be danged. But I suppose she went down the wrong road at some point and met her match."

"Who would have thought it would have turned out like it did?"

"So what are you going to do?"

I poured coffee into my cup and thought for a moment. "I'm

going to go see her. I think it's time we really talked. And I do mean *talked*. No more accusations from me. I just want to talk."

"Are you going to tell Vernon?"

That was a good question, one with an answer I didn't have quite yet. "I'll think about it," I said. "And I'll let you know how it goes."

I thought about it as I prepared the tuna fish pie for dinner and decided to call Vernon to tell him of my plan while on my way to the trailer park where Dee Dee and Velvet live. Of course, by then it was the same time as the shift change over at the sheriff's office so it wasn't much of a surprise that Vernon didn't answer his cell phone.

I elected not to call his office line.

I drove my car down the snowy path to the trailer Dee Dee and Velvet called home. It was an old single-wide with turquoise siding running around its base and cream-colored siding from there up. The small and dirty windows were book-ended with fading black shutters. There was a rickety latticed porch that rested beneath the peak of the trailer's center and front door. Lying catty-corner across it was a mop that appeared to be frozen stiff, and along the back of the steps were potted plants that had long ago tasted the bitter pill of death.

"Oh, Lord," I prayed. "Why have you brought me here?"

Not waiting for an answer, I opened my car's door and exited its warmth for the chill of the day. I looked up for a moment, hoping for any sign of sun in the gray sky, but found none. Heaving a sigh, I walked toward the porch, keeping my gaze on my feet, careful of where I stepped. Seconds later I was knocking on the door with my leather-gloved knuckles, then standing back in wait.

When Dee Dee opened the door and saw me, she sighed so deeply her shoulders visibly sagged. "What in the . . . what do you want, Evangeline?"

I arched my back so I stood a bit taller. "Do you have a minute?"

She closed her eyes and shook her head, then looked back at me. "For what? Another fight with you?"

"No." I swallowed. "Actually, I'd just like to talk to you. Like we used to do . . . when we were kids."

"When we were kids?" She coughed a laugh. "Evangeline Benson, you do beat all." She ducked her chin a bit. "Excuse me. Evangeline Vesey."

"Seriously, Dee Dee. I want to talk to you. Are you alone? Is Velvet here?"

"Velvet's at Wal-Mart working."

"Then may I come in?"

Dee Dee looked at me long and hard before stepping away from the door. "By all means. May as well warn you: it ain't Buckingham Palace, but it's a roof."

I stepped over the threshold. She was right. It wasn't Buckingham Palace. The place was clean but with stained green and yellow shag carpet someone must have stolen from the set of the Brady Bunch and furniture that screamed of the Spanish hacienda motif era. The pictures on the walls were mostly replicas of oil landscapes, no doubt purchased at a thrift store. Still, it was clean.

"I just made some coffee. Want some?"

"No." I watched her walk into the open kitchen of orange Formica and off-white linoleum floors that buckled here and there. "Thank you, though."

"Well, why don't you have a seat there in the living room?" She poured a cup of coffee into a chipped mug and then made what I felt was too big a production out of adding sugar and non-dairy creamer.

I moved into the living room and sat in the first chair I came to. I sat up just a bit to tug my coat tightly around me as I glanced at the oversized maple end table next to me. There was an ashtray with the telltale sign of a recently smoked cigarette (as though the trailer reeking of it wasn't enough), several five-by-seven and wallet-sized framed photos, and an old Bible.

When Dee Dee joined me, I jumped.

"That's some of my family." She moved to the other side of the table, then squatted down, holding the coffee cup with both hands. "That there," she said, pointing to the frame nearest her, "is my boy Darrin."

I looked at the handsome young man made all the more dashing by his army uniform.

"He's over in the Middle East right now. Not a day goes by but what I don't pray for that boy, even though I don't know him real well."

I remembered Vernon telling me that one of Dee Dee's children had been raised in a foster home. I nodded once in acknowledgment.

"He was mine and Danny's son. Danny was my fifth husband." She looked at me with a sharp eye. "I suppose you know I was married a bunch of times."

Again I nodded. "I've heard."

"Six times." Again she pointed to a photograph, this time of a man who looked old enough to be our fathers' age. "My husband Neil McGurk. Neil was my last husband. He died right before Velvet and me moved back here." I looked from the photograph to Dee Dee, who blinked back tears. "He was a good man, Neil was. That man loved me and he didn't care what my past was about. He just loved me."

"How'd he die?" I nearly choked on my words.

"Heart attack. Then a stroke. Velvet and I nursed him like he was a baby, but he died anyway."

"I'm sorry, Doreen."

"Yeah, me too." She paused before continuing. "Anyway, Danny and me had Darrin, but he was taken by the state when Danny and I were busted for selling marijuana."

I opened my mouth to ask how a woman got involved in such as that, but then closed it when she pointed to another photo of another young man, this one with a woman and small boy who appeared to be about four or five. "That's Dion."

"Dion? Like DiMucci? The singer from the fifties?"

"I got pregnant with him while listening to 'The Wanderer.'"

"It's amazing you can know that," I commented. I felt my shoulders relax, and I briefly wondered how she could squat for so long. Women our age—in our late fifties—can't usually stay down for that long.

"Well, it was a one-night stand in the back of a club."

I frowned and felt myself tense up again.

"Those weren't my best days. Anyway, I never married his daddy, whose name, for the record, is Paul. Paul actually owned the club, and I was his bartender, and one thing just led to another, if you know what I mean."

I didn't, but I just nodded.

"Paul was a pretty good guy, and he and his wife—"

"His wife?" The words flew out of my mouth before I had a chance to mull them over.

Dee Dee all but sneered at me. "Like I said, Evangeline, those were not the best of times. I was divorced, I had a child to feed, and I was lonely. Sometimes, when you're young, you think that men mean what they say when they say it and then you grow up and find out they rarely do." She took a sip of her coffee then. "Leastways, not when they're married, they don't. But, like I said, Paul wasn't all bad; he was just hot for me. In those days a lot of men were, but Paul was the only one who could make things happen for me, or so I thought. So I had this one-night fling with him, and he told me the next day he'd made a mistake and that he loved his wife, he really, *really* loved his wife and that I had a job as long as I wanted one." She barked another laugh. "Sure I did. As long as I didn't tell his wife. And I never did, even when I handed her Dion to raise."

"Oh, Doreen."

"Don't feel bad for me, Evangeline. I made my choice out of love and a little desperation. Paul knows, of course, that Dion is his. He knows but we never discuss it."

"What do you mean? How can he know if you never discuss it?"

"Because I named him Dion. That's all it took for him to know that I hadn't been with any other man. Anyway, I told Paul there was no way I could raise another child and asked if he and his wife would take Dion."

"How old was he? Dion?"

"About six months. Cutest thing you ever did see."

I smiled at her.

"So Paul and Connie—that's his wife—took Dion because Connie couldn't have children and thought that this was God's way of providing. In the meantime, they never kept me from Dion if I wanted to visit. They told him all along that I was his real mama and, in return, I never bothered them much."

"Is that his wife and son?" I asked, pointing to the photo.

"That's my baby and his baby," she said and smiled a crooked smile. "Little Dion Bunn Jr. We call him D.J."

"Has Dion ever asked you about his father?" I shocked myself at the forwardness of my questions, but I figured I had come here for answers, so I might as well ask.

She paused before answering. "No. But I think he knows. I think Connie knows, to tell you the truth, but no one says anything."

"How could they know?"

"Dion is the spitting image of his daddy."

"Like Donna is the spitting image of her mother? And Velvet too?"

Again Dee Dee laughed. "Yeah, I guess so. Except my girls are ten times prettier than I ever dreamed of being." At that she heaved herself up and moved to the sofa, where a pack of cigarettes and a lighter waited for her. She pulled one from its pack and lit it, then said, "Now you know my story."

I picked up the faded color photo that had been closest to me all along. It was of Donna, taken with Santa the Christmas before Doreen had left town, I imagined. "Not all of it, Dee Dee. What happened with you and—"

"The choir director? Horace Shelly?"

"Yes."

"Horace and I married after we moved to California and my divorce from Vernon was final." She drew on her cigarette and blew the smoke upward. "I was so stupid. I actually thought that dog of a man loved me. We'd move to California, get married, get involved with a church, and I'd be the beloved pastor's wife. But he said he couldn't work for God after what he'd done. He reminded me every stinking day of what his 'lust for me,' as he put it, had cost him. He took a job in a shoe store, I took a job in a restaurant—that's where I learned how to bartend—and then, after a year or so of pure misery, I met Steven."

I cocked my head in puzzlement.

"He's Velvet's daddy. He was from Alabama." She took another drag of her cigarette, leaned back against the rough cushions of the sofa, and crossed her legs. "Lord have mercy, but I was hot for that man." She laughed again. "He was in L.A. on business and just took to me, wham-bam. I ran off with him after knowing him less than forty-eight hours."

"Goodness."

"Shock you?" She sat up and thumped ashes into the ashtray on the coffee table.

"Ah . . ."

"Sure it does." She answered her own question, then leaned back again. "That's okay. That's why you're here, isn't it? To learn all my secrets?" She waved her hand at me. "Don't even bother to answer that." She took another drag of her cigarette before she leaned up again and ground it out. "Steven and me—our good days lasted about six months. Just long enough for me to get pregnant and realize I'd made a huge mistake . . . or, in this case, another huge mistake. I was drowning my sorrows in the bar where I worked—"

"While you were pregnant?"

"Gosh, no. I'd already had Velvet. She was about a month or so. I'd left her with Steven's witch of a mother who thought she was God's answer to motherhood and I was just some cat Steven had brought home from the pound. I went out and got myself plastered while Steven was on one of his 'business trips.' Oh yeah. I knew all about those business trips."

She paused long enough for me to take this in.

"So you divorced Steven?" I asked.

"No. He divorced me, right after he found out that while he was tom-cattin' around, I was kitty-cattin' around, if you get my drift."

I did.

"No doubt his mother told him. Anyway, Velvet and I left, I moved to another town, and that's when I met Paul. As soon as Steven found out about me being pregnant with Dion, he hauled my rear end into court and took custody of Velvet. Him and his mother, of course."

I took a deep breath, then blew it out. "Doreen, I am so sorry about all this. I . . . well, why didn't you just come back here? To Summit View? To your old home and your friends and . . . to Donna?"

"After what I'd done? No way in . . . you-know-where. Even after I heard that Mama died, I stayed as far away as I could."

"Until now."

Dee Dee lit another cigarette. "Velvet and her daddy had a falling-out when she was about sixteen, and she came to live with me and Mickey, my fourth husband. We've been together ever since—mama and daughter."

I was afraid to ask what had happened with Mickey. So far I felt like I'd fallen into a Jacqueline Susann novel.

"Velvet was the one who suggested we move back here. She wanted me to come first, to get things set up a bit, to get the lay of the land, so to speak. So I came. What blew my mind was that none of you even recognized me." She leaned up and took a sip of what I imagined was tepid coffee.

"You don't look the same, quite honestly."

"No. Years of smoking and drinking and going from one man to another and having one kid after another. This is what it gets you." She gave me a hard look as she drew on her cigarette. "Sin'll age a girl." She blinked before she said, "You're lucky, Evangeline."

I agreed with her there, with one exception. "I never had children, Doreen. And I'll never have a grandson like your little D.J."

She seemed to ponder my words before answering. "You got me there."

No, I thought. *You got me.* "Do you remember how, when we were kids, we used to play that little game with the folded pieces of paper?"

"To tell our fortune?"

I nodded.

"Good gosh, I haven't thought of that in years."

"I dreamed about it last night."

"You have weird dreams, Evangeline." She drew on her cigarette again.

I chuckled then. "Maybe. But what I was thinking was . . . how it all turned out . . . and really, how unfortunate your future was. Only we didn't see that back then. What I remember about the dream is that the game said you would marry a lawyer and have a few kids and live in a wooden house."

Dee Dee was quiet. She pursed her lips, then said, "Seems like no matter how many times we played that game, we got a different answer. But life isn't a game, Evangeline. It's a gamble, but it's not a game."

I looked over to the Bible lying on the table next to me. "Not according to the Good Book."

"That was Mama's. Mama believed without question what I have trouble believing even with the answers."

Maybe, I thought, *because certain Christians haven't made it too easy for you to believe the message of the book*. I looked back at her and, for the briefest of moments, saw the little girl who had once been my friend. "Look, Doreen . . . Dee Dee. I know you and I won't ever be close, and that's okay. But I would like to work with you as best as possible. We've got the catering business going, and you've got the bartending thing going—you and Velvet. We can at least keep it civil." I looked at the photos again. "It's helped, I think, knowing what you've been through."

Doreen appeared to size up my words before answering. "I want to try to make some kind of amends to my girl. Donna, I mean. And I want to see both my girls come to some sort of relationship. But that's going to take some doing."

"It doesn't have to." I shifted a bit in the chair.

Doreen snickered. "My Velvet . . . now there's a girl you'll have to watch. I take no credit for her nasty side. That was her grand-mother's doings. Old Lady James and her son with his endless stream of women. Not to mention Mickey."

So much for not asking. "Mickey?"

"I divorced Mickey when I found out that he had a bigger eye for Velvet than he did for me. Not that he ever touched her, but a woman can't stand for a thing like that. My girl came first, and I left as soon as she told me how he'd been looking at her and talk-ing to her."

Something—I don't know what it was—told me that Velvet had made it up. I had no reason to think that—plenty of young women today most certainly have been abused, even women in the church—but when it came to Mickey and Velvet, my intuition said different. "Did you ask him about it?"

"He denied it. But what man would admit it, I always say."

I took a deep breath, then stood. "Doreen, I have to go. Vernon will be home soon. I just . . . I just wanted . . . well, you know."

She shrugged. "I know. Okay. We're good here. We can play nice from now on. I won't bother you, and you won't bother me, and . . . if you can . . . maybe drop a good word to my daughter about me every now and then."

I only nodded, then turned and walked out the door without saying good-bye.

When I got in my car, I thought, *Poor Donna.* Something told me she was up against more than she knew with Velvet James, and I had no way to tell her. Maybe later, I thought, I'd tell Vernon, and he could tell Donna.

I started the car and backed away from the trailer, knowing all too well I'd never admit to anyone what I'd learned that afternoon. Doreen Roberts's secrets would remain my secrets.

Lizzie

24

Teatime Buzz

Immediately after tea with Michelle, Adam, and Esther Peterson, and while following the happy threesome in Adam's car to Lisa Leann's bridal boutique, I placed a call to Lisa Leann from my cell phone and told her, in no uncertain terms, that I was greatly disappointed in her decision to trick me with the bridal gown choice, that I thought she was my friend, and that—as far as I was concerned—her keeping this secret from me was in very low taste.

"Why, Lizzie," she said from the other end, obviously taken aback. "I don't believe I've ever heard you speak like this."

I took in a deep breath and attempted to steady my shaking, ever grateful for the hands-free phone system I'd recently installed in my car. "You most likely have not." My voice held a bit of staccato. "That said, I cannot imagine that you—Lisa Leann Lambert—having been the mother of a bride yourself, would stoop so low, just to make a buck."

"Lizzie, I—"

I shook my head as my foot pressed harder on the accelerator. "No, Lisa. I don't want to hear any excuses. I'm furious and you may as well know it now."

"My name is Lisa Leann."

I had to admire her attempt to stay in control of the conversation, but it wasn't going to work with me. I had raised a house full of children. I was the media specialist for a high school full of obnoxious teenagers. Staying in control of conversations was part of my on-the-job training. "I know your name. And don't switch the subject, Lisa."

"Why, Lizzie. I do believe you *are* upset."

I felt heat rising in my body. I reached over and turned the heater down in my car. "I will say this to you now so as not to ruin anything for my daughter when I see you in a few minutes. I am disappointed. I am upset. I had plans with my daughter today. Not you and my daughter." I took another deep breath. "In addition to this, and just so you know, I will not be serving at the shower—"

"I had always assumed you wouldn't be—"

"Well, good. Because I'm not. I think that, at least on this occasion, I'll simply enjoy being Michelle's mother. Thank you for listening. I will see you shortly."

And with that, I ended the conversation.

Lisa Leann bristled a bit around me at our "bridal gown" meeting, which Adam avoided by heading across the street to Higher Grounds for a chat with Clay, whom he said he had spied sitting at his usual table. "Tradition being what it is," he said with a wink to me, "I have no intention of seeing my bride in her finery until the day she walks down that aisle."

Tradition, my eye. Tradition is mother and daughter . . . oh, well. It is what it is, I decided. And what "it is" is mother, daughter, future mother-in-law, and one clucking bridal shop owner.

That evening—when it had been what it had been and when

everyone except Samuel and I had gone to bed—I said, "What do you think God thinks about Christians who drink?"

We were sitting on the sofa of the family room, the fire in the fireplace giving off the only light in the rustic setting. Samuel had brought an ottoman over and placed his feet upon it while I curled up nearby.

"Where'd that come from?"

"Do you have to answer every question with a question, Samuel? Can't you just answer?"

His face twitched a bit. "Well . . . I know Christians who have the occasional drink. Some of the guys from the bank—who I know all love and serve the Lord—will have a beer during a football game or a glass of wine with dinner."

"But what do you think God thinks? Not what do you think they think."

He took a few moments to ponder before answering. "Well, God's Word says nothing about drinking per se, but quite a bit about drunkenness."

"So then if a Christian—a solid believer—wanted to come home at the end of the day and have a drink, or, let's say, sit by a fire"—I nodded toward the fireplace—"and have an Irish coffee, or perhaps a nice glass of wine before bedtime to help relax before turning in . . . you think that would be okay with God."

Again he paused before answering. "I haven't thought that much about it, Liz. I've never been one to drink. Just never cared for the stuff. Even when I was in college and my frat brothers would throw parties, it just wasn't my thing. With it not being a part of my everyday life, I guess I just haven't thought much about what God might think. Like I said, I know where he stands on drunkenness. But this is . . . well, I don't know. I suppose one could argue that it's being 'like the world,' versus apart from it. But, I imagine Jesus is more interested in the heart of the situation than the action. What the motive is and that sort of thing."

I nodded as though in agreement, but inside my mind I fought to rationalize my own feelings and recent behavior. Not to mention my desire at that moment to have a nice glass of wine and then go to bed.

Then Samuel spoke again. "Now, you know Frank Holmes, right?"

"From the bank? Yes."

"He was telling me once that his doctor actually advised him to have about four ounces of red wine in the evening after dinner. Frank was having some digestive problems at the time, and he tells me it has cleared right up."

"So, for medicinal purposes? Like Paul said to Timothy?"

Samuel crossed his arms over his abdomen and scootched down on the sofa, then looked at the fire. "You know, Lizzie, I think we—even we Christians—can justify pretty much anything if we work at it hard enough. Maybe not everything, but just about." He closed his eyes. "I'm getting sleepy. Fire's nice and warm. My beautiful wife by my side."

I leaned over and put my head in his lap, closing my eyes as well. I shivered a little when he began to play with my hair, and—without opening my eyes—I smiled up at him.

"Hey," he finally said, so whisper soft I might have imagined it.

I opened my eyes and looked up at him.

"I know you were disappointed about Michelle and the dress today, but I think you handled it well."

I frowned. "I didn't tell you the part about telling Lisa Leann off."

He chuckled. "That might have been worth the price of admission."

The fire crackled and popped. I looked over at it, watched as a burning log shifted, then turned to ash and fell. "I'm not going to work the shower."

"I would think not."

257

We remained silent for a few moments before Samuel asked, "Is that what this is about? Drinking at the shower?"

I felt breath escape my lungs. If I were honest, I would say, "No, this is about the fact that to ease my personal pain and frustration of late, I have been enjoying a drink and some quiet reading in little out-of-the-way places you know nothing about." But, the shower was a good "out."

"Yeah," I said. "Just wondered how you felt about it, that's all."

I called my brother the following day. If my timing could have been any worse, I don't see how. "Lizzie," he said as soon as I'd identified myself. "I was just about to call you."

"Really?" With any luck, I thought, it would be to say that he and Mildred were ready to take on Mom's care again.

"Mildred had another small heart attack last night. Nothing like the last one, but she's back in the hospital."

I felt my shoulders droop. I was in the laundry room, sorting stinky socks from damp towels that smelled faintly of mildew and sweat. I dropped my sorting and walked out of the room, then up two flights of stairs toward my bedroom. "Oh, Charles," I said as I went along. "I'm so sorry. What do the doctors say?"

"Dr. Schnereger is her physician right now. He hasn't given me a complete report yet, but I'm hopeful for a good one. Mildred's color was back this morning when I was there. Last night, when the episode happened, she went ash white then a weird shade of blue. I'm telling you, Liz, I've never been so scared in my life. Not even the last one prepared me for this. I thought we were home free."

I felt for my brother; truly I did. How could I possibly tell him about Mom now? I sat on the bed, then laid back and stared at the ceiling.

"How are things there? Michelle getting ready for her big day?"

"The bank is having a very lavish shower. It's constantly one thing and then the other. Samuel is doing much better. Back at work, praise God."

"Be thankful, Liz."

I was. Truly I was.

"How's Mom?"

I allowed myself the privilege of answering mentally in two ways: *She's ☐ne. Good days and bad days. But mostly good.* "That's good," *Charles would say.* "I know you can take care of this." *Or, I could tell him the truth.* Not so good, Charles. In fact, the administrator of the assisted living facility says we need to discuss a nursing home. So what do you think? Can you get away any time soon so we can visit a few because, quite honestly, I don't think I can handle this by myself. *"You'll have to, Liz,"* he would say. *"I can't do any more than I'm doing right now."* And then I would say, *"Neither can I, Charles. What do you think I'm made of? What, in the name of all that is good, do any of you think I'm made of?"*

"She's fine," I finally said. "Good days and bad days. But mostly good."

I heard my brother exhale. "That's one less thing I have to worry about. Thank you for taking such good care of her. I have no idea when I can deal with Mom again. You're a good daughter. A good sister too."

I smiled, but I wasn't very happy.

That night, after everyone had gone to bed and I found myself unable to sleep, I slipped out of bed and went to the kitchen, where a bottle of red wine was now hidden in the back of the pantry. I poured myself a tea glass to nearly full, then shuffled into the family room. I turned on a small table lamp, curled up on the sofa with a book that had been sent to the library for me to review but that I'd yet to touch, and began to read.

And drink.

I woke with another headache. Samuel stood over me, shaking my shoulder, calling my name as though I were in a coma. "Lizzie. Lizzie, do you hear me?"

I opened my eyes. The room was bleary—even for so early in the morning—but after several blinks I was able to bring it back into focus. Samuel was in his pajamas and a robe, the sash untied. "What are you doing sleeping down here, hon?"

I attempted to sit up, but my head had other ideas. I moaned a response, and Samuel sat next to me. I watched in semi-horror as he picked up the empty wine bottle sitting on the end table next to the sofa and brought it to his nose. He frowned. "Liz?"

I made my best effort to wet my lips, but my tongue was just as dry. "What?" I finally croaked out.

"Is this what the questions were about? Are you drinking—how do they put this—in the closet?"

I closed my eyes. "I suppose it's according to how you look at it." I opened my eyes again.

Samuel held the bottle up a bit higher. "This is how I'm looking at it."

"I just needed something to help me sleep."

His eyes bore into mine. "And so you turned to liquor?"

I pushed myself up against the armrest of the sofa. "Oh, Samuel. Don't be so melodramatic. It's not liquor. It's wine. You yourself said you didn't see anything wrong with it."

"I don't think that's exactly what I said."

I pushed my fingertips deep into my forehead. "Samuel, you act like I'm ready for AA or something. With everything going on in my life, I just need some help shutting down. I need some quiet time and a way to relax during it."

"That's a far cry from a glass of wine with dinner."

I pulled my knees close to my chest so that I could slip my feet around his body and escape the line of questioning, but he was too fast for me. Especially this morning. His arm locked around my knees and held me in place. "Stop it, Samuel. I need to go to the bathroom, and I need to get ready for work."

"Lizzie, we aren't finished with this."

I wrestled free of his grip and stood, albeit very slowly. "We're finished. You don't want me to have a glass of wine here in the privacy of my own home, fine. I won't." I practically growled at him, something I—in all honesty—had never done before.

"Liz . . ."

I touched his shoulder with my fingertips and said, "I'm sorry, Samuel. I'm fine, really I am. Everything is fine."

"Promise me?" The early morning sunlight rested lightly on his face.

"I promise."

Good news came on the Thursday before Tim and Samantha's "move out" deadline.

"We've found a house," they said simultaneously around the dinner table.

My hands flew over my mouth. "You did!" I said behind them. "You found a house?"

Could my glee have been any more exposed?

"We did. And," Tim said with a twinkle in his eye, "it's just around the block from here."

"Around the block?" Samuel asked.

"We'll be over all the time," Kaci exclaimed.

"All the time?" I asked.

Tim chuckled. "Don't worry, Mom. We'll give you and Dad your space for a little while, at least."

"Who around the block is selling a house?" Samuel asked. Leave it to my husband to stay practical.

"The Whitlocks," Tim answered.

"James and Betsy?" Samuel asked. "I wasn't aware they'd put their house on the market."

"Grandpa, you can't know everything," our grandson Brent chimed in.

Samuel smiled at him. "As president of the bank, my boy, I typically can." He finished with a wink, and Brent snickered in the way boys do when amused by their grandfathers.

"Where are the Whitlocks moving to?" I asked.

Samantha reached for the Louisiana red beans and rice she'd prepared earlier and that I'd served in the vegetable bowl that is a part of my great-grandmother's dish pattern before spooning a bit more onto her plate. "Mrs. Whitlock's parents live in Denver and they're moving up there to help take care of them. Apparently, her father hasn't been doing well lately, and Mrs. Whitlock—being the good daughter—feels they should move into her childhood home and help out."

I felt a quick and sudden pang of guilt over my own mother. If I were such a good daughter, I wondered, would I move Mom in with us when Tim and Samantha moved out?

"Wonder what Peter thinks of that?" Samuel mused.

Michelle, who'd remained silent (even for her) during our conversation, nearly choked on the water she was sipping.

While Samuel slapped her between her shoulder blades, Tim reached for the beans and rice his wife was handing to him as he answered, "Actually, he's pretty cool with it. His job allows him to work out of his home—as you know—so he's just fine with picking up and moving."

"Peter and Connie never had any children of their own," I blurted out. "Makes it easier, I suppose."

Life came to a quiet halt. When I realized what I'd said—and my family's stunned reaction to it—I blushed and said, "Not that I would trade any of you for the easy load, of course."

Eventually Samantha said, "Of course not. As a mother myself, I know exactly what you're saying."

I smiled at her in appreciation, and the meal continued with a flurry of information about the new home, move-in dates (in a month, which was not soon enough, but I could now at least see light at the end of the tunnel), and talk of what furnishings would be kept from their home in Baton Rouge versus time for shopping amidst Michelle's wedding plans.

For a while, all seemed right with the world.

My breaking point came on Saturday.

Even now, to fully understand what happened, I have to take myself back to Thursday evening, after dinner and baths, when Kaci begged and pleaded for spend-the-night company on Friday evening. Jamie, she promised, was a great little friend, a good little girl, even a Christian good little girl, who was her best friend in the whole wide world and please, please, please MeMa, would you let her come here and spend the night? With everything else going on in our lives, I should have been smart enough to say no, but my granddaughter's angelic face, freshly scrubbed and framed by long dark hair, stole my heart and my good sense right along with it.

While Friday evening was uneventful, Saturday morning began with a crash. Literally.

When Samuel and I heard what sounded like glass shattering on porcelain tile, we bolted upright and looked at each other, saying, "What was that?" at the same time. We bounded out of bed, and Samuel, sleepy confusion etched on his face, opened our bedroom door. I stepped into the still-dark hallway first, but when his hand locked around my wrist with a slight tug, I allowed him to pass me. After all—and as any wife knows—if there is a burglar-slash-axe-murderer in the house, the husband should be the one to "go" first.

Even in the predawn, I noticed that Kaci's bedroom door was ajar, but the significance of that didn't register. Samuel slipped down the top floor stairs, holding on to the railing and with me close behind. When he reached the ground floor landing (our home is a split-plan) at the foyer, he peered around the doorway as though he were Lenny Briscoe from *Law and Order*. Then he turned back to me and whispered, "Kitchen light is on. Did you leave it on?"

"No," I whispered back.

When Samuel turned, he jerked suddenly and took a step backward, stepping on my foot in the process. I, directly behind him, fell against the bottom stairs. When I was able to regain my composure, I saw Tim and Samantha standing behind Samuel. They were dressed in adorable matching pajamas—which was nearly amusing at this early hour. Amid a flurry of "Are you okay?" and "What was that noise?" we were finally able to determine that whatever the noise was, it came from the kitchen, and that Samuel and Tim—who I now noticed was armed with one of Brent's baseball bats—were required to go check it out while Samantha and I held back in case someone needed to call the sheriff's office.

Samuel moved from the foyer to the large dining room, which segues into the kitchen, with Tim on his heels, while Samantha and I held back in the foyer. When the shadowed backs of our husbands were no longer visible, I held my breath until I heard "What in the world?" followed by "Honey, are you okay?"

It was then Samantha and I joined Samuel and Tim—and Jamie—in the kitchen, where my great-grandmother's vegetable bowl lay shattered on the kitchen floor. "Oh no!" I exclaimed, bending down to pick up the fragmented pieces. "Oh no . . . oh no . . . oh no . . ."

"I'm so sorry," Jamie said. I looked up at the child dressed in lavender Bratz pajamas. Her long blonde hair was tussled about her head and her sleepy blue eyes filled with tears.

"Young lady," I said in my best teacher voice. "What are you doing down here this time of night, and what are you doing with my great-grandmother's vegetable bowl?"

The tears began to flow down her cheeks as she explained between hiccups that she'd seen the bowl in the kitchen (I'd not yet put it back in the china cabinet where I should have put it, shame on me) and thought it was very pretty. She woke up and, unable to go back to sleep, decided to come downstairs to explore a bit because "Your home is just so pretty, Mrs. Prattle" and when she turned the bowl upside down to read the underside of it, it slipped and fell.

"I don't understand. Why would you turn it upside down?" I asked, still squatting but no longer picking up pieces.

"I dunno. That's what my mom does whenever she's looking at china, so that's what I did." The waterworks came fast and furious at this point.

"Well, what's done is done," Samuel said from above us.

"Sweetheart, let's get your face washed and make sure there are no cuts on you, and then I think you should go back to bed." Samantha reached for Jamie, and Jamie eagerly—too eagerly—went with her while Tim said, "Here, Mom. Let me get a broom and clean this up." He turned and stepped carefully toward the broom closet.

"Unfortunately, this can't be salvaged," Samuel said, "but there's no point in making the child feel worse than she probably does already, Liz."

I looked up at my husband. "You know how much I love this china," I said. "Oh, why did I even think to bring it out the other night? Why didn't I put it up after I'd washed it?"

His hand reached for mine. I set the broken pieces back on the floor and took his hand. "Let's go to bed, and Tim will clean this up right away," Samuel said.

"I've got it, Mom," Tim said, broom and dustpan in hand.

Samuel and I returned to our room, but I didn't go back to sleep. When the seven finally rolled into place on my digital bedside clock, I got up, took a long shower while my coffee brewed, and then prepared myself for the rest of the day.

I could not have possibly prepared myself for the rest of the day. By noon Jamie had managed to take everything out of Kaci's closet under the pretense of "organizing it" and had convinced Kaci to allow her to "style her hair."

This included cutting Kaci's hair. With Samantha now in an uproar over her daughter's new "do," and with my great-grandmother's china bowl lying in shards at the bottom of the kitchen garbage can, I decided to leave the house for a visit with Mom.

I no sooner got into the assisted living facility than I was, once again, accosted by Luke Nelson. "Mrs. Prattle, have you managed to find another location for your mother?" he asked without even saying hello.

I sighed. "Not yet. My brother's wife had another heart attack and I—"

"I'm so sorry to hear that. Is she okay?"

"She's much better, thank you. But he's been a bit preoccupied this week, you understand, and I—"

"Of course I understand, Mrs. Prattle, but I'd feel much better if I knew your mother had another facility lined up to take her when her Alzheimer's becomes too much for her to stay here. I would hate to have an unfortunate incident here at the Good Shepherd—"

"An unfortunate incident?"

"Yes. The Good Shepherd in Nashville—one of our Southern locations—recently had a resident who caught her kitchen on fire when she forgot she was making soup. Fortunately everyone got out okay, but as you can imagine there was extensive fire and smoke damage and—"

"I get your point, Luke. I promise you that I will take care of this on Monday. In fact, I'll take a half day from work and make this my sole priority. Would that satisfy you?"

Luke's face pinked. "I don't mean to be unfeeling."

I took in a deep breath and exhaled slowly. "Of course you don't," I finally said. "I'm going to go up and see my mother now."

"Of course," he said, stepping aside.

Mom was not having a good day. She was feisty and forgetful, and after an hour or so of helping her bathe and dress, and then settling her down in front of the television, I bent down to kiss her forehead and said, "I'll see you later, Mom." I'd spent as much time with her as I could reasonably deal with on a day that had begun entirely too early.

She nodded in response, totally fixated with the screen of the television. I glanced its way; *Steel Magnolias* was on, which had always been one of Mom's favorites. I patted her shoulder and said "I love you" about the same time as Olivia Dukakis says to Shirley MacLaine, "Ouiser, you know I love ya more than my luggage . . ."

Mom chuckled at the screen, and I slipped out of the apartment unnoticed. As I waited for the elevator doors to open, I pressed my back against the wall opposite the hallways, dipped my chin toward my chest, and began to weep. The elevator door opened and closed without my having entered it.

By the time I made it to my car I had sobered enough from my crying spell to drive without impaired vision. But my hands were unsteady, and I was forced to clutch the steering wheel with both hands. I was halfway home when my cell phone chimed, telling me I had a text message. I had reached a traffic light holding its own at red, and I slowed my car to a stop, then checked the message on the oversized face of my new Motorola Q.

It was from Michelle.

"Mom," it read. "LLL sez my gown may or may not be available in my size!! Hlp!!"

The light turned green, and as the cars in front of mine began to roll forward, I pulled over to the shoulder of the road, set my hazard lights, and sent Michelle a responding text.

"Don't worry, sweethrt. God made alt. shops. :o) We have 3 mths 2 spare! LLL just trying 2 feel important."

I reprimanded myself for the last sentence but sent the text anyway. Then I dialed Lisa Leann's home number.

"This is Lisa Leann," she sang.

"Lisa Leann, this is Lizzie."

"Goodness, what timing you have, Lizzie. I just got off the phone with Michelle. Do you know I just love those TTY operators! I feel like I'm a part of some spy show, sending out secret code, ending all my messages with 'go ahead.'"

"Lisa Leann, can you please tell me why you insisted on telling Michelle that her dress might not be available in her size? What possible reason might you have for this? I mean, we're what? Three months out? Do you not think for one single second that a good alterations shop might be able to handle this? Don't you have connections, for heaven's sake?"

"Why, Lizzie, you sound distraught."

"I *am* distraught, Lisa Leann. I have a lot going on in my life right now, and I certainly do not need my daughter, three short months from her wedding, in any sort of turmoil. She should be enjoying this time, not fretting through it."

"Now, Lizzie, if you will just calm down I will tell you that I always keep my brides informed of all the details. And I most assuredly told Michelle that we'd have plenty of time to find a seamstress. What kind of wedding coordinator do you think I am?"

I sighed so deeply, I'm surprised the car didn't blow off the side of the road. "Lisa Leann," I said after several deep breaths. "You are a fine coordinator. My nerves are just a little raw right now, and I should have calmed down before I called. My apologies."

"Apology accepted, of course."

"I'll let you go," I said. "I'm sure you have plenty to do without dealing with a crazy woman's hysteria."

I ended the call without a proper good-bye, then gauged traffic and slipped between two cars and continued toward home. But when I reached the next traffic light, I shifted into the left turn lane and turned my car toward Silverthorne.

On my way I called Samuel and gave him a bald-faced lie. "Hey, honey. I just got off the phone with Lisa Leann"—which was true—"and she insisted that I head over to one of the outlets in Silverthorne where some fabulous mother-of-the-bride sale is going on"—which was not true—"so, if you don't mind I'm just going to run over there and see what's what. By the way, how's the fort holding up? Is our home still a war zone?"

Samuel moaned in response. "Take me with you," he said, though his voice held a lilt to it. "I'll happily dress shop with you and never complain."

"Is the demon-child still there?"

"Liz . . ."

"Sorry." I smiled at the gloriousness of the country around me. "Well, is she?"

"Her mother called and said she'd be here in an hour."

"And when was that?"

"Two hours ago."

"You know, you don't have to stay there. You can always leave. Tim and Samantha are totally responsible for Kaci and Jamie."

"And leave what's left of your great-grandmother's china unprotected? Not a chance."

"Don't remind me."

"How's your mother?"

"Don't remind me," I repeated. "I'll talk to you later. Be home before too late." I disconnected the call and then turned the radio on. It was on K-LOVE, and I immediately changed it to an equally favorite country station, then sang as loudly as I possibly could until I reached the Swiss inn I'd grown so fond of.

I keep at least one book in my car for those times when I get stuck somewhere or need a good book to read. I was halfway through my third glass of wine and nearly finished with the book I'd brought in with me when my cell phone rang. It was the Good Shepherd.

I rolled my eyes. If Luke Nelson was calling me to find out if I'd done anything in the few hours since I'd seen him . . .

"This is Lizzie Prattle," I answered.

"Mrs. Prattle, this is Veronica Daniels at the Good Shepherd." The statement sounded more like a question than a fact.

"Is there a problem?"

"Yes, I'm afraid so. How soon do you think you could come up to the facility?"

"Is there a problem?"

"Mrs. Prattle, your mother has fallen. One of our residents from the first floor—"

"Is my mother all right?"

"She may have broken her arm. We have an ambulance on the way, and she'll be transported to the hospital in Breck."

"I'll be there as soon as I—" I stood. When I felt the blood rushing from my head and my knees at the same time, I returned to my seat. "I'm in Silverthorne. I'll call my husband and be there as soon as I can."

I took deep breaths as I waited for someone to answer the house phone. When no one did, I called Samuel on his cell. In the background I could hear a mild ruckus. "Samuel, where are you?"

"Higher Grounds. Took your advice and got out of the house. Tim and Samantha—"

"Samuel, Mom has fallen. She's being transported to the hospital and—"

"Is she okay?"

I pressed my upper front teeth into the thick pad of my tongue. "I don't know, really. Samuel, please. Go to the hospital and wait. I'll be there as soon as I can get there without speeding."

I wasn't speeding. If anything, I was driving too far under the speed limit. When I saw the Summit County marker I may have sped up just a bit, but I'm not sure. And my car may have been weaving ever so slightly onto the shoulder of the road. But only ever so slightly.

I'm also not sure how long the blue lights swirled behind me. When I noticed them, I felt a thousand and one pinpricks along my skin, and I groaned. The time I would spend on the side of the road going through the motions would be precious time away from Mom. But, a quick glance into my rearview mirror and I saw that it was only Donna. I breathed a sigh of relief. She was, no doubt, on the lookout for me and was going to escort me to the hospital.

I pulled over to the shoulder and rolled to a stop. She did the same, coming up behind me. I powered down the window as she approached, then turned my head to call out the window.

"Donna! Oh, thank goodness! Are you here to escort me?"

Donna stopped in front of the driver's door and stared at me for a good long minute. Fear began to grip my heart as I imagined something far worse than the apprehension of being pulled over by a sheriff's deputy. *Has something worse than a fall happened to Mom? Has she burned the Good Samaritan down to the ground, killing herself and many of the other residents?*

"What is it? Donna, what is it?"

Donna cocked her pretty blonde head as she furrowed her brow. "Lizzie? Have you been drinking?"

Donna

25

Steak Out

I shined my flashlight into Lizzie's confused face. She managed to stammer, "You've come to take me to my mother, right?"

"License and registration, please."

She dug into her wallet and handed me her MasterCard as she asked, "Aren't we wasting valuable time?"

"Lizzie, would you step out of the car?"

She looked at her credit card in my hand. "Oh dear." She reached into her wallet and pulled out her license, then traded with me. "Here you go."

I stared at her license then back into her glassy eyes. "I still need you to step out of the car, Lizzie."

She looked baffled. "Okay."

When she was standing before me I held up my pen. "I'm going to ask you to follow my pen with your eyes. Lizzie, can you do that for me?"

"Why?"

"Just give it a try." I slowly moved the pen in a horizontal then a vertical line. My heart sank as Lizzie's eyes jerked, showing mild nystagmus, a sure sign of intoxication.

"Lizzie, I need you to take nine steps forward, heel to toe, then nine steps back."

"I thought you were going to take me to the hospital."

"Are you ill?"

Lizzie swept her fingers through her graying bangs as if trying to stop her hair from dancing with the evening breeze. "No, I'm fine. Had a few glasses of wine, but I'm fine."

"Just try the walk."

I watched as she gently tilted first to the right, then to the left. *Oh boy.*

"So how many glasses?"

She tucked her hands into the pockets of her jacket and pulled her shoulders higher, as if she were fighting the chill. "I don't know, I was going to order dinner but didn't get a chance."

"Okay, can you stand with your arms to the side, then lift your left foot about six inches off the ground and count to ten?"

"How's that going to help?"

"Just humor me." I watched as she once again failed the test, having to lift her arms to keep her balance.

"You stay right there, I left something in the truck."

"Okay, but hurry."

I walked back to my cab to retrieve my Alco-Sensor, a small handheld breathalyzer. I'd have her puff into it, and if it indicated an alcohol level over .08, I'd have to arrest my friend and take her in to the station for a more conclusive blood alcohol test.

When I returned to my truck and opened my cab door, dispatch was broadcasting my call number through my radio. "Unit two, Summit View ambulance service has been trying to reach you about a patient they just delivered to the hospital."

My heart jumped and I grabbed my microphone. "Betty, anyone I know?"

"A David Harris told me to tell you not to worry. He wants you to keep an eye out for Lizzie Prattle and get her down to the hospital in Breck."

"What's wrong?"

"Her mother's in the ER."

"Roger. Is she okay?"

"Word is, it's nothing life threatening."

"Roger that," I said. "Thanks, tell him I've got Lizzie with me now and we're on our way."

I walked back to my tipsy friend, finally understanding her frenzy about getting to the hospital. "I'm going to take you to see your mother in just a second," I said, "but first, can you blow into this please?" I held up my Alco-Sensor.

"You think I've been drinking?"

"Well, you just said so."

"Oh. I did." She laughed uncomfortably. She shifted her weight from foot to foot, as if to hurry me. "But this is an emergency."

"I know, but let's just see how much trouble you're in."

"Trouble? You don't think I'm drunk, do you?"

I silently held up the testing device. "Let's find out."

Lizzie blew into the tube, and the digital readout registered a .07. I secretly breathed a sigh of relief. The number meant that what happened next was up to my discretion.

"Well?"

"I'm going to follow you to the off ramp, and I want you to leave your car in the parking lot across the way there. Then I'm going to take you to see your mother. We'll talk about your test results on the way to the hospital."

"Okay," Lizzie said, stepping back into her car.

A few minutes later, I had the siren blasting as Lizzie sat buckled into the passenger's seat beside me. "Lizzie, I've never known you to drink."

Lizzie's voice hardened. "Are you judging me? Because I didn't think you, of all people, were like that."

I picked up speed, passing cars as they pulled to the side of the road. "No, I'm just surprised."

Lizzie gave me a stern look then turned on her best librarian's voice. "All I can say, Donna, is if you were dealing with the kind of stress I've been under, you'd chill out with a glass of wine yourself."

"But Lizzie, you're drinking to the point of intoxication. You didn't exactly pass my breathalyzer test."

She sat stunned in the pulsating light. "I didn't?"

I ran a red light, watching as the cars yielded to my race. "It was right on the borderline. I'm thinking about having the hospital run a blood alcohol test to get a more accurate result."

Shock filled her voice. "You're saying I'm drunk?"

"Yeah," I said quietly then gave her a quick glance. Lizzie was staring out her passenger window as I asked, "Is drinking your way of self-medicating your stress?"

She spoke to the darkness. "I don't know. Maybe lately."

I zigzagged around cars that were trying to pull over. "That surprises me, Lizzie. I mean, you're a godly woman. I would think you would go to talk to a counselor or pray before you resorted to drinking."

Lizzie turned to me, trying to support her words with gestures that seemed a tad too sloppy for her usual prim demeanor. "I was just trying to get through these next few days. I'm not an alcoholic, you know, and besides, the Bible doesn't say it's wrong to drink."

"But isn't there some Scripture about getting drunk?"

Lizzie hesitated. "You're referring to Ephesians chapter 5?"

"See, you know this Bible stuff better than I do. I bet you can quote it, right?"

Lizzie hung her head, "Do not get drunk on wine, which leads to debauchery. Instead, be filled with the Spirit."

I sat silently.

Finally, Lizzie spoke, her words not as crisp as usual. "Still, I'm not an alcoholic."

"Well, all I know is that alcoholism can happen to good people, and you're one of the best people I know, so I'm worried, Lizzie."

"I've only been drinking for a few weeks, you know, just to relieve the stress, till this wedding, till my kids move out, and my mom—" She gasped. "Oh dear, my mom!"

"It's going to be okay. We're almost to the hospital."

"What are you going to do when we get there? I mean, about me being borderline while driving my car?"

"Honestly, I haven't decided. Though maybe I need to do something drastic to give you a wake-up call, so you can get help."

"I don't need help. I'm fine."

"But you may have already become alcohol dependent, and, well, have you considered that your actions may mean you're at least a problem drinker?"

She folded her arms across her tan jacket. "How can you say that, Donna? You only picked me up tonight because of that call that came in about my mother."

"Not true. You were weaving. I picked you up because you couldn't stay in your lane. I didn't get that call about your mother until after I stopped you."

Lizzie looked stunned. "Oh. I ah . . . Oh."

As we neared the hospital, I turned off my siren but kept my lights flashing. "I think I'm going to let you off with a warning this time, but don't drink and drive again. I don't want to have to scrape you off the grill of an eighteen wheeler."

I pulled up to the double doors and turned to my friend. In the rotating glow of red and blue, I could see she was trembling. "Aw,

Lizzie, you go check on your mom, I'll be inside in a minute. But in the meantime, I'm asking you to ask yourself a hard question."

Lizzie unbuckled her seat belt and stepped out of the car before leaning back in. "What's that?"

"Can you find another way to cope with your stress, besides drinking? You know, go for a walk, read your Bible, knit something? If you can't, then you need help. Maybe you need to talk to a counselor or join a support group."

"Okay. Yes, I'll look into that."

"One more thing . . ." I reached into the hidden compartment of my console and retrieved a piece of gum. "Here. Chew this. You need it to ward off the smell of wine on your breath."

Lizzie frowned but took the gum anyway. "Thanks," she said before hurrying through the doors of the ER. I switched off my rotating lights and pulled the truck behind the Summit View ambulance that was parked around the corner from the entrance. I reached for my clipboard and started to write up my report when someone tapped on the window. I lowered it. "David! How's Lizzie's mom?"

"She's going to be okay. She tripped over her shoes, which she'd left in front of her recliner, and fell full force on her coffee table. At first I thought she broke her arm, but now it's looking more like a deep bruise."

I shook my head and sighed. "Poor Lizzie. She does have her hands full these days. I'm going in to check on her mom in just a minute, soon as I fill out this report."

David looked hesitant, then leaned his head closer to mine, dropping his voice. "While I have you, do you wanna talk about our upcoming date? I mean, I know you were working around the clock this week to cover for Clarence, but what about next week?"

I nodded as I looked into his brown eyes, eyes that seemed to pull me into a closeness that frightened me. "Yeah, though next week is crazy with the upcoming Prattle shower. So what would you say to a weeknight date, maybe Tuesday?"

A lopsided grin spread across his face. "Sounds good. Do you have a favorite restaurant?"

"Well, would you mind going to the Mountain Bell Tower Resort's restaurant? I have a few things I want to check out there, undercover, more or less."

David looked amused. "So, now you're a detective?"

"Well, when the circumstances call for it, yeah."

"Just who are we investigating?"

"If I told you, I'd have to kill you," I teased.

David held up his hands in mock defense. "That won't be necessary, Deputy. But you've got a date."

Tuesday morning of my day off brought the latest that Lizzie was moving her mom, bruised arm and all, to another nursing facility. I'd been hoping she'd call and talk about the other night. But so far, silence.

In the meantime, I was feeling guilty for not dropping by to help Lisa Leann with all the catering preparations, but I was in a panic over my date. I mean, I couldn't wear my brown deputy's uniform, could I? And besides, David was taking me to a pretty swanky restaurant, so I needed to run down to the Silverthorne outlets and figure out how to look fashionable.

After I made a few phone calls to set up the night's covert operation, I drove over to Silverthorne. The tall brunette saleswoman (Ellen, according to her name tag) in the Jones of New York outlet was actually a big help. She steered me to a nice pair of black pants and a black satin V-neck sleeveless tank, which she topped with a soft black shawl with a topaz and rust paisley woven into the Italian wool. "These pieces are essentials," she'd emphasized. "But what about your jewelry?"

"I don't really wear much of that stuff."

"But jewelry will absolutely make the look rock," she said. "Here, let me show you."

"You're not related to a woman named Lisa Leann, are you?"
I asked.

"Who?"

"Never mind."

Soon Ellen had selected a dainty gold-tone chain belt with tiny topaz-colored crystals between the loops, along with a short gold-tone necklace and matching earrings.

I looked at myself in the full-length mirror, a bit surprised. The amazing thing was I looked like a girl a guy might *want* to date, and, well, I was rusty. I mean I hadn't really dated since my partying days, after my failed rescue above Boulder when I'd lost my grip on a baby I was trying to rescue from a car submerged in a flash flood. The incident had caused me untold agony, mainly because it had finally made me come to terms with the loss of my own baby over a decade earlier.

I blinked back the bad memories and focused on the petite woman in the mirror before me. "Don't you think all this bling bling is overkill?" I asked the clerk.

"Absolutely not. What you've chosen is simple yet elegant. You look wonderful."

I wasn't convinced; still, I pulled out my Discover card. All I can say is thank goodness everything was on sale or I might have been tempted to wear jeans and a turtleneck for a more affordable "look."

When I was done at Jones of New York, I stopped by one of the shoe outlets and picked up a pair of strappy heels in black leather. I couldn't wear my tennis shoes or the white heels I'd worn at Dad's wedding. Still, I was chagrinned to find that black dress shoes were pricey. I was suddenly glad I had overtime pay coming.

On my final stop, I dropped by Angie's Hair Hut to get my hair styled. Now that I no longer wore my blonde curls military short, I needed a new look. As it was, my hair was starting to look like a frizzy mop.

When Angie was done combing and clipping, she handed me a mirror.

I stared. "Ah, well, that's different."

Angie fluffed my curls as her dangling earrings bobbled beneath her short apple-red hair. "It's hot." She whirled my chair so I could see the back of my head in the wall mirror. "It's easy care, and you look adorable."

I watched myself frown. "In my line of work, 'adorable' could be a problem."

"Well, you looked adorable when you came in, even in black sweats. Now you look even better." Angie turned to the stylists working on other clients. "Girls, what do you think of Donna's new hairdo?"

Irene, who was wearing cropped embroidered jeans topped with a red boat-necked tee, stopped clipping her client's hair. She waved her scissors and said, "Donna, you should have done this years ago."

"You don't think this cut makes me look like Tinker Bell?"

"Far from it," Janie from behind the register said. "You look hot."

Angie laughed. "That's what I told her."

Later that night, I'd lightly applied a little tinted moisturizer, blush, and eyeliner and brushed my lashes with a wave of mascara, as Lisa Leann had taught me just before my last court date. Then I slipped into my new black pants and tank. I even added the jewelry, though I thought it created a "look" that went over the top.

As I stood in front of my mirror inside my closet door, I barely recognized myself. All too soon, I answered David's knock at the door. When I let him in, I caught a whiff of his spicy cologne. He looked great in his dark suit coupled with a white shirt. "Wow! Donna!" David said when he saw me. "You look amazing."

"Wow yourself. But are you sure you want to be seen with me looking like this? I feel like I'm in a costume."

David grinned. "You look nice. You're undercover, right?"

"That's my excuse. What's yours, Mr. Fancy Pants?"

He pulled my hand into his. "I'm your undercover date, remember?"

"Yes." I stepped back to retrieve my shawl, which I'd draped across the top of my couch. David helped me nestle it around my shoulders. Before we left, I walked to my kitchen table and grabbed my ragged, purple quilted handbag, which had been in hiding on the top shelf of my closet, a leftover from the nineties. I guess I should have gotten a small black clutch, but I had to have something big enough to put my camera and notebook inside, and of course, my gun.

"Are you ready?" David asked.

"Guess so."

Once I was in his Mazda, I didn't know what to say or how to act so I began to fidget with my wrap.

"Are you okay?" David asked.

"Not really. I don't even know what to say to you, dressed in this getup."

"Just be yourself." David adjusted his CD player, which began to croon "Unbreak My Heart" by Il Divo. "That's the girl I admire."

I turned and stared at him. "You admire me? Why?"

"Well, you're funny, smart, and I think you're pretty cute."

When I didn't answer, he gave me a sideways glance. "Did I just embarrass you?"

I gave a little nod. "I admit it, I'm feeling uncomfortable."

David chuckled.

"What's so funny?"

"You are."

I crossed my arms. "Well, what about you?"

"Me?"

"Yeah, here you are, some kind of millionaire paramedic from

Hollywood. You could be dating starlets. Not small-time deputies from the Colorado outback."

"I like real women. I'm not interested in starlets."

"Yeah, but you were interested in Velvet," I pushed on. "Speaking of, what did you say to explain things to her?"

David shifted uncomfortably before turning the music down. "I . . . I reminded her I only wanted to be friends."

"Oh? How did she take that?"

"She hung up on me."

"Ouch."

"How did you explain things to Wade?"

"Wade and I, we're not dating. So, what's to explain?"

His eyes shifted from the roadway back to me. "You didn't say anything?"

"David, our date tonight is an experiment. I mean, maybe when you get to know me a little better, you'll lose your infatuation. Maybe Velvet will seem like your dream girl."

He tried to hide a smile. "That's not possible."

I pulled my shawl closer. "You think I'll swoon and fall all over you, don't you?"

David raised his eyebrows and stared at the highway ahead. "Would that be bad?"

"You're not getting through this process based on your good looks, you know."

He laughed out loud. "So, you admit you think I'm good looking?"

I sighed loudly. "Stop grinning."

"Yes, sir, Officer. But I have an idea. Let's try to relax and maybe even enjoy the evening."

I took a deep breath. "Okay, I'll try. But don't forget, we're undercover. So, follow my lead and never look surprised."

"Yes, ma'am. I'll do as I'm told."

I grinned then. "Now that's the attitude of a man I could be attracted to."

"Like you're not already."

"Better not push your luck, bucko."

"Don't worry. Tonight, I'm playing by your rules."

Later, after we'd been seated in the restaurant, the waitress dropped by. "Would you like anything to drink?"

"I'll have water with lemon," I said after David ordered an iced tea. I looked up at the blonde whose hair was so neatly pulled back into a ponytail, and she greeted me with a single raised eyebrow. I closed my menu and turned to David. "I'm off to powder my nose," I said, grabbing my purse. "I'll be right back."

David watched as I slipped out of the seat. "I'll be waiting."

A few minutes later, I stood in a closed bathroom stall when the door of the bathroom opened. "Donna?" a soft voice whispered.

I stepped out. "Trisha, appreciate you dropping in." I opened up my purse and pulled out my digital camera and handed it to my old high school classmate and showed her the zoom feature.

"You don't think I could lose my job over this, do you?"

"Just don't get caught."

"Well, he's with LaRita now. They're supposed to walk out of the hotel room in exactly five minutes."

"Wow, how do you know that?"

"I've got their MO down, and besides, LaRita is set to take over my shift, since she thinks I have to take off for a family emergency."

"Okay, then you'd better hurry; I'll meet you back here."

Trisha slipped out of the restroom. I waited until she returned. Her cheeks were pink, and she held the camera over her head. "I got it!"

I hugged her. "Did they see you?"

"No, they were preoccupied. See."

She handed the camera to me, and I turned on the review feature and watched the colorful shots of Clark Wilkes kissing a very young redhead through an open hotel room door. "Wow. Good work."

"Thanks to the zoom on your camera," Trisha said. "Well, I gotta get back to work so LaRita can relieve me."

"Yeah, I bet David is wondering where I went."

Trisha paused at the door. "He's hot."

I bit my lower lip and nodded. "Yeah. So he tells me."

Trisha scurried down the hallway, and soon I slipped back into my chair across from David.

"I thought maybe you got lost," he said.

"Nope, just, ah . . ."

"Sneaking around undercover?"

"Keep your voice down."

No sooner than I gave the warning, Trisha approached our table with LaRita, a young redhead with flashing green eyes. Trisha said, "I'm about to go off duty for the night, and LaRita is here to take your order."

As Trisha headed back toward the kitchen, I smiled sweetly at the waitress. She was a cutie, tall, long hair, and she looked all of eighteen. I said, "LaRita, you look familiar, aren't you from Summit View?"

"Yeah, I was a cheerleader up till last year, but I'm a graduate now."

"I thought I recognized you. So, is this your regular job?"

"Yeah, though I've recently made some connections, and I'm expecting better opportunities here at the resort."

I tried to look impressed. "Oh, that's nice."

David was still staring at the two of us. I hesitated. "Did I introduce you to David Smith, my fiancé?"

I stared David down with a look that said, "Don't react."

She turned to David and smiled. "Nice to meet you."

"We have an appointment tonight with Clark Wilkes to talk

about our upcoming wedding this summer. We're planning it here at the hotel. Do you know Clark?"

She nodded. "Yeah, he's actually the one who's going to promote me."

"Really, so he's a nice guy?"

She nodded and smiled shyly. "Yeah, he's okay."

"I know him from church," I said. "He's a swell family man."

LaRita raised her eyebrows. "What do you mean?"

"His wife is one great lady. You've met her?"

Her eyebrows shot up. "He's married?"

"Oh yeah, with kids too. He and his wife make the perfect couple."

LaRita looked angry, then embarrassed. She seemed to catch her breath before she said, "Look at me, I almost forgot to take your order."

David said, "Well, I'm going to have steak, medium rare with all the trimmings."

"I'll have the same."

In a flash, LaRita was gone.

David stared me down. "Fiancé?"

I reached across the table and squeezed his hand. "Thanks for playing along."

"I take it we have a meeting with Clark Wilkes to, ah, plan our wedding?"

I shifted in my chair. "You said you wouldn't act surprised, remember?"

He sighed. "Will he help us plan our honeymoon too?"

"Don't bet on it."

David smiled as if he had other ideas.

"Stop it," I said, trying not to smile at his mirth.

"You started it."

"I know this is awkward, but I appreciate you being a good sport."

"Why not? I'm having the time of my life."

As we were finishing our shared dessert, death by chocolate cake, Clark Wilkes dropped by the table. He was a handsome man, a man a woman like Lisa Leann would certainly approve of. Judging from his haircut and the cut of his suit, he looked like he was stepping out on the red carpet. He said, "The maître d' pointed the two of you out to me. I was wondering if I could escort you on a tour of our facility."

David said, "We haven't paid our bill."

"Oh, don't worry about that. Dinner's on the house, Mr. Smith. Your lovely Donna here is thinking of serving our steaks at your wedding rehearsal dinner. I hope you enjoyed them."

David looked at me. "They were excellent."

I smiled sweetly. "Yes, we would like to take the tour of the ballrooms."

David helped me with my chair and my wrap, then we followed our host down to the Tabor Grande Ballroom. Clark opened the door. "Take a look, I think this room would meet your requirements."

David said, "Dear, how many people have you invited to our wedding?"

I smiled. "Now, we've discussed that, darling."

"Well," Clark continued, "this room will easily seat the five hundred on your guest list."

I exchanged looks with David. And he nodded with a silly grin on his face as he said, "Sounds like what we were looking for."

"Now, let me take you to our Silverheels Room. I think it would be perfect for your wedding reception." We walked down the hall and he opened another set of double doors.

"Ah," David said, "this is perfect."

I smiled up at him. Clark turned to us. "Would you like to see your complimentary honeymoon suite?"

I shook my head, but David said, "Oh yes, we're quite interested." He draped an arm across my shoulder. "Aren't we, dear?"

I had no choice but to nod as I meekly followed the men down to the suite. Clark opened the door to a masterpiece of a suite, rich with designer couches, desks, flat-screen TVs, a liquor cabinet, and a wide open door to a master bedroom glowing in lavenders and mauve. David made a beeline through the master bedroom door and sat down on the bed. Clark followed him, and I trailed behind. David patted a spot beside him. "Try it, dear."

"Oh, I, ah . . ." I looked at Clark, who said, "You two make yourselves at home. I'll step down to my office and wait for you there. You know the way, don't you, Donna?"

"Yes, I do."

Clark discreetly closed the door behind him.

David lay back on the bed. "I think I like undercover work."

I turned and kicked at his foot. "Cut it out, you knucklehead. Let's get down to Clark's office."

David laughed as he stood and followed me to the door. "Your wish is my command."

Soon we were sitting in front of Clark's desk, looking over the pricy contract. *Zow!*

I looked at David, then looked at Clark. "Do you mind if we take a minute alone?"

"Sure. I need to run to the restaurant to check on an employee matter. I'll be right back."

As soon as he left his office, I stood and stared at his desk and noticed a paper only partially covered by his telephone.

"So, it's Clark we're investigating," David said. "But aren't you performing an illegal search?"

"Not if I find something out in the open that gives me probable cause. Say, what's this?" I leaned closer to peer at the paper listing female employees, complete with special notations.

David walked around the desk and looked over my shoulder.

"What did you find?" He read the hand-jotted words beside LaRita Jones's name. "Excellent in bed?" He looked up at me, concerned. "You say this guy goes to our church?"

"Not for long." I pulled out my camera from my purse and began snapping pictures of the document. David went and stood by the door then whispered, "Donna, better wrap it up. I think he's coming."

Quickly, David and I slipped into our chairs just as Clark opened the door. I pushed my camera into my purse and smiled as if nothing had happened. I looked up with all innocence. "Do you mind if we take these contracts home and study them, then I can call you with my questions."

"Sure, if I can't trust a deputy, who can I trust?"

David and I stood to go, and Clark shook David's hand and mine. He said, "I'm looking forward to your call."

Half an hour later, as we neared Summit View, David asked, "So, do you take all your first dates to honeymoon suites?"

"You're the first. But what about you? Do you bounce on the bed with everyone you go out with?"

David shook his head. "Believe it or not, I'm an old-fashioned guy. What about you?"

Before I could stop myself, I blurted, "I'm . . . I'm celibate."

After a stunned silence, David grinned. "Ah, I see."

I frowned and studied my hands, which I'd folded into my lap. "Yeah, and I'm guessing that's a deal breaker for you."

"Well, Donna, I'm not looking for a party girl. I'm looking for someone I can build a life with. So, actually, it's nice to hear you've been celibate."

I felt my face burn. "Well, ah, we all have a past."

David slowly nodded. "Let's think of the future and—"

So help me, I snapped. "I just can't be pressured, David, I can't."

David looked surprised. "Well, since I played your fiancé tonight, you can't blame me for merging our undercover assignment with a little wishful thinking."

"Take a reality check. I'm only getting to know you. I'm not ready to think of the future with you or anyone else, for that matter."

"Fair enough." David pulled onto my street. "Maybe, though, we need to try another date. Just to see where this thing is going in the short term."

I leaned back into my seat and stared up at the mountains glowing beneath the starlight. "Okay, you were a good sport tonight." I smiled. "And I had a good time."

He pulled into my driveway and wiggled his eyebrows. "Good enough for a good-night kiss?"

So help me if I didn't say, "Why don't you step under the porch light with me and find out?"

Moments later, he did. When he wrapped his arms around me, our lips touched, and my heart stirred in a way I hadn't expected. Our lips lingered before I could push away. "Good night, David."

"Good night, Deputy. And you're a good kisser."

I smiled shyly. "Then that makes two of us." I slipped inside my front door, my heart hammering. I shut the door and leaned against it, almost in a panic. I had to slow this situation down.

I looked out the kitchen window as David pulled out of my driveway. *Oh Lord, what am I getting myself into? This will never work. It can't. Besides, Velvet will never forgive me.*

Lisa Leann

26

Dicey Meeting

Chopping onions is always a great smoke screen for a good cry. At least, that's what my mama always said, and today, it was certainly true.

I laid down my knife and wiped away the gathering dampness with the back of my hand, careful not to rub onion juice into my eyes. *How is it that everything in my life is so out of control?*

I hopped off my stool and went to rinse my hands in my large stainless steel sink while my eyes continued to water, not so much from the pungent onion but from an overflow of heartaches.

Maybe I was crying because Lizzie, the mother of our little bride, had accused me of sabotaging her daughter's wedding dress. (How could I have known Esther was butting in where she shouldn't?)

Or, maybe it was because I missed Henry. How could he have left me for a church mission trip at a time like this? Not only did I desperately need his help, he had unwittingly left me alone to face a lovesick Clark.

I blotted my eyes with a tissue and turned to look at the clock on the wall.

Or maybe it was because not one of the Potluckers had shown up to help me. Here it was, 10:00 a.m., the day before the shower, and I was the only one preparing for our big day.

I understood that Goldie and Donna had to work, and of course, I couldn't expect Lizzie to help, being the mother of the bride and all. But where were Vonnie and Evie? They'd promised to come and lend a hand first thing this morning.

When the phone rang, I felt a pang of hope. I put on my headset and picked up. "Potluck Catering."

"Well, if it isn't Lisa Leann."

I put my hands on my hips. "Clark, I asked you not to call me."

"This is a business call," Clark said, as if he was teasing me. "I'm calling to confirm our meeting tonight."

I picked up my knife and continued to chop onions. "What meeting?"

"Didn't Beverly tell you? The three of us are going to do a walk-through of your event about 7:00 tonight. We'll go over everything, just to make sure we can pull off this bridal shower without a hitch."

I sighed loudly. "Beverly did not inform me of these plans. Can the two of you make do without me?"

"Oh, I'm afraid not. Since you're the outside caterer, I will definitely have to go over some codes and regulations concerning both the city of Breckenridge as well as the hotel, you know, to make sure everything's in order."

"Okay. I'll be there."

I hung up before he could say more. *What's next?*

"Hello?" a voice called from the front of my wedding shop. I called back, "Evie, is that you? I'm back here in the kitchen."

Evie came in, tugging off her beige coat before hanging it on the coatrack. She was dressed in a pair of jeans and a fuchsia sweatshirt.

She pushed up her sleeves, ready to get to work. "Goodness, where is everyone?" she asked, walking to the sink to wash up.

"It's only you and me, and hopefully Vonnie. Tomorrow, we'll have the whole gang, minus Lizzie."

Evie laughed. "We'll excuse Lizzie, just this once."

Vonnie stuck her head in the back door. "Sorry I'm late, I had a heck of a time getting Mother squared away for the day."

"Oh, Vonnie, I'm just glad you made it," I said, watching as she too slipped out of her coat then popped one of my pink aprons over her head before tying the sash in the small of her back. I went to the refrigerator and pulled out my ball of cheese dough I'd placed in a large ceramic bowl and topped with plastic wrap. I placed the bowl on the workstation next to my king-sized roll of wax paper and a stack of baking sheets. I nodded toward Vonnie. "Why don't you wash up?"

But instead of turning toward the sink, she blocked my path. "Why Lisa Leann, have you been crying?"

I pointed to my large bowl of chopped onions I'd been preparing for the salmon mousse. "No, no, it's only the onions."

Vonnie looked at me carefully, as if trying to read the thoughts behind my eyes. "There's something more, something you're not telling me. What's wrong, Lisa Leann?"

Evie walked toward me, looking concerned as she tied on her apron, looping the extra sash around her middle. I shook my head and forced a laugh. "Oh, I'm fine." I took a deep breath. "I'll admit I'm feeling the stress, especially without Henry here to help me."

Vonnie turned to wash her hands in the sink while Evie continued to stare. "Where is Henry?"

I tried to be stoic. "Mission trip to Mexico. It's with the youth of our former church in the Woodlands."

I could tell my performance hadn't convinced the girls. "Are you sure nothing else is wrong?" Evie asked.

I began to busy myself by rolling out two long lengths of wax paper and dividing the dough in half.

"Honestly? I'm missing Mandy and the baby. I found out she had a baby shower, and no one even told me about it till after the fact."

Vonnie, who had just finished drying her hands on a paper towel, turned and hugged me. "It must be tough to be so far from your grandbaby."

I simply nodded and sniffed my nose as I tried to gain a new level of calm. Evie said, "Okay, Lisa Leann, we're yours for the day. Show us what you want us to do."

Within minutes I began demonstrating the cheese stick making procedure by rolling a small piece of dough between my hands and into a long, thin strip. I twisted the strip for a decorative flair and placed it on one of the cookie sheets. After my demonstration, the girls got to work, and I returned to my chopping job, now slicing bok choy into tiny strips for the spring rolls.

I was glad to have help, as long as we could avoid the topic of my personal life. Soon, though, I had changed the subject, directing Evie to tell us more about life as a newlywed.

"It is so different from life as a single," she'd said with a shy smile. "Now I have to always consider Vernon in my every decision. I mean, I used to be the center of my world, and now my focus has shifted to Vernon."

"That's really the secret to marital happiness," Vonnie agreed as she twisted a small cylinder of dough. "To focus on the one whom God has given you to be your soul mate."

"I always thought the so-called 'soul mate' thing was a myth."

Vonnie laughed. "Not every couple is as happy as Fred and me. Of course, we've had our rough times, like recently, when my long-lost son showed up on our doorstep. But I've always believed it's possible to change a normal marriage into an exceptional marriage, just by being a loving spouse. Of course, that philosophy won't work in every situation, but it will help most."

"Is that your secret?" Evie asked Vonnie. "Is that how you and Fred have lasted all these years?"

"Pretty much," Vonnie said. She turned to me and asked, "How about you, Lisa Leann? How have you managed to stay so close to Henry?"

I was now chopping sugar peas into skinny strips as I admitted, "Actually, my marriage hasn't always been healthy. You know, Henry was so engrossed in his work at Exxon, and I was always so busy with church and my club activities. That's why we decided to leave Texas and take early retirement. We agreed we needed to concentrate on each other."

Evie raised an eyebrow. "How's that working?"

I felt heat tingle my cheeks. "Well, great. That is, except for this week with Henry out of the country and all."

"When does he come back?" Vonnie asked.

"I pick him up at DIA Monday."

The afternoon flew by as I continued to feel emotionally stronger. It helped to be busy and it helped to have my friends around me. We spent the day stirring, chopping, laughing, and baking as we told funny stories on each other as well as ourselves. I also treated the girls to a lovely lunch of grilled chicken sandwiches and frozen grapes, plus we got to sample the first of our cheese sticks, all toasty from the oven. As the five o'clock hour approached, I was surprised at how much we'd accomplished: the cheese sticks were baked and bagged as were the pumpernickel crisps, the salmon mousse had been poured into large fish molds and refrigerated, the spring rolls had been stuffed and wrapped and now lined my baking pans, ready to be baked fresh tomorrow afternoon, so we could keep them warm in our portable warming ovens for the party. Plus we'd wrapped our scallops in prosciutto. Earlier, I'd pulled the tiny petit fours out of the freezer to thaw. They looked like adorable ivory and chocolate gift boxes, all tied in ribbons of silver icing.

"What time should we get here tomorrow?" Vonnie asked.

I began to brew a fresh pot of coffee in my coffeemaker, and I set a few of our petit fours on a serving plate for the girls to sample. "Things are really coming together," I said. "All we have left is the chocolate fountain and the crimini mushrooms, plus moving and set up. Which, believe me, will be a chore."

"I've got David signed up to help with the moving back and forth," Vonnie said.

"Yes, and my Vernon too," Evie added.

"Great! Then, let's plan to meet back here about nine," I said. "I'll have the work schedules made out by then, so everyone will know their jobs."

"This is so exciting, girls!" Vonnie said. "The way we're organized, what could go wrong?"

What could go wrong, indeed, I wondered as I drove toward Breckenridge later that evening, chagrined that I had to see Clark with my husband nowhere to be found. Well, at least Beverly would be there to act as my guardian (whether she knew it or not).

Soon, I walked into the marbled lobby of the Mountain Bell Tower Resort and turned down the hall leading to Clark's office. I knew Michelle, Adam, and Tim worked in some of these back offices, but they'd probably all left for home by now. I knocked then poked my nose inside Clark's office to see him busy working at his desk. "Is Bev here yet?"

He stood. "Lisa Leann, Bev will be here momentarily." He walked around the desk and took my hand. "She just called and said she's running a little late. But while we wait, let me show you the setup for your catering team."

I shrugged. "Okay." I followed him down the hall. He smiled at me then. "Oh, and I appreciate you sending me the Harris-Vesey wedding. I met with your deputy friend the other night and I think she's going to sign on the dotted line any minute."

I stopped dead in my tracks. "David and Donna are getting married? Here?"

Clark studied me. "Didn't you know? I know she's trying to keep it all hush-hush, especially after pretending Hollywood Harris's name was Smith, but I saw through their little ruse. I know they're just trying to protect their privacy from the media crush the news of their wedding will surely spawn."

I nodded, shell-shocked. How could I have missed seeing Donna and David's romance develop? And why hadn't she yet come to me to help plan her wedding?

When we bypassed the conference room where the shower was to be held, I stopped. "Clark, just where are you taking me?"

"To the room where you're going to set up your catering operation," Clark said, as if he were puzzled by my hesitation. He stopped in front of a nearby door and inserted his master key. "This way," he said as I entered ahead of him.

The door shut behind us, and I reached for the wall to see if I could find the light switch. But before I was able to flip it on, Clark pulled me into his strong embrace. I tried to push away. "Clark, what do you think you're doing?"

"I told you, Lisa Leann, you belong to me," he said, kissing me gently on the forehead.

"Stop it, Clark."

He whispered in my ear, "I know you love me, Lisa Leann. I know you want me. Why else would you have come tonight, with Henry out of town?"

"No! I . . . I came to meet Bev."

"Really? I don't believe she'll be here till tomorrow afternoon. That means we've got the whole night to ourselves." Clark continued to back me through the room until I bumped into the edge of the bed with my legs.

"Clark, stop it. No!" I shrieked as he lowered me onto the plush mattress. He began to tug at my clothes, his kisses heavy on my mouth. I squirmed my face away from his. "Stop! Help!" I cried, hoping I was loud enough to be heard by someone passing by.

The room door rattled open as a backlit figure stepped into the darkness.

"Who's there?" Clark asked, kneeling on the bed above me. He switched on the nightstand lamp.

I gasped out loud when I saw a face materialize in the lamplight. There stood Donna Vesey dressed in her deputy's uniform with one hand resting on her holster.

"I got a tip from one of the staff that something was about to go down in here. I was just outside the door when I heard a cry for help. Is everything all right?"

I jumped off the bed and ran to her, tugging my red sweater back into place. "No! Donna, thank God you're here."

Clark ran a hand through his disheveled hair. "What is this? How did you get in here?"

Donna pulled a passkey out of her pocket with her free hand. "I've got connections," she said. She held up a photograph of a document and continued, "And, I've got evidence. In fact, Clark, I was just on my way to hand-deliver it to you."

Clark climbed off of the bed and took a step toward her as he tucked in his shirt. "What do you mean?"

Donna opened the file folder, which contained enlarged photographs of Clark kissing a young redhead.

"What is this?" Clark demanded.

Donna handed him the file. "Some photos we snapped yesterday, plus some sworn statements that you've been sexually harassing some of the staff. This file is for you, Clark. I have another copy of it down at the station."

Clark thumbed through the pictures and photocopies and looked back at Donna. His voice rose. "What are you planning to do with this?"

Donna frowned. "Actually, it's up to Lisa Leann to decide."

Clark's eyes bore into mine. "What's your part in this?"

"I'm just as surprised as you are, Clark. I'm surprised by this 'evidence' as well as your behavior tonight. But I like where Donna is going."

Clark wore his little-boy pout that I'd once found so adorable. "But I was only doing what you know you wanted."

I took a couple of cautious steps toward him. "No, Clark. You were doing what you wanted. I've long come to realize that getting involved with you was the worst mistake of my life. Tonight proved it."

Clark looked shocked. "But we were in love."

"No, we were in lust. What we did was wrong in the eyes of God."

Donna handed me the glossy photo of Clark in a major lip-lock with a young redhead. "Don't feel too sorry for Clark; from the looks of things, you were only one of many."

I nodded as I stared down at the picture. "I can see that." I looked back up at Clark and narrowed my eyes. "I can't believe I betrayed my husband for you."

Donna put her hand on my shoulder. "Lisa Leann, what do you want to do?"

I folded my arms and gave Clark the once-over. "It looks to me that there are other victims you need to talk to besides me. But if it were up to me, well, I'd expose Clark for what he is."

"You're kidding, right?" Clark said. "Because if you tell on me, I'll certainly tell Henry about us."

I felt a strange sense of calm. "I've already made up my mind to tell Henry. When you showed up at my church, I realized that telling the truth was the only way I could finally be rid of you. I don't know how Henry will take it, but I'm willing to bet my marriage just to prove to you we're over."

Donna looked at Clark. "You heard the lady. I'll be expanding my investigation to see if there are more sexual harassment complaints from your employees."

"That's outrageous."

"Outrageous is a word I'd use to describe your behavior," Donna said.

Clark blinked, and Donna grabbed my arm and tugged me toward the door. "Time to go home, Lisa Leann. I think we've concluded our business with Clark."

With my heart still pounding, I followed her into the hallway without looking back. I leaned against my friend. "Oh Donna, I had no idea Clark was capable of something like this."

"I know."

We walked down the corridor and into the parking lot, where the evening's chill cooled the hot flush that had engulfed me.

"Come sit in my Bronco for a minute, we need to talk."

I climbed inside as Donna slid into the driver's seat. She turned to face me. I folded my arms across my stomach. "Since when did you get engaged to David Harris?"

"Oh." Donna laughed. "We're not engaged, we were just undercover."

My eyebrows leaped. "You were what? Girlfriend, you've got a lot of explaining to do."

Evangeline

27

Savory Prayers

Saturday Evening, March 25

My husband of approximately two months stood at the door of our bedroom. He leaned against the doorframe, dressed in an impressive dark blue suit, and gave a slow whistle. He crossed one ankle over the other. "Look at you, Evie-girl." He whistled again.

"I could say the same," I said, "if I knew how to whistle." I turned away from his boyish good looks and back to my reflection in the mirror. "Are you sure I don't look too . . . I don't know . . . fancy or manly?"

Vernon pushed himself from the door and came up behind me, then placed his hands on my shoulders. "Lisa Leann's idea?"

I nodded. Lisa Leann had insisted we wear a woman's tux with crisp pink tux blouses, which would, of course, blend beautifully with our pink chef's aprons. Though I'd never thought I'd live to see the day that I would wear a tux of all things, I had to admit I looked pretty sharp. I'd curled and styled my hair to perfection, applied just the right amount of makeup for a woman my age (Lisa Leann would, no doubt, do flips over it), and, in my new duds, held my shoulders back and kept my chin up.

"You look hot," Vernon said. "And I don't mean in terms of temperature." I caught his face in the mirror. He winked. I blushed. Even after two months of intimacy, the man still made me feel a little unnerved. Vonnie insisted this was a good thing.

To break the tension, I glanced down at my feet and pointed a toe. "What about the shoes? How do you feel about these puppies?"

Vernon's gaze went south, and he chuckled as he took in the sight of the other item Lisa Leann had insisted upon: black leather classic Walker Hush Puppies. "Well, I suppose they're practical. After all, you'll be on your feet most of the evening."

I frowned. "How'd I get myself into this?" It was a question that didn't require an answer. "Let's go. If I'm more than a minute late, Miss Texas will have a fit."

We arrived in Breckenridge and at the resort only a short while later. We'd spent all afternoon the day before doing the setup— Vonnie's ficus trees adding the perfect touch—but still I wasn't sure which door we should use. "Let's just go through the lobby," Vernon suggested. It sounded good to me.

Of course, Lisa Leann was already in the large ballroom—dimly lit by lowered-light chandeliers and the twinkling lights on the ficus money trees, and elegantly laid out with small round tables, each adorned with floral arrangements and a single candle—flitting about. I noted her arms were laden with the clear acrylic cocktail napkin holders we'd ordered. "Finally," she said when she saw us, then jerked her head to a doorway behind her. "Why didn't you come in from the back?" She had already donned her pink chef's apron, our name and logo in its center. Other than that—and her Hush Puppies—she looked as though she could have been attending the event rather than catering it. Her hair was beautifully coiffed, and she was wearing just a tad too much makeup for my taste. Still, I had to admit, she looked fetching.

I shrugged. "Wasn't sure which way to come, to be honest with you."

Lisa Leann sighed dramatically. "Well, go get your apron. I'm almost done setting these things out, and then I'll fill them with the personalized napkins." She took her eyes off me for a millisecond in her babbling and over to Vernon. "My, my, Sheriff Vesey. Don't you look debonair?"

Vernon pressed the palms of his hands to his chest and ran them down his suit's lapels. "Thank ya kindly, ma'am," he said in his best Texan drawl.

Lisa Leann giggled. I turned to Vernon, took his hand in mine, and squeezed it lightly. "I'll be back. Don't you dare let that redhead talk you into working. You are a guest here this evening and don't you forget it, Vernon Vesey."

Vernon gave me a light peck on the cheek. "Yes'm."

I felt my brow go up. "Since when don't you kiss me on the lips?" I whispered.

He leaned in and whispered back, "Since you started wearing pink stuff on them."

"Gloss," I countered. "It's called gloss."

The door to the kitchen opened wide, slicing harsh light into the romantically set ballroom. We looked toward it. Velvet and Doreen were pushing their way through, each carrying large, obviously heavy, boxes. Vernon did what any man would do, I suppose. He stepped away from me and over to them. "Here, let me help you with that, ladies," he said.

I shot a look over to Lisa Leann, who did the same to me. She shook her head lightly and mouthed "No, no," as if to say, "Don't go there, Evie. Stay calm."

I went to the kitchen, where my job, according to Lisa Leann's what-to-do-list, was to begin the final steps of preparation for the strawberry punch. I only hoped that—with the open bar—the punch would be partaken of at all. As I stepped into the kitchen I heard Vernon say, "Good to see you, Doreen." I looked over my shoulder at them. He took the box from her arms with a grunt and added, "Goodness, woman. How'd you manage to pick this up?"

"You'd be surprised what bar-backs can lift," she answered with a throaty chortle.

About that time I felt a hand on my other shoulder. I turned with a start. Donna stood before me. "Don't let it get to you," she said.

I smiled a weak smile at her. *At least*, I thought, *she's being nice to me.*

"Have you had a chance to talk to your mother much?"

She shrugged. "A little. I'm still a bit wary around Velvet, but . . . time will tell." Her blue eyes softened as she looked past me. I turned again, witnessed what she was seeing: Vernon and Doreen pulling bottles from the box and setting them on the bar while Velvet removed various sizes of glasses from the opposite side.

This was Donna's blood family, or a part of it, at least. I could not begin to imagine what she was feeling at this moment. "I never thought I'd live to see the day when my mother and father were in the same room, much less in the same section of it," she continued. I looked at her again, and she brought her eyes to mine. "Does it bother you? At all?" she asked me.

I had to think about that for a minute. Did it? After my time with Doreen, my feelings had truly changed toward her. For that I was thankful to God. But in the secret places of my heart, I wasn't so sure I was ready to see her and Vernon shoulder to shoulder. For any reason.

Then I saw everything through Donna's eyes and felt my shoulders relax. "No," I said finally. "It doesn't. They are, after all, your mother and father. Nothing in this world will ever change that."

Donna leaned over and kissed my cheek in the very same place her father had a few minutes earlier. When she leaned back I placed my fingertips where their lips had been and pressed. Tears formed in my eyes and I pressed harder, preserving the memory while willing myself not to cry.

Family, I decided, was not only built on blood. Sometimes family was built on mutual respect and love.

And kisses.

When the party was over, when the last of the guests had departed and all the leftover food had been put away, we—the ladies of the Potluck Catering Club—pulled padded banquet chairs around one of the cleared tables and sat slack-shouldered and weak-backed. It had been a wild success, this shower. As my father used to say, "We done good." Michelle and Adam would be well-set financially and the Potluck Catering Club would be the talk of the Summit View business elite. Lisa Leann, I had by now decided, could keep her job as head honcho of our catering club. She'd done a first-rate job, and I, for one, wouldn't want it any other way.

"I am pooped," Lizzie said.

Vonnie reached over and patted her hand. "I am impressed you stayed to help with the cleanup."

Lizzie—dressed in a dazzling satin pewter-colored cocktail dress with matching sequined jacket and wearing eye-catching multi-colored rhinestone accessories—smiled at us all. "I told Samuel I wanted to be—as Kaci puts it—with my peeps. Besides, you girls were terrific. I can never thank you enough." We'd managed to pour a serving each of punch from the bowls, and she took a sip. "Whose recipe is this? It's incredible."

"Mama's," I answered. "That woman knew how to make punch."

"I remember," Vonnie said.

"Me too." Lizzie set her cup down. "Did anyone besides me notice how little the bar was used and how this nonalcoholic punch flew out of the bowls, so to speak."

Donna leaned back and crossed one tuxedoed leg over the other.

"Can't say I'm surprised. Sometimes nonalcoholic just suits better." She gave Lizzie a long look, and Lizzie nodded, pressing her lips together.

"Hear, hear," Lizzie then said, raising her glass. We did likewise and drained our glasses.

"How's your mother, Liz?" I asked her, setting my glass back on the table.

Lizzie shrugged. "She's okay, I think. We've got her settled, at least. And, time will tell."

"Time will tell for sure," Vonnie added. "Lizzie, how is it you and I managed to have our sons and mothers create such chaos in our lives at the same time?" Vonnie, I noted, looked as though she'd aged five years since David's arrival and her mother's injury.

Lizzie giggled. "Must be God's way of keeping us humble," she said.

"Speaking of David," Lisa Leann said, seeming to spring back to life and turning a bit to look at Donna. "You and David sure did look chummy this evening."

Even in the soft lighting I could see Donna blush as she uncrossed her legs, then crossed them again. She looked to Vonnie before answering. "Like you said, time will tell. I'm not so sure I'm up for anything heavy right now."

"I thought you and Wade . . ." Goldie spoke up for the first time since we'd gathered around the table, but then became quiet again.

Donna reached for her empty punch cup and began to fiddle with it. "I dunno. Wade and I . . . maybe we're just the past trying to catch up with the present." She cocked her head to the side and studied her index finger as it etched around the rim of her glass. "I shouldn't say anything. Once you say something, it's out there. But I guess if I can't talk to you girls I can't talk to anyone." She moistened her bottom lip with the tip of her tongue. "I will always love Wade. He and I have a very personal history. And maybe it's too much. I don't know. Maybe he is 'the one.' And maybe right now—what with everything going on with Pete—maybe right now isn't the best time for Wade. Family wise." She looked up. "And David. David is fun. A lot of fun, actually." She smiled broadly. "And a pretty good kisser."

"And crazy about you," Vonnie added after we'd all giggled like schoolgirls.

"And crazy about me." But there seemed to be no joy in her words, I noted. How could one woman have so many men in love with her and be without joy in her words?

We were silent for a good minute before Vonnie said, "Well, you never know, my girl. Maybe—just maybe—the man God has set aside to be your husband is neither Wade nor David." Vonnie was sitting next to Donna, and she patted the area between her shoulder blades maternally.

"Maybe you've not even met him yet," Goldie said, sitting straighter in her chair. "Wouldn't that be something, girls?"

We all mumbled in agreement. Donna, in an effort—I'm sure—to change the subject, looked across the table at Goldie and said, "Enough about me. How are you?"

Goldie became misty-eyed. "I've decided that while one day I'll get through a day without crying, I'll never ever experience a day when I don't miss my daddy."

"I can vouch for that," I said.

"Me too." Lizzie raised her hand in agreement.

We became quiet again, perhaps too tired to talk, until Lisa Leann said, "Girls, I needed to talk to you about something. It's going to come out soon enough, and I . . ." She cut her eyes over at Donna, then straightened and leaned over, resting her elbows on the table and bowing her head as though in prayer. When she looked up, tears were streaming down her cheeks. "I wanted to tell Henry first, but he's still away on the missions trip, and I . . ."

She swiped tears from both cheeks with her perfectly manicured fingertips.

"My goodness, Lisa Leann. What in the world could be so earth-shattering?" I asked.

"Girls, I feel I can trust you. I can, right? Because if this were to get out . . ."

All my friends exchanged glances, that is, except for Donna, who continued to look down. *What in the world?*

I was the first one to speak. "Lisa Leann, you can trust us."

She looked hesitant, and I saw her glance toward Donna, who gave her a reassuring nod.

Lisa Leann turned the color of our aprons. "I . . . I haven't always been faithful to Henry," she said, "and in the last few days, my indiscretion caught up with me, right here in this hotel." She took a breath but quickly resumed. "It was wrong, I've repented, I broke it off, but Clark Wilkes followed me here and tried to restart the affair I thought I'd left behind in Texas."

"Clark Wilkes? That nice man who just visited our church?" Vonnie asked.

"He's not as nice as he looks."

Donna spoke up. "I'm filing charges against him on Monday. A quick investigation showed that Mr. Wilkes has sexually harassed some of the female employees here at the hotel."

Lizzie put her hand to her chest. "Michelle . . ."

Donna said, "Lucky for her, she didn't work in his department."

Lisa Leann continued. "The difficult part is, I'm going to have to come clean with Henry and tell him what I've done. It's the only way to really protect my marriage from Clark, because as it is, our secret leaves Clark with an open door. A door I have to shut."

We sat in stony silence until Lizzie cleared her throat. "Donna, you really are something, you know that?" Then Lizzie looked at everyone and said, "A week ago Donna pulled me over, but instead of taking me to jail, she gave me a second chance." Now tears were coursing down *her* cheeks. "Did you ladies know that?" It was obvious she was speaking through a knot in her throat.

"For speeding?" Vonnie asked. "Why would you go to jail for speeding?"

Lizzie and Donna shared a knowing look, then Lizzie answered. "Not for speeding, Von. For driving under the influence." She nodded while we swallowed our collective gasps and then continued. "I have learned something, my friends. One, I'm apparently sensitive to the sugar and alcohol combination. Two, when life hits hard, your knees should hit equally as hard on the floor of your closet, so to speak. Alcohol—no matter how much or how little—will never settle a problem . . . be it too many people under a roof, a husband's injury, a mother's dementia . . ." She looked at Goldie. "Or a husband's infidelity or a parent's passing." Then to Vonnie. "Or a strained marriage after a past secret—like an unknown son—has been revealed." Then to Lisa Leann. "Lisa Leann, I don't know how Henry is going to take your news, but I know this: if we band together and pray, God will take each one of our secrets and draw them to the quiet places of his heart. And that's the real truth of the matter."

"All God's children got secrets," Goldie said whisper-quiet.

"That's right," Lizzie continued. "But all God's children got prayer too." She reached over and took the hands of the two beside her—Goldie and Lisa Leann. Lisa Leann took Donna's hand, who took Vonnie's, who took mine. I looked over at Goldie, who was extending her hand toward me.

Our hands clasped, and then we all looked toward the center of the table, where a single candle flickered light against the soft pink petals of a rose bouquet.

"Shall we pray?"

The Potluck Catering Club Recipes

Double Chocolate Brownies

2 6-ounce bags semisweet chocolate chips
3 tablespoons butter
¾ cup granulated sugar
3½ tablespoons water
2 eggs
¾ cup flour
¾ teaspoon salt
powdered sugar
2 cups walnuts or pecans (optional)

Preheat oven to 325 degrees. In a medium saucepan, combine 1 bag of chocolate chips with butter, sugar, and water. Cook and stir over low heat. When melted, stir in the second bag of chocolate chips and dissolve/melt into mixture. Next, stir in eggs, flour, and salt. (Optional: stir 2 cups of walnuts or pecans into batter.) Stir the thick, lumpy batter before pouring into (sprayed) 9-inch square pan. Bake for 30 to 35 minutes then set on rack to cool. Top with dusting of powdered sugar.

Yield: 1 pan of brownies

Donna's Cook's Notes

I know I don't look like I eat brownies by the pan full, and I don't. But if I get a craving and make a pan, I share them with my pals at the station as well as whenever I run into cute paramedics. I always think I might freeze the rest, but that never happens because they disappear before I get around to it.

Chocolate Cheesecake

CRUST

> 1¾ cups graham cracker crumbs
> 2 tablespoons sugar
> ⅓ cup melted butter
> ¼ teaspoon salt

Combine graham cracker crumbs, sugar, butter, and salt. Press mixture into side of greased 10½-inch springform pan. Chill.

FILLING

> 2 8-ounce packages cream cheese
> 8 ounces of chocolate chips
> 2 eggs
> ⅔ cup corn syrup
> ⅓ cup heavy cream
> 1½ teaspoons vanilla

Preheat oven to 325 degrees. Cube cream cheese and set aside to soften. In microwave-safe bowl, microwave chocolate chips on high for 1 minute. Stir. If chips aren't completely melted, microwave for another minute then stir again.

Next, in separate mixing bowl, beat eggs, corn syrup, cream, and vanilla until smooth. Slowly add cream cheese cubes. When filling is smooth, slowly pour in melted chocolate and beat until well blended.

Finally, pour filling into pie shell and bake for 50 to 55 minutes, until firm. Set aside to cool, then cover to freeze or to refrigerate.

Yield: one cheesecake—slice as thinly as possible to save calories.

Lisa Leann's Cook's Notes

Nothing like a bite or two of chocolate cheesecake to take the blues away. That's why I always have one in my freezer in the garage, for emergencies. Just try not to have too many emergencies, or you may have to change your dress size.

Chocolate Macaroons

¾ cup sugar
4 large egg whites
4 cups shredded sweetened coconut
3 tablespoons matzah cake meal
3 tablespoons cocoa powder

Preheat the oven to 375 degrees. Line a baking sheet with parchment. Set aside. Combine the sugar and egg whites in the top of a double boiler over simmering water (boil 2 inches of water in the bottom of the double boiler and reduce the heat to simmer). Cook the mixture, stirring until the sugar is dissolved. Stir in the coconut, cake meal, and cocoa until smooth. Spoon 24 mounds of macaroons onto the baking sheet and bake for 15 to 18 minutes, until the tops are just golden. Allow to cool completely before removing from the baking sheet.

Yield: 24 macaroons.

Evangeline's Cook's Notes

Naturally this is a new recipe for the girls and me, but from what I hear they turned out pretty yummy. So yummy, I decided to try it myself. Vernon made an absolute pig of himself!

Lemon Chicken

⅓ cup flour
1 teaspoon salt
1 teaspoon paprika
1 frying chicken (2½ to 3 pounds)
3 tablespoons lemon juice
3 tablespoons Crisco
1 chicken bouillon cube
¼ cup green onion, sliced
2 tablespoons brown sugar
1½ teaspoons lemon peel, grated
chopped parsley for garnish

In paper or plastic bag, combine flour, salt, and paprika. Brush the cut-up chicken with lemon juice. Add 2 to 3 pieces of chicken at a time to the bag and shake well. In a large skillet, brown chicken in hot Crisco. Dissolve bouillon cube in ¾ cup boiling water; pour over chicken. Stir in onion, brown sugar, lemon peel, and remaining lemon juice. Cover, reduce heat, and cook chicken over low heat until tender, 40 to 50 minutes. Garnish with chopped parsley.

Serves 4.

Goldie's Cook's Notes

Sally is a real doll for sharing this recipe with me. She says she found it in an old cookbook of her mother's and that nothing but nothing her mother ever cooked came out bad. One taste of this recipe and you'll be a believer in old cookbooks too!

Texas Hash

1 pound ground beef
3 small onions or one large onion, sliced
1 green pepper, chopped
1 can (16 ounce) tomatoes
½ cup uncooked rice
2 teaspoons salt
1 to 2 teaspoons chili powder
⅛ teaspoon pepper

Preheat oven to 350. In a large skillet, brown meat, onion, and green pepper. Drain off fat. Stir in tomatoes, rice, salt, chili powder, and pepper; heat through. Cover and bake 1 hour in skillet or 2-quart casserole.

Serves 4–6.

Lizzie's Cook's Notes

For busy wives/mothers/grandmothers and otherwise working gals like me, this recipe is easy and filling. Try it and you will quickly see why it is one of my husband's favorites!

Southern Pecan Pie

⅓ cup Crisco
½ cup brown sugar
1 cup white sugar
½ cup whole milk
3 eggs
pinch of salt
1 teaspoon vanilla
1 cup chopped or halved pecans
pie crust

Preheat oven to 425 degrees. Cream Crisco and sugars. Add remaining ingredients and blend. Pour into unbaked pie shell and then place in the oven. Bake 10 minutes, then turn heat back to 350. Bake another 25 minutes. Let cool.

Goldie's Cook's Notes

When I told Mama about the cookbook I saw, she pulled out her mother's pecan pie recipe and said that Grandmother's didn't call for corn syrup like so many others do but she couldn't ever remember her mother's recipe coming out bad.

Italian Casserole

1 pound ground beef
½ cup chopped onion
1 teaspoon garlic powder
1 (15 ounce) can tomato
   sauce
1 (4 ounce) can mushrooms
1 teaspoon sugar
½ teaspoon oregano
½ teaspoon basil
¼ teaspoon salt
¼ teaspoon pepper
½ cup sour cream
2 cups Bisquick
½ cup milk
1 egg
8 slices American cheese
¼ cup grated Parmesan
   cheese

Preheat oven to 400 degrees and grease 9-by-9 casserole dish; set aside.

In a 10-inch skillet, brown ground beef, onion, and garlic powder, then drain. Stir in tomato sauce, mushrooms, sugar, oregano, basil, salt, and pepper into the beef mixture. Heat to boiling while stirring constantly. Reduce heat, simmer, and occasionally stir (about 10 minutes). Remove skillet from heat and fold in sour cream. In separate bowl, mix Bisquick, milk, and egg. Divide the dough in half and press first half into bottom of the pre-greased casserole dish. Pour contents of skillet over dough then top meat mixture with 4 cheese slices. Sprinkle slices with Parmesan cheese. Next, drop spoonfuls of the remaining dough on top of the cheese, like biscuits. Bake uncovered until light brown for 20 minutes. While dish cools, top with remaining cheese slices.

Serves 6.

Vonnie's Cook's Notes

I love Bisquick. It's been one of my best kitchen friends. You don't think I made everything for Fred from scratch, do you? But that can be our little secret.

Petit Fours with Glaze Icing

1 cup butter, softened
3 cups white sugar
7 eggs
1 tablespoon vanilla extract
3 cups all-purpose flour
¼ teaspoon baking soda
¼ teaspoon baking powder
1 cup sour cream

Preheat oven to 325 degrees. Grease and flour a 9-by-13 pan. In a large bowl, cream together the butter and sugar. Add in and beat the eggs, one at a time, mixing well after each. Stir in the vanilla. Combine the flour, baking soda, and baking powder, add to the creamed mixture and mix until all the flour is absorbed. Stir in the sour cream. Mix for 1 or 2 minutes. Pour the batter into the prepared pan. Bake 45 to 60 minutes or until a toothpick inserted into the center of cake comes out clean. Cool cake completely before cutting with petit four designed cutters. (You can use petit four molds, if you desire.)

THE POTLUCK CATERING CLUB RECIPES

SUGAR GLAZE

> ½ cup confectioners sugar
> 2 teaspoons warm water
> ¼ teaspoon vanilla extract

Sift sugar into a small bowl. Sprinkle warm water and vanilla over the sugar and stir until smooth. If the glaze seems stiff, add more water, drop by drop, until it reaches drizzling consistency.

To use the glaze: drizzle over cooled petit fours with a fork. Alternatively, scrape the glaze into a sturdy plastic bag, snip off a tiny portion of the corner, and use the bag to pipe the glaze decoratively on cakes. The glaze should be made shortly before using, since it hardens quickly on contact with air.

Decorate the tops of the cakes with little flowers or designs made from colored icing.

Evangeline's Cook's Notes

"Petit four" is a fancy way of saying "little desserts," and is a term that Lisa Leann likes to throw around a lot. I think it makes her feel more . . . chichi, as she puts it. These little cakes are bite size, served at "low tea" (according to one of my new books on the subject), and almost too pretty to eat. Here's a recipe I managed to wrangle out of Lisa Leann for the ones she served to Beverly Jackson and, subsequently, to us.

Eggs Florentine

1 10-ounce package chopped frozen spinach
pinch of nutmeg
1 to 2 tablespoons water
3 eggs
salt and pepper (to taste)
3 tablespoons grated cheese
cream

Let spinach thaw then spread into bottom of large skillet. Season spinach with nutmeg and add water. Cook over medium heat till spinach is hot. Crack eggs onto spinach. Sprinkle with salt and pepper, turn heat down, and top skillet with lid. A few minutes later, the eggs will be steam-cooked.

When the eggs are almost done, top with cheese. Return lid to pan until cheese is melted. Drizzle cream over dish and serve.

Serves up to 3 people.

Donna's Cook's Notes

This is a lot for one person to eat by herself, but sometimes I do the "brunch thing." This goes down great before a long, cold night shift too. And really, it's not that much fuss to make.

Thyme Roasted Chicken

4 large chicken breasts
1 cup olive oil
½ cup vinegar
5 cloves garlic, thinly sliced
zest of 1 lemon, slivered (outermost part of rind)
1 teaspoon thyme
1 teaspoon salt
½ teaspoon pepper

Rinse chicken breasts then pat dry with paper towels. Place chicken flat in a baking dish. In a small bowl, combine oil, vinegar, garlic, lemon zest, thyme, salt, and pepper. In dish, pour marinade over chicken, coating each side. Cover dish and refrigerate chicken for at least one hour or overnight.

Heat oven to 425. Season the chicken with pepper and salt. Roast chicken until golden brown, about 20 minutes. Reduce heat to 375. Continue to roast until the chicken is thoroughly cooked (about 40 minutes more). Top chicken with pan juices before serving.

Serves 4.

Lisa Leann's Cook's Notes

I got this recipe from the chef at the resort. Henry loves it, but then so do I. I know it has an oil coating, but olive oil is really good for you, so no worries.

_____

_____

_____

_____

_____

_____

Cream of Potato Soup

8 potatoes, peeled and chopped
3 carrots, diced
2 green onions, sliced thin
2 stalks celery, diced
1 onion, diced
1 cup diced ham
5 cups water
4 chicken bouillon cubes
1 tablespoon dried parsley
1 tablespoon chives
1 teaspoon salt
½ teaspoon dill
½ teaspoon pepper
¼ cup margarine
1 (13 ounce) can evaporated milk
½ cup shredded cheddar cheese
¼ cup sour cream

Add everything except milk, cheese, and sour cream to Crock-Pot. Cook soup on high for 5 to 6 hours. Add milk, cheese, and sour cream half an hour before serving. Stir well to blend.

Vonnie's Cook's Notes

If you make this early enough, you can run errands all morning, then come home to a hot bowl of rich, satisfying soup.

Apple Rolls

4 cups apples, diced
1 cup pecans, coarsely broken
2 cups sugar
3 cups flour
2 teaspoons baking soda
¼ teaspoon salt
¼ teaspoon nutmeg
¾ teaspoon cinnamon
¼ teaspoon allspice (the secret ingredient!)
1 cup butter or margarine, melted
2 teaspoon vanilla
2 large eggs, slightly beaten

Mix apples, nuts, and sugar; let stand, stirring often until juicy, about 1 hour. Sift flour, soda, salt, and spices. Add apple mixture and stir well. Stir in butter, vanilla, and eggs. Pour in 2 loaf pans. Bake in preheated 325 degree oven for 1 hour and 15 minutes. Test with cake tester inserted in center. Cool on wire rack. Serve hot or cold.

Lizzie's Cook's Notes

I have no idea why these are called apple "rolls," but that's what Mom always called them. Apple rolls will forever remain a memory of comfort and joy for my family and me. Now that I know the truth about my mother and father's love for them, they are even more special. And that, I believe, is the true secret ingredient!

Bread Pudding

4 cups milk
2 cups bread crumbs (not toast)
2 eggs
⅓ cup sugar
3 tablespoons butter, melted
1 teaspoon vanilla
¼ teaspoon nutmeg
1 cup raisins

Preheat oven to 350 degrees. Scald the milk and allow to cool. Soak bread in milk. Beat the eggs. Add sugar, melted butter, vanilla, nutmeg, and raisins to beaten eggs. Add this to the milk and bread mixture. Pour into a buttered 9-inch baking dish. Set in a pan of hot water and bake about 40 minutes, or until firm. Serve hot or cold, with or without cream. Nuts may be added. Yield: 6–8 servings.

Evangeline's Cook's Notes

My mother always said this was the best way to use your day-old bread. I was never one for making it, but she made it on a regular basis. I'm just grateful that my sainted mother passed her recipe on . . . to Sally!

Hero Sandwich

DRESSING
: ½ cup mayonnaise
1 tablespoon honey mustard
1 teaspoon prepared horseradish

SANDWICH
: 1 loaf French bread
6 slices deli Swiss cheese
8 slices turkey
8 slices American cheese
8 slices ham
1 green bell pepper, thinly sliced
1 tomato, thinly sliced
lettuce

Cut bread in half lengthwise. In small bowl, combine dressing. Spread dressing on both halves of loaf. On bottom slice of loaf, arrange cheeses, meats, green pepper, tomato, and lettuce. Top with loaf topper. Cut diagonally into 8 slices.

Donna's Cook's Notes

Sometimes, I'll make the whole sandwich, then feast on it for every meal for the next two days. Other times, I cut the recipe in half (literally). That way, since I don't always have a way to share a meal, I won't get burned out on a good thing. Be sure to save the leftover dressing to put on your salad or on a future sandwich.

Pineapple Muffins

1⅓ cup all-purpose flour
½ cup sugar
⅓ cup light brown sugar, firmly packed
1 teaspoon baking powder
½ teaspoon baking soda
½ cup chopped pecans
⅔ cup oatmeal
1 cup buttermilk
½ cup melted butter or margarine
1 large egg
1 can (15 ounces) crushed pineapple, drained
½ cup shredded sweetened coconut

TOPPING

⅓ cup light brown sugar
¼ cup all-purpose flour
¼ cup shredded sweetened coconut
2 tablespoons oatmeal
3 tablespoons butter

In a large bowl, mix together flour, sugar, brown sugar, baking powder, baking soda, pecans, and oats. In a separate bowl, blend buttermilk, melted butter or margarine, and egg. Pour into flour mixture. Stir dry ingredients until moistened but do not overmix. Gently fold in drained pineapple and coconut. Spoon batter into large, well-greased muffin tins, fill about ⅔ full.

To make topping, mix brown sugar, flour, coconut, and oats. Cut in 3 tablespoons butter (unmelted) with a pastry blender until coarse crumbs have formed. Sprinkle topping crumbs over pineapple muffin batter. Bake muffins at 400 degrees for about 20 minutes until light brown and firm. Cool on rack. Yield: 12–18 muffins.

Lisa Leann's Cook's Notes

You know what I like about this? It's fussy, fun, and good. A great muffin to make if you have a group you'd like to impress. It sure beats the run-of-the-mill blueberry muffin, any day.

Roast

3–5 pound roast
1 onion, chopped
2 teaspoons flour
1 tablespoon butter
5 or 6 large carrots, peeled
4 or 5 potatoes
1 package Lipton onion soup mix
1 cup water

Chop onion and place in skillet then sprinkle with flour. Add butter and sauté then pour into bottom of Crock-Pot. Place roast on top of onion.

Mix soup mix with water and pour over roast. Cover and leave on high. Peel then chop potatoes and carrots before adding to the pot. Turn on low and cook for 6 or more hours.

Vonnie's Cook's Notes

Who would think this hearty meal was so simple to prepare?

Daddy's Favorite Banana Pudding

1 box vanilla wafers
3 to 4 ripe bananas
¾ cup sugar, divided
3 tablespoons all-purpose flour
dash of salt
4 eggs
2 cups milk
½ teaspoon vanilla extract

Before cooking pudding, prepare layers of wafers and bananas in glass 3-quart casserole.

Combine ½ cup sugar, flour, and salt in top of double boiler. Mix well. Mix in 3 egg yolks (save and set aside the whites) and 1 whole egg. Add 2 cups cold milk, stir until well blended. Cook uncovered, stirring constantly until thickened. Remove from heat and add vanilla. Pour over wafers and bananas already prepared in casserole.

Beat 3 egg whites until stiff but not dry. Gradually add remaining ¼ cup sugar until mixture forms stiff peaks on top. Top pudding with meringue.

Bake in preheated 425-degree oven until browned, about 5 minutes. Serve warm, then refrigerate leftovers (if there are any!).

Goldie's Cook's Notes

Some people have told me they're not sure what they will miss more, Daddy or his banana pudding. I know what I'll miss: having banana pudding and a hot cup of coffee with Daddy on Sunday afternoons after church, our big family meal, and a nap. Daddy's favorite pudding following that nap was as sure as he was.

Mystery Mocha Cake

1½ cups sugar
2 cups sifted all-purpose flour
4 teaspoons baking powder
¼ teaspoon salt
2 squares (2 ounces) unsweetened chocolate
4 tablespoons butter
1 cup milk
2 teaspoons vanilla
½ cup brown sugar
½ cup sugar
4 tablespoons cocoa
1 cup cold double strength coffee

Preheat oven to 350 degrees. Mix and sift first four ingredients. Using a double boiler, melt chocolate and butter together over hot water; add to first mixture, blend well. Combine milk and vanilla; add and mix well. Pour into greased Bundt pan. Combine brown sugar, ½ cup sugar, and cocoa. Sprinkle over batter. Pour coffee over top. Bake for 40 minutes. Serve warm or cold.

Lizzie's Cook's Notes

When the pan is turned upside down to place the cake on a cake plate, you'll understand the mystery to the cake. You'll have both cake and icing, all at once!

_____

_____

_____

_____

_____

Wade's Mean Bean Chili

1 ½ pounds ground beef
2 teaspoons vegetable oil
1 small onion, chopped
½ teaspoon minced garlic
2 (16 ounce) cans red kidney beans
1 (16 ounce) can Great Northern beans
1 (15 ounce) can tomatoes
1 (15 ounce) can tomato sauce
2 tablespoons chili sauce or catsup
1 tablespoon oregano
1 tablespoon chili powder
¼ cup picante sauce
1 teaspoon salt

Brown ground beef with vegetable oil, onions, and garlic; drain the grease. Rinse beans. Add meat, beans, and remaining ingredients to slow cooker. Cover and stir occasionally. Put on low heat in the morning and serve for your evening meal.

Donna's Cook's Notes

Wade makes this all the time. The only thing it's missing is a little bit of Beano. Otherwise, it would be perfect. Oh, and I like to eat it with Fritos.

Sally's Meatloaf Sandwich

thick slices of leftover meatloaf
coleslaw (should not be too runny, so drain it well)
tomato slices
Swiss cheese slices
bread slices

Warm meatloaf in 350-degree oven. Place cheese over meat and allow to melt just a bit. Take out of oven and place on wheat, white, or rye bread. (Toast bread if desired.) Top with tomato and coleslaw, and a final piece of bread. Slice sandwich in two and serve with potato salad, curly fries, or onion rings.

Evangeline's Cook's Notes

This has always been a favorite dish of mine at Higher Grounds Café. Not just there, but at home too. Meatloaf sandwich is a great way to eat leftover meatloaf. You can serve it cold, of course, but it's so much better served warm.

Cheese Sticks

1 cup flour
1½ teaspoons baking powder
½ teaspoon salt
⅛ teaspoon ground cayenne pepper
4 tablespoons butter or margarine
½ cup shredded cheddar cheese
3 tablespoons sour cream

Combine dry ingredients into mixing bowl. Blend in butter and cheese. Slowly add sour cream. Shape the dough into a ball and chill 2 hours. (You can freeze for later too.)

On a lightly floured surface, roll dough into 1/8-inch-thick strands. Cut strands into strips ¼-inch wide and 3 inches long. Give the strip a twist (for decorative purposes) then bake at 425 degrees for 8 minutes.

Lisa Leann's Cook's Notes

I broke down the recipe so you could make a smaller batch than what I made for the shower. I love this recipe because it's simple, easy, and tasty. I always have a fresh batch of dough in the freezer. Then, give me a day's notice, and I'll have hot cheese sticks—just for our little get-together.

Tuna Fish Pie

3 tablespoons butter
3 tablespoons chopped onion
1 cup chopped bell pepper
3 tablespoons flour
1⅔ cups milk
½ teaspoon salt
1 tablespoon lemon juice
1 10-ounce can tuna, drained

CHEESE ROLLS
　　1½ cups flour
　　3 teaspoons baking powder
　　½ teaspoon salt
　　⅛ teaspoon pepper
　　2 tablespoons shortening
　　½ cup milk
　　¾ cup cheddar cheese, shredded
　　2-ounce jar pimiento, chopped/drained

Melt butter in a medium saucepan. Add onion and pepper. Cook over low heat until soft. Add flour. Stir until well blended. Add milk slowly, stirring constantly until thick and smooth. Add salt, lemon juice, and tuna. Pour into buttered 7-by-11 baking dish.

Cover with cheese rolls and bake in preheated 400 degree oven for 12 to 15 minutes or until brown.

Cheese rolls: Sift flour, baking powder, salt, and pepper into a mixing bowl. Add shortening and mix with a fork. Add milk to make soft dough.

Toss lightly on floured board until smooth. Roll out into a rectangle 8 by 12 inches. Sprinkle with cheese and pimiento and roll as jelly roll. Slice 1 inch thick and lay on tuna mixture with ring side up.

Evangeline's Cook's Notes

Can you believe this? Me, Evangeline Vesey, cooking to such an extent? It looks difficult, but trust me, it's not. If I can do it, you can too!

Louisiana Red Beans and Rice

1 cup red beans, washed and drained
3 cups water
bacon drippings, ham, or seasoning meat of choice
1 medium onion, chopped
1 clove garlic, chopped
1 rib celery, chopped
2 tablespoons parsley, chopped
1 large bay leaf, crushed
2 tablespoons sugar (optional)

Cook beans in water. Season with salt and bacon drippings, ham, or seasoning meat of choice. Cook on low to medium heat for 1½ to 2 hours, then add onion, garlic, celery, parsley, and bay leaf. Continue to cook over low heat for another 30 minutes to 1 hour. If beans become too dry, add heated water. If you really want to make this recipe zing, add 2 tablespoons sugar. Serve on rice.

Serves 4.

Lizzie's Cook's Notes

According to my daughter-in-law, leaving behind the delectable Cajun cuisine is one of the toughest things about moving from Louisiana. A sample of some of her favorite recipes have left me with no doubt on this!

Marinated Steaks

4 beef round (sirloin) tip side steaks, cut 1-inch thick (about 8
   ounces each)
½ teaspoon salt
⅛ teaspoon ground black pepper

MARINADE
   ⅔ cup prepared balsamic vinaigrette
   2 tablespoons Dijon-style mustard

In small mixing bowl, combine marinade ingredients. Place steaks
and marinade into a plastic bag and shake bag to coat meat. Seal
bag and refrigerate steaks for 15 minutes to 2 hours.

Remove steaks from bag and place on grill for 12 to 14 minutes for
medium-rare doneness, turning once. (I usually cook 7 minutes per
side.) Season steaks with salt and pepper.

Serves 4.

Donna's Cook's Notes

*I tried this later at home (cutting recipe to serve one), and it was great. Glad the restaurant chef
shared his secret marinade sauce with me. Now it's our secret.*

Bok Choy Spring Rolls

20 large spring roll wrappers (see freezer section in grocery store)
1 bunch cilantro
2 large carrots, peeled and grated
3–4 heads baby bok choy, cut lengthwise into 1/4 inch strips
20 snow peas, cut lengthwise into matchstick-size strips
1 pound ground lean pork
1 tablespoon toasted sesame oil
2 tablespoons peeled minced fresh ginger
½ teaspoon salt
vegetable oil for brushing

To Make Filling

Chop cilantro, grate carrots, and slice bok choy and snow peas; set aside in bowl. In skillet, fry the meat in sesame oil with minced ginger and salt. Drain off excess fat. Spoon meat mixture into additional bowl and set aside. Use skillet to sauté cilantro, carrots, bok choy, and snow peas in two tablespoons of water. Cook until vegetables are just limp. Drain excess water (if necessary) then combine mixture with meat mixture. Stir.

How to Stuff Spring Rolls with Filling

Brush each spring roll wrapper with oil; turn wrapper so they are positioned like diamonds (not squares). Spoon portion of filling into center of wrapper, creating a line of filling across the wrapper. Fold side corners inward, then roll up to make a neat tube.

Repeat till all rolls are stuffed. Place spring rolls on lightly greased cookie tray or cake pan. Bake at 350 for about 30 minutes, until golden brown.

Serve with plum or other store-bought sauce.

Yield: 20.

Lisa Leann's Cook's Notes

I prefer baking spring rolls over frying them because they are not only easier to prepare, they are healthier to eat. We had to make ten batches of these for the Prattle shower. They disappeared fast.

Strawberry Punch

10 ounces frozen cut strawberries
6 ounces lemonade
1 pint lemon-lime sherbet
1 quart ginger ale

Approximately 2 hours before preparation, place frozen strawberries in refrigerator to thaw. Prepare lemonade according to favorite recipe (whether fresh, frozen, or dry) and place in refrigerator to chill. Just before serving, combine berries, ginger ale, and lemonade, add sherbet, and gently stir until sherbet is dissolved. Use ice ring in punch bowl to keep punch cold.

Evangeline's Cook's Notes

Prepare enough for one punch bowl, and you'll be sorry. I've yet to serve this when I didn't need at least two bowls. For the shower, even though alcohol was served at the bar, we poured more of this than the bartenders could have dreamed possible.

_____

_____

_____

_____

_____

_____

_____

_____

_____

For more information about the women of the Potluck Catering Club, go to www.PotluckClub.com.

Linda Evans Shepherd is an author, international speaker, media personality, leader of Advanced Writers and Speakers Association, president of Right to the Heart Ministries, founder of Stepping into Destiny Conferences, and publisher of Right to the Heart of Women Ezine. (See www.VisitLinda.com.)

In addition to the Potluck Club series and now the Potluck Catering Club series, Linda has authored and coauthored over twenty books including *Share Jesus Without Fear*, published in over fifty languages, and the upcoming *Be Your Own Prayer Project* from Baker Publishing Group.

Linda been married to husband Paul for almost thirty years, and they have two children.

Award-winning author and speaker **Eva Marie Everson** is a Southern gal who's not that crazy about being in the kitchen unless it's to eat! She has been married to a wonderful man, Dennis, for three decades and is a mother and grandmother to the most amazing children in the world.

Eva's writing career and ministry began in 1999 when a friend asked her what she'd want to do for the Lord, if she could do anything at all. "Write and speak," she said. And so it began.

Since that time, she has written, co-written, contributed to, and edited and compiled a number of works, including the recently released *Reflections of Israel* (which includes her photography among the spectacular photographic works), *Sex, Lies, and the Media* and *Sex, Lies, and High School* (co-written with her amazing daughter Jessica), and *Oasis: A Spa for Body and Soul*, in which she gets to talk about two of her favorite subjects: the Word of God and pampering.

Eva Marie is both a graduate of Andersonville Theological Seminary and a returning student. She is a mentor with the Jerry B. Jenkins Christian Writers Guild. Eva Marie speaks nationally and internationally about her passion: drawing believers to the heartbeat of God. In 2002 she was named AWSA's first Member of the Year. Also that year she was one of six journalists chosen to visit Israel for a special ten-day press tour. She was forever changed.